Three Time Travelers
Walk Into…

Other Books by Michael A. Ventrella

Terin Ostler and the Arch Enemies
Terin Ostler and the War of the Words
Terin Ostler and the Axes of Evil
Terin Ostler and the Zombie King (and other stories)
Bloodsuckers: A Vampire Runs for President
Big Stick

Anthologies edited by Michael
Tales of Fortannis
Baker Street Irregulars (with Jonathan Maberry)
Baker Street Irregulars: The Game is Afoot! (with Jonathan Maberry)
Release the Virgins!
Across the Universe (with Randee Dawn)

Novels edited by Michael
It's a Wonderful Death (by Derek Beebe)

Nonfiction
Long Title: Looking for the Good Times: Examining the Monkees
Songs (with Mark Arnold)
Headquarters: The Monkees Solo Years (with Mark Arnold)
How to Argue the Constitution with a Conservative

Three Time Travelers Walk Into...

edited by Michael A. Ventrella

Collection © 2022

Copyright page continued on page 283.

Cover art by Lynne Hansen, www.LynneHansenArt.com

Fantastic Books
1380 East 17 Street, Suite 2233
Brooklyn, New York 11230
www.FantasticBooks.biz

Simultaneous hard cover and trade paperback publication
June 27, 2022

Hardcover
ISBN: 978-1-5154-4778-8

Trade Paperback
ISBN: 978-1-5154-4779-5

First Edition

Contents

Trudging Through the Slush Pile, or How Time Was Not on My Side
Michael A. Ventrella

My novel *Big Stick* was selling well—not great, but not terrible, either—and the publisher wanted a sequel. The book is a rousing steampunk adventure with Teddy Roosevelt, Mark Twain, Harriet Tubman, and a slew of other people from that time period. With dirigibles. And rayguns.

But a sequel? Hmm, what sort of adventure could they get into next?

Anyway, I'm skimming over Facebook, avoiding doing any real work, when an ad pops up for online courses, with an illustration of Teddy Roosevelt, Jesus, and Beethoven. *Ooh*, I thought. *Wouldn't it be fun to get those three together and have an adventure?*

Ultimately deciding not to do a time travel story, I instead began work on a sequel involving the explosion of the *Maine*, Rough Riders on clockwork horses, and an exciting conclusion at the Battle of San Juan Hill. With dirigibles. And rayguns.

But I kept coming back to that idea of three famous people from various times going on an adventure.

After all, I love time travel stories. I've used time travel in one of my novels and in a short story, and may do so again. One of the very first adult science fiction novels I ever read when I was in high school was David Gerrold's *The Man Who Folded Himself*, about a guy who uses a belt that allows him to travel through time. And come on, who doesn't like *Back to the Future* and *Time Bandits* and *Bill and Ted's Excellent Adventure*?

So when I later spoke to Ian Randal Strock, publisher of Fantastic Books, I brought the idea to him. He agreed it could be a fun project.

We used a Kickstarter campaign to fund it—that way we know we can pay our authors. We got some Big Name Authors to commit, which helps to entice everyone to pitch in to the Kickstarter campaign.

One of the things that I sometimes can't get over is how so many of the authors I grew up reading I have now edited in various anthologies. It geeks me out sometimes. I've become friends with Spider Robinson and Peter David and Jody Lynn Nye and Gregory Frost and Lawrence Watt-Evans, and you know that guy who wrote that first adult science fiction novel I read, David Gerrold? Him, too. (And if you have read that novel, you'll like his time travel story here.)

So once we had our Big Names and our funding, I put out the word that I was looking for more stories. It's always great to have a ton of submissions to read from many different writers so that I can pick the very best to accompany the invited authors.

"Take any three famous people from history, toss them together, and have an adventure," I wrote. "How they got together is up to you—you could do an origin story of how they first met or you could write the story as if they had been adventuring for years. You can use a time machine or a rip in space-time or quantum magic or whatever. You could have some sort of universal translator or you can have the language barrier be part of your plotline. And these three people should be really separate if possible, from different cultures and times. That's part of the fun...."

I had asked for writers, if at all possible, to avoid fictional characters. Some stories ignored that, but were good enough to accept anyway. You'll see.

I have edited or co-edited almost a dozen anthologies by this point, but I never expected the response I received. While this means more work for me, it's a very good thing. It means I could be very picky. I could choose only the very best. And that's good for you, the reader, too. ("The very best," of course, is entirely a matter of opinion. Another editor reading the same stories could pick completely different ones.)

Once I finally was able to narrow down the stories to the final selection, I then had the problem every editor faces: How to make them all work together.

You see, editing an anthology is like making a mix tape. Or, for you youngsters out there, a Spotify playlist. You want a good variety. You don't want all the stories to be too serious or too funny; you don't want to have more than one story with the same basic theme or plot; and then you want to arrange them in such a way that by reading them in order, they flow well.

One of the problems with choosing stories was that many character. in the submitted stories appeared often, and I didn't want to repeat characters if at all possible. Some good stories got rejected for that reason. (Maybe if there is a sequel anthology…)

So what characters appeared most often in the submitted stories, you ask? Well, I was curious, too, so I went back through all the stories submitted and counted them up. Believe it or not, the most popular character who appeared in most stories was Joan of Arc. I have no idea why. Close behind were Cleopatra and William Shakespeare, followed by Amelia Earhart, Benjamin Franklin, Marilyn Monroe, and Vlad Wallecha (a.k.a. Dracula).

Eve (as in "Adam and") appeared more than once, as did Jesus, Lilith, and Noah. I found a lot of writers traveling through time—the most common being Jane Austin and Mark Twain—but also Kurt Vonnegut, Edgar Allan Poe, H.P. Lovecraft, and (not surprisingly) H.G. Wells. Scientists who appeared in more than one story included Albert Einstein, Nikola Tesla, Stephen Hawking, and Thomas Edison. Politicians included George Washington, Abraham Lincoln, Theodore Roosevelt, and Donald Trump (who was the "comic relief" in every story in which he appeared).

I also had duplicate stories with Hedy Lamarr, Wolfgang Mozart, Harry Houdini, Florence Nightingale, Marie Curie, Oscar Wilde, Annie Oakley, Mary Wollstonecraft Shelley, and Jimmy Hoa, who apparently had disappeared into time.

In the end, I hope you'll enjoy the selection.

Now to get back to that *Big Stick* sequel.…

In the Chocolate Bar
Jody Lynn Nye

"That's just it," Steven Mentzel wailed, clasping his hands on the bar table. "I don't have the recipe. I never did! They'll think I stole it because when I opened the vault this morning, it was empty. I'm the holder of the key, and one of only four people who know the combination to the safe. But there it was, sitting empty as my wallet is going to be, if they fire me. I might end up in jail! But I swear I didn't steal it. I have always done *everything* to be a trustworthy steward. The original document is priceless! It's centuries old. Irreplaceable! It's the cornerstone of the whole Abelard empire! It says right there in the corner of the paper, 'This is proof of ownership.' I'm one of the few people who has ever been allowed to see it." He lowered his head to the tabletop. "I mean, the disaster has already happened. It's hours after the press conference was supposed to take place. It's gone! I don't know why I should even go back to my office."

The three seated with him at the table in the quiet corner of the old-fashioned Boston bar regarded the young man with sympathy.

Julia Child patted the man absently on the arm. Even seated, the auburn-haired woman towered over him, making her gesture even more motherly. "There, there, dear. I'm sure we can help you. From how long ago does the recipe originate?"

"It's supposed to have come from the New World not long before the great fire of London in 1666," Steven said, raising his head. His misery was almost instantly abated by a scholar's enthusiasm, and his pale blue eyes lit up. "Well-to-do Englishmen couldn't wait to try the new beverage from the Americas that the Spaniards and French were already enjoying. Drinking chocolate became a sensation! Once serving rooms began to appear in the city, one man, John Abelard, became absolutely the most popular proprietor in London. They said that his chocolate drink was liquid magic! Of course, the English had already added sweetening to the traditional Aztec form of the drink, but his was widely known to be the best anywhere. He refused to sell the secret of his formulation, and no one could surprise or threaten it out of him. His children were sworn to secrecy, on their honor, and with the threat of losing any hope of their inheritance if they leaked it. The recipe has been passed down through the family for generations. In 1910, the sixth great-grandson of Sir John Abelard made the mixture into a candy bar. It premiered at the World's Fair in Brussels, and swiftly became the most popular confection in the world! But the formulation is a deep, dark secret. No one who aids in the manufacture has had the complete recipe. Ever! The main factory even buys some ingredients as a blind, so no one can guess by the incoming shipments what or how much goes into them. But they're always delicious."

"I've eaten Abelard Bars with great pleasure," Julia mused, mulling over the flavor in her mind. Her skill at breaking down a recipe began to tease the various facets out. In no time, she was certain of at least seven ingredients, but four more left her a bit puzzled, and she wasn't at all sure of the proportions. Perhaps Dr. Carver could put his finger on those. "I had no idea that its history went back so far."

"They're for sale in the general stores in my university town," said Dr. George Washington Carver. The dark-skinned academic sat back in his chair and hooked his thumbs through his suspenders. "They are a fine treat. I admit trying to duplicate the recipe for myself and my family. In the end, it was cheaper and less worry to buy them. Three cents apiece isn't worth my time. I've got a thousand projects in the works."

"Was Abelard one of those sweet, sticky brown masses that you brought to me?" asked Im-Hotep. The Egyptian noble felt uncomfortable in the heavy charcoal-gray woolen suit and thick black leather shoes Julia had insisted he wear. True, the weather necessitated more than the linen kilt and sandals to which he was accustomed. Julia had also required him to leave his heavy linen wig behind, so his shaved head was cold. "The fragrant sweetmeats?"

"Well, yes," Dr. Carver said. "The one in the blue wrapper. You said you liked it."

"Not the mess, however," the Egyptian said. "You said it wouldn't soil my fingers."

"That was the M&M's, my friend," the professor said, with a genial chuckle. "The panning process of the sugar and corn syrup makes the candy shell resistant to melting at body heat."

"The magical pastilles," Im-Hotep said, with a knowing nod.

Steven Mentzel looked puzzled at the conversation between Carver and Im-Hotep. How could the American professor understand the foreigner's gibberish and vice versa? Mrs. Child's eyes widened at his bemusement.

"Oh, of course!" she exclaimed. She reached into the capacious black handbag at her side and emerged with a flat blue disk about the size of a half-dollar coin. "Eat this, dear man." She pushed it toward Steven's mouth. "Universal translator. A bit ahead of your time—and even mine—but necessary for people in our occupation. I've goosed the mixture a little. The originals taste so *clinical*."

Against his better judgment, Steven opened his mouth. Rather than needing to be chewed, the disk melted on his tongue and spread down his throat. He gagged, feeling the fragrant liquid rise up toward his sinuses, penetrating into his brain. Then, suddenly, the bronze-skinned man's words made sense.

"...I attempted to copy the process of the em-and-ems to contain medicines for the Pharaoh. She never cared for the flavor of tansy or other healing herbs, even though she needed them. Her Majesty did enjoy the em-and-ems, and they did her much good. Yet, in the end," Im-Hotep emitted a great sigh, "she more greatly needed protection from her own machinations. Those of us who loved her deeply were no match for the one who despised her. No pill can cure hatred."

"Who are you?" Mentzel said, eyeing them all with a fearful gaze. "I know this lady from television, but she looks a lot younger than I've seen her. And you two—are you from history?"

"Not from our point of view," Dr. Carver said, with an easy smile. "We live in our own times, most of the time. It's circumstances like this one that make us meet up and try to solve problems." He chuckled again. "I find it refreshing. Allow me to introduce myself. I'm George Washington Carver. My friend here is Im-Hotep, from the 18th dynasty of Egypt. His Pharaoh is Queen Hapshetsut, a tough lady you might have heard of. Dates to about 1620 B.C. Mrs. Julia Child you already know. Now, what exactly do you need, young man?"

Time travelers! Steven had to force the concept to make sense. Part of him was frightened out of his mind at the notion, but all three pairs of eyes fixed on his were sympathetic and intelligent. "M. Pepin didn't explain it to me. He just said he knew people who were able to help people who needed… um… unusual assistance. I never dreamed she… I mean, you were one of those."

That made the three seated at the table with him laugh. Mrs. Child broke into a high-pitched whinny that was at the same time strangely musical.

"Unusual, yes," she said. "I thought I had lived down my reputation! But we and others who do what we do have become good friends, despite or perhaps because of our diverse backgrounds. When Jacques referred your problem to me, it seemed to me that you needed the three of us in particular. Dr. Carver is an expert in chemistry and microanalysis. Lord Im-Hotep is a physician as well as an architect. He understands complex construction, since your concern involves a locked room mystery—which I, too, find most intriguing. I worked for the OSS during the war—World War II to you—so I'm well-versed in confidential documents and the lengths people go to, to preserve their classified information. And we all love good food!"

"Ma'am, I defer to you on knowing more about food than the two of us," Dr. Carver said gallantly, "but I think you've defined our talents as far as this young man needs."

"You're quite right, dear doctor. Tell us all about it, Steven."

Mentzel looked around the bar to make certain no one was close enough to overhear him. The server in the tuxedo vest with curly gray hair who had brought them their drinks stood a couple of yards away, wiping down a table. When Steven glanced in his direction, the waiter started toward them, but Steven waved him away. The man went back to his tasks. No one was seated at any of the nearby tables. He lowered his voice.

"I got to work a few minutes late today—it is still today, isn't it?" he asked the others. They nodded. "Well, I have a checklist of tasks I have to take care of every day. I check my inbox, both the basket on my desk and the one on my computer.… Uh, okay, you don't need all of that. But item number eight is to go through the strongroom and make sure all the built-in safes are closed and locked, and that there's no request for any of the artifacts or documents to be brought out for educational purposes, or the press, or some presentation. So, I went in there." He trembled, remembering the horror that kept replaying itself in his memory. "The safe at the end of the room was ajar! I rubbed my eyes, thinking I had to be mistaken. I went to examine it, but it was empty! The document is in a big blue folder. That was there, but it was empty! You can imagine that my heart just stopped!

"I heard some rustling around, and some voices. I ran out to see if I could catch the person who took the recipe. No one was there!" He raised pleading eyes to the others. "I need the parchment back in my hands. Or I'm responsible for a candy empire falling into ruin. It's the center of the whole operation, the most important thing we have."

Lord Im-Hotep regarded him with narrowed brown eyes. "You claim the contents of the scroll are a secret, but they are already spread across the known world. The confection is made in more than one place, so others have knowledge of the contents. What you want returned to you is the symbol of that empire. I can call upon the finest scribes in Upper and Lower Egypt to duplicate it for you."

Mrs. Child held up a hand. "No forgery will do in this case, am I correct? Photographs or photocopies of this document exist?"

"Yes," Mentzer said, miserably. "If they compare a replica, I'm still out of a job. If word got out that the recipe is missing, the trademark is in jeopardy. The Abelards have always held tight to the concept that possession of the document constitutes proof of ownership. If someone else got it, *they'd* own the rights to manufacture Abelard chocolate."

"Then you require the original." Dr. Carver slapped a hand down on the table. "I'm game to help with that."

"As am I," said Im-Hotep, drawing down his black brows. "Woe betide he who steals written documents. The gods will curse him."

"I hope we will not have to involve any higher powers," Julia said, with an indulgent smile for her friend. She signed to the waiter. "Check, please, Henry!"

The gray-haired waiter bustled toward them and presented the check. Waving away Steven's attempts to pay the bill, Julia fumbled in her capacious black leather handbag and produced a handful of money.

"There you are, dear," she said to the waiter. "We should be back later."

"Yes, Mrs. Child." His expression said that the tip she left was generous. Steven found him liking her more and more.

The bar wasn't busy at that hour of the evening, though a few well-dressed people came and went through the revolving glass door. Mrs. Child looked around as they headed out.

"Who are you looking for?" Steven asked.

"Myself," she said, peering up and down the busy Boston street. "It's not a good sign. I usually come back to reassure me that we've succeeded. I wonder what's holding me up?"

"Maybe it's just a delay," the clerk suggested, concerned by the look on the tall woman's face. "You couldn't get back in time?"

"It's time travel," Julia corrected him. "There's always time to get back where you started." She straightened her narrow shoulders with an air of resignation. "Perhaps it's our last journey. It was bound to happen one day."

Steven was alarmed. "Maybe you just didn't go?" He didn't want to put anyone in harm's way, even if it cost him his job. Still, he really needed their help.

"No," Im-Hotep said firmly. "Once our word is given, we go, regardless of danger. Now I am curious about the challenge you have set us."

"So am I," Dr. Carver added. He straightened his shoulders. "Well, I never wanted to die in bed. Let's go."

Steven followed them, feeling reassured and worried at the same time.

"We had better begin at the beginning," Mrs. Child said, pushing Steven forward through a checkpoint at the Public Broadcast Station's main door. The uniformed guard there seemed surprised at first, then recognized one of the system's greatest stars. With a big smile on his face, he waved them through. "We should examine the scene of the crime, at least a little before it happened."

She guided the group through the maze of the studio, stepping carefully over cables that snaked everywhere, dodging past technicians pushing equipment, and nodding to worried young women in headsets with arms full of papers, and into a small room. She flicked a switch, and a sign over the door lit up that said RECORDING.

"That way no one will disturb us," she said, shutting and locking the door behind her. From her handbag, she produced a glowing blue ring about eight inches across. From an inside pocket, Carver removed a similar ring, but gold in color. Lord Im-Hotep's ring was green. Mrs. Child grabbed Steven's hand.

"Hold tight," she said, her eyes twinkling. "I don't want to lose you between here and last week." She let out a peal of laughter at her witticism. Her companions grinned. "Dr. Carver, would you make the adjustments?"

"Gladly," the inventor said. He twisted parts of his ring as if he was rotating the tumblers of a safe, then nodded. "Ready."

Trembling, Steven clutched Mrs. Child's fingers as the three of them touched the rings together. He squeezed his eyes shut and braced himself for an impact, a drop, an explosion, but...

...But, nothing.

Well, not nothing. His nose twitched at the familiar smells of chocolate, furniture polish, and old wood. He opened his eyes. His three companions were studying the wood-paneled room with its heavy-sashed windows and slightly crooked venetian blinds, varnished paintings on the walls.

"We're... in my office?" he said, uncertain even as the words left his lips. The old-fashioned partners desk that he shared with his secretary was empty. He looked at the clock. It said seven A.M. "How did we get here?"

"Well, isn't this where you intended us to be?" Mrs. Child asked. She swept an arm around. "I've been here before, of course, on Abelard's three-hundredth anniversary. They gave me a most comprehensive tour. What a wonderful celebration that was!"

"But... I mean, when?"

"A little adjustment of Earth's rotation," Dr. Carver said to Steven, with a smile. "We can't always get this close, but it saves the walk."

"By the angle of the sun, we are here before you arrived and discovered the strong room had been opened," Im-Hotep said. "Show it to us."

Steven pulled his wits together. "Right this way," he said. The room with the safes in it was beside his in the high-ceilinged corridor.

"Do you smell kerosene?" Mrs. Child asked. The others looked blank.

Dr. Carver shook his head. "Perhaps someone is using it to take stains out of something. It's got many uses besides fuel."

Steven felt his hand trembling as he pulled out his key ring. The room should be completely safe. No visitor knew that the heavy wooden door had been reinforced with steel on the inside and multiple bolts that held it as securely as a bank vault. He inserted the longest and most complex key into the lock under the knob.

"I'm the only one on site with a key," he explained. "If I lost it, they'd have to get another from the safety deposit box at the First National Bank."

"We can wait in here until someone makes the attempt to break in," Dr. Carver said, glancing around. "Then Steven here can catch the crook."

"But he didn't see us when he came in later," Mrs. Child corrected him. "Something must have prevented us from waiting, just like stopping me from appearing to reassure us that we succeeded. And I do smell kerosene."

Steven pulled open the door.

"That is because the crime has already been committed," Im-Hotep said. "Behold!"

A light came on as the door swung open. Six man-height safes flanked the room like an honor guard to protect the shorter, older strongbox at the end of the small room. But they had not done their job. The seventh safe stood open. Steven ran to it.

"No!" he wailed. Nothing was in the safe except a large blue folder. "It's already gone! I never let the key out of my sight!"

"Then there is another way in," Mrs. Child said. "Under the floor? Through the ceiling?" Steven scanned the plasterwork above his head.

"Not another way," Im-Hotep said, examining the walls with an expert eye. "The wall between your office and this room is too thick. I have done similar work in stone. A compartment must be here somewhere." He pounded on the wood paneling with the heel of his hand. One of the panels sounded hollow. The Egyptian pulled at it with his fingertips. It sprang open.

A man with long silver hair glared out at them. A small, old-fashioned lantern swung from one hand. In the other, he held a large yellowing square of paper. The Abelard recipe!

"That's not yours!" Steven bellowed, diving for him. "Give it to me!"

With a wry smile, the man shook his head. He stuffed the precious paper into the top of the lantern. Fire flared up, making the paper curl and blacken. Steven grabbed at it. Fire burned his hand, but he tried to save the document. It broke into hot ashes. Steven gasped at the pain. The stranger ground the fragments underneath his heel.

Im-Hotep leaped for the man, but the stranger pulled a yellow ring out of his pocket. Before the Egyptian's arms closed around him, he vanished.

Steven threw himself to his knees beside the smear of ashes and let out a horrified wail. It was no longer a case of recovering the recipe. The priceless artifact had been destroyed! Nothing could save him now.

"Well, well," Dr. Carver said, rocking back on his heels. "Another time-traveler. There's more going on here than we thought."

"Mr. Mentzel!" An appalled female voice came from behind him. "You know there is no smoking in these offices! I will call for the janitor right now!... Hello, Mrs. Child!" The voice turned simpering. "We didn't know you were coming today. I'm Tessa Burton. We met at the Abelard Christmas party two years ago."

Mrs. Child immediately rose to the occasion. "Why, yes, I remember you, Ms. Burton! I was in the area and thought I would... drop in. Mr. Mentzel kindly offered us a cup of coffee."

Im-Hotep helped Steven to his feet. The clerk turned to face his nemesis. Tessa Burton, an assistant to the CEO and inveterate snoop, was always looking for ammunition to make others look bad. If she figured out what had just happened, she would make a huge fuss. He might even be arrested for destruction of private property!

The thin woman ignored him and focused on the celebrity guest. "Please allow me to take you to Mr. Snodgrass's office. Mr. Snodgrass has the *best* coffee. I would be delighted to make some for you!"

"Is he here yet?" Mrs. Child asked, edging so she was standing between Tessa and Steven. "I would love to say hello."

"Not yet," Tessa admitted. "He is coming in later on for a press conference. Abelard is announcing a merger with the London Chocolate Company! We're going to take over their operations. They used to be part of Abelard," she confided, dropping her voice. "But Abelard's dominance in the field due to its wonderful candy has outstripped them for more than a century! The press is going to be admitted to the safe room to see the original recipe! Well, the folder, actually. No one gets to see the recipe." She sniffed pointedly in Steven's direction. "I'm sure Mr. Snodgrass would be thrilled to have you at the conference! You're such a big celebrity and everything!"

"I have an appointment this morning, but I suppose I could be here this afternoon," Julia said. She must have picked up on Steven's despair at Tessa's arrival. No words could have been more telling than his expression. She took the woman by the arm and turned her away from the smear on the floor. "Don't let me keep you. My friends have come a long way to have a talk with Mr. Mentzel. See you later!" She gave Tessa a gentle shove to send her on her way.

Fortunately, the woman took the hint. She set off down the corridor, occasionally looking back with bemusement. Mrs. Child waited until she was out of sight.

"Is there any hope of restoring it?" she asked.

"No," Im-Hotep said. "This papyrus was too old and dry. Nothing remains that could be pieced together."

"Parchment, surely?" Mrs. Child asked, looking puzzled. "Such an important document dating from the seventeenth century would have been inscribed on parchment or vellum."

"Im-Hotep's right," Dr. Carver said, rubbing ashes between his fingertips. "This is plant-based. Looks like it was paper after all. Wish we were still using good quality like this. Modern paper wouldn't last three hundred years."

"Who was the destroyer?" Im-Hotep asked, gesturing out of the door.

"I don't know," Steven said, woefully. "He looked kind of familiar, but I don't know why." All he could think of was the loss of the priceless document.

"Never mind," Mrs. Child said. She smiled at Steven. "You need a replacement, so we have to go directly to the source. Lock the door! We're going back to the studio!"

S teven plucked at the heavy brushed corduroy of his costume. Dark blue breeches, slashed around an embarrassingly prominent codpiece, belled out from his waistband. The white linen shirt felt itchy and hot underneath the tailored coat that buttoned right up to his neck. He poked a fingertip underneath the starched linen ruff tied around his neck to scratch. Why did the outfit have to be narrow on the top and huge on the bottom? And the shoes! Huge bows adorned each of his toes. He even wore a tricornered hat over a long, curled wig. If anyone from the office had seen him, he would have died.

All four of them were dressed similarly, including Mrs. Child. The tights under the balloon breeches showed off good legs with muscular calves that rivaled either of the other men. She had combed her hair out so it touched her ruffled collar. People passing up and back on the crowded street paid no attention.

"Without makeup I can pass for a man," she said, holding open the door of the shop. A burst of noise exploded from inside. "Women aren't allowed in these places! Ridiculous, but there you are."

Abelard's Chocolate Room was doing fantastic business. The room was so tightly packed voices echoed off the high, ornately painted ceiling. A thin man with thinning hair answered the tall "man's" hand signal, and gestured to a small circular table in the corner of the room near one of the crazy-quilt glass windows. Steven followed the others through the crowded room, trying not to let his pantaloons hit any of the other customers in the shoulder. The bulk of Im-Hotep's long-skirted silver-trimmed coat over his breeches made the stocky Egyptian even wider.

Steven tried to make sense of the fact that he was back in 17th century England, in the very chocolate shop that had made his employer's ancestor famous. The clothes, hair styles, décor, shapes of the chairs and tables, were all strange and exotic to his modern eyes. The only thing that was familiar was the aroma. He smelled that mixture of chocolate and spices every working day of his life. He inhaled deeply. The scent gave him a tiny bit of confidence.

"We'll get Sir John to write out a new recipe for us," Mrs. Child had explained while they rifled the public television studio's costume department for clothing. "If it looks identical to the one that man destroyed, Abelard can't be disgraced or endangered."

The thin man got them seated. "D'ye require tobacco, too, m'luds? Pastries?"

"No, thank you," Dr. Carver said, with a smile. "Just drinking chocolate. Is Sir John Abelard here today?"

"Aye," the thin man said, nodding toward a burly, bearded man in peach-colored brocade leaning against a pillar in the middle of the room. "'Tis him o' there."

"If we might make our respects to him?" Dr. Carver asked.

"I'll see if he's busy," the server said. He glanced down at the coin Mrs. Child pressed into his palm. "Aye, sure that he's got the time."

Steven looked around at the chocolate shop. From his studies he knew that chocolate predated coffee or tea as a popular drink. Chocolate shops were conversation salons, much more genteel than bars or pubs. Men had glanced up as the four of them entered, then gone right back to intense conversation.

"Um, I don't mean to be offensive, but…?" Steven bit his tongue.

"But they don't notice I'm black or my friend here is brown?" Dr. Carver asked, with a smile. "There were visitors to these isles from many southern nations during this time as well as the slaves in the Americas. We're gentlemen and dressed accordingly. Clothes make the man, sad to say."

The thin man appeared. He set a tray down on the table and dealt out saucers, cups, and spoons to each of them. In the middle, he plunked down a silver shaker with a pierced top. The last thing was a tall, narrow covered pot with a handle sticking out one side.

"I'll pour, then, m'luds?" he asked.

"Yes, please," Mrs. Child said.

Steam rose from the spout as the velvety brown liquid gurgled into each cup. It smelled so good Steven wanted to seize his and guzzle it. He managed to make himself wait until the server retreated.

Julia lifted her cup. "To your very good health, gentlemen. And to the King!"

Dr. Carver's mouth twisted in a wry grin. "To the King!"

Im-Hotep and Steven echoed the toast. Steven took his first sip of genuine, original Abelard chocolate. The smooth, fruity, warm liquid melted over his tongue like the language lozenge Mrs. Child had given him. The familiar taste of the spices was even more pronounced than in the 20th century candy bars. His taste buds wanted to dance for joy. It was good. No, it was great!

"Brilliant!" Mrs. Child said, savoring her first mouthful. "It's a symphony of flavor! No wonder he became famous!"

The thin server made his way to the well-dressed gentleman in the center of the room. Sir John lowered his head to hear his employee speak under the hubbub. With a grin, he waded through the crowd to their table.

"Welcome, me lords!" he said. Dr. Carver slid sideways on his bench to make room. The chocolatier sat down in a swirl of expensive coat-tails. "How may I serve?"

"I have had chocolate in many places, but never any as good as yours," Mrs. Child said, holding up her now-empty cup.

"Why, thankee," Sir John said, with satisfaction. "It's true. No one's is as good."

Julia nodded to her companions. "We would be interested in opening more shops under your name in our own cities, sir. Would you consider such a partnership? You would get half of our profits."

The humor in his chuckle didn't extend to his eyes. "And cut off me own business, me lord? Nay. I'm not ready to expand yet."

Julia leaned a little closer. "Isn't there any way we can persuade you, sir? What would be enough of a surety to convince you that we have your best interests in mind."

"As well as your own? Nothing. Nothing at all. Me recipe's me own, and thus it will remain." Sir John stood up and brushed down his clothes with an air of finality. "Is there anything else, me lords? I've got others I must attend to. Pray enjoy yourselves! Your second pot is on me. I'll send the boy."

Disappointed, Steven watched him plow toward another customer and strike up a conversation.

"That's it," he said. "I'm doomed. Abelard is doomed."

"Not so fast," Dr. Carver said, holding up his cup. "I think I have figured out most of what's in this."

Mrs. Child beamed at him. "So have I! Let's compare notes." She felt in her pockets. "Good heavens, I didn't bring my notebook! It's still in my purse back at the station."

"Nor did I," Dr. Carver said. "Don't concern yourself. Our memories are good enough."

"I have the implements for writing," Im-Hotep said. From the broad pocket in the skirts of his coat, he drew sheets of yellow-white paper, a reed pen, and a round jar with a stopper.

"Excellent, my friend," Mrs. Child said. She sipped from her cup and lifted her eyes toward the ceiling. "Take this down: chocolate liquor, milk—no, cream—refined sugar, cloves, ginger, cinnamon, cardamom, a hint of black pepper...."

"The thickening has to be flour or corn starch," Dr. Carver said. "Nutmeg, I'm sure of it. Allspice, but not too much."

"Grains of paradise," Im-Hotep added. "But no saffron, turmeric, mustard, nothing woody or that leaves a colored residue."

"I believe you are right, my friend!" Mrs. Child exclaimed. "But what's that last flavor? Sumac? Anise?"

Dr. Carver smiled. "It's not common anise, my friend. It's star anise. Trade with the orient was well-established by now."

"Yes! Delightful."

Their second pot of chocolate arrived. The three continued to discuss the ingredients. Im-Hotep made notes in a backward scrawl that Steven couldn't decipher, sanding out notations as the others corrected him. A third and a fourth pot arrived. Steven asked the pot boy for directions to the "necessary," and found it was a smelly outhouse behind the long narrow shop in the alley. He was grateful to return to the table, where a fifth pot of chocolate had arrived and Mrs. Child had taken over the pen.

"Very well, then," she said. "Let's make a clean list. Perhaps we can persuade Sir John to copy it out for us. We'll tell him we will respect his confidence."

She spread out one of the new sheets of papyrus. Im-Hotep took a small knife from his kit and shaved the reed pen's nib smooth.

"How was it written out on the original document, Steven?" Mrs. Child asked.

"It's a list of ingredients, by proportion," he said. "Sir John has really neat handwriting. I know it started with a pound of chocolate, 'ground small.' That's what it said."

"Can you recall if we have deduced all of the spices?" Dr. Carver asked.

Steven clutched his hair and got handfuls of his borrowed wig. "I don't know! I think so! I just can't remember. I'm not a cook."

"Well, we'll do our best," Mrs. Child said, soothingly. She dipped the pen into the jar of ink. "First, chocolate, one pound, ground small. There! Next?"

"Cinnamon," Steven said. He watched the pen point glide gracefully over the page, and had a tremendous sense of déjà vu strike him. "Yes, that's just what it looked like."

"Good!" Dr. Carver said. "Then we're getting it."

"No!" Steven exclaimed, feeling elation fill his belly. "I mean, it's *exactly* what the Abelard recipe looks like!" He stared at Mrs. Child. "It was in *your* handwriting!"

Julia's eyes widened, and she beamed. "*We* came up with the formulation for Abelard chocolate?"

"Well, that's convenient," Dr. Carver said, slapping Im-Hotep on the back. "And it means our friend here was right! It was written on papyrus, not parchment."

"Let's finish jotting the ingredients down before we forget any," Julia said. She went on writing. Steven's spirits rose with every further notation. It was the Abelard recipe, for sure!

"We will have to determine the proportions," Im-Hotep said. "Precision makes all the difference in flavor and effect."

Mrs. Child nodded. "You are right as always, Lord Im-Hotep. Sir John won't help out with that at all. Well, that will take some experimentation. My kitchen or your laboratory, Dr. Carver?"

"How about the lab?" Dr. Carver asked. "I can obtain this whole list of ingredients in town. It might take a few days to test. My palate gets confused after three or four samples."

"Mine, too," Mrs. Child said. "Best to space out the tests."

"But that could take weeks!" Steven protested. "Months!"

Mrs. Child rose to her feet and patted him on the shoulder. "Stay here. We won't be a moment!"

She and Dr. Carver made their way out of the door, followed by Steven's puzzled glance. He started to rise, but Im-Hotep held him back.

In a moment, the two returned. Mrs. Child was beaming. Dr. Carver looked as though he had a stomach ache.

"Those three weeks were hard on my digestion," he said, shaking his head. "Too much chocolate!"

"Can one ever have enough chocolate?" Mrs. Child asked. She handed Steven the rolled document. He opened the papyrus and scanned it. The proportions were there. Now that he saw them, he was certain they were right. And at the bottom, Mrs. Child had written *This is proof of ownership.* "There! Although it doesn't say whose proof. No one will know but the four of us." She gave them a conspiratorial smile. "Your job is safe, young man."

Steven looked at them in despair. "But we have to get it back to the office in time for the press conference!"

"Time travel," Mrs. Child reminded him. Her expression changed, and she tapped him on the arm. "Look there!"

Steven glanced up. Sir John was having an argument with a silver-haired man. To Steven's horror, he recognized him as the intruder they had confronted in the office strong room. The clerk sprang to his feet.

The man recognized them, too. His eyes went wide with horror. He stormed toward the door, pushing customers out of his way. Sir John looked puzzled.

Mrs. Child grabbed Steven by the arm and pulled him down onto the bench.

"We have to go after him!" Steven exclaimed.

"No, we don't," she said, gently. "We have all the time in the world to correct the recipe, even to make multiple copies of it with the genuine ink and paper, in the genuine handwriting of the original." She let out her trilling laugh. "Me! Even if he destroyed them all, I can just write out another one."

Lord Im-Hotep peered at Steven. "You said you recognized him. Who is he?"

Steven urged his memory to fit the face to a place and time. He was certain he had seen the man in the office somewhere. The office....

The paintings!

"He's an Abelard," Steven blurted out. "He's... Roger Abelard, Sir John's older brother. He's the one who founded the London Chocolate Company and tried to compete. The family journals said he was always jealous of John. He never got knighted, you see."

"Hmmm," said Mrs. Child. "So, he moved in time to try to sabotage the empire that his brother created. Absolutely, he must be in league with his own descendants. I wonder if he's tried before?"

"Jealousy is a powerful spur," Im-Hotep acknowledged.

"But he loses again," Dr. Carver said. "Someone will have to work out how he got a hold of a travel ring, but that's a job for enforcement, not us."

"And close up that place of concealment, Steven Mentzel," the Egyptian said sternly. "If it has served once, it could again."

"I will!" Steven said, joy bubbling through him. He poured more chocolate for all of them and held up his cup. "Thank you! All of you!"

Julia Child sipped her toast. "And I have just figured out why I didn't come back to let myself know that we succeeded."

"Why not?" Dr. Carver asked.

"Well, we have to be at that press conference!" she said, and smiled at Steven. "And so do you, young man. I know you'll get there just in time."

The Jurors

Lawrence Watt-Evans

T hree time travelers watched as the young man walked into the room and took the chair on the opposite side of the table. He set a small rectangular object on the table; colors flickered across its surface.

He cleared his throat. "Good morning," he said. "My name is Tobe Carlsen, and I am here to explain your situation."

The younger of the male time travelers folded his hands behind his head, leaned back, and said, "Please do. I understand we are in what we would consider the future?"

"That's right, Mr. Fitzgerald. You are roughly a century and a half from the time of your death."

Fitzgerald frowned. "Go on."

"First, I don't know whether you've introduced yourselves. Ms. Wollstonecraft—"

"Mrs. Godwin," she interrupted.

"I'm sorry," Carlsen said. "Mrs. Godwin, then. This is Mary Wollstonecraft Godwin, who died in 1797, at the age of thirty-eight, from complications of the birth of her second child."

As this exchange took place, Fitzgerald sat up and unfolded his hands, giving the woman a curious look.

Carlsen turned to the older man. "General William Tecumseh Sherman, U.S. Army, retired. Died of pneumonia in 1891, aged seventy-one." Fitzgerald gave Sherman a startled glance, then returned his attention to Carlsen as the man said, "And Mr. F. Scott Fitzgerald, died of heart failure in 1940, aged forty-four."

"If we are dead, how is it we are here?" Sherman demanded. "Surely this isn't the afterlife."

"No, it isn't," Carlsen agreed. "This is the city of Seattle in the year 2096, and you were brought here by means of a machine that allows us to travel through time. We abducted each of you from as close as we could manage to the instant of your death, brought you to our own era, and cured you of the ailments that killed you, keeping you asleep while we did so. We also made lifeless copies of your bodies, dressed them in the clothes you were wearing when you died, and left them in your places, so that your absence would not be noticed."

"I assume you realize this is quite incredible," Sherman said.

"Oh, I know. It's still true. You may be wondering why we did this— why abduct anyone, and more specifically, why you three."

"Yes," Godwin said. Both men nodded.

"Recently a person named Rasheeda Cho led an insurrection against the governments of Europe and North America. Rasheeda was defeated and arrested, and was to be brought to trial, when we encountered a difficulty. Our law requires an impartial jury. Well, in Rasheeda's case, we couldn't *find* an impartial jury." He tapped his rectangular device. "We have methods of communication that had allowed everyone to watch the events of the insurrection, and everyone we approached already had a very strong opinion on Rasheeda's guilt or innocence.

"At the same time, the scientists—I'm sorry, Mrs. Godwin, that word is from beyond your time; the scholars—who had recently constructed a time-traveling machine were eager to find a way to put it to use, and suggested that we draw our jurors from the past, as a demonstration that their work could be of practical value. We agreed.

"We required jurors who read and speak fluent English, since the trial would be conducted in English. We needed people where we knew enough of the details of their deaths to be able to *find* them, and take them without being seen. We preferred people who had written extensively, so that we could analyze their attitudes and beliefs. From the candidates who met these standards, you three were chosen for your clarity of thought and your experience of revolutions and their effects."

"Experience of revolutions?" Fitzgerald asked, startled. "*I* was? I mean, Mrs. Godwin saw the French Revolution first-hand, and General Sherman fought in the War Between the States, but what did *I* do?"

"You closely observed the class conflicts of the Jazz Age and the Great Depression," Carlsen replied. "A social revolution, rather than a political one."

Fitzgerald grimaced. "I think you got the wrong man."

"Why only three of us?" Sherman demanded, before Carlsen could respond. "Or are there nine more in other rooms somewhere?"

Carlsen sighed. "I was coming to that. The operation was under way, and you three had been retrieved, when the entire project was shut down."

"Why?" Fitzgerald asked. "You decided it was too dangerous?"

"No. Because Rasheeda was assassinated while awaiting trial."

"Assassinated?" Sherman asked.

Carlsen nodded.

"So you don't have any use for us?" Fitzgerald said. "You went to all this trouble for nothing?"

"That's right." He shifted in his chair. "Well, not really for *nothing*. We proved our methods worked. You're here, and alive."

"All right," Fitzgerald said. "I suppose we should be grateful for that, but now what? Are we going to be returned to our deathbeds? Or rather, these two to their deathbeds, and I to the living room floor?"

"No. We are not going to save your lives only to kill you again. You will stay in this time, and you are free to go. We will assist you in adjusting to our era."

"You aren't taking us back to our own times?" Fitzgerald asked.

"No," Carlsen said unhappily. "We don't dare. We're afraid your presence would alter the course of history, so that our own time would not exist."

"I do not understand that," Godwin said.

"It is recorded history that you, Ms... Mrs. Godwin, died in 1797. If you were to be found alive in 1798, the world would change in ways we cannot predict—though in *your* case, we do know one change that would alter our world. If you had lived to raise your daughter Mary, she would almost certainly not have written the novel *Frankenstein*, with its theme of parental abandonment. The development of modern literature would be completely different."

Godwin's eyes widened. "What? What are you saying?"

"I hate to say it, Mrs. Godwin, but he has a point," Fitzgerald said. "*Frankenstein* was *unbelievably* influential, and not just in literature."

"My Mary became a writer? A novelist?" Godwin looked thunderstruck.

No one answered her. "That's fine for her," Sherman said, "but what about me? I was retired and no longer doing anything of importance, just giving speeches."

"We cannot say what effect your survival might have had, General. It's true there is nothing as obvious as *Frankenstein*, but you were still politically influential, whether you intended to be or not."

"I did not."

"Nevertheless."

"And I suppose you're afraid I might actually write that masterpiece I wanted to write," Fitzgerald said. "A book added, rather than lost."

"Yes, Mr. Fitzgerald. You understand. Though you will be interested to know that Edmund Wilson published your unfinished final novel, *The Last Tycoon*. Had you been able to complete it… but you weren't."

"He did… what? Well, damn!"

"If we can't go back, then what *are* we supposed to do?" Sherman demanded.

"Whatever you wish. I'm sure historians will be eager to interview you, and you might become speakers or lecturers—you are, of course, more knowledgeable about your own times and your own works than anyone born in our century can ever be, and many people are interested in hearing about your experiences. Your speeches will be in as much demand here as in your own time, General, though the crowds will be virtual, rather than filling lecture halls."

"What does *that* mean?"

"We'll explain that."

"I will want to read my dear child's novel—what was the title, again?"

"*Frankenstein*," Fitzgerald replied. "It's very good, but… perhaps not what you might expect."

Carlsen cleared his throat. "We will need to acquaint you with the basics of modern civilization. Simply putting you out on the street without guidance would be cruel. Mrs. Godwin, in your case we think we should also provide an interpreter; English has changed somewhat in the last three hundred years."

"I would appreciate that," she said.

"Good." Carlsen nodded, then rose. "We'll install one. I will be back in a moment." He turned, and left the room.

For a moment the three sat silently. Then Fitzgerald said, "Install?"

"That is what he said," Sherman said. "What he meant I cannot say. This entire situation is extremely strange."

"You can say *that* again!" Fitzgerald agreed. "It's something I wouldn't expect to find in the most lurid pulp magazines, let alone experience first-hand!"

"Pulp magazines?" Godwin asked.

"Well, the General would know them as dime novels, I suppose, but I'm damned if I can think of an equivalent from your time. Newgate Calendars, perhaps?"

"Oh," Godwin said, looking only slightly less puzzled.

"I might not be entirely convinced this is real, even yet, if not for the incidental details such as these 'pulp magazines'," Sherman said. "I'd say this must be some last-minute delirium, save I don't believe I have the imagination to come up with it all, even in my death throes."

"And that from one of the more imaginative military men in our history," Fitzgerald remarked. "The idiots in command in Europe in 1914 hadn't half your intelligence or imagination."

"Was there a war in 1914? I wouldn't know," Sherman said, a bit stiffly.

"Of course not. But there was, and rest assured, the best of their generals were bumbling fools compared to you. I read your memoirs— you're a brave and talented man, General. The men running the Great War were not. I volunteered in 1917 because I thought serving under them would be a more respectable way to die than outright suicide, but I didn't get sent to the front in time to pull that off."

Godwin listened to this with growing interest. "You wished to die?" she asked.

"Well, I thought so at the time. I got over it."

Sherman snorted. "I suppose a woman was involved?"

"Ah, you know romantic young men too well, General." He glanced at Godwin. "I seem to recall that your posthumous memoir mentioned suicide attempts. I concede you had more reason than I."

She blinked. "Posthumous memoir?"

"Your husband published it. I haven't read it, merely descriptions."

"It is very strange to hear that anything I wrote might be considered posthumous, since I am yet alive."

"Personally, I'm glad you are," Fitzgerald said. "I confess I haven't read any of your work, Miss Wollstonecraft, but I would like to."

"Hm," Sherman muttered.

Fitzgerald looked at him. "Her reputation as a writer and philosopher was much improved in my time over how she was viewed in yours, General, and that she was chosen as we were is intriguing."

"Not to me."

"I wonder how long they'll keep us waiting?" Fitzgerald asked.

"No telling," Sherman said. "At least here we don't have all those confounded moving images and colored lights and hums and clicks that were all over my hospital room."

Fitzgerald shrugged. "I made my living from moving images. Or at least, from words intended to accompany them, though most of what I wrote never made it onto the screen."

Sherman frowned at Fitzgerald. "And was this a respectable way to earn a living, where you came from?"

"Not really. It's what I was reduced to when my novels stopped selling."

"You were primarily a novelist?"

Fitzgerald sighed. "I like to think I still am, despite how I earned my bread for the last few years before they kidnaped me. Apparently I am sufficiently remembered as such that they considered me worth fetching here." He glanced at Sherman. "And I must say, General, that it is an honor to be treated as your peer."

"Hmpf."

"Excuse me, gentlemen," Godwin said, rising from her chair. She walked to the door they had entered through; it slid aside as she approached, and she stepped into the corridor beyond.

The door closed behind her.

"What's *that* about?"

"A call of nature, I suppose."

"I suppose." Sherman cast a look at the door, then turned back to Fitzgerald. "I would not be too sure it *is* an honor to be considered my peer, sir; the fact that they have put me in the company of a notorious and wanton madwoman like Mrs. Godwin does not speak well of my reputation here."

"Madwoman?" Fitzgerald threw a glance at the door, then smiled wryly. "Oh, she's no madwoman, whatever the people of your time may have thought. Believe me, I know a madwoman when I see one. I was *married* to one, and Mrs. Godwin is nothing like her, nor like any of the others I've met when visiting my wife in the asylum."

"You are doing nothing to dissuade me from my opinion."

Just then Carlsen reappeared, followed by three others, a man, a woman, and one whose gender was not immediately obvious; all of them wore blue pants and white tunics, similar in cut to the pale blue pants and tunics the time travelers had been issued. Each held two rectangular objects about the size of a children's book. "Where's Ms. Godwin?" Carlsen asked.

Fitzgerald gestured toward the door. "She didn't say."

"Ah. Well, I'll start with you two, then. General Sherman, this is Darine Ramirez." The clearly female person stepped forward. She handed Sherman one of the rectangular things.

"It's an honor to meet you, sir," she said. "This is your tablet; come with me and I'll explain how to use it."

"Perhaps we'll meet again, Mr. Fitzgerald," he said, as he allowed Darine Ramirez to lead him away.

The clearly male new arrival stepped forward. "Mr. Fitzgerald? I'm Caspar Tranh." He proffered a tablet. As Fitzgerald accepted it, the door opened and Godwin reappeared.

"Mrs. Godwin," the third individual said, stepping forward. "I am to be your tutor in your brave new world."

They reached out a tablet, and Godwin accepted it. "And your name?" she asked.

"Robin Walters. If you will follow me?"

She glanced at Fitzgerald.

"It has been a pleasure, Mrs. Godwin," he said.

"Farewell, Mr. Fitzgerald." Then she followed Walters.

Fitzgerald turned to Carlsen. "Will I ever see them again?"

"That's up to you," Carlsen said. "Now, if you would accompany Caspar…"

Fitzgerald did so.

One year later, Scott Fitzgerald sat in a café sipping some weird descendant of Coca-Cola—there were so many varieties that he did not try to keep them straight, but simply took whatever the machines first offered—when Mary Godwin walked in and looked around. He waved, and she crossed to his table.

"Mr. Fitzgerald," she said, as he rose and pulled out a chair for her.

"It's been over a year since I did that for a lady," he said, as they both sat.

"Many of the old niceties do seem to have been lost," she agreed.

A machine rolled up and set a glass of tea and a plate of tiny sandwiches on the table, then moved smoothly away.

"I do find some of the changes improvements, though," she said, sipping her drink.

"You ordered online?"

"Yes."

"I don't really have the hang of that yet. I always get some detail wrong."

"For my own part, I find these intelligent machines quite agreeable." She sipped tea again. "Will General Sherman be joining us?"

"I hope so. I did not get a straight answer."

She nodded. "And how have you been faring this past year?"

"Well enough. Carlsen was right that I would have an audience for whatever I might want to say, but I could wish for a *better* audience. I am very tired of answering stupid questions about *The Great Gatsby*."

"Your… third novel, was it?"

"Yes. And it seems to be the only one anyone remembers. I am further mortified that that fool Wilson published the fragments of *The Love of the Last Tycoon*, rather than doing the decent thing and leaving it alone."

"At least you are remembered for *your* work, even if not as you would have chosen. There are a handful of scholars familiar with my work, and I am credited by them as one of the early visionaries whose writings helped bring about the equality of the sexes now taken for granted, but to the vast majority of the population I seem to be known only as the mother of the author of *Frankenstein*. I am constantly being asked about a child who was barely ten days old when last I saw her, and about whom I know almost nothing."

"Did you read the novel?"

"I did. I found it tremendously sad. If I could only return to my own era and raise little Mary in a loving household!"

"Then it would not have been written."

"And would that be a tragedy? Perhaps she might write something joyous in its stead."

"Well, *I* would regret its loss—assuming I knew of it, which of course I wouldn't." He frowned thoughtfully.

"I also read my husband's *Memoirs of the Author of A Vindication of the Rights of Woman*. It is absolutely not what I would have published, had I lived."

"It did not serve your memory well," Fitzgerald agreed.

"Oh, here is the General!" Godwin exclaimed, waving.

A moment later Sherman joined them at the table, and accepted a glass of some amber-colored beverage from a serving machine.

"General," Fitzgerald said. "A pleasure to see you again."

"Is it?"

"Why, yes," Godwin said.

"You prefer a relic like me to the popinjays and perverts of this time?"

The others exchanged uncomfortable glances.

"A relic, sir?" Fitzgerald asked.

"What else would you call it? I have neither friends nor family, and serve no purpose in this place. I have accepted several speaking engagements, but they have all been done as talking images, rather than standing upon an actual stage, and the audiences are far less congenial than those of my own times. Interviews with historians have also proven less than enjoyable. I must thank you, though, Mr. Fitzgerald, for mentioning the generals of the First World War. I have been studying them, and I find it a far more appealing topic of research than this new world; I can *understand* them, and see where they went wrong. I wish I had been there to tell them what fools they were, and perhaps put them on a better path. Tens of thousands of lives could have been saved."

"It seems we would all prefer to return to our own times," Godwin said. "I to raise my daughter and see that my husband did not make a hash of my memoir, you to show the generals of Europe how to avoid needless slaughter, and Mr. Fitzgerald to finish his novel. Would that it was possible!"

Fitzgerald said, "You know, it's not actually *impossible*; it's simply forbidden."

"Oh?" Godwin said.

Fitzgerald nodded. "I've been studying it—time travel, I mean. They won't allow us to return to our lives because they're afraid we'll change history, but it's not that we *can't* go back. The machine that brought us here can take us back."

"You are sure of this?" Sherman asked.

Fitzgerald nodded. "Absolutely. And I have been studying the theory involved—not the actual physics, that's beyond me, but the theories regarding causality and what would happen if we *did* change the past."

"Go on, Mr. Fitzgerald," Godwin said.

"I'm afraid this is… well, it sounds insane, frankly, but the physicists…"

"The what?" Godwin interrupted.

"Physicists. People who study the science of physics."

"Go on," Sherman said. "What do these mad scientists say?"

"Well, the basic argument is that you cannot change what has already happened—which seems obvious enough, doesn't it? At any rate, if we were to return to our former lives, the universe in which we died would not be changed, because it can't be; it already existed, and if it didn't, we wouldn't be here discussing it. Instead we would create an entirely new version of reality existing alongside this one. They even have a word for this theoretical creation—a 'timeline.' Theory says that there can be multiple timelines, and that if we returned to our own times, we would create new timelines, entire new universes that would follow their own paths, while *this* universe, where we died on schedule, would continue to exist, blithely unaware of any changes. Our Mr. Carlsen and his friends are worrying about nothing in their determination to prevent us from going back; this reality will not be changed, and will be unaware a new one has been created. I read several articles saying as much. Apparently there is a consensus among physicists, but the politicians reject it."

"New universes?" Sherman said doubtfully.

"I was not aware the word 'universe' could have a plural," Godwin said.

"Say 'worlds,' then." Fitzgerald replied. "Or realms. Think of the worlds where we return to our old lives as realms like Faerie."

"And you say the time machine can take us to this Land Beneath the Hill, where we will have our friends and family around us again?" Godwin asked.

Fitzgerald nodded. "Of course," he said, "that would mean giving up everything we have here that was not invented yet in our own times. No medical miracles that brought us back to life and cured us of the diseases that killed us. No tablets that can answer every question. No foods brought from every corner of the world, regardless of the season."

"I'll take that," Sherman said. "No constant buzzing and humming from machinery everywhere, no flashing lights and moving pictures, no creatures who are neither men nor women."

"I quite like some of the machinery, though its ubiquity can be disconcerting," Godwin said. "I confess that I am not entirely comfortable with some of the changes in society, however, even though I argued for many of them; I am still a creature of my own upbringing, as are we all. But this is all nonsense; we have no choice. Perhaps the machine can take us back, but its keepers will not allow it."

All three were silent for a moment, though the café was anything but; there was a constant buzz of conversation, and unpleasant music playing.

Then Fitzgerald said, "I have a long history of doing things that weren't allowed. True, most were when I was either young and stupid or very drunk, but still. And since they repaired my heart and liver for me, I feel twenty years younger; I think I'm capable of being quite stupid again."

"I have never felt the need to let others dictate my actions," Sherman replied. "I think we can find a way."

"They did choose us for our familiarity with rebellion," Godwin mused.

"I have an idea of how we can get to the machine," Fitzgerald said. "We are celebrities, after all, and that gives us power. I don't know how to operate it, though."

"Perhaps I can help," Godwin said.

"Really?" Fitzgerald cocked his head.

"As I said, I have taken quite an interest in electronic devices, and I have made friends these past few months who are very knowledgeable," she said. "We may need some time, though."

"That can be arranged," Sherman said, "if you two are serious about this."

Fitzgerald smiled crookedly. "As serious as a heart attack," he said.

"I think this is a wonderful idea," Tobe Carlsen said. "I'm glad to see the three of you finally enjoying your celebrity. You know, I'd had some concerns about how you were adjusting, Mr. Fitzgerald."

"Scott," Fitzgerald said. "Please, call me Scott."

"Scott," Carlsen said, smiling.

"Are the cameras getting it all?" Fitzgerald asked, looking at the swarm of drones cruising around the laboratory.

"I'm sure they are." He glanced back as Mary Godwin and someone he did not recognize followed them into the big room.

"Mrs. Godwin wanted to bring a friend," Fitzgerald said. "I trust that's not a problem?"

"Oh, not at all! I'm pleased she's made friends!"

"That's good. I believe General Sherman may have brought a few, as well." He turned to the structure occupying the center of the laboratory. "So this is it, then?"

"That's it. Of course, it's shut down now."

"Of course." Godwin and her companion came up to stand beside Fitzgerald as he studied the time machine. It was smaller than he had expected.

Behind them General Sherman entered the room, accompanied by two very large men.

"Do you think you could turn on the power?" Fitzgerald asked. "Just so the lights come on, to make it look a little more exciting. You don't want our viewers to think the project has been completely abandoned. I mean, one point of today's exercise is to convince them that the money spent here wasn't wasted."

"I think we can do that," Carlsen said. He ran a finger across the miniature tablet on his wrist, and a dozen screens and indicators on the time machine lit up.

"Thank you, Tobe—may I call you Tobe?"

"Of course!" Carlsen smiled, bathing in his own sense of self-importance.

Sherman had joined the party, his two men hanging back. Godwin was now close beside Fitzgerald, and her companion had stepped back a little as well, where she was doing something with a tablet.

"You're on in five," a voice said from somewhere overhead.

"Thank you," Carlsen said. He turned to face the largest of the drones, which had dropped down to eye level. A red light came on.

"Dear viewers," Carlsen said, "welcome to our special presentation on the International Physics Consortium's time travel program. I'm sure you've all heard about it, and perhaps even seen interviews with some of the people involved, but today we have the three people brought from the past, who have agreed to appear together for the first time..."

He rambled on for what seemed like hours, but Fitzgerald knew it was really just a few minutes. He noticed that Godwin looked nervous. Sherman looked alert, but calm.

Carlsen introduced each of them, and asked a few questions, which they answered. Then Fitzgerald saw Godwin's friend with the tablet nod.

"May we go inside?" he asked Carlsen. "Just the three of us? I don't think we can fit any more; it's not very big."

"Inside?"

Fitzgerald nodded. "I mean, we were unconscious when we were in it before, and I'd like to see what it looks like."

Carlsen looked uncertain.

"We don't mind if the drone comes in with us," Fitzgerald said. "I mean, we aren't going to break anything."

"Well, I suppose..."

"Won't your viewers want to see the inside, as well?"

"Yes, of course! Good idea. Ms. Godwin, General...?"

The three of them clambered through the hatch into the machine, Fitzgerald first, Sherman next, and Godwin last, a drone squeezing in between Sherman and Godwin.

And the instant Godwin was inside, the hatch slammed shut and the machine shifted from standby mode to powering up. Panels lit, and a loud hum sounded. The drone in the machine with them fell to the floor, inert.

"It seems your friend knows her stuff," Fitzgerald said.

"I trusted her, and I do not trust lightly," Godwin replied, tapping commands on her own tablet.

Something pounded on the hatch from the outside. Fitzgerald looked up.

"Don't worry," Sherman said. "My men know their job."

"You're sure you can trust them?"

"They were two of Rasheeda Cho's most devoted troops. They have no love for the government here, and will make sure no one prevents our departure."

"Mary?"

"There!" she said, with a final triumphant click. She looked at Fitzgerald. "I do hope you gave me the correct time and place."

"I hope so, too," he said, as the air around them began to shimmer.

They had not given much thought to the fact that there were dead bodies in their respective places, but the solution was obvious. Sherman and Fitzgerald heaved Fitzgerald's corpse into the machine just as Sheilah Graham entered the room.

"Scott, what the *hell*!" she exclaimed.

"Just a moment," Fitzgerald said. Then he stepped back as the hatch closed.

Harry Culver, the building's manager, was close behind Graham. He stared as the time machine flickered and vanished.

"What the *hell*," Graham repeated.

"What was that?" Culver asked.

"How about," Fitzgerald said, "we pretend none of this ever happened? Because I can't give you a reasonable explanation, but I can assure you it won't happen again."

"But... are you okay?" Graham asked. "I thought you were dead!"

"I'm fine," Fitzgerald replied. "I'm fine. And I'm not going anywhere."

Aboard the time machine, Sherman and Godwin both stared at Fitzgerald's corpse with distaste. There was no room to move more than a few inches away from it, but they did their best not to touch it.

"I'm afraid you'll have my body as well for the final leg," Sherman said.

"I will bear up," Godwin replied.

"I'm sure you will. While I may have entertained unkind thoughts about your beliefs and morals, Mrs. Godwin, since meeting you I have never once doubted your courage and resourcefulness." He hesitated, then asked, "What do you plan to do with this machine, once you reach your home?"

"I intend to send it into the distant past, where no one will have any notion what it is, or how to operate it, or how it came to have three cadavers in it."

Sherman nodded. "A good solution." He turned his attention from Fitzgerald's dead face to Godwin's very alive one. "How *did* you learn to operate it?"

"I did not think to study time travel, as our friend did," she said, gesturing toward the corpse, "but I found the devices of that place fascinating." She held up her tablet. "I learned as much about them as I could, with the help of Robin Walters and our friend Kris. There are those who teach themselves to use these machines illicitly; they call themselves hackers, and take pride in gaining access to forbidden information. Kris is one such. She was able to find out everything I needed to know to operate this machine; it is, after all, merely a larger device. All of their electronic devices operate on the same principles." Then she looked at her tablet, and said, "Shall we deliver you to your deathbed, General?"

Godwin's control of the machine had improved, and the two remaining travelers were prepared for the task of manhandling a body into the time machine, so they were able to manage the transition in Sherman's New York home more smoothly than the one in Fitzgerald's Hollywood residence. Godwin launched herself for home before anyone caught more than a faint glimpse of her transport.

At her final destination, though, she required her baffled husband's assistance in loading her doppelganger into the machine. After the machine's disappearance he demanded an explanation, and she told him, "You must consider it a miracle, dear William, and accept it as such. I cannot tell you more unless you would think me a madwoman. Know only that I am here, I am well, and I am eager to spend the remainder of my life with you and Fanny and Mary."

The Godwin family thrived, and no further mention was ever made of the strange apparition and miraculous cure. William inquired about the curious tablet his wife had acquired, and the manuscript she hastily copied from it—*Frankenstein, or the New Prometheus*—but received only evasion, and no real answer. The tablet went dark forever after a month or so; as for the manuscript, Mrs. Godwin refused to publish it, but presented it to young Mary on her twenty-first birthday. Whatever explanation she gave her daughter remained between the two of them.

The feminist movement led by Mrs. Godwin took root and grew, as well, though far more slowly than she liked.

"It is faster than it was previously, at least," she said to her husband, and once again she refused to provide an explanation.

After his miraculous recovery from pneumonia, General W.T. Sherman surprised everyone by taking ship for Europe, where he seemed determined to track down certain French and British officers and engage them in extended conversation about military history and practice. Upon Germany's surrender in 1916, several of the victorious generals credited their success to Sherman's tutelage.

F Scott Fitzgerald's *The Love of the Last Tycoon* was published to critical acclaim in the spring of 1943; wartime paper shortages severely hampered sales, but in 1945 a second edition landed on the bestseller list. Fitzgerald's sixth novel, *A Time of Strangers*, took an unexpected turn into science fiction, but was nonetheless well received.

In October of 2097, Tobe Carlsen stared in horror at the empty space at the center of the laboratory floor. He waited for the world he knew to vanish around him, to be replaced by something alien—or by nothing at all.

Nothing changed.

He lost his job, of course, even though that final webcast became a popular success, with over three billion views. He checked feverishly to see whether he could find any difference in the world, but the histories of Mary Wollstonecraft Godwin, William Tecumseh Sherman, and F. Scott Fitzgerald were all just as he remembered them.

He tried very hard to ignore the possibility that his own memories had changed, along with all records.

Several people told him that this simply proved the diverging timeline hypothesis. Others suggested that the inexperienced people from the past had been unable to handle the machine properly and were lost in time, or had simply ceased to exist.

The two Rasheedists who had held security at bay during the hijacking were apprehended, tried, and convicted, but served only six months.

The time machine never reappeared.

In a fifth timeline, a mysterious metal box containing three corpses appeared out of nowhere on the island of Hokkaido during the later Neolithic era. The cult that grew up around this phenomenon became the foundation of the Ainu Empire that ruled much of Asia for some 1,100 years. Later archeologists studying the remains concluded that the box was a tomb of some sort, but no consensus on its origins was ever reached.

Star Rat's Tale
Allen Steele

Let me tell you about my friend Star Rat. It's a strange tale and you probably won't believe a word of it. I didn't either, not at first. And then… well… maybe I should give you his story and let you decide.

Star Rat was a guy I knew in college, many years ago in the '70s. He was another student at the liberal arts college in New Hampshire where I went to learn how to write, drink without throwing up, and climb into bed with as many girls as I could without contracting a social disease (the last two were my easiest subjects: the drinking age was still 18 and no one had heard of AIDS yet). Star Rat was already there when I arrived as a freshman, and he was still there when I graduated four years later, and when I came back for my five-year reunion he was still there, unmatriculated and unchanged, ever and always Star Rat.

I didn't know his real name. No one did. I asked him that once, during one of those rare occasions when he was sober, and he mumbled something that could've been Paul and Phil or Pat or Pete—a single syllable that began with a P, that's all I heard—and shambled away. If anyone asked where he got his nickname, he would say that he'd taken it from a palindrome, *rats live on no evil star*. On his right forearm was a tattoo of a bemused-looking rat lounging atop a five-pointed star, joint hanging from his hairy snout. A nice bit of skin art, etched there by a skilled craftsman long before tats became fashionable; I've never seen another like it. Star Rat must had paid a tattooist well for this, but I have no idea how long he'd had it.

With a nickname like that, you can be sure that the person who has it isn't a Boy Scout—well, *maybe* not a Boy Scout—so if you assume that Star Rat was a hippie, then your deductive reasoning is flawless. Star Rat was a hippie for the ages, a beatnik for all seasons. He stood about five-six, a skinny white kid with black hair that grew down past his shoulders and was seldom combed or washed; his face was framed by an untrimmed beard that covered most of his acne and but not his nose, a large, rodent-like proboscis befitting his moniker. He didn't brush his teeth every day, but at least he didn't smoke. Cigarettes, that is; his breath, like everything else about him, perpetually reeked of pot. An hour or two with a barber, a dental hygienist, and a steady girlfriend to insist that he clean up his act might have changed all that, but if Rat truly wanted to change, I'm sure he would've done so on his own. He was a person comfortable in his own skin, however unwashed it may be.

Star Rat almost never talked about himself, not even with friends like me, so what little we knew about him was rumor and hearsay. Campus legend had it that he was the scion of a wealthy Colorado family, western old-money that made its fortune in the 1800s from gold, cattle, or railroads. But he was the black sheep of the clan, the rebel heir who didn't want any part of the family business. A trust fund recipient who'd never need to get a job, he was too weird and embarrassing for the family to have hanging around, so they shipped him off to a small school on the other side of the country whose academic standards were low enough for him to get in. Star Rat Senior quietly paid the college to keep Star Rat Junior there forever so long as he behaved himself, without ever demanding that he keep up his grade-point average (which was probably 0.0; I never once saw him in class, and didn't know whether he'd even declared a major). He never graduated so far as I know; even the seniors who'd received their diplomas during my freshman year treated him as an old classmate when they came back for Homecoming. He was an ageless campus fixture, untouched by reality. He was Star Rat.

As you might also expect, he was a Deadhead, a devoted fan of the Grateful Dead (with a name like Star Rat, do you think he would've been into Abba?). Just about every T-shirt he wore was a Dead shirt; his denim jacket had a skull-and-roses patch on the back. If you visited his off-campus apartment—he'd been thrown out of the dorms years ago; the college had *some* standards, at least—you'd find the walls covered with Grateful Dead concert posters and silkscreen tapestries, and he always had a Dead album or concert tape on the stereo. And indeed, it was an indication of his hidden wealth that Rat had the best equipment Pioneer, Sony, and Bose produced in the '70s.

And, of course, whenever the Dead came through New England on one of their East Coast tours—usually in autumn or early winter—Star Rat would buy tickets for every show, pack up his '72 Volkswagen Beetle with Dead stickers all over the windows and fenders, and drop everything to spend weeks on the road, traveling with the Dead from Connecticut to Rhode Island to New York to Massachusetts to Maine, crashing in motels with other Deadheads and subsisting on a diet of junk food and cheap wine.

He was always high. Always. In the four years that I saw Star Rat nearly each and every day—except when he was touring with the Dead—I can recall only two or three times when he wasn't obviously stoned. To his credit, Rat never used anything addictive. He stayed away from heroin, despised cocaine, and never touched hard liquor. But he loved marijuana like it was a woman; indeed, one of the reasons why I made friends with him was because he had great weed and was always willing to share a joint. Not for him any crappy New England grass; Star Rat smoked only the finest from California, Oregon, and Hawaii, and occasionally laid his hands on gourmet herb from Mexico and Central America or black hash from the mountains of Afghanistan.

It was acid, though, that Rat enjoyed most of all. He tripped at least once a week, sometimes nonstop for days on end. His appetite for LSD was bottomless and his tolerance was legendary; he claimed to have never had a bad trip, and not to anyone's knowledge did he ever OD. I'd occasionally drop acid, too, back in the day, but not nearly as much or as often as Star Rat did. I can't recall how many times I encountered Rat when his eyes were bloodshot and looked like black marbles and he was babbling about things I couldn't understand.

Star Rat was a cosmic cowboy, an acid astronaut. If he hadn't been such a nice guy—and Rat really was a sweet person, a kind and harmless soul—his bohemian appearance, neglect for personal hygiene, and forever stoned behavior might have made him unbearable. Most people who knew him liked him, though, at least well enough to put up with his deficits.

Then he went to a Grateful Dead show where something happened that changed everything. An incident that led him to become obsessed with the picture on the back of an obscure Dead album, and how it caused him to question the nature of time itself.

That particular concert was on the Dead's winter tour of '79: January 15th at the Hartford Civic Center Arena. I wasn't there; I couldn't afford a ticket and never went to a show without one, unlike the scores of Deadheads who'd show up at the venue begging for "miracle tickets" other 'heads would sometimes give away when a friend or date couldn't make it. But Star Rat was with a bunch of friends who'd car-pooled down from our school in New Hampshire, and although most of them would later tell me all about the show that night, with everyone raving about a long, sweet jam of "Terrapin Station" that was the highlight of the second set, Rat had a different tale to tell.

I often wish iPhones had been invented long before they actually were; I might've been able to record him relating the incident that would haunt him long thereafter. But Rat repeated it often enough that I have no trouble recalling the details. Although most of our friends laughed it off, it stuck in my mind. It wasn't just its weirdness that made the story memorable; it was the fact that Star Rat adamantly insisted that it really and truly happened.

According to Rat, "Terrapin Station" had just phased into that part of the show which Deadheads know as "Space Drums," when percussionists Mickey Hart and Bill Kreuztmann launch into an improvisational drum duet that can last twenty minutes or more. That's when he decided, as Deadheads often do, that now was a good time to take a leak.

As always, Rat's seat was on the arena floor in front of the stage (although no one with floor seats for a Dead show actually use them, except to briefly sit and roll a joint on their knees). So he picked his way through the hand-waving, ass-shaking, dog-whistling and war-whooping crowd to the nearest exit and, once out in the mezzanine, went in search of the nearest men's room.

The closest one was just a little way from the arena entrance and he sailed right in. By that point of the evening, it was probably hard to say which was more messed up, the piss-stained floor or Star Rat's mind. He couldn't recall how many tabs of blotter acid he'd already consumed, but it wouldn't have been less than three or four; the Rat had developed such a tolerance for LSD that he had to take more than most people just to get a proper buzz. And who's to say how many joints he'd smoked on the way down from New Hampshire and out in the parking lot? So a quick trip to the john was more like a moonwalk for him; he was probably just barely aware that he was on Earth.

Everyone else with seats in that section were still inside, so the restroom was deserted. But as he stood before a urinal emptying his bladder of all the Diet Coke he'd consumed over the past few hours, he heard someone walk in behind him. The newcomer went straight to the row of urinals and took the second one to the right of where Star Rat was standing. Another Deadhead, he figured, but when he looked over at the man who'd just joined him, Rat noticed that he was unusual even for this crowd.

Deadheads, particularly hard-core 'heads who make the effort to get floor close to the stage, have a certain look: shoulder-length hair and beards, patched and faded jeans, long peasant skirts for girls and, most of all, the garish, tie-dyed T-shirts that don't look like anything actually worn by hippies in the '60s. That's how they dressed in the late '70s and pretty much how they still dress today, but this fellow was different.

Tall and skinny, he was totally hairless, with a shaved scalp that no guys except punk rockers had in 1979 (and no self-respecting punk would've been caught dead at a Dead show). Because he had no hair, it was difficult for Star Rat to pin down his age; somewhere in the ball park between 18 and 100, he guessed. And instead of the usual hippie gear, this chap was dressed entirely in black. Black shoes, black trousers, black T-shirt… the last a subtle fashion *faux pas* for Dead shows, since only one person was allowed to wear a plain black T-shirt and that was Jerry Garcia. If anyone else came to a show wearing Jerry's signature apparel, he'd get cold looks and snide comments until he got the message and went over to the souvenir stand and purchased a tie-dyed tour shirt, or just took off the offending shirt, threw it away, and went bare-chested for the rest of the night. No one wore plain black T-shirts except the Dead's leader (until Jerry himself sported red T-shirts for a while during the '80s, a period Deadheads remember with baffled horror).

This individual had been standing beside Star Rat for a minute or two before he became aware of the stoned kid regarding him with eyes the size of robin's eggs.

"Are you enjoying the concert?" he asked.

"Oh, yeah," Star Rat replied. "The Dead are just so far out." (Yes, he did indeed say this. Star Rat was probably the last guy, even among hippies, to use the expression "far out" without a trace of irony.)

The bald man smiled and laughed a bit. "Yes, they are… far out," he said, repeating what Star Rat had said as if he'd never heard it before. "I'm surprised how good they were."

Whenever Rat retold his story, he'd stress that part of the conversation. "That's what the dude said," the Rat would say, then slowly repeat his words. "'How good they were.' *Were!* Past tense, man… *past* tense!"

However, Star Rat apparently didn't notice this odd comment at the time. He figured that this person had never been to a Grateful Dead concert before, which explained his unfamiliarity not only with the show's quality, but also the way you were supposed to look. Before Rat had a chance to become wary, though, and suspect the bald man was a narc, the stranger asked, "What's your favorite Grateful Dead album?"

A harmless small-talk question, common among people attending their first show. "*American Beauty*," the Rat said without hesitation, "although I love *Blues for Allah*, too. And *Anthem of the Sun*. And *Workingman's Dead*, too. And—"

"What do you think of *Skeletons from the Closet*?"

That's an odd question to ask a Deadhead. *Skeletons from the Closet* was the Grateful Dead's first best-of album, put out by Warner Brothers Records in 1974 as a compilation of already-released studio tracks the band considered to be their best single-length songs of the time. While it's a good album for someone to sample the Dead for the first time, those who truly love the band usually ignore it. Just a few years later, Warner Bros. replaced it with *What a Long, Strange Trip It's Been*, the two-record collection that was longer and considered by fans to be much more definitive. Since then, the Dead have released so many compilations that *Skeletons from the Closet* has become all but forgotten.

"It's okay," Star Rat said. By now he'd pegged this fellow as a newbie. "Got some good stuff, y'know."

"Have you ever looked at the back cover?" the stranger asked. "The art, I mean."

Another odd question. Dead albums usually had remarkable cover art, but it's not a topic Deadheads often discuss. "Uhh… yeah," the Rat said. "Sure, it's cool."

The man in black nodded. Now there was a sly smile on his face. "Would you like to see something just like it? Something else that is also… cool?"

Star Rat nodded. "Yeah, man. What is it?"

The bald man stepped away from the urinal. "Follow me and I'll show you."

L et's pause for a moment to consider what this individual (whom we'll simply refer to from here on as the Stranger) was talking about. Like most Grateful Dead albums—until the mid-80s, that is, when band photos started being used instead—*Skeletons from the Closet* had wonderfully surrealistic artwork for its front and back covers. The front jacket, a group portrait of Botticelli's Venus, a grinning black dude wearing hipster shades, and a joint-smoking skeleton spinning a record on his upraised middle finger, is amusing but doesn't concern us here. It's the back-cover painting that requires description for those unfamiliar with it.

The picture shows three men seated around a table in what appears to be a sidewalk diner or maybe a bar. On the table are a cheeseburger and fries, a soda, a salt shaker, and bottle of ketchup; also present are a matchbook with the '70s ecology symbol on the cover and a small Earth globe balanced atop a cone. Through a window in the background behind the table can be seen a tear-shaped Dymaxion automobile, the flying saucer from *The Day the Earth Stood Still*, and a streamlined Frank Lloyd Wright-style building. But the three men at the table are the painting's most interesting subjects.

From left to right, they are: Marlon Brando, in the biker outfit he wore as Johnny in *The Wild One*; Jesus Christ, wearing an academic cap and gown as if he's just come from a college graduation, and Cesar Romero, dressed in the embroidered Mexican jacket and sombrero he wore when he was the Cisco Kid in western movie-serials of the '40s. Each is holding a handful of cards; Johnny seems to be worried about the hand he's been dealt, but Jesus and the Cisco Kid are casting sly smiles to each other, as if sharing a secret poor Marlon doesn't know about.

It's a clever and intriguing scene. While I was in college, I used to spend a lot of time gazing at it, usually while smoking a bone and listening to the Dead album it came from. And like many other people who've studied the painting, I wondered just how these three guys came to be together, grabbing lunch and playing cards in a place that never was.

How indeed?

O kay, back to the story:
Star Rat and the Stranger left the restroom and began walking down the mezzanine. The drum duet was over and once again the mezzanine was filled with twirlers, Deadheads who spend the show

dancing as only Deadheads do, ecstatically spinning about on their toes and heels, nearly colliding with one another but somehow managing to stay apart, light on their feet and blissfully stoned. The two of them gently made their way through the dancing mob—the only way to safely traverse twirlers is to do a little twirling yourself; Star Rat was an expert, but the Stranger had apparently never done this before—and it was only once they'd reached the other side that Rat realized where the bald man was leading him, toward the roped-off area directly behind the stage that's off-limits to everyone but the band and their road crew.

It's the fondest wish of every Deadhead to go backstage during a show. Very, very few people are given this privilege; even groupies aren't allowed there, or at least not without specific invitation. And although Rat didn't see an adhesive backstage pass affixed to the Stranger's black shirt or trousers, his companion strode toward the rope and the opaque drapes behind it with the self-assured confidence of someone who belonged there. And then it dawned on Star Rat that, by some stroke of outrageous fortune, his years of devotion had finally been noticed and he'd been chosen to enter the Grateful Dead's inner circle. Can you say hallelujah?

Yet before they reached an opening in the rope where a roadie with the show's guest list and a uniformed security guard stood like a pair of Chinese temple lions, the Stranger veered toward a door in the cinderblock wall just a few yards away. It was an ordinary metal door with the sign *Authorized Persons Only*, and as the bald man halted before it and reached into his pocket as if to retrieve a key ring, Star Rat saw his fantasies of sharing a joint with Phil Lesh or having Bob Weir invite him onstage to sing "Truckin'" dissipate like so much pot smoke.

"Hey, dude… where're you taking me?" he asked.

"Don't worry," the Stranger said, "you'll love this."

With that, the door opened. Star Rat couldn't recall later having actually seen the Stranger produce a key and fit into the lock; the knob simply turned the moment the Stranger touched it with his left hand, his right hand remaining in his trouser pocket. "Come, hurry," he said as he glanced at the roadie and the cop nearby. "Go quickly."

It was pitch black on the other side of the door, as dark as the Stranger's clothes. The lights were off, but the Rat hurried in anyway, and the moment he was through the door, the Stranger slammed it shut behind him.

In that instant, Rat no longer felt floor beneath his feet. He was falling, falling as if they were in a skyscraper elevator whose cables had just been severed. Star Rat had the terrifying sensation of plummeting through a starless midnight sky. It happened so quickly, he didn't have a chance to yell or do anything more than suck in his breath. And then...

He landed.

Although it had felt like he was falling from a great height, when his shoes touched the floor, it was with no more impact than if he'd hopped off a stepladder. The abrupt arrival startled him so much, though, it barely registered on him that he was in a brightly lit room. His legs collapsed beneath him, and Star Rat fell upon his hands and knees, and a moment later he was throwing up the veggie burrito he'd bought for dinner from a parking lot vendor.

"Oh, no." A pair of hands settled upon his shoulders. "I'm sorry, so sorry," the Stranger said. "I should have realized this would be a new experience for you and given you some warning." He gently massaged the Rat's shoulders, offering comfort. "My most sincere apologies, Mister... uh..."

"Star Rat, man." His guts now empty, Star Rat sat back on his haunches, raising his head to look around. The room was vacant except for him and the bald guy; no furniture, only a circular chamber like the inside of a drum, its bare walls the color of a newly minted penny. There was a window on one side of the room, dark and unreflective, and beside it was a narrow door with no knob or handle.

"Where the fuck are we?" he asked. "What the fuck's goin' on?"

"We're no longer at the concert, if that's what you're asking." The Stranger slid his hands beneath Star Rat's arms, and carefully hoisted him to his feet. "Where we've gone will take some explanation, I'm afraid. And as for—" a pause, as if he was trying to utter an unfamiliar expression "—'what the fuck is going on,' well, Mr. Star Rat Man—"

"Star Rat... just Star Rat."

"Very well, Mr. Rat," the Stranger said, which made Rat smile; no one had ever called him Mister before. "If you'll come with me, I'll try to explain things."

His companion gently guided him toward the door. They'd almost reached it when Star Rat heard a faint hum behind him. He looked over his shoulder, and saw that the puddle of vomit he'd left there was gone. The floor was as clean as if it had just been mopped.

"Whoa, dude… where's my puke?"

"Recovered. Matter-energy conversion. If you'd like, it can be analyzed and reconstituted to its original edible form. Are you hungry? Would you like to eat?"

"Uhh… no, that's okay, thanks." One veggie burrito was enough. And besides, Star Rat wasn't in the practice of eating his own vomit.

The Stranger laughed as if Star Rat had just said something clever. Then the door opened on its own, and they walked out into a place that obviously wasn't the Hartford Civic Center.

At this point in the narrative, which Star Rat related to me and his other friends many, many times, the story's details often became vague and inconsistent. It wasn't as if Rat was lying. It was more like his conscious mind, inhibited as it was by LSD, was fabricating a hallucination so vivid that Rat could only interpret it as being real. And indeed, Rat often admitted while he was reiterating the story for the umpteenth time, he was "peaking" while all this was happening, acidhead vernacular for the period in an acid trip when the drug takes full effect and kicks into high gear.

So, for better or worse, this is what Star Rat said he experienced. Be as skeptical as you like; I never believed it either. Not until much later.

Star Rat followed the Stranger into another room on the other side of the door, larger but dimly lit, where several men and women—sometimes just five or six, other times a dozen or more; the number tended to change with each telling—were seated at rows of workstations, intently watching computer flatscreens above consoles filled with self-illuminated buttons ("looked like NASA, man," he'd invariably say, "like fuckin' Mission Control."). The men were all dressed like the Stranger, entirely in black, their heads shaved bald; the women wore sleeveless, knee-length black dresses, and although they all had the same hairstyle and color—black bowl cuts with no hair touching their necks or foreheads—Rat had the impression they all wore wigs and they were actually bald underneath. They all they stared at Star Rat "like nobody ever seen a hippie before" but no one said anything as the Stranger walked him through another door on the other side of the room that opened "just like *Star Trek*… *wsssh!*"

On the other side was a long corridor with closed doors on either side. As the Stranger led him down the hall, they'd gone just a few steps when one of the doors opened. Out came one of the women with a Moe haircut ("y'know, like Moe in the Three Stooges"), and right behind her was another person.

"An' I swear to God, man," Star Rat said, "it was Carl Sagan... Carl fuckin' Sagan! Mr. Billions and Billions of Stars himself!"

Did he really see the most famous astronomer of the century? Star Rat swore he did... until another occasion when I heard him tell the story again, this time a bunch of people at a party sitting in a circle and passing a bong around. Then it was Leonard Nimoy ("Spock, man! Fuckin' Dr. Spock himself, ears and everything!") who came through the door. And yet another, having lunch in a pizza joint near campus, I overheard him tell some guys sharing a large pepperoni and olive that it was "the guy who walked on the Moon... can't remember his name but, y'know, *that* guy!"

Whether it was Sagan, Nimoy, or Neil Armstrong, he barely glanced at Star Rat as he was escorted back the way Rat and Stranger had just come. The control room door opened to let them through and whispered shut behind them. Star Rat asked the Stranger why Carl Sagan (or whoever) was there, but the man in black said nothing as they continued down the hall.

They passed another door. It was half-open and slowly closing as if someone had just walked in; Star Rat paused and managed to catch a glimpse of the room on the other side. Two men were seated in comfortable leather armchairs, a bottle of red wine and a couple of glasses on a table between them: a man who could have been the Stranger's brother, and "an intense little dude" in mid-1800s' apparel with a trim mustache and straggly black hair receding from a broad forehead. "I remembered seein' his face in school," Rat said later, "and think it was the guy who wrote that poem we had to read in English class. Pie or Pee or Poe, somethin' like that."

They continued down the corridor without stopping again until they reached the last door at the end. It opened when the Stranger paused in front of it, and although it wasn't dark on the other side, Star Rat hesitated before going in. But the Stranger assured him that it was going to be all right and they weren't about to be "transferred" again, so he reluctantly let his leader take him in.

"And, man, there I was... in the same place that's on the cover of *Skeletons from the Closet*." Star Rat's eyes were wide as he said this, giving me a chance to check his pupils. I was expecting to find them dilated, but they were normal size; he wasn't tripping, at least not then. "This old-time diner with a lunch counter on one side and booths on the other and tables in between, and it's identical, man, one hundred percent *identical* to the one I seen."

"Uh huh," I said. "And what did you do?"

"I said, 'Whoa, dude! It's the place on the album!' An' the bald dude tells the guy who did that picture was someone else who'd been brought here, and he musta subconsciously remembered what he'd seen because after he got back he did that painting. And I said, 'Shit, man, that's awesome!' an' he says, 'Yeah, it sometimes happens.'"

That wasn't all. The diner was fully occupied, as busy as if it was lunch hour, with waitresses in short-skirted uniforms and aprons, their hair coiffed in '50s and '60s styles, walked among the tables and booths, taking orders and delivering food on trays they carried through a swinging door behind the counter: burgers and fries, chili, grilled cheese sandwiches, chicken-fried steak, shakes and sodas. At each table was someone in black, a man or a woman, and with them was a person who looked like they'd been brought there from some place else.

"Some of 'em I didn't know," Star Rat said, "they looked like, y'know, just regular people. But I knew a lot of the others. I saw Albert Einstein an' Jane Fonda an' Jacques Cousteau an' Muhammed Ali an' Marilyn Monroe an'…"

Each time Star Rat told the story, the notables in the diner would change a little. Einstein was always among them, but otherwise the cast of characters were often different. In some iterations, Rat saw Pigpen, the Dead's original keyboardist; in others, he saw Michael Jackson, either when he was a kid or when he was an adult. On one retelling, he claimed he saw both Paul Newman and Robert Redford sitting together in a booth, as they'd looked in *Butch Cassidy and the Sundance Kid*. In any case, the celebrities who were in the diner were never consistent, except they all came from twentieth century America.

There was an empty table at the center of the diner; the Stranger led Star Rat there. As they sat down, Rat happened to gaze out the long plate-glass windows that ran alongside the booths. Sure enough, the futuristic building was there, but he didn't spot either a flying saucer or a three-wheel Dymaxion car. Instead, a stagecoach pulled by a team of horses trundled by as it had just arrived from the Old West. As it went by, an enormous, bat-like shadow swept across the street, and when Star Rat looked up he saw that it was being cast by a giant pterodactyl gliding overhead.

A waitress appeared, ready to take their orders. There were no menus on the table, but the Stranger told Rat he didn't need one, he could have anything he could think of and not worry about paying for it. Star Rat ordered his favorite, a foot-long Coney Island hot dog with relish, ketchup, and mustard, with onion rings and a Coke to go with it. The waitress nodded, not bothering to write anything down, and sashayed away. When she was gone, the Stranger, who hadn't ordered anything, got down to business.

If I tried to repeat what Rat told me exactly as he said it, you probably wouldn't understand it; I had to listen to his babble two or three times before I was able to get any coherent meaning out of it. It came down to this:

The Star Rat had been taken through a bridge in spacetime to a locus that exists between planes of the multiverse, a junction where countless parallel universes touch like an infinitely long pin that's been thrust through an infinitely thick stack of paper. That was where he was now: a world out of time, out of space, out of anything most people would call reality.

In some of these universes, the version of humankind that lived there —not our own, not yet at least—had developed the means to navigate through the multiverse, thereby travelling not just through our timeline but through other parallel timelines in all their endless variety. The Stranger's breed of spacetime-hopping humans had chosen to use this ability as a means by which they could study the histories of other universes.

One aspect of particular interest were those instances in parallel history where human culture had developed in ways that were similar or even identical to those in adjacent timelines. For example, each timeline of humanity had managed to invent pecan shortbread cookies. No one knew how or why; the fact simply remained that one could travel through dozens, hundred, even thousands of parallel universes, and find pecan shortbread cookies in every single one of them.

Likewise, in every universe no matter how different it may otherwise be, there was always a traveling musical ensemble like the Grateful Dead.

The group in the universe Star Rat belonged to was the only one called the Grateful Dead, and the musical repertoire was usually different, yet nonetheless something much like the Dead existed in every plane of the multiverse visited by scholars, as were the Deadhead-like subcultures that had evolved around them.

So the time scholars were presently studying the Grateful Dead in all its variations. And as they often did with anything they were researching, one method they'd developed was to find someone in a timeline, briefly "borrow" him or her (a nicer word than "abduct") and bring that person to the locus, where he or she could be interviewed at leisure. It often helped to get a first-person perspective from a native of that particular timeline, whether that individual was famous and influential or merely an obscure bystander. The trick was to borrow them when no one else was around; Star Rat wasn't famous, he just happened to be in an empty men's room at the right moment.

This diner was located in a research center established between universes for the particular purpose of interviewing contemporary subjects. Although some people were less disoriented if they were interviewed in private, just as Edgar Allan Poe and Carl Sagan had been, others could be brought to a more relaxed environment where they could have a meal and talk for a while. And once the interview was over, they'd be taken back to the transfer room where the multiversal portal was located. From there, they would be sent back to the exact place and time they'd come from, after first being administered a harmless drug that would delete all memories of the experience they'd just had.

Well, all this sounded just fine to Star Rat, especially since by then he'd decided all this was just a particularly vivid acid trip. So he sat with the scholar for an hour or so, having one of the best Coney Island dogs he'd ever tasted ("like, man, it was perfectly roasted, not boiled or steamed, and the relish was *amazing*") while he told the Stranger about the Dead shows he'd seen, the Deadheads he'd met, which concert venues were the best and which were the worst. And just about the time the acid was about to wear off, the Stranger decided that he'd learned enough and the time had come to send Star Rat home.

So they left the diner and walked back down to the portal, passing "the guy who did *The Twilight Zone*" along the way, and just before the Stranger left him in the transfer chamber, he pulled out something that looked like a small syringe gun, placed its barrel against Star Rat's neck, and gave him a dose of the amnesia drug. Then he left the room, the lights went out, there was another sensation of falling, and when Star Rat's feet touched solid floor again, he found he was back in a janitorial closet in the Hartford Civic Center, where through the walls he could hear Space Drums coming to an end as the Dead segued into "Casey Jones."

But here was the thing: the amnesia drug failed to erase his memory. Star Rat recalled everything, or at least as much as he could considering that he'd been tripping on acid the entire time. Rat thought it was because he'd built up such a tolerance to LSD over the years that the drug the Stranger gave him simply had no effect. He had a clear memory (if inconsistent) of what he was supposed to forget, and although he was supposed to believe that he'd wandered into the closet by accident and passed out there, instead he remembered all that happened from the moment he'd met a bald guy while taking a whiz in the men's room.

"But, dude, no one believes me," Rat would say to me later. "Everyone thinks I was just trippin'. They all say I was stoned and laugh, an' no one believes a thing I say."

Star Rat stopped and looked me straight in the eye, and when he did it I realized that this was one of the few times I'd ever seen him straight. "Man, you got an open mind," he said. "I know you read a lot of sci-fi and stuff, so you'd know what I'm talking about, parallel universes an' all that. You believe me, don't you?"

Rat was pleading with me, trying to get me to say that I understood everything he'd told me and accepted it as truth. But while I more or less comprehended what he'd said, I couldn't bring myself to tell him that it was a true experience.

"Dude," I said, "I hate to say this, but you *really* need to stop doing drugs."

Star Rat stared at me for a moment or two, then for the first time since I'd known him, I saw him get angry. "Oh, fuck you, man," he said. "You're an asshole." And then he got up and walked away.

S tar Rat didn't speak to me much after that. He was still cordial whenever I saw him, but he'd never again ask if I wanted to share a joint with him or come over to his place to listen to the new Dead bootleg he'd just received in the mail. Our friendship had been damaged by my honesty; he thought I'd said he was lying, and although Rat didn't much care what people thought of him, he didn't appreciate having his honesty questioned. And he'd long since become sick and tired of people telling him to give up drugs; anyone who did so was relegated to his "asshole" category.

I graduated from college about a year later; I collected my diploma and left the little town in New Hampshire where I'd spent four glorious years. Star Rat stayed behind, just as he'd stayed behind class after class, year after year. He was still there when I returned five years later, and because I continued going to Dead concerts, I occasionally spotted him there, usually in the parking lot or on the floor of whatever concert hall, arena, or stadium the Dead happened to be playing.

He always looked the same, just a little wider and grayer as time went on, but whenever I walked over to say hello he seemed to only vaguely recognize me. I'd gotten older, too, and once I cut my hair apparently he no longer remembered me. Or maybe he remembered the way I'd rejected his story and still considered me to be an asshole. But he was no longer just hanging out in the Dead scene; it always seemed like he was moving through the crowd in search of someone or something that would validate a strange experience he'd once had.

The years passed by and I stopped seeing Star Rat altogether. When I visited my college again for my 25th anniversary homecoming, he wasn't still on the campus or in town, and although my classmates all remembered him, no one had seen or heard from him in decades. And although I still occasionally went to a Dead show after Jerry Garcia died and the band renamed itself Dead and Company, Star Rat was never there. I'd look for him, but he was no longer part of the scene. I figured that either he'd finally grown up and changed his act, or he hadn't and drugs had finally killed him; either way he was gone and I thought I'd seen the last of him.

Then one Saturday afternoon, I was in a used record store in Worcester, Massachusetts. I was in town for a campus SF convention at Worcester Polytech, and since I'd remembered this store as having a great collection of classic vinyl, I made time to drop in and see what I could find. I was combing through a bin of Hot Tuna LPs, trying to find a pristine copy of *Burgers* to replace the one I'd worn out years ago, when someone came up beside me, put a copy of *Skeletons from the Closet* before me, and said, "Have you ever listened to this?"

At first I didn't recognize the person standing beside me. He was a short, thin guy of indeterminate age, his head shaved bald and with no facial hair, wearing only a black T-shirt, black trousers, and black moccasins. Then I happened to look down at his right forearm, and there was a tattoo I hadn't seen in many years, a sly-looking rat sitting on a star, a joint hanging from his mouth.

"Star Rat?" I asked, incredulous. "Rat, is that you?"

"Yeah, it's me." He grinned, and when he did I recognized him from his nose; no one else had a rodent-like schnozz like his. "Good to see you again."

"Holy crap! Star Rat! It's really you!" Holding out my arms, I stepped toward him. My first impulse was to give him a guy-hug, and in the old days he would've returned it, but this time he took a step back, deliberately putting distance between us.

I stopped myself, dropped my arms. "Hey, Rat," I murmured, taken back by the cool reception. I couldn't help but feel a little hurt. "How've you been?"

"I'm good," he said quietly. "Doing fine." His eyes were clear, his voice wasn't slurred, his demeanor totally sober. If it hadn't been for the tat, I would have never recognized him. "I saw you over here, just wanted to say hello." He then smiled and tapped the Dead album he'd placed before me. "Remember this?"

I looked down at the album, seeing for the first time in years the clever and enigmatic illustration on the back cover. "How could I forget? Do you...?"

I stopped myself before I could finish what I was about to say: *do you still think what you saw was real?* For it was then that I noticed how he was dressed, realized that his hair was gone and beard was missing, and how that reminded me of the story he'd told me and all his friends and anyone else who'd listen to him.

Star Rat must have known what I was about to say, because he slowly nodded. "Yeah," he said. "I think it's real. I *know* it's real. In fact—" he paused to glance about, making sure no one else could hear us "—would you like to see for yourself?"

I looked at him, then the album, then him again. "Are you asking if I'd like to—?"

"Sure. C'mon. I'll show you." Star Rat took another step back from me, but this time he held out a hand, a friendly invitation to join him. "C'mon, man," he said again. "This way."

Behind him was a door with an old Yes poster stapled to it; *Employees Only* was the sign above it. "Umm…" I said, and stepped toward him.

Then I remembered the story he'd told me.

The shop's front door was behind us. I stepped backward toward it instead. "Thanks, man," I said hastily, "but I gotta be somewhere. But, hey, it's great to see you again. You're looking good. Maybe another time, like the next Dead show…"

I kept talking all the way out the door, and as soon as I was through it, I turned and headed down the sidewalk as fast as I could without running. Halfway down the block, I looked back to see if I was being followed.

Star Rat was nowhere in sight. I never saw him again.

A Vampire, an Astrophysicist, and a Mother Superior Walk into a Basilica

Henry Herz

Instead of lounging on my sofa, contemplating my next astrophysics research project, I found myself bolting upright from a black leather office chair. I stood in an austere conference room with drawn window blinds and two thriving potted plants. Blinking repeatedly and pinching myself failed to restore me to my living room couch. *The data suggest I'm not dreaming.*

The room's two other occupants also gazed at their surroundings in disbelief. A petite, middle-aged woman wearing a simple white-and-blue nun's habit sat to my right. Her hazel eyes radiated kindness from a sun-weathered face. A mustachioed man in archaic garb glared at me from across the table. Long brown hair tumbled down to his chest from underneath an ornate red cap bordered with pearls. His fur-collared red cloak sported intricate golden buttons.

"Hello," I tried.

The man only stared at me, his eyes dark pits and fists balled in agitation. His body odor crossed the space between us like a slap to the face.

"Blessings," the woman replied with an accent I couldn't identify. She pointed at the polished wood conference table. "Do you know why we're here? And where here is?" Her expression remained serene, despite our bewildering circumstances.

I raised my hands, palms-up. "Sorry, no."

"I'm Mother Teresa. Nice to meet you."

The one that died in 1997? I gave her a smile. *Yeah, sure you are. That rascal Bill Nye must be trying to punk me for a YouTube video. Might as well play along.* "The pleasure's mine. I'm Neil deGrasse Tyson." I tilted my head at the man eyeing us suspiciously. "It seems our friend here doesn't speak English."

Teresa turned to him and made four attempts to communicate. She shrugged. "Nor does he speak Bengali, Albanian, Serbian, or Hindi."

Our companion's face flushed, perhaps with frustration.

Hmm. Maybe those three years of college German will finally pay off. "Guten Tag?" I tried.

His shoulders relaxed and he introduced himself in a dialect of German not fully comprehensible but completely unbelievable.

Yeah, sure you are, pal.

I translated for Teresa. "He claims he's Vlad Tepes, warlord of Wallachia. You know… Dracula."

Her eyes widened. "Surely you can't be serious?"

I nodded. "That's what he told me." *And don't call me Shirley.* I scanned the room for hidden cameras and shook a fist. "I'm gonna kick your ass, Bill."

Her brow furrowed. "Language, please."

Got to hand it to her for staying in character. I dipped my head. "My apologies." *Hmm. Let's collect more data.* "What year is it, Teresa?"

She straightened. "Are you joking?"

I nodded. "Serious as a supernova."

"It's 1952."

Interesting. "And if I may be so bold, how old are you?"

"I'm forty-two."

Interesting. "Me too… except I'm forty-two in the year 2000."

I queried our companion. "Vlad's also forty-two, but in 1470." I couldn't resist the urge to sneak a glance at his canine teeth. *Normal length.*

Teresa's fingers touched her lips. "Is there something special about that number?"

I closed my eyes in concentration. "Forty-two is the sum of the first six positive even numbers. It's a pronic number, an abundant number, a Harshdad number in base ten, a Catalan number, a meandric number, and the third primary pseudoperfect number. It's the atomic number of molybdenum, the critical angle rounded to whole degrees for which a rainbow appears, and the hypothetical efficiency of converting mass to energy by orbiting a mass around a black hole."

Teresa stared blank-faced. "Which means?"

I shrugged. "I've no idea."

Before I could probe further, a brilliant flash of light filled the room. A beatific seven-foot-tall figure appeared before us. He wore radiant, intricately detailed silver armor. A sword hung from his belt, and he gripped a glowing staff. His piercing ice-gray eyes scanned us as he extended white-feathered wings from wall to wall.

"[I am the archangel Barachiel,]" thundered soundlessly in my head.

My heart raced. *Now that is some serious special effects, Bill. Hologram with subsonic audio? I may have a boatload of college degrees, but I never took Angelology 101. Looks like archangels are badass.*

Vlad leaped to his feet as if readying to fight, while Teresa remained remarkably calm, bowing her head reverently.

"[I charge ye with a holy quest. To thwart Satan, a mighty weapon is needed. Ye shall bring me a link from St. Peter's Chain, a crucifixion nail, and a barb from the Crown of Thorns.]"

Fun. They've added a scavenger hunt component to the prank. I hope there's a pie-eating contest too. "May I ask, why us three?"

Barachiel folded his wings. "[Archangels may not intervene directly in mortal affairs. Thou possess remarkable intellect, Mother Teresa unwavering faith, and Warlord Tepes savage ferocity.]"

Not bad. And flattery never hurts. Still, we need more clues. "Wouldn't holy relics be extremely well-guarded?"

At the graceful sweep of Barachiel's left hand, three items appeared on the tabletop.

More holograms.

"[These items shall aid ye. The Concido dagger can slice through any material. The Opulentia purse yields unlimited currency appropriate to the bearer's locale. The Salio wand can transport ye to any place and time.]"

A wand that can fold space-time? Nice! Now that's *a big production budget.* I crack myself up.

Teresa uttered in Latin what I assumed was a prayer.

Vlad asked a question.

Barachiel aimed a withering gaze at him. "[A mortal can only bear one of these items at a time. And take care, for the Salio wand can only transport ye six times. Utter a destination, desired date and time, and travelers' names to invoke its powers. When thy task is complete, return to this room in Jerusalem's King David Hotel at midnight on the thirty-first of October, 2020. Only then shall I return ye to thy homes.]" The archangel raised his staff and vanished.

2020 Jerusalem, huh? If I can grab a newspaper, I could make a killing in the stock market. Ha.

At the mention of Jerusalem, Teresa rushed to a window and opened the blinds.

Vlad's gaze remained locked on the "heavenly" gifts.

Those items, if real, certainly would be useful to a conquering warlord. I joined Teresa at the window. The golden Dome of the Rock shone unmistakably in the distance. *There's no way they could have flown me to Israel. These "windows" must be video monitors.*

Teresa turned and examined the purse.

Vlad claimed the dagger. *Just like any warlord worth his salt.*

I reached for the slender metal rod encasing glowing shards of stained glass. *It's solid! Holograms can't be solid. Oh, I bet "Vlad" placed these three props on the table when my back was turned.* "Nice try, Bill," I muttered to the mic I felt sure was concealed in the ceiling. "But I'm still an agnostic."

Teresa proposed we first jump back in time to see Jesus with our own eyes.

I wonder who they got to play Christ? Gary Oldman's a chameleon of an actor. When I translated Teresa's suggestion for Vlad, he scowled. "That moves us no closer to our goal."

I set my mind to solving the puzzle. *The sooner we finish filming, the sooner I can get back to my research… and planning a revenge prank.* "Well, with this wand, time isn't an issue. And I wouldn't mind jumping back to meet Sir Isaac Newton. But I agree with Vlad. We should wait until *after* we have the relics. We don't know how many jumps that'll take. Teresa, do you know where the relics are stored?"

She nodded. "The holy chain was kept in Rome's Basilica of Saint Peter in Chains. I suggest we go to the year 450, prior to the Vandals' sack of Rome. The earlier the time of our visit, the simpler the security will be."

Smart. Sure, why not? "And then?"

"A crucifixion nail and two thorns from the Crown of Thorns were located in the Basilica of the Holy Cross in Jerusalem which, despite the name, is also in Rome. It's less than three kilometers from the first basilica."

I do love Italian food. "But, what if the items aren't in Rome?"

"Religious relics were also stored at the Sainte-Chapelle in Paris as early as 1300," she replied.

Vlad tugged at his sleeve. "Our clothing may look odd to Romans of 450."

Okay, I told myself. *Just have fun with this and commit to the prank.* "True." I raised a hand, palm-up. "But we could simply jump to our destination in the dark of night, take what we need, and proceed to the next target."

I raised the Salio wand and commanded, "Behind the Basilica of St. Peter in Chains in Rome on midnight of January first, 450. Mother Teresa, Vlad Tepes, and Neil deGrasse Tyson."

The wand glowed. Frigid darkness enveloped us, muffling all sounds.

450 C.E. Rome, The Basilica of St. Peter in Chains

The synesthesia of flashing afterimages that somehow smelled of fire rendered me momentarily disoriented. *Damn.*

Teresa, Vlad, and I stood outside in the dark at the deserted rear of a brick church. Their mouths hung open in astonishment. I realized mine was also agape. *How the hell did they manage a nearly instantaneous set change?* I shivered in the wintery air, starting to question my assumptions. *This is starting to feel more* The Truman Show *than* Candid Camera.

Vlad pointed toward the building. "Let us see if the entrance is guarded."

In the absence of alternatives, I set aside my rational disbelief. *This is kinda fun.*

We moved to the right rear corner, then crept along the wall, halting at the front of the basilica.

Vlad gestured for us to wait. He stole a glance around the corner. "Single guard," he whispered with military economy. "Helmet and laminated-strip cuirass. Sword and short thrusting spear." He raised his dagger meaningfully.

I know it'll be fake murder, but I have a queasy stomach. "Vlad, what if you slip behind the building to the other front corner. Teresa will approach the guard from this side. While he's looking at her, you creep behind him and smack his head with the dagger pommel."

They nodded agreement, and Vlad headed around the rear of the church.

Teresa gave him two minutes to get in position before approaching the guard.

I remained behind the corner, not wanting to risk the guard seeing me. Instead of the expected sharp metallic thud, a gasp from Teresa reached my ears. Rushing to her, I discovered Teresa praying through tears. My gut twisted.

Vlad wiped his bloody blade on the dead guard's shirt sleeve. "The dagger *is* sharp."

I dropped to my knees, putting two fingers on the side of the guard's throat. He was sure seemed real but lacked a pulse. The blood felt warm. I gagged.

With a grim smile, Vlad turned to the locked church entrance and sliced through the bolt as if it were made of gray cheese. He dragged the guard through the doorway.

Playing along, I kicked dirt to hide the spilled blood and followed Vlad and Teresa into the basilica, shutting the thick wooden door behind us. "Why'd you kill him?"

Vlad glared back, candlelight flickering in his eyes. "Because a dead guard cannot wake and attack us. Do not be a child. We have a relic to collect."

My face flushed at his disrespectful tone, but since he held a dagger and my Bill Nye/*Candid Camera* hypothesis had unraveled, I reined in a sarcastic riposte.

Teresa's eyes met mine, her unspoken message clear. *We cannot trust him.*

I gave her a curt nod. The interior stretched before us in a long rectangle, the nave lined by Doric style columns of fluted marble, ten to a side. The far side of the basilica featured two small chapels flanking a large central apse for the high altar. Light from the full moon trickled through small windows in the nave walls above the arcades.

Wait. Full moon? *Last night was a* crescent *moon!*

Teresa led us forward. Beyond the transept stood a confessional and a crypt with exquisite carvings. In a voice faltering with emotion, she explained, "These depict the miracle of the loaves and fishes, the resurrection of Lazarus, the Samaritan woman at the well, Peter refuting Christ's prophecy of denial, and the giving of the Law."

Unmoved by art or spirituality, Vlad scowled.

Teresa took us to a niche shrine on the high altar. There, in an ornate golden reliquary, hung St. Peter's Chain.

Vlad wasted no time slicing a piece off the relic. He yelped as he seized the fallen link.

It burned you, vampire? If only I had a clove of garlic to conduct an experiment...

Teresa muttered a prayer, and reverentially took possession of the link. "We should go now. Our next destination is the Basilica of the Holy Cross."

I raised my hand. "I suggest we walk there. It's only three kilometers. Let's preserve a jump we might need later."

The others agreed.

Vlad strapped the dead guard's sword belt around his waist.

My striped button-down shirt and blue jeans will look odd to ancient Romans. I removed the guard's cloak and wrapped it about my shoulders, shivering at despoiling a corpse.

While we plundered, Teresa crossed herself and uttered a prayer for the man's soul.

450 C.E. Rome, The Basilica of the Holy Cross in Jerusalem

Teresa led us through empty residential streets toward the Basilica of the Holy Cross. A cloud eased in front of the moon, cloaking us in welcome darkness. She pointed to a church a hundred yards away. A half-dozen guards milled in front of the building.

Damn. "What can you tell us about the layout, Teresa?"

She closed her eyes to aid her memory. "It has the standard rectangular interior. An elliptical atrium leads to a central nave lined with columns along both sides. A ciborium and altar urn rest in front of the apse containing sepulchral monuments. There's a bronze snake and a carving of Moses drawing water from a rock."

"Get to the point, woman. Where are the relics kept?" Vlad replied when I translated.

I asked her much more politely in English.

"There are two separate rooms behind the apse, the chapel of St. Gregorio on the left and the chapel of St. Elena on the right. The reliquary's in the latter."

Vlad's gaze returned to the basilica, and he sighed. "Fierce I may be, but even I cannot defeat six soldiers in a fair fight."

"Allow me to propose a less violent solution," I whispered, reluctantly having accepted the bizarre reality of our situation. "This way." Giving the soldiers a wide berth, I led us to the rear of the basilica. I pointed at Vlad's dagger and raised my eyebrows. "Barachiel said it can cut through *any* material…"

Vlad offered me a grudging, "clever." He turned and thrust the dagger into the wall, which resisted no more than soft clay. Gouging half-foot-square blocks, he tossed them aside.

As he continued, I squatted and grabbed a piece. My heart skipped a beat. *This is* real *stone. How's that possible?*

In short order, Vlad carved a three-foot-wide by two-foot-high entry at ground level. We scrambled through the opening.

The taper-lit, marble-walled chapel had a single exit, presumably leading to the apse. Vlad slipped toward the doorway to listen for a patrol, while Teresa and I each took up a candle to aid the search among the staggering wealth of silver and gold relics.

"I found a crucifixion nail," whispered Teresa, staring in awe at a silver reliquary in the shape of a candelabra.

The slow tread of booted feet reached my ears.

"Guards. Hurry!" Vlad whispered.

We had no more time. Two pairs of footsteps grew louder. My hands trembled, my body accepting the scenario even though my mind resisted.

As the guards crossed the threshold, Vlad lunged from a crouch like a striking snake, thrusting the dagger upward through the first guard's chin. He yanked the blade free as the guard toppled to the ground.

The other guard scrambled backward in fear, losing his footing.

Vlad jumped on him, stabbing his heart, but not before the soldier shouted a cry of alarm.

"That will bring more guards," Vlad hissed. "Do you have the relics?"

"O—o—only the nail," I replied, my heart pounding from shock at the sudden violence.

The horror on Teresa's face at Vlad's brutality mirrored my own. But her countenance calmed as she whispered a brief prayer. "No more murder. I will delay the other guards. Have Vlad help you find the thorn." After I translated, she passed Vlad her candle and moved toward the threshold, withdrawing the Opulentia purse from a sleeve.

Several pairs of booted footfalls echoed from the nave, followed by the tinkling of metal on the stone floor.

She's distracting the guards with gold coins. Clever girl!

"We're out of time!" I cried, dropping his candle and raising the Salio wand. "Inside the treasury of the Sainte-Chapelle on Île de la Cité in Paris on midnight of January first, 1300. Mother Teresa, Vlad Tepes, and Neil deGrasse Tyson."

Again, frigid darkness enveloped us.

1300 C.E. Paris, Île de la Cité, Sainte-Chapelle

The coppery smell of the guards' blood lingered in my nostrils. My heart pounded in my chest. *I'm actually holding a wand that folds spacetime.* I shook my head. *Maybe Barachiel's an alien. The universe is under no obligation to make sense to you, Neil.*

Teresa whispered, "The mad warlord will kill us when he no longer needs us."

I put my hand on her shoulder. "Ironically, his greed protects us. Remember, Barachiel told us a mortal can only wield one item at a time. So, if he murders us, he cannot return home without abandoning the purse and dagger."

She smiled. "The Lord works in mysterious ways. We must fulfill our holy task."

I was about to disagree with her premise but, being honest with myself, her faith-based explanation was just as good as my alien hypothesis. *The only thing worse than a blind believer is a seeing denier.* There was also a practical consideration. *Angel or alien, Barachiel would be a far more formidable opponent than Vlad. We have no choice but to proceed.*

We were fortunate that Teresa had known of a second church preserving holy thorns. And it was dumb luck that Vlad still gripped the candle from Rome, as we arrived in an otherwise unlit vault. A sparkling array of riches surrounded us.

Vlad's eyes shone with avarice. He tilted his head at me, his question clear.

"I brought us directly inside the church treasury to avoid killing more guards." After estimating the room's dimensions, a quick calculation reassured me we had roughly four hours to find a holy thorn before carbon dioxide poisoning took its deadly toll.

But with a single candle casting scant illumination, the search progressed glacially. The clinking of metal objects echoed in the enclosed space. I observed small gold jewelry make its way into Vlad's pockets. I tapped Teresa's elbow. "See what he's doing?"

She nodded, frowning. "Yes. He's a bloodthirsty warlord driven by greed for power. I saw pleasure in his eyes at the taking of life." Teresa uttered another prayer.

For Vlad's soul? Do vampires have souls?

Teresa took my hand. "For the sake of his countrymen, we must deliver him home without anything that enhances his power."

"Love thy neighbor, eh, Teresa? Easier said than done." I sighed.

Teresa nodded. "God doesn't require us to succeed, He only requires that you try." Her eyes twinkled as she conveyed her plan to send Vlad home.

I admired her instinct to restore him to the proper timeline. *That will minimize the disruption to the flow of history.* And I made a mental note to never underestimate the deviousness of a mother superior. I turned to Vlad. "Tell me of your country. I've not had the pleasure of visiting Wallachia."

A grin flashed across his face at my mention of his realm. "I rule from Tepes castle in Târgoviște. It is a mighty fortress atop a steep-sided hill." He offered further details at my encouragement as we searched for the Crown of Thorns.

"I found it," cried Teresa. "Praise the Lord." Hands trembling with awe, she raised a woven crown of thorns, encased within a stunning gold lattice torus studded with emeralds and sapphires.

I'm neither religious nor impressed by wealth, but the relic still took away my breath.

Teresa prayed, drawing a sneer from Vlad.

I suppressed a smile, imagining Teresa slapping the impious warlord's wrist with a ruler.

She reverently removed a thorn and secured it in a pocket.

At a nod from Teresa, I raised the wand and declared, "The great hall of the Tepes castle in Târgoviște on midnight of January first, 1470. Mother Teresa, Vlad Tepes, and Neil deGrasse Tyson."

* * *

1470 C.E. Târgovişte, Wallachia, Tepes Castle

"W hy are we here?" Vlad demanded at the unannounced change in plan.

I gazed wide-eyed at the splendor of his great hall. Colorful tapestries depicting Vlad's triumphs adorned the walls, along with impaled skeletons of the vanquished. "Your description so moved me, I had to see it."

As planned, Teresa swooned, and I "only just" caught her before she fell. I helped her sit at the long dining table. "She needs to recover her strength."

Vlad nodded. "I shall order refreshments." He summoned a servant, issuing orders in a language I did not speak.

Undoubtedly the food will be poisoned.

Teresa asked me a question, which I conveyed to Vlad. "While we wait, she wonders if she could admire the Concido dagger."

His left hand brushed against his sword pommel. "Certainly."

I suspected the vicious warlord felt secure in the heart of his domain.

Teresa set the purse on the tabletop as Vlad approached.

With unlimited wealth, you could raise a mighty army to push back the Ottomans and the Hungarians... and alter the flow of history.

Vlad passed Teresa the dagger, handle first.

She admired it briefly before slashing the purse in half with a flick of her wrist.

"What have you done?" screamed Vlad, transfixed in shock.

Before he could draw his blade, I cried, "Barachiel's room in the King David Hotel on midnight of October 31, 2020. Mother Teresa and Neil deGrasse Tyson."

2020 C.E. Jerusalem, The King David Hotel

I bowed theatrically to Teresa in the hotel conference room. "Had you not devoted yourself to God, you could have been a successful actress."

An immodest grin split her face as she tucked the dagger in a sleeve. "I simply use His gifts to serve Him." She placed the three relics on the tabletop. "I pray to the Lord for wisdom to do His will. We overcame one challenge, but another remains."

I raised an eyebrow.

Before she could elaborate, Barachiel appeared at the far end of the table near the wilting potted plants.

Having finally resigned myself to the idea that there were some things science couldn't explain, including archangels, I bowed like Teresa.

Barachiel's voice echoed in my mind. "[Thou may rise. Where is the warlord?]"

"We returned him to his proper time and place," Teresa replied, standing.

"[Ye have done well.]"

"Thank you." Teresa reverentially gathered up the three relics.

Barachiel took a step back as she neared him. "[Hold.]" He waived his hand, and a small, wrought iron-bound ebony box materialized on the tabletop. "[Place the items in this reliquary.]"

The barest hint of a smile appeared on Barachiel's face when she did as he asked. As he reached for the box, Teresa stabbed him in the heart with the dagger. The blade shattered.

What?

Barachiel howled like a thunderclap. He burst into purple flames, knocking Teresa backward. The stench of brimstone filled the room as his outline twisted into a demonic form before crumbling to dust. The carpet smoldered.

Coughing, I helped Teresa to her feet. "For heaven's sake, why'd you do that?"

She exhaled, trembling. "Precisely for heaven's sake. He was not an archangel, but rather the fallen angel, Batârêl."

Still struggling to grasp what had transpired, I managed, "How did you know?"

She collapsed into a chair. "I didn't know, but I had faith." Her hand rose to her throat. "When he first appeared, the crucifix under my habit warmed."

I shrugged. "Odd, but that isn't conclusive proof."

"True. He raised further doubt in my mind by giving us the dagger, an instrument of murder. And he instructed us to return at midnight on October 31." In response to my blank stare, she added, "All Souls' Day? The Day of the Dead? Samhain?"

I slumped into a chair next to Teresa, my brow wrinkled. "I shudder to imagine the heinous use of the relics Batârêl intended."

"Indeed. I thank the Lord for lending me His strength." She pointed at the potted plants. "Did you notice those wilted in proximity to Batârêl? And the closer I approached him, the hotter my metal crucifix got." Pulling down the collar of her habit, she showed me her blistered skin.

My eyebrows rose.

She continued. "Did you see him step back from the holy relics, instead telling me to put them in the box?"

I smiled. "Ah. He didn't want to touch them. You're a woman of remarkable piety, resourcefulness, and bravery."

She inclined her head. "Thank you. Kind words' echoes are truly endless."

I laughed. "Well, my wife would agree I talk endlessly. I don't know about you, but I've had all the chaos I can handle. And I'll have to revise my view of how the universe works." I raised the wand. "It has two jumps remaining. Shall I take you home?"

She collected the ebony box, nodded, and told me the location.

1952 C.E. Kolkata, India, Missionaries of Charity Headquarters

Surprised nuns surrounded us, welcoming Teresa home.

When my stomach rumbled, the nuns giggled and brought us a simple meal, which we wolfed down after Teresa said grace.

She pushed back her plate. "Who would have thought a mother superior and an astrophysicist could work so well together?"

I smiled. "I've long felt that if my philosophy isn't unsettled daily, then I'm blind to all the universe has to offer."

Teresa winked. "Including God? I'll ensure the holy relics are restored to their rightful homes."

"Your return of items missing for centuries will surely be viewed as miraculous." I winked. "Maybe you'll even be canonized someday."

Her eyes twinkled impishly. "What a *Nobel* sentiment. May the Lord lift up His countenance upon you and give you peace."

"I've never been to India before," I mused aloud. "With the wand, I can afford a few days to see the sights, sample the local wines, and still arrive home precisely when I left."

And on to my next research project—figuring out how the Salio wand works and whether I need to adjust my understanding of physics... or theology.

The Greatest Trick
Louise Piper

It's late afternoon, but what day is it? It happened three days ago, on Thursday, so it must be Sunday. *Damn it, Daddy... I s'pose you woulda liked dying on the same date as Martin Luther King, Jr.*

I spit my cigarette butt through the window before closing it against the dampness rising from the lake. Big Lake. Imagination isn't too ripe in these parts—that's what Daddy used to joke anyways—before splayed spindle-legs and a meeting of the minds stopped him dead. He woulda found it funny. Taken by a headbutt from a moose! Geez, yep, he woulda hooted at that one. "Them's the most stupid animal you'll eva meet, Vickie," he told me every time we crossed the New Brunswick border, laughing, "When Dr. King warned us 'sincere ignorance' and 'conscientious stupidity' are 'the most dangerous things in the world' he was including moose in that evaluation, you bet!"

Underneath the window, the old family credenza is laden with flowers from neighbors. *Huh,* never knew most of 'em existed 'til now. Drooping blooms, stuffed in jam and pickle jars, are sitting in piss-yellow water. My hands run through my hair. I turn to the mirror. Goddamn greasy... and is that my first gray?

The rain stops at last and I sit in the quiet. *What you got stashed in that cardboard box anyways?* It's resting in your spot, close to the hearth. Grief spills from my nose and I sniff it back, swallowing a glug of mucous. My fingers tap, tap the top of the box lightly. It hasn't yet been sealed—Daddy was putting stuff aside for the Salvation Army like he did every spring. My index finger worms its way to the hole in the middle of the folded flaps, and tugs gently until the opening expands.

A hit-you-in-the-guts smell escapes, carrying me through the woods on my father's shoulders once more. *Don't drop me, Daddy.* Both hands pull open the box completely. A pilled blue sweater lies on the top. I lift it out and press it to my nose and mouth before I pull it over my head, pushing my arms, that seem so skinny, through his wide, threadbare sleeves. I roll the cuffs several times to recover each of my hands.

Ah! My goodness, I've not seen this for years. Geez, I used to love this singing bowl. Daddy had used it when I was a little girl. He would tell me the tale of how he had once helped a Tibetan refugee named Dawa find a new life here. In gratitude, the man had given Daddy the bowl and shown him how to use it. He could make it sing endlessly, until my eyes would droop, and I crossed the threshold to elsewhere.

I lift the bowl from the box and take it over to the small wooden table, pushing the pile of unpaid bills underneath the condiments. Taking the puja from the bowl, I sense the warmth of Daddy's grip beneath mine. The first strike makes me jolt.

I close my eyes. *Come on, Daddy, howd'ya do this?* Loosening my grip, I make the bowl sing briefly with a circular motion of the wood against the rim. I move the puja rhythmically. There are a few false starts, and a promising ringing subsides before it gains its own momentum. Geez, it's like the promise of an orgasm, but when a thought creeps in, it just kinda fades away. Daddy always said there'd be less bother in the world if people would make the time to get laid. Smiling, I shake my head and pick up the puja again. *Come on… I want it to last this time!*

A low humming is building volume. *Don't think about it! Keep going! It's like riding a bike—just keep going.* I become lost, and I'm startled when I open my eyes to see the room is now silent and gloomy, save for an early evening glow. There is a knock at the door. *Who the hell is this now—more flowers?*

"*Excusez moi,*" an eccentric-looking man, who looks like he stepped out of the nineteenth century, coughs politely, raising his hat in deference.

"Can I help you?"

"My name is Charles… Charles Baudelaire."

"Are you the funeral director?"

Charles puffs his disdain loudly, "*Non*. I am a poet! But I can see my *austère* dress-code meets the occasion. *Oui*? My sincere condolences." He dips his head reverently.

I'm still standing at a guarded distance. "Have they sent you to write the eulogy?"

"You tell me, *ma chère*, you summoned me here."

"I did?"

The stranger places his hands on my shoulders. In a soft tone, he confides, "*Oui*, I work by invitation," lifting his eyes to a bottle of wine on top of the mantle, "and I know your father feels I may be of service to you." At the mention of Daddy I can't help but relax, and I gesture for him to come inside.

Charles positions himself in front of the mantle. "*Du vin, ma chère?*" Clad in a black three-piece suit and topcoat, he picks up the half-empty bottle, ejecting the cork with a flick of his thumb. After taking a swig, he proffers it to me. "Come, *ma chère*, make yourself comfortable. And we'll begin." I accept the bottle and take a couple of swigs, wiping my mouth with the sleeve of Daddy's sweater. "Begin what?"

Charles chuckles, "Don't be so coy! You want me to explain the art of," Charles licks his lips and raises his eyebrows, "… *faire l'amour.*" What in hell's name is he going on about? "Specifically, you want to know how to make it last." Charles cocks his head to one side.

"Geez, don't think you're getting any, punk!"

"*Mon dieu!*" Charles chuckles again, draining the last of the wine, before saying more gently, "*Ma chère*, the flesh, *hélas, est très…* soft. But don't tell anyone. I have a reputation to keep. Now, do you want to know my secrets for long, exquisite orgasms or not?" He shakes the empty bottle at me like I'm a waitress in a bar. "Any more? One should always be drunk, *ma chère*, so as not to feel the pain of living… either that or anesthetize yourself with love-making."

I'm mesmerized for some reason, so I stutter, "No, not, no, not up here… in the cellar."

"*Ooh*, a wine cellar?" Charles rubs his hands together and makes his way down the rickety steps. I notice a volume of poetry on the bookcase: *Les Fleurs du Mal* by Charles Baudelaire. I pick it up and read the publication date—1857. *Daddy, did you send Charles? You've got to be kiddin' me!* I drop the book, and cover my mouth with my hand. *You've sent a horny, drunk poet?* Charles returns with two bottles of wine and glances at the floor. "*Ah!* You've found my musings."

I sit back at the table, burrowing my nose into the crook of my elbow, so I can inhale Daddy. The bills I had earlier pushed aside beckon me. I pause over the foreclosure notice and shake my head. *Daddy, why didn't you tell me things were this tight?* I'm gonna need a miracle to sort this out! *Humph.* I turn the bills face down on the table, pick up the puja, and circle the rim of the bowl again. *Come on, Daddy, I need someone to help me make money outta nothing.* The singing of the bowl grows more persistent. *Any rich ancestors I don't know about, Daddy?*

The bowl is still singing when there is a rap at the door. I drop the puja and step to the window, parting the drape to peer outside. It's now dark, but the full moon casts light enough for me to make out the form of a woman.

"Can I help?" I'm taken aback by the manly brows that greet me.

"Cousin Vick?" Sunken eyes peer at me.

I go to close the door, "Sorry, I think there's—"

The woman braces a not insignificant-sized foot against the doorframe.

"—No, it's definitely you, Vick!"

The middle-aged woman's thin, mean lips break into a delighted smile, revealing tiny child-like teeth.

"I heard about poor Uncle Vernon and I've come to help."

"But I don't know who you are!"

"How can you say that, *ma chère*? This is your kin, Cassie Chadwick."

Catching on more quickly this time, I retort, "The great Canadian fraudster from a hundred years ago has come to help me?" *Really, Daddy? This?*

Cassie reaches out for my hand and gives it a pat, "We're here to pay our respects."

"Look, it's getting late and the funeral's tomorrow. Why don't we chat then?" But I already know they aren't going anywhere.

"But we've come so far, Vick. Can't you put up with us 'til after the funeral? We want to help." Again, the baby teeth.

As I open the door wider, Cassie bustles past me while Charles snoops in the cupboards for wine glasses. They sit at the table and drink.

"So, did Uncle Vernon ever mention me?" queries Cassie with earnest eyes and a hand upon her heart.

"Not in a very kind way—you brought shame on the family."

"I did what I needed to do to survive." Cassie dips her chin indignantly.

"Remind me again—how are we related?"

"You must know of Vernon's older brother, Dan Bigley, married to your Aunt Annie? Well, Aunt Annie is my great-granddaughter." I nod my head vaguely while Cassie lifts her long skirts and rummages in her bloomers, pulling out a scroll of legal-looking papers from between her legs.

"I'm not sure this is the way to help *ma chère*—nobody likes *des trucs*," Charles wags his finger at Cassie.

"This is exactly what she needs. It's gonna help her a lot more than your go-to talk on the art of using a feather!"

"But that's a crucial tool in the art of seduction and pleasure," Charles pouts.

"I dare say, but it's not gonna keep the bank at bay, eh?"

"Well, maybe if she tried it on the manager!"

Mr. Pilsbury? I imagine his naked belly quivering in front of me, rolls of pasty flesh that haven't seen the light of day for decades. "*Eww!* I'm not prostituting myself," I object.

"Of course not," Cassie reassures me. "Look," she lays out the papers, "these are the deeds to the family farm back in Eastwood, Ontario." She wets her index finger and separates a document from the bottom of the pile, "And this is their will—leaving everything to you."

"Is this genuine? Not another one of your scams?"

"They were elaborate plans, if you don't mind, and I didn't gain from anyone who couldn't afford it. See me as a Canadian Robin Hood!"

"You redistributed to the needy?"

"Well, I was certainly needy. You've no idea how difficult things were in those days. Anyway, I'm here helping you now, aren't I?"

"But how does this help me with this place?" I look at Cassie, who is rocking at the edge of her seat as her master plan takes shape, and then at Charles, who is leaning back in his chair, hugging a full glass of wine to his chest, his cheeks and nose rouged, and his eyelids drooping slightly. "Collateral!" Cassie winks.

Charles' attention has been caught by the wilting flowers. "So many poppies, *ma chère*," he smiles.

"Yes, Daddy said the town is a lucky spot—enough rain and sun."

"*Oui*, a lucky spot indeed."

"What are you up to, Charles?" Cassie tilts her head.

"I need to sleep on it, but I too may have a business proposition to help *ma chère*."

When I come down the stairs the following morning, Charles and Cassie are both busy. Charles is sitting at the table which is covered with cut flower stems; the floor around his feet is strewn with poppy petals—both white and red. He holds a razor blade in his hand, cutting the poppy pods which are weeping a thick, white fluid he is catching on the leaves. Cassie is carefully lining the laden leaves onto the south facing windowsill.

"What are you doing?"

"Potentially solving all your worries, *ma chère*. We'll know later if this has worked and whether *le* quality of the opium *est très bon*."

"Opium? Isn't that illegal?"

Charles looks to Cassie, who ushers me into a chair. "Look, Vick, I think you're gonna have to bend a little to get outta this hole."

"And besides, *ma chère*, life is a game. Do you wish to be a winner or a loser?" Charles' eyes twinkle.

"He's right… just look on this as a challenge, a chance to take lots of money from incredibly stupid men." Charles winces before curling his lip in agreement.

Just a week ago this was our home, but things are turning real strange, and now there are two weirdos sitting at our table. I won't be able to stomach those Sunday-morning piles of pancakes, bacon, and maple syrup sitting there anytime soon. *Ugh!* I'm ashamed to even be thinking about sorting out money stuff on the day of the funeral. *Oh Daddy, will you think I'm a loser if I don't save the cottage?*

"If I were to go along with your plan, what would I be doing?

"You'd go to the bank this morning."

"But I need to get ready for Daddy's funeral."

"Daddy don't care what time he gets put in that hole in the ground. Now go and put on your finest clothes—dark and sombre, but also show off those curves a little."

"I've told you, I'm not prostituting myself." But I've already shown my hand by asking about the plan.

"Look, honey, Walter Pilsbury will be parting with more money than you can imagine, and he won't be laying a finger on you, I promise. Look, if I got away with it with this face, your lips and bosom are a surefire winner!"

Mr. Pilsbury is sitting in a black leather chair at his desk and farting noises escape every time he moves. His wrap-around hair style covers his bald spot; a long clump has fallen out of place and hangs on the short-haired-side of his head. It flutters slightly. He doesn't seem to notice, and I have to sit on my hands so I don't reach across and fix it. I imagine the grease of Brylcreem catching beneath my fingernails as I weave it back into place.

He is thumbing through a thick file, Daddy's thick file. When he stops, I produce the legal documents, and he picks up a magnifying glass to scrutinize them. "*Uh-huh, uh-huh,*" he nods. Looking up, he scrunches his mouth to one side as if chewing tobacco, "Okay, Victoria," he pauses to clear phlegm from his throat, and I watch his Adam's apple rise and fall with his swallow, "these documents appear to be in order, but I fail to see how they help. Vernon's estate owes a lot of money, and foreclosure is the only viable way for us."

My resolve crumbles. What am I doing here? I look out of the window onto the parking lot, and I'm alarmed to see Charles and Cassie staring back at me. Cassie has her hands cupped under her breasts which she is jiggling, while Charles has pulled his shirt collar away from his neck and has pursed his lips.

I recall the lines and actions I had practised with them, shuffling my chair closer to the desk. "My dear Mr. Pilsbury, don't you understand just how desperate I am?" I plead, just as I'd been directed by Charles, leaning forward, giving him a flash of my cleavage, before continuing, "These documents clearly show you I am the sole benefactor of my cousin's estate in Ontario. I am prepared to leave both the will and the deeds in your safe custody. You have my word I will honor Daddy's debts. He looked after me all these years, and I always look after those who look after me." I eye Pilsbury intently and give him the merest wink of my eye.

Mr. Pilsbury straightens his tie, "Well, I guess we could keep these documents; they would give some leverage."

I lean fully across the table, my exposed cleavage heaving below his chin, and exhale deeply and softly through my nose into his shirt collar, before whispering in his ear, "I knew I could rely on you."

"My dear lady, I'm at your service," he gives me a full smile, revealing some crumbs of burned toast in his teeth. "Is there anything else I can do for you?"

"Well, as you know, it's the funeral today. There will be other bills I need to pay urgently. Is there any way I could withdraw $500 cash?"

"Of course, my dear, follow me."

"*M*a chère, your seduction technique was exquisite!"

"I told you it was easy to get a lot of money from a stupid man!" Cassie picks up the wad of cash from the table. "So now you have your home and some money to get by until we find a way to get some more. Look, we'll meet you at the church, give you some quiet time here."

Alone in the cottage, I wrap Daddy's sweater around my shoulders and sit again with the singing bowl at the table. I am sick, thinking of how I spent the morning of his funeral. *I know I should be grateful for their help, Daddy, but it feels wrong. It's as good as stealin', and I'm worried how far I could sink, y'know?* I make the bowl sing. *Please, Daddy, help me find my way.* The clock on the mantel chimes and I drop the puja, grab my purse, and leave the cottage.

Standing at the edge of the pit, the scene where Hamlet jumps into Ophelia's grave flashes before my mind's eye. Mrs Simpson once set an assignment asking us to explain why the character had done this, but I failed the paper. My knees bend, ready to jump into the hole so they can't bury Daddy and take him away. I am teetering until I feel someone's arms pull me back from the brink. He's a short, well-groomed Black man. I sort of recognize him, but can't place him exactly. I give him a small, sad smile, and turn my eyes back to Daddy's coffin about to be lowered into the hole in the ground. I could write that essay now.

Nobody ever told me how macabre a funeral is—I mean the horror of it. While Daddy is being lowered, I imagine his elbows knocking the sides of the coffin; I can see the fists of the pallbearers whiten with the strain of holding the strap, and I fear the coffin will topple into the ground head first.

There's no dignity in death.

I can hear laughter coming from the cottage as I open the front door. Charles and Cassie are both drunk already. "Come, *ma chère*, have some wine and let's toast your dear father. *Hic!*" I drink as I've been bidden, but the wine sits acidly on my stomach. "Great news! I've sampled the opium and it is excellent. *Hic!* You will be able to demand a high price for this," he adds.

"Leave the poor girl in peace," booms a deep voice. I turn and see the man from the funeral who I now recognize. His tight curls are gray and sparse in places. The warmth in his brown eyes soothes me. He extends his arm to greet me, "Hello, I'm Martin Luther King, Jr."

I know I should feel overwhelmed, but for the first time since the accident, I feel some peace is within my grasp. "Has Daddy sent you?"

"You called for me earlier today, child." He looks over at Charles and Cassie, sitting at the table, "Are they bothering you?"

"They've been helping me."

"With what, exactly?"

I glance at the empty bottles of wine stacked on the kitchen counter, recall Cassie stuffing the wad of bills I brought home from the bank into her bloomers, and feel Pilsbury's warm, moist breath on my heaving cleavage earlier that morning. I shrug my shoulders, and tears of shame smart in my eyes which now look to the floor.

Dr. King sits me in the rocker and kneels beside me. "You have fallen into a dark pit, but you won't find a way out digging in the dirt... you need to look to the light."

"But I'm gonna lose his home."

"Why do you need to save it? He doesn't need it anymore."

I pick up the cardboard box lying on the floor next to the chair. "But what about his stuff?"

"Your father isn't in that box, Victoria."

I shudder. No, he's in that box buried in the earth. *Oh, Daddy! Tell me what to do.* I watch Cassie and Charles laughing together, her baby teeth and his drooping lids. I meet the gaze of Dr. King. "But I can't see the way forward," I sob.

"Can you see the next step? That's all you need."

"Can I ask you something?"

"Anything at all."

"Why hasn't Daddy come to me?"

"He knows you can work this out for yourself."

"Then why am I so afraid?"

"That's the brain trying to keep you safe. If it could, it would seal you in that cardboard box with your father's belongings!"

Geez, that's suffocating... in fact, this town, never mind that box, is choking me. And how can I live a Daddy-shaped life without him here? ... Shit! What happened to my life? I feel foolishly duped. Dr. King is looking at me, waiting for my next question, so I nod, then ask, "Do you still think 'sincere ignorance' and 'conscientious stupidity' are the most dangerous things in the world?"

Dr. King smiles and looks across to Charles and Cassie, who are sitting in a drunken stupor. "Well, don't you?" He leans over to pat my leg. "Wrap yourself up and get some sleep. I'll sit with you while you settle." He lifts *Les Fleurs du Mal* from his lap where his index finger holds his place. "I'm intrigued to read more of this," he winks.

Cocooned in the warmth of Dr. King's aura and Daddy's sweater, I drift into sleep.

M y neck is stiff. *Goddamn it!* I can tell by the brightness of the sunshine that it's late morning and the place is lighter—not just brighter. I see all the bottles, jars, and vases have been cleared away. The credenza is empty save for the cardboard box which is now sealed. Everything is immaculate—no dregs of wine, dead foliage, or opium residue. On the table sits a clean vase with freshly cut poppies. Next to this sits the singing bowl. I panic when I wonder where all the unpaid bills are. I pull out the top drawer of the credenza and there they are—with the thick bundle of dollars.

I pull out the bundle together with an envelope. I place them on the table and make myself some coffee and toast. As I breakfast, I put the bills into the envelope, root in my jeans pocket for my house key, and drop that in, too. I pull the lid off the pen with my teeth and, between mouthfuls of toast, write, "Mr. Pilsbury," onto the crisp white envelope, which I leave propped against the vase.

I lift my backpack and coat off the peg on the door, and stuff Daddy's sweater and the singing bowl inside. I fasten my coat and take one last look around the room. *Goodbye, Daddy.*

I step out of the door and stretch my arms toward the big sky.

The Mystic Lamb
Gail Z. Martin

Present—Ghent, Belgium, April 9, 1934

“The ghosts are panicking, Edgar. This isn't going the way we planned.” Maggie Fox didn't raise her voice, but her tart tone made the urgency clear.

“Hold steady. Stay in contact with the ghosts. Harry needs us.” Edgar Cayce couldn't afford to have his spirit medium lose her focus, not when the prize was almost within reach.

“Give me a report, Maggie,” Edgar replied, keeping his voice firm and steady. “Harry's life depends on us. The fate of the world depends on Harry.”

Maggie's lips twisted in an annoyed moue, but she stayed at her post. Her all-black mourning dress accentuated a pale complexion and angular features. The center-parted hair and tight bun added severity. Polished jet buttons and earrings—her only adornment—glinted in the gaslight.

“He's in the room with the artwork,” Maggie recounted from her ghostly spies. “Already at work stealing the panel we need.”

Edward glanced away from the telescope where he had been watching the main entrance of the Saint Bavo Cathedral. The little flat they had rented for the week had the perfect view. Edgar ground his teeth in frustration as he watched a unit of Nazi soldiers take command of the area, trooping inside like they owned the place.

And not just any soldiers. These were the elite SS officers tasked with building Hitler's occult armory.

“Dammit! They weren't supposed to steal the panel until tomorrow.”

Maggie arched an eyebrow. “Maybe the theft just wasn't discovered until the tenth. Ever think of that?”

“Have your ghosts sound the alarm,” Edgar told Maggie. “Harry needs to know company's coming.”

* * *

Then—April 8, 1939, Virginia Beach

*I*n his vision, Edgar watched the banners of the Third Reich burn, and saw the Nazi Party's monuments and statues bombed and blasted. Images flashed, and he glimpsed Hitler, dead. Planes emblazoned with the swastika fell from the sky trailing smoke, while the once-powerful German army surrendered in utter defeat. Wewelsburg Castle, the pride of the Ahnenerbe, burned like a Lughnasadh bonfire.

The scene shifted, and Edgar recognized the facade of the famous New Yorker Hotel. He glimpsed a thin, white-haired man with a face so gaunt it looked like a death's head, and piercing, uncompromising black eyes.

"Watch for me—I am coming to you," the man said, and Edgar could still hear the stranger's voice in his mind. "I can give you twenty-four hours to change history and save the world."

Edgar Cayce woke with a gasp, the vision still clear in his mind.

That wasn't a dream—it was a vision. But could such a thing actually come true?

He had dozed off in the sunshine on a park bench, one of the few simple pleasures still available amid the privations of the war.

America had joined the Allied nations against the Axis powers when the bombing of the U.S. East Coast left no alternative. While the two factions were well-matched in numbers and conventional munitions, the Third Reich's obsession with the occult was paying off and threatened to change the balance of power.

Edgar's vision had conveyed knowledge beyond the images—he *knew* that unspeakable horrors powered the Nazi juggernaut. Blood magic, demon possession, and the ability to revive soldiers no matter how horrific their injuries to unleash an un-killable army of the dead and damned—all of them propelled Hitler's legions toward a victory that would doom the human race.

People called Edgar "The Sleeping Prophet" because his visions only came to him while he slept. He had gained a following among modern Spiritualists and truth-seekers, those who were open to questioning old assumptions and exploring new ways to acquire knowledge. Usually, Edgar's readings focused on a client's concerns for health or prosperity. A vision on the scale that he'd just experienced was unprecedented, and it shook him to his core.

Twenty-four hours to save the world. Could something I do possibly prevent the future I saw in my vision? I would do anything to keep those monsters from winning!

But before he set out to save humanity, Edgar needed to find a restroom.

Fortunately, the park had public facilities, an elaborate Victorian building complete with a cupola. When Edgar walked inside, he frowned, looking around in confusion. The outside of the building had seemed much larger, but the white-tiled room in which he found himself was the size of a large closet without any plumbing fixtures.

And it was already occupied—by the man he had glimpsed in his vision.

"There's very little time," the stranger said brusquely. "I'm Nikola Tesla, and I was instructed in a dream to find you, bring you my time machine, and send you off to change history—and save the world."

"I thought this was the men's room." Edgar was in favor of stopping the Nazis, but he really did need to pee.

Tesla rolled his eyes. "There's a door over there. Be quick about it."

When Edgar returned, Tesla stood with his arms crossed, tapping the toe of his shoe like a metronome.

"It takes an enormous amount of energy to power this craft, and I can't maintain that for longer than a day," Tesla told him.

"Where am I going? What do I need to do?" Edgar tried to wrap his mind around the strange turn his afternoon had taken and the obvious urgency of his unlikely task.

"You need to steal a painting five years ago, in Belgium. I've analyzed all the possible intersections and probabilities, and this single event is the nexus which, if changed, will alter the course of the war." Tesla shoved a piece of paper at Edgar, with an address scribbled on it, and beneath that, dates and coordinates.

"I don't know how—"

"Look to your vision, Edgar. The answers have been supplied."

Two names came to Edgar's mind: Maggie Fox and Harry Houdini. "All right. What do I need to do?"

"The dates and locations on the paper I gave you are where you must go to accomplish the mission. I've worked them out with precise mathematics, so do not deviate from the plan," Tesla admonished. "First, you have to persuade your accomplices to accompany you. Then, you steal the artwork, evade the Nazis, and return your helpers to their times. I will navigate the time machine remotely. When you come back here, history will—hopefully—be changed, and the course of the war altered."

"All that, in twenty-four hours? What happens if we're late?"

Tesla fixed him with a look that scorched his bones. "Bad things. Avoid that."

"When does the time start?" Edgar's mouth had gone dry at the abrupt change in his day.

Tesla looked at his watch. "Now."

Then—1859, near Hydesville, New York

"Y̶ou want me to help you steal a painting—in my future, your past?" Maggie Fox, the oldest of the famous trio of sister mediums, looked at Edgar as if he'd slipped a cog.

"Hear me out," Edgar replied, relieved she hadn't started screaming and gotten him arrested. "I have a special gift, just like you and your sisters. Where you can talk to ghosts, I get visions of the future. My visions come true—unless something happens to alter what sets them in motion."

The severe hairstyle and somber black dress made Maggie look much older than her twenty-five years. She and her two sisters were world-famous for their ability to speak to the dead and channel them during séances. While Edgar knew that some of their mediumship would eventually be debunked as showmanship, he believed that they did have a genuine gift.

The Maggie Fox from 1859 wasn't bitter yet from being mistreated by reporters and her own kin. She hadn't pushed herself to burnout to entertain audiences that would later turn on her without hesitation. Her ability was at its strongest, and most importantly, she still believed in it.

He sat down in a rocking chair next to her, on the wide hotel porch overlooking one of the many Finger Lakes. It hadn't been easy to catch up with her—the sisters were at the peak of their fame and traveled almost constantly. But Tesla had pinpointed a weekend at a lodge when Edgar could find Maggie alone and have a conversation about changing the history of the world. At least he knew the details—he had dozed in the time machine, and the missing pieces revealed themselves.

"In Germany, seventy-five years from now, a very bad man—Adolph Hitler—will come to power. He'll build an army like the world has never seen and wage a war that will kill millions of people. In my original timeline, he wins, and the world is enslaved in darkness and flames." Edgar hoped he could get through to Maggie, because if there was even the barest chance to subvert that future, he had to make it happen.

"I had a vision that another future—a much better one—was possible. In my time, Hitler's army and guns weren't his greatest strength. In 1934, he sent a thief to a cathedral in Belgium to steal part of a painting that held the key to an occult treasure," he told her.

"The 'Just Judges' panel—part of Van Eyck's *Adoration of the Mystic Lamb*—is the key to a map that leads to the Arma Christi. The Arma Christi is made up of three objects: the crown of thorns worn by Christ on the cross, the Holy Grail, and the Spear of Destiny," Edgar knew Maggie was listening, but remained unsure whether she believed a word he said.

"Anyone who controls all three of those items gains supernatural powers, including the ability to reanimate the dead. In my time, Hitler's people stole the panel, decoded the map, and found the relics. They and their armies of the dead were unstoppable, and the rest of mankind became their slaves. Hundreds of millions of people died." Edgar's heart hammered just recounting that horror.

"We need to steal the 'Just Judges' panel before Hitler's people get there. Then the Nazis won't find the Arma Christi, and they'll never have gained those infernal abilities. They'll lose the war, and the world will remain free." Edgar would never have believed that the fate of mankind would rest on the whim of a twenty-five-year-old woman, but then again, he knew better than most people that stranger things had happened.

"Interesting. Suppose I believe you," Maggie Fox said, toying with her fan. "How do we get to the cathedral—in 1934?"

Edgar smiled and pointed toward the brightly painted wooden cabanas that dotted one side of the lakeshore. "I came in a time machine. It's the green cabana on the end."

She raised an elegant eyebrow, and her lips thinned in derision. "Oh, really?"

She thinks I'm a madman. Before she could raise a hand to signal hotel security, Edgar dug into his pocket and withdrew a handful of coins and bills. "Wait! Look at the dates on the coins and bills."

He held them out to her, and she examined them, clearly skeptical. "These could be forged."

"What do the ghosts say?" The vision had left Edgar desperate to find a solution, and he had no intention of failing.

Maggie's eyes lost focus for a moment, and he assumed she was communing with the spirits. Different emotions flitted across her features, ending with a canny look he didn't dare try to guess.

"They vouch for you. So I guess I shall have to believe you." Maggie snapped her fan open and shut a couple of times, and Edgar assumed it was a nervous gesture as she gathered her thoughts.

"You'll bring me back to this very place, this very afternoon, when we finish?"

Edgar nodded. "Yes. And while I can't guarantee your safety, I will do everything in my power—to the loss of my own life—to protect you."

"Let's hope that's not necessary," she replied. "One more question: why me?"

He smiled. "Because you're the best. Do we have a deal?"

A smile twitched at the corners of her stern mouth. "I believe we do, sir."

Present—Ghent, Belgium, August 9, 1934

"One of the ghosts has a message from Harry." Maggie turned to look at Edgar, who still stood by the telescope trying to count the number of Nazi officers who entered the cathedral.

"What did he say?" Edgar felt his stomach twist, worried both about his thief and the fate of the world.

"The ghost wouldn't repeat Harry's comments word-for-word because he said they weren't suitable for a lady's ears," she replied with a hint of mockery. "But I believe it boils down to saying he'd cause a distraction and he had a plan."

Edgar sighed. "Let's hope he's as good for real as he is on stage. That cathedral is crawling with Nazis, and Harry needs to get himself and the art panel out safely, or this whole expedition goes to hell in a handbasket." *And so does history.*

"Much as it pains me to say it—knowing what he says he thinks of people like me—he seems like a reliable fellow," Maggie said, and despite the edge in her voice, Edgar thought she meant it.

He couldn't fault her pique with Harry, who had made it a mission in life to debunk fraudulent Spiritualists. He had, of course, heard of the famous—or infamous—Fox sisters, and he had been surprised that Edgar had chosen one of them as his medium on such a critical mission.

For her part, Maggie regarded Harry with dismissive disdain. Edgar knew that he'd plucked her from a point in the timeline thirty years before she and her sisters would be pressured by family squabbles and the burnout of fame into an ill-advised "confession" that would ruin them all.

Then again, he'd pulled Harry out a year before his death from a ruptured appendix. As grateful as he was to both of them for saving history, he didn't dare tell them what he knew to save them from their own destinies.

Then—National Theatre, New York City, December 8, 1925

"You're quite a cheeky fellow to come seek me out, considering what I do," Harry Houdini said when Edgar walked out of the closet in his dressing room after the performance.

"I know what you do, and I'm not afraid. If you weren't the best, I wouldn't be here," Edgar replied. "If my visions weren't true, I wouldn't be here, either."

Harry used cold cream to wipe away the theatrical makeup, and changed out of his stage costume without false modesty. In street clothes, his short stature might make him easy to overlook if it weren't for his muscular form and the blazing stare of his eyes.

"So you want to hop almost twenty years into the future in your *time machine* and have me steal a famous painting from a cathedral to stop crazy German anarchists who think they can find the Holy Grail and rule the world?" Houdini's expression made it clear he thought Edgar was mad.

"That's the gist of it, yes. You're the best illusionist and escape artist who ever lived."

"They still say that about me, where—when—you come from?" Houdini looked skeptical, but the sop to his ego got his attention.

"Absolutely. There have been many imitators, but no one as good."

"Huh. Guess the future isn't too exciting. Say I agree. We go to Ghent, I sneak into the cathedral and heist the painting—"

"Not the full work. There are twelve panels. We only want one specific panel. And we only need half of it."

"Sure. Let's go with that," Harry said, clearly appeasing the crazy man. "I get out, we all fly away, and you drop us off at the curb in our own time. How do I know you aren't just going to take off with the painting and sell it in the future, make yourself rich?"

"The missing half of the panel has never been found." Edgar pulled out an art history book he'd chosen for its lack of potential to give away spoilers for the future and flipped to the marked section. He handed it to Harry. "Go ahead, read the passage. Do you think I printed up a whole textbook to lie to you?"

Houdini regarded him with an inscrutable expression. "Stranger things could happen." He paused and read the page, then read it again. Harry thumbed to the front matter and frowned when he read the copyright before handing it back to Edgar.

"I've seen a lot of elaborate frauds. Usually, there's some sort of get-rich-quick hook and a victim who never knows what hit him. But what you're proposing—I can't get what's in it for you," Houdini said.

"I don't want to live in that future," Edgar replied. "With the unfair magical advantages the Third Reich gains from the Arma Christi—which they found because of the map in the painting—the armies of the world couldn't stop them. I was resigned to that reality until my vision showed me that one small change in who steals the panel changes the fate of the world."

"Tempting. Noble. I assume we'd be the kind of heroes whose derring-do must remain a secret for the good of mankind?"

Edgar refused to jump at the bait of Harry's mockery. "Probably for the best."

Harry leaned forward from his seat at the mirror. "So… dispel my doubts. Show me your time machine."

Edgar nodded toward the closet. "It's in there."

"Your time machine is in my closet? How convenient."

"Don't take my word for it. Go have a look. I'll wait here. Nothing up my sleeve and all," Edgar replied.

Harry glared at him, but a moment later he got up and walked across the small dressing room, yanked open the closet door, and stared inside, gape-jawed.

"Well, damn. Guess you were telling the truth after all."

Present—Ghent, Belgium, April 9, 1934

"I don't like what I'm hearing from the ghosts," Maggie said, drumming her fingers. She had candles and a cloth embroidered with arcane runes and sigils was spread across the old oak table, items that she said strengthened her gift. "The soldiers have rounded up all the priests and put them in handcuffs while they go looking for the painting. Harry's among them."

Damn. "That's all right. If there's anyone who can get out of a pair of cuffs, it's Houdini."

He knew the magician was clever, and between his illusions and his ability to get out of chains, ropes, and straitjackets, Edgar felt certain that Harry would somehow escape and evade his captors.

His confidence didn't stop the knot in his stomach from twisting or his mouth from going dry with anxiety. If Harry couldn't slip his bonds, ditch the Germans and get out with the painting, they were all in a lot of trouble—and humanity was doomed.

The minutes crawled by, and Edgar forced himself not to pace. Maggie remained in contact with her ghost spies while Edgar watched with the telescope. Unfortunately, they had no way to see inside the cathedral.

"The soldiers are everywhere. But... Harry's gone from where they're keeping the rest of the prisoners, and now the spirits can't find him. I hope he's already got the painting and gets out of there. We're running out of time," she fretted.

Edgar grinned. "If the ghosts can't find him, that's a good sign because odds are, the Nazis won't either. After all, he *is* Harry Houdini."

"You say that like it means something."

"It will someday. Just like how people remember you and your sisters."

Maggie cast a glance over her shoulder. "You don't have to play to my vanity."

He shrugged. "I'm not. It's true." Edgar wondered whether anyone would remember him for as long, and if so, what would remain. The thought made him melancholy. He shook himself out of his mood and focused on the work.

"The ghosts are distracting the soldiers as instructed," Maggie said. "Slamming doors, knocking on woodwork, pushing objects off shelves. Cold spots and orbs. Soldiers are a superstitious lot. They're frightened."

"Good. Keep it up."

"The soldiers are searching everywhere for the missing panel," Maggie shared the ghosts' report a few minutes later. "But they haven't found Harry... or the art."

"That's because he's just that good," Edgar murmured with pride.

Edgar knew that the Nazi officers sent on this mission were dedicated to finding and acquiring occult objects. Their belief in the supernatural made them more susceptible than the average soldier to believing—and fearing—paranormal activity.

He hoped that frightening the soldiers would make them leave. But as Edgar watched with the telescope and cursed under his breath, he saw that the headstrong, arrogant captain in charge of the mission wasn't willing to retreat.

How in the hell Harry intended to smuggle a five-foot-tall painting out of a cathedral crawling with Nazis, Edgar didn't know, but he trusted his new ally to figure it out.

"The ghosts spotted him. They said he came out of the floor." Despite herself, Maggie sounded excited.

"It's Harry. He probably did. Make sure the ghosts lead the soldiers on a merry chase." Edgar forced himself not to watch the second hand on his watch ticking down their time. He knew Tesla and his time machine would not be late.

Just then, Edgar saw a priest in a long cassock with a hood emerge from a side door. The man walked slowly, arms clasped in front of him, posture rigid. *That has to be Harry. But where's the panel? It's is almost as tall as he is. He must have it down the back of his robe.*

The priest shuffled, not moving quickly enough to cause alarm. One of the soldiers accosted him, and the priest just kept his face downcast and shook his head as if he was hard of hearing.

Edgar's heart sped up, fearing the worst. One wrong move, and not only would Harry get re-captured, but the panel of the 'Just Judges' would be confiscated, making their journey for naught.

He wished he could hear the conversation, but at this distance, all he had were gestures and body language to guess the direction of the discussion.

"Can the ghosts move beyond the cathedral?" he asked Maggie.

"Some can." She managed a faint smile. "You need them to cause a commotion?"

"Please."

Just as Edgar feared that the stern soldier would grab Harry to force him back inside the cathedral, a distraction off to one side claimed his attention. Harry bumped into the guard on his way past, but whatever ruckus the ghosts had engineered had all of the soldiers running into a side street, completely forgetting the short priest who now moved more quickly toward their hotel.

Edgar checked his watch, seeing only fifteen minutes remaining. *He's cutting it fine.*

Harry burst into the room, wearing street clothes with the painting wrapped in his stolen cassock. "I gave the person at the front desk the keys I pickpocketed off the soldier, so someone can set the priests free. Would have been here sooner, but I hid the painting in a damn priest hole when I knew they were going to catch me, and I had to go back for it," he told them as Maggie and Edgar hurriedly gathered their gear.

Footsteps thundered on the wooden stairs, growing closer.

"Time to go," Edgar said, pushing them all into the small bathroom as a kick splintered the hallway door.

Nothing around them changed, but the swoop in his belly told Edgar that Tesla had yanked them back from the brink of disaster.

"Nice work," he told Harry and Maggie. "We made one heck of a team."

"What now?" Maggie asked.

"I take you both home and go back to my time," Edgar said. He could already feel them altering course. When the door opened, they looked out on the lake where he had met Maggie.

"Thank you," he said. "And please, don't try to get back at your sister. You'll fight, but trust me on this: vengeance will destroy all three of you." The words were out of Edgar's mouth before he realized he had made the decision to warn her how to change her future.

She gave him a strange look, as if she understood more than what he'd said. "I'll take that to heart." Then she stepped out into the sun and sand, and the "cabana" disappeared.

"Guess this is the end of the road," Harry said when the momentum shifted again, and the door opened into his dressing room.

"We all owe you a debt," Edgar said. "And Harry, never let a stranger punch you in the stomach, and if you have a bellyache, don't put off going to the doctor."

Harry's eyes narrowed, trying to parse out Edgar's meaning, and then nodded. "I appreciate the tip."

The door shut, and Edgar was alone with the stolen painting, left to wonder if he could ever completely believe what had just transpired. *How will the world be different? Did we win? Did I save Harry and Maggie, or did fate find another way to claim them?*

When the door opened one last time, Tesla stepped inside. He looked up from the chained pocket watch on his vest and snapped the cover shut.

"Down to the wire, but on time nonetheless," he said. His gaze flickered to the cassock-wrapped art. "You did it."

Edgar shook his head. "Harry did it, with lots of help from Maggie's ghosts."

"You rallied them, and it was your fervor that made them agree," Tesla replied. "Now, if you'll excuse me, I have one last stop to make." He waved his hand toward the door. "Go up the steps, and you'll be back at the park."

"What will you do with the painting? Even by my time, no one's ever found it."

Tesla nodded soberly. "It's far too dangerous to return to time going forward. The Arma Christi must never be recovered. Which is why I intend to store the painting in the past: in the Library of Alexandria. If it's ever needed, a time traveler can go back before the library's destruction to retrieve the art. Otherwise, it will be outside the reach of any who seek it for all time."

Edgar smiled. "You did some nice driving, maneuvering the machine. I barely even got carsick."

Tesla sniffed. "I should hope so. It's my invention, after all." The barest hint of a smile touched his thin lips. "Don't forget to stop by a newspaper stand. I think you'll find the headlines to be... enlightening." He conveyed his thanks with a curt nod, which Edgar returned.

Edgar climbed the steps and stepped out into the sun. He felt sure that retracing his path would find only an unremarkable public men's room.

He hurried across the street to a kiosk covered with magazines and papers. "A copy of the *Times*, please." He dug payment out of his pocket and realized that the coins on his palm were no longer anything special.

"Here you go, bub. Looks like our boys have the Jerries on the run," the man said proudly as he handed over the newspaper. "It's about time."

Edgar scanned the front page, heart thudding as the headlines corroborated that the Allies did indeed have the upper hand, with no mention of dark magic or the resurrected dead. He looked up and spotted a broadside tacked up in the bus stop heralding an upcoming performance by Harry Houdini on his farewell tour. When he got home, Edgar resolved to look up whatever happened to Maggie and her sisters, but he suspected their fortunes had improved.

"It certainly is."

Episode in Liminal State Technical Support, or Mr. Grant in the Bardo

Gregory Frost

1:47:23 P.M.

It is his one hundredth, his final, session with Dr. Hartman, whom he calls "my mahatma." You would think it would be easy sailing by now: He lies back on the blue couch, closes his eyes, and waits, drifting. He should right now be seeing blossoming, exploding and recurring Rorschach patterns, saturated with color. Instead, when somebody shakes his shoulder, he's finds himself lying on a thick cushion that's red as a field of poppies.

He expects it will be Hartman shaking him. Certainly not one of the staff. Interruption of a patient's LSD therapy session is strictly verboten, so who but his mahatma would intrude? Instead, however, an oddly jointed blonde woman stands above him. She has a pageboy haircut and looks strikingly like Eva Marie Saint, whom he hasn't seen since they wrapped shooting on *North by Northwest*. Her couture is strange, too, a pants outfit somewhere between Flash Gordon and Busby Berkeley, with winged shoulder pads and a spiral sequined design from top to bottom, with flared pantlegs. There's something uncanny and artificial about her demeanor—a too perfectly smooth face, for one thing. All of this dampens his annoyance somewhat at being pulled out of his final session with psychedelics. Maybe if he just closes his eyes, he can go back to looking inside himself and she'll go away. He tries it, although no sparkling visuals appear.

After a minute, the woman says, "Good evening, sir."

He opens his eyes again. She's still there, with a clipboard.

"Could you go away? I'm trying to enjoy my pareidolia." It's at that point he realizes he's in a completely different room. No maple paneling, no blue couch, no desk for Hartman. Everything's translucent, and the overhead light diffuse, as if the entire ceiling is the light.

He sits up. He's wearing the same cashmere sweater, the same linen slacks and dark socks. Same tan to his hands, and so presumably the rest of him. His loafers are on the floor beside this crystalline daybed. He considers the woman again. Her head is tilted to one side like the R.C.A. pup. "You probably get this all the time. But am I dead?"

She smiles, as if the question has activated her. "That's what we need to determine," she explains. "You've been transported here to Liminal State Technical Support, and death is one possibility."

"Liminal Whowhat?"

She consults her plastic clipboard. "It's our job—*my* job—to determine your fate, whether you're alive, dead, reborn, or transmogrified."

"Just the four choices? What about gayly intoxicated?"

"I don't know what that means." She taps an index finger at the clipboard. "You, sir, fell off your timeline."

"Pardon me. The only thing I fell off was a couch."

"Well, you must have hit your head. Fallen through a surprise wormhole. *Something*." She studies the clipboard again. "Strange, it doesn't say on your chart. I suppose that's why I'm here, to determine your fate."

"If it's all the same to you, I don't want my fate determined. That's why I'm in therapy." He smooths his dark hair going gray at the temples, feels around for a bump or a dent. There's nothing. "If you're technical support, what exactly is it you're supporting anyway?"

"Why, the stability of the universe. There are beings, like you, who fall off the timeline. While some are *supposed* to disappear, most are not. It is our job to ensure all outcomes are correct."

"And, what, my hitting my head destabilizes the universe? My goodness, I must be the Grand Poo-Bah!"

"I don't know what that means."

"No, of course not. So you make people disappear?"

"Yes, we do."

"You sound like Murder Incorporated. What do you do with people once they fall off this timeline thing?"

She brightens at this question she can answer. "They're placed in a state of suspended animation here in our facility, until such time as we are able to place them in a similar, compatible timeline."

"You're giving me a headache. What is a similar compatible timeline?"

"Another timeline within the myriad of multiverses where we can insert them without any ripples."

"For the record, when I wake up, I expect Hartman to explain to me how can I be making up this dialogue when I don't even understand it." He shakes his head as if to clear it. "All right, alive, dead, reborn, or transmogrified—is that actually a word?" He gestures around himself. "So, what would this be then?"

"It *might* be rebirth. It is difficult to tell, as this is merely a way station. Of course I need to confirm your information."

"Rebirth is what I was engaged in accomplishing for myself before you interrupted. I mean, am I talking to you or just talking to myself and thinking there's a 'you'?"

"Well, I am truly sorry, Mister"—she peers at the clipboard—"Mister Clementine."

He blinks. "Oh my darling. Listen, Leach or Grant, I answer to both. But there's no Mr. Clementine in here." He raps a knuckle against his head. "Though I believe we have located the source of the problem."

"What?" She studies the clipboard, shakes her head. "Oh, no, that can't be right."

He smugly crosses his arms. "No, it can't, can it? I am or was in Dr. Hartman's office for *my* final session. Maybe you were supposed to collect his three-o'clock."

She looks ready to burst into tears.

"Listen," he says, "if it's any consolation, I'm very likely imagining you and your conundrum anyway, and if you'll just send me back to where I was, I'll peel you off the inside of my eyelids, and we can forget the whole thing. At least, I will. Happily." He considers the clear daybed, the red pad on top of it, now notices various toggles and lights on the wall behind it as well as a row of four buttons in red, green, yellow, and blue. "You *can* send me back?"

"Oh, yes. If this turns out to be our fault, you'll just lie down again and I'll press that blue button over there, and you won't even know you were gone."

"Blue for alive, I hope?"

"Of course. Red for rebirth. Yellow for death, and—"

"Yes, I think I've got it."

"If you'll just lie down, I will go and find out what's happened to Clementine."

"Lost and gone forever, I imagine."

"I don't understand that."

"Dreadful sorry." He gives her a big smile, then sits back down. "So, I'll just wait—"

They're interrupted by an alarm that seems to sound from everywhere around them. The woman sweeps her hand across her clipboard. No lines appear in her face but somehow she frowns. "Oh, no."

"What's the matter now?"

"Oh, Judge Crater's escaped again!"

"Is *he* still running around?"

"He's due to be under an aquarium. Oh, dear. I'll be right back."

Speechless, he watches as she turns away and glides across the small chamber. A door slides open where there was no door, and she's gone. There's no obvious belt or moving panel in the floor. How did she skate like that? However, the door remains open. The alarm has stopped sounding, but lights flash on and off in the corridor.

He considers everything, finally deciding that, somewhere, he is lying on a blue couch above gray shag carpeting and this is his damn hallucination, so he can do as he pleases in it.

He puts on his shoes and walks through the open door and into a long corridor. Both sides contain nothing but translucent chambers identical to his own. He walks across the way. A new door slides open. Inside is the mirror image of his own chamber. The figure lying on the red pad there is an elderly man who looks vaguely like Mark Twain, though his hair is more gray than white and he needs a shave. The fellow is dressed in a collarless shirt, brown vest, tan dungarees. His pointed-toe boots, on the floor beside him, are roughly worn and hand-tooled.

A gentle shake on the shoulder produces no effect.

He circles around to the same panel on the wall as was installed in his own chamber. Knowing what the four buttons do, he leaves them alone, instead considers the odd toggle switches. What can it hurt? This is all in his mind anyway. He flips one of the toggles. The figure is bathed in intense red light for a moment, and begins to stir.

He goes over to him and the man opens his eyes, reaches up for assistance. He pulls him upright.

The older man stretches with a grimace. Glances around himself while clearing his throat. "Where's this?" he asks. "Sure as hell it isn't Chihuahua."

"There's a novel idea. Frankly, I'm not sure where this is, but you're the first to bring Chihuahua into it. By the way, who would you be?"

"Bierce. Ambrose Gwinnett Bierce. And you?"

Well, in for a penny... "Grant. Cary Archibald Leach Grant. Say, you aren't 'Chicamauga' Bierce, are you?"

"I am. Proclaimed one of America's three greatest writers." He seems to find the very idea absurd.

"And who are the other two?"

"William Dean Howells," Bierce replies without cracking a smile.

"Well, he must get around a lot."

"Not as much as me, he hasn't. Been all through the South, visiting graves of men I killed in the war, before I crossed through Texas to Mexico, joined Villa's army and reported there on the Battle of Tierra Blanca. I wrote of it to Blanche, and that's about all I remember. I was setting out..." Stops and shakes his head. Bierce's demeanor is dour, not so much troubled as resolved.

He nods at all of this information, as if understanding it, but truly all that he recalls of Ambrose Bierce's life story is that he vanished without a trace, and that various conflicting tales claimed to "explain" his whereabouts. "What happened to you that you ended up here?"

"Firstly, I should like to know where here is," says Bierce.

"Wouldn't we all? What do you say we wake somebody else up? Maybe they'll know more than we do."

"So long as you mean to explain." He grabs his boots and pulls them on.

"Well, listen, do you remember what happened to your character in 'An Occurrence at Owl Creek Bridge'?"

"You've read it?"

"I have. And you and I would seem to be in that illusory location between the escape and the hanging. Personally, I would prefer a different outcome, if it's all the same to anyone."

Bierce, looking gloomier, says nothing but follows after him. They walk along the corridor while lights continue flashing on and off. Finally, he turns to Bierce in some frustration. "Anybody could be in any of these compartments. There's nothing to identify one from the other."

"Except for those." Bierce points to a dully lighted strip of characters above the nearest door.

"Yes, but can you read it?"

"No, sir, I can't. That's no lingo I've ever seen."

"Me, either. So I say, what the hell. Let's take our chances and hope we don't wake up Attila the Hun." He walks over to the one in front of him, and the invisible door magically defines itself and slides aside. "Shall we—?"

"Might as well," says Bierce. "Can't dance."

He grins as the old man passes him. "I'll have to remember that one."

Inside, the compartment is identical to the other two he's seen. A slender middle-aged woman lies on the red pad here. Her dark blonde hair is cut short and shaggy. Her eyes are closed but her mouth, slightly open, reveals a gap between her front teeth. She's dressed in a pale blue shirt beneath a leather aviator's jacket, above khaki trousers. One of her socks has a hole in it. Something about her seems familiar.

"How do we wake her up?" Bierce asks.

"Oh, like this." He crosses around to the wall and flips the same toggle as before. She is bathed in red light and, shortly, her eyelids flutter open.

Bierce bends over her. "Hello, there," he says. "How you feeling?"

The woman looks up in a daze. "Are you God? Am I dead?"

Bierce smiles in some embarrassment. "No, madam, I am not." Introduces himself.

Her bright eyes widen with recognition at his name, and she sits up. "Why, you disappeared. I remember hearing of it." She considers for a moment. "And I suppose I must have disappeared, too. I know we were lost, coasting on fumes, and Fred thought the 20B receiver wasn't transmitting on the right frequency, or maybe the antenna had broken off." She glances around, notices him at the controls. He gives her a friendly smile. "Is Fred here, too?" she asks him. "Fred Noonan?"

He shakes his head. "He might be, somewhere. We've only just found you, Amelia."

"I—you know me?"

"Only the same stories that everyone knows: the greatest female aviator, an inspiration to thousands of women pilots in World War II."

"There was a world war two?"

"And a one?" Bierce interjects.

"Oh, dear. There's a good deal happened after you two disappeared. And rather more for you to absorb, Ambrose, old thing."

Earhart asks, "And who are you?"

"A fair question." He introduces himself. The name obviously doesn't register. But by 1937 when she vanished he had only been in a couple of films.

"And how did *you* disappear?"

"Ah, well that's the thing, you see. Far as I know, I didn't disappear at all. These birds mistook me for someone named Clementine."

Earhart and Bierce both laugh.

"Yes, I thought it was hilarious, too, the first time."

"But where is this place?" asks Earhart. "Why are we here if we disappeared somewhere else?"

He does his best to explain what the eccentric attendant told him, including the four possible outcomes, determined by the panel on the wall behind them.

Bierce replies, "What's it even *mean* to say somebody fell off their timeline? Makes it sound like a bicycle."

"I can only assume it means there was some pre-ordained outcome for you and you didn't take it."

"'Two roads diverged in a yellow wood, and sorry I could not travel both and be one traveler, long I stood,'" Bierce recites, then continues gravely, "I certainly chose a less traveled way. At least I would have, had they let me be. Road where I come to my end. Guess that didn't jibe with the universe's plans. Probably it couldn't."

"Why is that?"

"Because where I truly want to go is to Carcosa."

Earhart, puzzled, says, "Where?"

Bierce nods. "A place I invented once upon a time. A great city, but my narrator, who was a ghost, only remembered its splendors, long past. I always thought I should like to arrive in its heyday, see what I might make of myself there. I've done about all I need to on *this* road."

"You want to go to a place that doesn't exist," he says.

"Why not? I've seen enough of reality—and I'll tell you, it's nothing but the dream of a mad philosopher." Bierce points to the four colored buttons. "So, which of those will send me there?"

"None of them, I think. We're in Miss Earhart's chamber. We'd have to go back to yours."

"All right, then." Gathering himself up, Bierce turns and strides out into the corridor, where the lights are no longer flashing.

"I have a feeling they've caught up to Judge Crater," he tells Earhart.

"Judge Crater, the missingest man in New York?"

"Believe it or not," he says as he takes her by the arm, "he's the reason you're up and about. And if they've managed to catch him, we don't have a lot of time for goodbyes."

They hurry down the corridor and follow Bierce back into his chamber, where he plops down on the bed, tugs off his boots, and asks again of the buttons, "Which one is it?"

He crosses to the panel. "According to the attendant, the green one. The only one that doesn't simply kill you or return you somewhere you've been. Magical transformation, I think it means, which sounds like your Carcosa."

Bierce lies back down on the red pad, crosses his hands like a body in an open coffin. "All right," he says. "I'm ready."

"You'll probably need to be asleep first." He flicks the same toggle as before. It bathes Bierce in red light, which fails to put him to sleep.

He flicks the other toggle. A deep blue light surrounds Ambrose Bierce and almost immediately he's unconscious.

"I swear, everything here is color-coordinated, like a bespoke tie and handkerchief."

"Are you certain about this?" Earhart looks worried.

"I'm not even sure I'm awake. Imagine me explaining to Doctor Hartman how I spent an afternoon with you and Ambrose Bierce and at the end of it, sent Bierce off to a place he invented. I'll have my very own rubber room by dinnertime."

From the doorway comes the cry of "Stop!" It's the attendant. He sees her now from head to foot—only there are no feet. Her legs end in wheels.

"If this isn't real, I am going to need even more therapy."

The attendant glides into the room. "You mustn't do that."

"Why not? It's what he wanted."

"What is what he wanted?"

He explains what Bierce has said, where he wants to go.

She holds up her clipboard. "I have an exhaustive set of questions for him to answer yet. How did you find this out without the proper forms?"

"We listened to him," replies Earhart.

"Oh." The attendant seems momentarily lost, as if she's wandered into the wrong chamber. "Green button," she says.

"Well, that's a relief," he answers and presses the button.

Bierce vanishes in the same instant.

"And how is dear old Judge Crater?" he asks her.

Focusing upon him again, she replies, "He is now where he was destined to be."

"Under an aquarium, you said. I'll bet that was fun for him."

"What about me?" asks Earhart. "And Fred."

"Yes, what about Fred Noonan," he inquires of the attendant.

She consults the clipboard, which he notes now has nothing on it. He's beginning to suspect it's something other than a clipboard. "He's gone," she says. "We had no trouble inserting him back into a timeline."

"I'm not sure I want to know what that means. And Miss Earhart?"

"I do not know what it is she desires nor where she goes."

"What's that mean, what I desire?" She's asking him, not the attendant. Her eyes brim with tears, no doubt for the loss of her friend and copilot, but he can't help feeling some tenderness toward her. She is, in this topsy-turvy universe, only seven years older than he is—or rather she was back in 1937—a world-renowned heroine, someone who does things.

Gently he tells her, "You know, when I started in with this LSD therapy, I didn't know what I wanted. Just how miserably unhappy I'd been forever. Inside was this little boy, Archie, who believed for much of his life that his mother had deserted him, hated him, and so also believed that he must be worthless. Archie was walled off by the persona I built named Cary Grant, which protected him but also allowed him to thrive and undermine every relationship I had. Every woman was my mother and Archie had it in for her. Even after I learned the truth—that she had been put in an asylum by my father—Archie continued to destroy everything. But now I've seen what inner peace looks like. He's done plenty, but my future doesn't include him anymore. That's what I want. I want to fall in love right for once." He looks at her with what he hopes is enticement. "Or maybe twice."

She stands there, silent for a moment. When she speaks, though, it's not what he was hoping to hear.

"I guess everything started for me on December 28, 1920, when Frank Hawks took me up in his plane at the state fair. After that, it was simply all those times flying with Neta, with Snooky. That was the best. Well, would have been if I hadn't had to endure all of those sinus operations. That I can do without if you can make it possible. Otherwise, yes, if there's anyplace I'd like to be, it'd be with Snooky again on those training flights. I think she felt that way, too. And maybe all the good years with George? That would be fine." She smiles at him, and, reluctantly, he nods, smiling tightly back.

The attendant consults her board. "A closed loop, then, circling forever."

He can't help barking a laugh. "Isn't that figuratively what she's doing in the public imagination anyway?"

"I suppose. Well, then, let's find your timeline. Come along."

She rolls into the hall and along to the open chamber. She pats the red cushion.

"Lie back on the frame," she instructs Earhart.

"Which button for her?"

"Red of course, for rebirth."

"Rebirth." He hesitates. "You're sure?"

"Oh, yes. And she'll be reborn without the pain she spoke of, and endure forever in the sphere of time she's chosen. It's closed and thus interrupts no other timeline."

"Thank you," Amelia says to him just before the blue light douses her and she falls asleep.

"Don't thank me," he quips, "I'm just—" Stops speaking because the red padded frame is empty.

The attendant turns and efficiently glides over to him. "And now, Mr. Clementine?"

He stabs a finger at her. "You know, the problem with your system is it's too rigid. I am not now nor have I ever been a practicing Clementine. It's Grant."

"Suit yourself." She rolls out of the empty chamber.

"I intend to," he says to nobody, "all the rest of my days." Then he follows her out.

Back in his chamber, he slips off his shoes and lies back.

"How are you feeling, then, Mr. *Grant*?" she asks.

"Blue," he replies, and gestures at the four buttons. "*Decidedly* blue."

The attendant flips the toggle.

1:47:24 P.M.

The Eternal Library
L. Penelope

Makeda's skin rippled with unease as the sound of bells receded. The melodic ringing had once accompanied her every movement. From the tiny chimes that had encircled her ankles, to the decorative baubles threaded into her hair, to the hand bells rung by royal attendants announcing her passage through the palace hallways. Every step she'd taken during her life as a queen had been done in harmony. Now, the high-pitched jingling surrounding her as she stepped through a portal of golden light only reminded her that she walked alone.

The gilded glow retreated when the portal closed, swathing her in the arms of the night. Solitude was her only companion now. She had been deposited upon a low, grassy hill overlooking what was once a magnificent city. However, the grand seat of empires was currently in flames.

The nearest stone gate was being smashed in, its thick walls crumbling as soldiers poured through, taking their orders to sack and destroy everything they could reach to heart. Every time Makeda watched Babylon be demolished she clucked her tongue at the waste of it all.

Once she would have turned to Senteu, who rarely left her side, to commiserate about the destructive acts of mankind. But she was alone and her heart was a harder, colder thing than it once had been. She had little emotion to spare and even less time. Fleeing refugees would soon make their way to this hill, and she had work to do.

She turned away from the city and traced the marks etched into her skin with a finger. One whirling pattern had called the portal through which she'd arrived, another was for entering the library. Instead of bells and golden light, this passageway was all darkness. Makeda stepped through the folds of reality into the stacks.

The Megaannum Library existed across space and time. It lay tucked into what twentieth century AD scientists would call "dark matter"—built alongside what humans could perceive but hidden from them. The particular collection housed in 7th century BC Babylon concerned agriculture and seed technology for early human communities. Tome after tome was filled with knowledge and recollections taken from the interviews each human had with researchers upon their deaths. As a lover of learning in life, Makeda took her afterlife job quite seriously: these stacks were part of her domain as administrative librarian. She'd received a report from one of the visiting scholars that repairs were needed to the shelving. Unfortunately, it was disappointingly vague as to the exact location and nature of the problem. The library was literally infinite—and expanding all the time—and all she'd been given was a year, 689 BC, so she turned her attention to locating the shelf in question somewhere in this time.

The faint jangling of bells sounded again, and she braced for an intrusion into the peaceful atmosphere. Sure enough, a swirl of dark fog announced the entrance of another. Zora materialized through the fold, splitting reality to step into the stacks.

The woman eyed Makeda with a raised brow but remained silent. Makeda crossed her arms, irritation seeping in. "Did you need something?"

Zora let out a deep, throaty chuckle and held up the volume in her hand. "Not from you, Your Majesty. This was mis-shelved in Sumeria, 16th century BC. You know how I hate when folk don't put things back in the right place." They all hated that, but Makeda didn't get the chance to respond before Zora stomped off down the aisle of one of the towering shelves.

The woman knew exactly where she was headed, belying her familiarity with this place. Of course, librarian was an after-lifetime commitment. And a few million years—*myr* for the uninitiated—was plenty of time to know where to shelve a book. Still, Makeda followed, partly out of curiosity and partly to ensure the task was done correctly. It's not that she didn't trust her co-worker... but these days trusting anyone was difficult.

They stopped partway down an aisle where, high above their heads, the gap in the spines of the books stood out like a missing tooth. Zora traced one of the patterns etched into the back of her hand, and rose into the air to replace the bound manuscript.

"Who was even given permission to check out anything in this section?" Makeda's irritation flared anew.

"Damned if I know," Zora answered, floating back to the ground and straightening her hat. She'd chosen a physical appearance to mimic that of herself in her mid-forties, and while Makeda, like most of the librarians, preferred a more time-neutral wardrobe, Zora's cream-colored dress, wide belt, and heeled shoes spoke of the 1930s AD.

A bit guilty for the impulse to micromanage, Makeda opened her mouth to thank the woman for going out of her way—this wasn't her assigned section, and shelving was most definitely not in her job description—when a shudder rippled across the floor.

"What was that?" both women said in unison.

Makeda whipped her head around, her long, beaded braids clinking together. Zora traced the largest pattern on her hand, blocky and simple, unlike the complex swirls Makeda bore. Between the blinks of an eye, the woman's wardrobe changed, and she shifted into her warrior form.

Charged with the Megaannum's protection, along with the enforcement of its many rules, guardian librarians were fearsome fighters equipped with armor—a dark gray plating that could withstand just about any material attack—and other gifts. Like the ability to grow the way Zora was doing now, gaining over a foot in height, her skin thickening and toughening, becoming a nearly impenetrable hide. A sword made of auric energy appeared in her grip, blazing bright gold in the darkened stacks.

"It came from over there," she said, her voice richer and deeper, everything enhanced in this form. Makeda could stand back and let the trained warrior investigate, but this was *her* section. True, her job entailed mostly requisitioning supplies, allocating resources, and budgeting her team's allotment of aurium—the "dark matter" which the library and all its contents were made of—but she reasoned that as the admin, she needed firsthand knowledge of everything happening in her domain. Zora had often called this inclination mere nosiness. As if *she* was known for minding her own business. Regardless, the compunction made Makeda follow the guardian's hulking form and creep down the aisles on silent feet.

Bookcases spread out into eternity on either side—you could access the entire library from here if you had a few million myr to spend and preferred not to use the portals. Makeda traced a small pattern for perception that allowed her senses to expand—but there was no one in this section. No other librarians and no patrons. This area was open to researchers, but they had to check in, and would be perceivable by her.

Just as she was beginning to think that whatever happened had been an aberration, another quake rocked the ground, followed by a roar.

Volumes slipped from the shelves, and Makeda just barely held herself back from picking them up again. There would be time to tidy later, now something was very wrong.

Zora sped her pace, with Makeda following. The guardian was fast, but Makeda kept up, spurred on not by any special energy or skill but rather pure outrage that someone or something would dare disturb her domain.

They turned a corner, then skidded to a stop almost comically. Eyes wide, her fear was secondary to disbelief as she looked up at the source of the sound. It was… a bookworm?

She knew there wasn't any such creature as a bookworm, and certainly not one that could survive in a realm with no natural plant or animal life, but it was the best descriptor she had. The insect was the size of a bus—one of the double long vehicles popular in large cities from the twentieth century AD. It was silvery gray in color, with two antennae taller than Zora's current height poking out of its head and an uncountable number of legs. The creature had wedged its massive bulk in the aisle as it munched on one of the shelves with immense jaws.

Shaking off the shock of its existence, she screamed, "Noooo!"

Disappearing down the giant maw went volume after volume of completely irreplaceable knowledge. The Megaanuum Library was the last repository of the history and accumulated scholarship of humankind. Once something was gone from here, it was gone forever. No future researcher or scholar from another realm would be able to partake in the knowledge. That's why they took theft so seriously—thwarting thieves was the main role of the guardians.

Makeda scanned the call numbers on the nearest shelf. Two hundred millennia of food gathering techniques from Homo bodoensis of the Middle Pleistocene age had disappeared right into this beast's belly. Pure vexation motivated her to get them back. The books were all crafted from aurium, so even the giant creature's stomach acid shouldn't be able to destroy them. Zora would just have to defeat this thing and use that sword of hers to cut into its belly to retrieve the tomes. A messy job, to be sure, but a necessary one.

Using her enhanced perception, Makeda reached out to sense the books. She stretched and strained, but couldn't find them. Connected as she was to everything under her administrative domain, she should have been able to perceive them only a few dozen feet before her, even inside an impossible insect's digestive tract, but they were gone as surely as if a thief had spirited them off to another dimension.

Zora's war cry was the embodiment of everything Makeda felt inside. The guardian's glowing sword shone through the dim lighting of the stacks. The monster opened its jaws wider, bellowing its own battle sound and displaying row after row of spiky teeth.

Makeda retreated as Zora advanced. As an immortal librarian, she hadn't felt true fear in more myr than she could count. Well, that wasn't precisely true. She'd been heartbroken when Senteu left, afraid she'd never be whole again, but that wasn't the kind of panic she was experiencing at the moment.

"Zora, be careful!" she shouted. "The creature must have anti-auric properties. It may be able to seriously harm you." Its ability to crunch through the shelves and disappear the books meant it likely could bite through guardian armor and pierce otherwise indestructible flesh. An anti-auric weapon could undo the life-giving properties of the library and send an immortal to a true death.

Zora merely snarled and raced forward, sword blazing. In response, the beast rose, displaying its true size. Not a bus then, not even an aeroplane. This thing was as gigantic as a thirty-fourth century AD space ferry. Even with her guardian gifts, Zora would stand no chance against it. However, the woman didn't know the meaning of the words "back down," and ran forward anyway, heedless of the danger.

"Zora, no!" Makeda screamed as the guardian leapt a few dozen feet into the air. Her sword struck, glancing off the behemoth hide, not even scratching it.

Black, beady eyes the size of satellite dishes seemed to sharpen as the creature focused on the tiny annoyance attacking it. The thing turned its massive head and snapped its jaws. Zora barely avoided the bite.

Makeda made an executive decision. One guardian alone would not be able to defeat the beast. And Zora would die before admitting as much. So Makeda traced the patterns inked under the knuckles of her four fingers, initiating an administrative override. Cloaked in her most potent ability, she began a mandatory evacuation.

"We're retreating. Now!" she called out, but Zora, locked in a battle haze, either didn't hear or ignored her. As the guardian geared up to attack again, Makeda coiled the woman in auric energy and physically towed her away, pulling her thrashing form through the air to beat a hasty retreat.

The giant roared with earsplitting volume and fixed its eye on Makeda. Only one was visible due to the angle of its head, and from this distance its black lens was glassy and reflective, like the surface of a still, dark lake. Every bone in her body began to hum with a subtle vibration. Her muscles stiffened and her heartbeat increased. Her pace slowed, legs struggling like she was walking through mud. She forced herself to continue moving backward, certain that if she stopped, her feet would be locked in place. But it was as if the creature's gaze was slowly turning her to stone. What's worse—she was somehow unable to look away from it.

Finally, the corner of a bookshelf blocked her view. No longer in visual contact with the impossible animal, she was released from its unnerving spell. She inhaled a jagged breath, unsure of what had just happened.

The foul words spewing from Zora's mouth burned her ears. The woman demanded to be released and allowed to return and fight, but Makeda didn't relent. It was management's responsibility to ensure the well-being of their employees, and while she wasn't Zora's supervisor, she certainly wasn't going to watch the woman face true death from pure stubbornness. She hauled her through the fold in reality, right through a portal, and back to headquarters.

M akeda stalked down the halls of the residential building, holding her limbs stiffly to hide their quaking. The first shift had just begun, so most employees were ensconced in their duties; she passed few people on her way to the portal pavilion. Today, like every day since that first beast attack, she had awakened from slumber, shaking from vivid dreams in which she was forever caught in the gaze of those enormous black eyes. What should have been restful sleep was spent rigid with anxiety. The knowledge that thus far no one else who had faced the creature had reported a similar experience was inconceivably odd. No one else had been locked in place, unable to move. No one else had felt like they were being turned to stone from the inside out. Only her.

And by now, dozens of librarians had faced off against the giant insect. Entire squadrons of guardians had attempted to fight the thing and failed. While none had yet succumbed to true death, many were gravely injured, their armor and otherwise impervious warrior forms no match for the monster's devastating jaws. Precious, irreplaceable knowledge had been consumed by the beast's insatiable appetite. All librarians were on high alert and no one traveled through the stacks without at least one guardian present. Makeda and the admins were busier than ever, assigning roles and trying to keep track of the destruction the creature had caused.

As she walked, she slid her finger across the mark etched into her hand, the one that could locate any of the library staff. Like she did every day of the myr since he'd disappeared, she first searched for Senteu. But as always, she could not sense him. He truly was gone. Still an employee, according to the roster. Not listed as missing or incapacitated. Just off on assignment. And without a word to her. But that was an old pain, a hurt she'd buried many myr ago. She traced the pattern again, searching for the one she needed to talk to now. Someone she'd recently realized might be able to help.

When she stepped onto the open pavilion inside the circle of portal generators, a breeze from the whirling flow of energy caused the folds of her aurium skirt to swish around her. The gown was inlaid with a flourish of gold embroidery, just a tiny reminder of her former existence as the Queen of Sheba. She'd foregone her normal wardrobe and dressed up a bit to boost her confidence, desperately wanting this gambit to pay off. Squaring her shoulders, she stepped up to a portal and set it to travel to the seventeenth century AD, to a hot and humid stretch of hilly earth, where dusk was falling. She'd intended to go straight to the stacks of this time, where she assumed the librarian she sought would be, but her enhanced perception made her pause and turn to the scenic view behind her. There, on a nearby hill overlooking a small, bedraggled village, sat a woman.

Instead of opening another portal, Makeda made the trip on foot just to enjoy the crunch of the grass under her feet. The setting sun cast long shadows, but its golden purplish light was calming. The seated woman apparently thought so as well. Her eyes were closed, face tilted up as if absorbing the sunset. Her chosen attire was period appropriate: a thick woolen dress covered in a white apron, dingy with time and overuse. She appeared around thirty, with warm brown skin and a thick black braid hanging down her back.

Makeda sat beside her. The woman's eyes opened, training an eagle sharp gaze toward the humans at the bottom of the hill, who were erecting a gallows.

"Tituba, why do you come and relive this?" She kept her voice soft, mindful that the woman was viewing her own past, something they were not forbidden from doing, but most avoided.

Tituba, the once famous instigator of the Salem witch trials, exhaled. She glanced over briefly at Makeda, then refocused on the scene below. "I like to remind myself of the consequences of my actions." Her face and voice were impassive, but Makeda sensed potent emotions beneath the surface.

"Do you regret it?" Makeda asked, something she'd long wondered. Tituba's testimony—false, elaborate tales made up on the witness stand accusing many in her community of witchcraft—had been the spark that lit the blaze of the witch trials. Nineteen souls would perish, but not her.

It was a long time before Tituba answered. "I did what I had to in order to survive. They thought to torture me for a confession, so a confession I gave. Didn't expect it would go so far, but once that spark hit the fuel, nothing could have stopped the burning. I forgave myself a long time ago. Now I just need to remember." Her nostrils flared as she inhaled. The scent of grass was fresh in the air. "But you didn't come to ask me that, did you?"

Makeda had always appreciated Tituba's forthrightness. "You're an expert on anti-auric beings. Do you have any insights on the creature?"

"The bookworm?" Tituba's voice was wry. "You know, I offered my services to the Head Librarian, and received a form letter declining my aid. I've been trying to get an audience with her to plead my case."

"I saw your name on the visitor's list at her office and that she didn't meet with you. That's why I came to find you."

"You've spoken with Ninmah?"

Makeda nodded. "I was the first one to see the, ah, bookworm. I told Ninmah of my experience, but she didn't believe me. Went so far as to say I was imagining things, but I know what happened."

Tituba's interest was piqued. "What was that?"

"The creature affected me somehow, in a way no one else who's faced it has mentioned. I don't know why or how but it got in my head." Makeda swallowed the feeling of panic that both the encounter and the dreams left her with. The loss of control. "What did you want to tell Ninmah?"

Tituba searched Makeda's face for a moment before answering. "I believe I can affect the... being with my gift."

It had been what she'd hoped the other woman would say, still it was difficult to believe. "But you are not a warrior."

Tituba shook her head rapidly. "See, that's the wrong attitude. Why does everyone jump straight to violence?" She threw up her hands. "Why has no one asked where this beast came from and what it's doing? Why is it consuming the library? Does it need the energy to survive? Is that its food source? How did it come to be here in the first place? Those should have been the first questions, not the last. But the Head Librarian would prefer to query a corpse."

Chastened, Makeda acknowledged the woman was right. That line of inquiry had quickly been brushed aside, and she couldn't even remember why.

"We've met the bookworm only with aggression," Tituba continued. "What do we expect it to do other than defend itself? But whenever it appears, the guardians are immediately sent out, not researchers or experts, and so we never learn. We need to know its story. And *that* happens to be my area of expertise."

Makeda studied the backs of her hands, the intricate swirls and lines representing her library-given abilities. "What if you could get to it before the guardians were alerted?" she asked quietly.

Tituba whipped her head around to stare, wide-eyed. "How would I be able to do that?"

"If you knew where it was going to strike before it arrived."

Wind rustling through nearby trees was the only sound for long moments. "Is that something you know, Makeda?"

She finally looked up into the woman's brown eyes. "I dream of the creature. Every night. And I began to realize as the attacks continued that I was seeing them before they occurred."

Tituba's jaw dropped. "And the Head Librarian doesn't believe you? You could easily prove it."

"Ninmah is stubborn and set in her ways. She's overseen the library for billions of years and refuses to listen." Makeda clenched her fists as the old frustration boiled within her.

"But you know when and where the next attack will be?" Tituba's voice was hushed.

"Yes. And if we leave now, we can make it."

The research librarian rose, swiping the back of her hand as she did, changing her outfit from 17th century AD garb to the official uniform of the Megaannum, a gray formfitting jumpsuit based on popular fashion from the 47th century AD.

"Where are we headed?" she asked as Makeda opened a portal before them.

"Alexandria."

The portal deposited them on a sandy beach at the edge of the Mediterranean Sea, at the very fringe of a thriving city. In the distance, an entire fleet of ships docked in the port was on fire. Flames licked up the old wood of the docks and had already spread to the land. Makeda turned away before she could catch a glimpse of the Great Library of Alexandria burning. The destruction caused a sharp pain in her gut each time she witnessed it.

The entire collection had been preserved in the Megaannum, lost to living humans but available in the afterlife and for visitors to this planet and dimension, but still the ruin was devastating.

Tituba shook her head and clucked her tongue. "So much waste."

Makeda smiled. She sounded like Senteu—it was nice to have someone to commiserate with again. But her expression grew grim once more as she faced her purpose. The scent of smoke and char tainted the air, and she was eager to get away.

Tituba took another look around before turning as Makeda opened the fold to enter the library. "Are you certain we shouldn't have a guardian with us?" she asked, pausing on the threshhold.

"Weren't you the one just spouting off about studying the creature and not attacking it?"

"Yes, but I'm not a fool. We may still need protection. Besides, there are other enemies in existence besides gigantic bookworms."

Makeda rolled her eyes, but a new voice broke in. "Now that sounds like somebody with good sense."

They both spun around to find Zora stepping out of a golden portal—the light of its glow mixing with the flickering flames from the city beyond.

Tituba crossed her arms. "The great Zora Neale Hurston," she said acidly. "Falsify any cultural research lately?"

"Ms. Tuba," Zora said with a wink. "Send any innocent farmers to their deaths recently?" When Tituba glared, the guardian turned to Makeda. "Your Highness."

"Why are you here?" Makeda asked, not even trying to hide her annoyance.

"Just because I'm not speaking to you after that little stunt you pulled doesn't mean I won't follow when you're walking around looking suspicious."

Tituba pursed her lips. "Last I heard, you were occupied with a certain bloodthirsty Zulu king."

Zora grinned. "Well, Shaka and I have finally come to an understanding."

"I thought you had an *understanding* with that Amazonian general."

"I can understand more than one thing at a time," the guardian said with a smirk. Makeda rolled her eyes. She had no interest in Zora's various romantic entanglements. "But I don't like being left out of schemes," Zora continued. "And with you two together, there's bound to be a scheme afoot." Her finger wagged back and forth between them.

"Ask and you shall receive," Makeda said to Tituba, sweeping her arm towards the guardian the woman had requested.

"Somehow I'm less than comforted." Tituba sniffed and then stepped into the stacks.

"So what has you all jumpy, Your Majesty?"

"I have a feeling that this collection will be receiving an unwanted guest very shortly."

"And our goal," Tituba added, "is to get information, *not* make a mindless assault."

Zora snorted and shifted to her warrior form anyway, stepping to Makeda's side. Solemnity cloaked the shelves stretching out on either side of them. And so a queen, a witch, and an anthropologist walked into the darkness together.

Makeda led the others through the towering shelves. Whoever the administrator of this collection was, they needed to go back to training. Instead of the neatly organized rows of bookcases present everywhere else she'd been in the library, this place was a maze. Aisles ended abruptly, shelving was placed at diagonals, and the path between them narrowed to a point in some places and grew wide as an avenue in others.

Books had been tossed onto the shelves haphazardly, crammed into any available space, spine inwards on many so it was impossible to know what they were. The urge to fix the mess was strong, but she tamped it down, focusing instead on locating the section of the holdings she'd seen in her dream—Philology, Nonverbal communication techniques from over one hundred millennia ago in eastern Asia.

They walked this way and that, making turn after turn, back tracking again and again after dead ends until they were in the very heart of this time's collection amidst shelves of manuscripts containing recollections of posture and body language techniques for negotiating land disputes. And still no beast.

But it was coming.

"Be ready," Makeda warned, her intuition firing. Only moments later, the bright golden glow of a portal lit up—right in the center of the stacks. This was impossible. Portals could take you to a date and location in the mortal world, but not *inside* the library, and yet they were seeing it. Of course, this would explain how the creature could travel so stealthily, appearing and disappearing without a trace.

The three women stiffened, and Zora edged in front of them in a protective stance. Perhaps one hundred yards away, the portal grew wider and taller until it could accommodate the massive form of the behemoth that emerged.

Makeda tried to peer around the hulking body to get a glimpse of its origination point. Wherever it had come from was dark and smoky and radiated a deep indigo light, but she could see nothing clearly.

"All right," she whispered to Tituba. "We don't have long before the guardians arrive. See what you can do."

Tituba stepped up to Zora's side and raised her hands, a single finger following a design on the back of each before spreading them apart above her head. Then she began to speak in a commanding manner.

"Emerging from the portal, the mighty one measures the forces arrayed before it. But it does not underestimate the opponents, small though they may be." Her voice grew like a cloud of smoke, filling the air.

"With wisdom and humility, it sizes up its adversaries, fear growing within its great belly, for they carry with them a pure and eternal power, a gift from the very creators of the universe. The same beings who created the library. They are imbued with the ability and will to protect and defend this place. The mighty one feels small in their presence, and growing smaller, inside and out. Its anger wanes, its fear subsides. It sees no enemies before it."

Tituba's voice had a warm, scratchy tone that forced listeners to both hear and pay attention. The beast was not immune. Her library-given gifts enhanced those she'd held in life. She now wove a tale that had the power to bend reality.

"Without rage, without terror, the mighty one grows smaller, lighter, no longer weighed down by the heft of overwhelming emotions." Sure enough, her words wrapped around the massive carapace and the body grew smaller. The story was becoming a reality as she spoke it. Her power did indeed work on the creature, and Makeda held herself steady with cautious relief.

Even so, Zora palmed her incandescent sword, shifting her stance warily. Makeda kept an eye on her as Tituba continued weaving her story, speaking of the gentleness and the calmness of the insect, and it continued to shrink. Now it was down to the size of an aeroplane.

Makeda slid her hands behind her back, feeling the patterns by memory to initiate an administrative override. She coalesced the same bands of energy she'd used to tow Zora to safety and wrapped the beast in them. Her goal was to keep what was looking more and more like something that could accurately be described as a bookworm subdued.

Until this point, she had purposely avoided staring into its eyes, but now that it was a manageable size, she dared. A gasp left her lips. She had no name for the confusing mélange of emotions that swept over her: panic, dread, relief, longing. They were not her own, she was feeling what the monster felt. Perhaps the animal's smaller size affected the overwhelming intensity of its power, but Makeda was not locked in place like before. There was no feeling of her skin and muscles turning to stone. Instead, the empathic link between the two of them became something she could parse. Something she was beginning to recognize.

As Tituba continued to weave her tale and the creature continued to shrink—it was now merely the size of a bus—Makeda realized Zora was no longer next to them. The guardian had crept around the side of the overgrown bug and was raising her sword of light, ready to remove the worm's head from its body.

The black eyes shifted, taking in the danger, and a bolt of pure fear shot into Makeda. "Wait!" she cried out as Zora's blade hovered in the air.

Jaws opened to screech out a deafening roar, the animal's anger returned like a tidal wave. It broke free of the spell Tituba had constructed, and began to thrash and buck and grow larger by the second.

Zora spewed a string of curses and leapt to meet it, slashing with her sword and actually piercing the thick plating, now much smaller and thinner than before.

"Why did you stop me?" she screamed as she rained blow after blow down on its back.

"Because we're not here to kill it!" Tituba shouted, her hands in fists.

The bookworm was growing larger, faster than it had shrunk, and broke loose of the bands of energy Makeda had wrapped it in. A bookcase to the left toppled over as the gigantic form tried to retreat from Zora's attack: an attack whose usefulness was quickly fading as the body she battled continued to swell.

No. They couldn't kill it, not now. Not when she finally understood what it was.

Makeda approached the furious animal, craning her neck to look up at its rapidly expanding height. She swiped all of the patterns on the backs of both hands with two heavy brushes of her palms, pulling every ounce of energy into herself. Far beyond an administrative override, this level of power was only for absolute emergencies, like a library-ending event. Perhaps this didn't count and she would face the consequences, but for her, they would be worth it.

Engorged with power as she was, she tossed Zora away with a flick of her finger. The woman sailed through the air to land in a heap four aisles down.

Makeda spread her hands out on either side of her, gathering all of her strength into a writhing ball of auric energy. Then she threw it at the embattled creature before her, screaming out a command with every ounce of intention and heart. "Change back!"

The bookworm shuddered, then froze in place. It was as rigid as Makeda had felt that first time looking into its eyes. Then it began to shrink, much faster than before. In the blink of an eye, it was the size of a tall man. Then it *was* a tall man. One swathed in a shadowy energy that slowly churned and formed into a brightly colored cloth of red and orange wrapped around his lean torso. Rows of necklaces beaded with seeds and stones graced his neck, with bracelets around both wrists and ankles, the traditional trappings of a Maasai warrior.

He fell to his knees, breathing heavily, then looked up at her. Fathomless dark eyes, nearly as dark as his skin, peered at her in recognition and wonder.

"Senteu!" she cried, and then collapsed.

M akeda came back to consciousness staring up at a starry sky. Nearby a fire crackled, its warmth heating her right side. She groaned and sat up, struggling for a moment, before a strong hand pressed against her back, giving aid.

Senteu was next to her, his familiar face sparking a cascade of joy. She wrapped her arms around him, not quite believing that he was actually here again. When she pulled back, she found Zora and Tituba seated on the other side of the fire. Zora was still in her warrior form, sword resting across her thighs. She cast distrustful looks at Senteu. However, Tituba's eyes were bright.

"All right, she's awake. Now will you answer our questions?"

Makeda rubbed her head, which still ached. "When… are we?"

"Sixth century AD Ireland, eastern coast of Lough Neagh." Zora spat out the words.

"Is there a collection here?" Makeda wondered, brain somewhat foggy.

"No. That's why we're here. Until we get answers, we need to be in a place less trafficked. We narrowly avoided the guardians on our way out of Alexandria, but they might be looking for us."

Makeda leaned into Senteu's side as her spinning thoughts settled. He rested an arm around her. "You haven't told them anything?" she asked.

"Not until you woke up. I knew you'd want to hear it too, but you pulled too much power." His deep voice was chiding.

"You're welcome," she croaked.

He chuckled, the sound vibrating through her. She wanted to stay like this forever, but Tituba was pulsing with curiosity and Zora looked like she still might stab him. "You'd better get to explaining. What do you remember?"

He shook his head. "Not much. Just bits and pieces of the last—how long was I gone?"

Makeda swallowed down her grief as she tried to also control her joy. "Nearly five myr."

He sucked in a breath. "So long?" His eyes met hers, full of unspoken apologies and more questions than she wanted to deal with in front of others.

"I—well, the last thing I remember is leaving you one morning to go on duty. Ninmah had requested a guardian accompany her to the Khmer Empire—I don't recall what century. She said she was concerned about the state of some of the older shelving and suspected sabotage."

His free hand rubbed his closely shorn head as if that would help his memories return more clearly. "And then... there was smoke. An indigo haze surrounding me and then darkness. I would wake sometimes to commands that I was unable to resist..."

A look of horror slowly overtook his face. "I was ordered to destroy the library. And I couldn't stop. The beast had no mind of its own, it only followed the commands of its master, and I was locked inside, unable to do anything."

"So, it has a master," Zora said icily.

"Yes, but I can't say who. I—" His brow furrowed as he tried to remember. Then he blew out a frustrated breath. "I'm sorry I can't be of more help."

"No, it's all right," Makeda said, stroking his arm. "We know much more than we did before."

"Are you certain this curse is broken?" Tituba asked.

Senteu frowned, and Makeda detached herself from him. She swiped at a pattern on her hand. The power was weak, it would take time to regenerate all she'd lost, but it was enough to check him.

Hope warred with fear within her as she stretched her senses. When Senteu had been the worm, she hadn't recognized him. But they'd still been connected. He'd unwittingly drawn her into his nightmare of fear and helplessness night after night, and she was finally able to identify him thanks to Tituba's story. And since he was a library employee, her overloaded administrative powers had forced him to change back to himself.

Now, she used her senses and stared into his eyes, searching for any remnant of whatever power had caused his transformation and imprisonment. Anything that didn't fit.

She leaned back, relief loosening her muscles. "The curse is gone," she announced, certain it was true. "But the library is still at risk."

Senteu enfolded her in his arms again, squeezing her tight. She hugged him back, countless years of sadness and loneliness taken away by the embrace.

"We're going to have to find out who targeted the library and why," she announced.

Tituba nodded grimly. "Whatever they were trying to do, it's unlikely they'll stop until it's complete."

Zora shifted back to normal with a flash, and tilted her hat back on her head. "Then we'll just have to stop them." Her lips turned up in a slightly menacing grin that Makeda found comforting.

They would find answers and eliminate the threat. This wasn't over yet. But for now, she would enjoy this moment, rest, and regain her strength. And soon face the challenges ahead.

"Yes, we will stop them," she said. "No one messes with our library." The others agreed, and the crackling of the fire sealed their resolve.

The Man Who Broke Time
David Gerrold

Even after Steve graduated, we stayed in the apartment on Romaine, partly because it was still a good office for me, but mostly because we'd spent so many nights here wrapped up in each other's arms, it was our private little hideaway. It wasn't very big, just a bedroom, a bathroom, a kitchen, a small closet, and a diagonal space that served as a living room. The furniture was leftovers and hand-me-downs—but it was all we needed right now. And even though I never said it aloud, it was my escape plan—if maybe Steve and I didn't work out.

Which was why I felt invaded when I came in the front door and found three strangers sitting in the living room.

No, not strangers.

Not exactly. Harlan Ellison and Dorothy Fontana on the green couch. And the third one, sitting in the blue chair. That was the real shock. Dog was parked in his lap.

"What the hell—"

And then I had to stop mid-sentence, because why would Harlan Ellison and Dorothy Fontana come visiting me? We weren't friends. We weren't even acquaintances. They were writers, I wasn't. I'd seen them on a couple panels at the Writers Guild, how to break into the business, and then again at a local science fiction convention. I was surprised they even knew who I was.

The third person? He was me. An older version of me. Short hair, going gray, puffy face, a paunch—I hadn't aged well. He looked exhausted. In fact, they all did. They looked a lot older than they should have been. Harlan had white hair. Dorothy's was an artificial dark red. Dog looked confused. He got down and trotted over to me.

I think I handled it well.

I went into the apartment's little kitchen. Dog followed. I put down the grocery bags. I put the sodas and eggs in the fridge. I put away the cans of dog food and the other items too. I gave Dog a cookie.

I leaned on the sink to catch my breath, and tried to make sense of what I'd walked into. I turned it over and over, upside down and inside out. It was impossible, but there it was—the only possible explanation.

Finally, Dog and I walked back into the living room. "Dorothy, do you want some tea? I think I have some Lipton's or something. Harlan, you want Perrier, of course. And you, Older Me, do you want a Coke?"

"Sit down, kiddo," said Harlan.

"Please," said Dorothy.

"I'll explain," Older Me said.

"You're time travelers, right?" I picked up Dog and held him in my lap.

Older Me looked to the others. "Told you he'd get it. I'm smart."

"Yeah. That's why we're here." Harlan was a lot more mellow in person than on the stage, but he was still Harlan. He said, "Look at him. He's too young. He's not going to believe us."

I looked from one to the other. "Why should I?" I didn't know any of them very well, only from the occasional run-in at some fannish event or other. So why were they here? Why me? "You let yourself into my apartment. What do you want?"

Older Me said, "Well, first we need you to trust us. You know who I am. It's not too hard to figure that out. And Harlan and Dorothy—they're two of your best friends in the world."

"Uh. I don't think so. Maybe they're two of yours—"

"Shut up, kiddo." That was Harlan. He pointed to Older Me. "That man—the one you might become—is one of the most courageous men I've ever known. You might be him someday. But right now, shut up and listen."

I shut up.

But I was tired of listening. I'd heard all the explanations. Too many explanations. It had taken a while, but I'd finally figured it out. Explanations are the booby prize. They don't produce results. I had lots of explanations. And no results.

My television career had fizzled out for reasons I never understood. Maybe I just didn't understand the industry. The only show I had wanted to write for had been cancelled after its first season. Right now, Steve was supporting both of us while I struggled with the Great American Science Fiction Novel and the occasional small pitiful sale to *The Staff*. I was desperate.

But Steve still believed in me. Sometimes I wondered how long that would last. He was beautiful, he was successful. I was neither. And it scared me. One day, Steve would probably figure it out, he'd realize what must have been obvious to everyone else. And then I'd be left alone with no one but Dog. Dog was loyal, not judgmental.

Older Me said, "You have no idea, do you?"

"I have no ideas at all," I said. "Do you want the whole list of producers who've shut me down. Even my agent gave up—"

"It's Chinatown, Jake." That was Harlan. I had no idea what he meant.

"Please listen to us. This is important," said Dorothy.

Older Me leaned forward, steepling his hands in front of himself. I recognized that gesture. I did it myself. "You're important."

"I don't think so. Almost everyone I know tells me that I'm not. The only one who thinks I'm special is Steve. So why should I listen to anyone else?" I held Dog close.

"Because everyone else is wrong," said Harlan.

"And you're the only one who can do this," said Dorothy.

Of all of them, it was Dorothy—something in her voice—that made me shut up. I looked to her.

"It's that article you wrote," she said.

"The one in *The Staff*," Harlan said.

There are people who believe in alien space lizards, Sasquatch, yeti, and Nessie. There are people who think the Earth is flat and others who insist that Hitler is still alive and living in Argentina. There are people who are so disassociated from reality they shouldn't be allowed out of the house without a keeper. They assume every unexplainable fact is evidence of something impossible—and the lack of evidence is evidence of a conspiracy. The more bizarre the idea, the more they embrace it.

I said, "This is about the murders, isn't it?"

Harlan nodded. "Yeah, kiddo. This is about the murders."

Older Me said, "I know you meant your article as a joke, but… well, here we are."

He was referring to a piece I'd written for L.A.'s second most popular underground weekly. The most popular had been *The Freep*, (short for *The Free Press*) until it ran into financial problems. Most of the staff had quit to start a competing weekly, appropriately called *The Staff*. I'd sold a few small articles to them, but I'd never been able to bootstrap that into a regular column.

The most recent article—I'd intended it to be a semi-satirical speculation, so of course, most of the paper's terminally stoned readers immediately accepted it as hardcore truth, a revelation of the way things really were.

There had been murders—murders are always page one stories. But these were particularly interesting. The FBI had been tracking a serial killer for almost a decade. He (or maybe she) seemed to kill at random. If there was any kind of a pattern, it remained unknowable. And apparently, there were other murders not publicly included in the official count.

It was a very odd list. There was no sense to it.

Charles Whitman in Texas, Thomas Hagen in New York, James Huberty in San Ysidro, John Wayne Gacy in Chicago, Ted Bundy in Washington State, Lee Harvey Oswald in Texas, James Earl Ray in Memphis, Sirhan Sirhan in Los Angeles—all of them apparently killed with the same 9mm weapon. The rifling on the bullets was a forensic match. The imprint of the firing pin on the shell casings was a forensic match.

Some of these were explainable. Somebody had pissed off somebody else. Maybe the Las Vegas casino magnate had offended another mob boss. Maybe the Australian broadcaster had angered a business rival. Maybe someone with a grudge had hired a prolific hit man, which might explain a few of the others. But then why the movie star's fiancé? Why the draft-dodger? Why the favored son of a rich Saudi family?

It had to be random. Except somebody had gone to a lot of trouble to get to some of the victims. A random killer wouldn't do that. But the forensics matched up, so it wasn't random—that was the problem. It looked like the same weapon had been used all over the world, but mostly in the United States.

The prevailing theory—at least the only one that fit the available facts—was that it was not the same gun. It couldn't be. There had to be some quirk in the manufacturing process of that particular model of gun, whatever it was, something that allowed multiple copies to all produce the same rifling and firing pin impressions. That was the only logical possible explanation.

But just for the fun of it, because that was the way my mind works— and because I had always wanted to write science fiction—I postulated that an aggressive time traveler was taking out murderers and assassins and terrorists before they could commit their terrible acts of violence.

It was a joke. Really.

Because if there really were time travelers, weren't there bigger and better targets?

Good questions, Right?

But not to be taken seriously.

Until three time-travelers showed up in my living room.

"Yeah," said Harlan. "You have questions. It's kinda brain-melting, isn't it?"

"Yeah," I said. "If you're really time travelers, then why are you here? Why didn't you kill Hitler?"

"Because if we had, you wouldn't have been born. Neither would any of us. Now stop being so smart."

"It's complicated," said Dorothy. "It'll take a while to explain."

"And even longer to understand," said Older Me. He held up what looked like a briefcase. "This will help. It's a laptop."

"What's a laptop?"

"It's a personal computer. It fits on your lap."

"Bullshit. Computers are as big as refrigerators."

"We're time travelers, remember? This is future technology. Don't panic, you'll figure it out. There's even a book of instructions. *Laptops For Dummies*."

I folded my arms around Dog. He grunted: he knew the gesture, he knew what it meant. I didn't believe a word of it.

Older Me said, "I know it's hard to accept. I didn't want to believe it either. But this laptop contains a whole library. All the resources you'll need. Books, articles, videos, documentaries." Older Me put the bag on my desk, next to my treasured IBM Selectric typewriter. "It's going to change your life."

"It'll do more than that," said Harlan. "It'll change the world."

"Um, wait—wait a minute," I said. "Do I understand this correctly? You're giving me the resources to change the future?"

"No," Harlan said. "We're giving you the resources to unchange the future."

Dorothy cleared her throat. Both Harlan and Older Me looked to her. She was holding a thick spiral-bound manuscript. Very thick. "This is the important part. You need to read this first."

"What is it?"

"It's a printout. The whole file is on the laptop, too. It's a history of the 20ᵗʰ century that didn't happen. It's not your history, it's not this history, but it's the one that might still happen."

"If what?"

Harlan said, "If you don't listen." He looked annoyed.

Older Me said, "I know you like alternate histories, but you're not gonna like this one. It's a very scary read." He took it from Dorothy and put it on my desk next to the case containing the laptop.

"Okay, fine. You're giving me a science fiction book. Is there anything on that laptop thing that you wrote? That I'm going to write?"

"No, there isn't."

"Why not? You could have saved me a lot of work."

Harlan interrupted. "Because if you don't write them yourself, you won't learn how to write."

"That doesn't make any sense."

"It will after you write them."

"I don't believe you. I don't even believe in that laptop thing. If I know anything at all, it's that everyone has an agenda."

"Yes, we do," said Older Me. "But it's your agenda. Or it will be soon enough."

Dorothy spoke then. "We went to a lot of trouble to get here. That's how important this is—not just to us, but to you, too."

"Okay, fine. Whatever." I don't know why I felt so annoyed. Maybe it was because they'd interrupted my frustration. I had my own plans. I didn't want theirs. "What else?"

Older Me said, "We've outlined it all for you, the steps you need to take. Read the history, then you'll know what's next—what we need you to do."

"Okay." I pointed to the black case at his feet. "What's that? What's in that box?"

He picked it up carefully and held it on his lap, but he didn't open it. "A 9mm pistol. A Sig Sauer with padded grip and a laser sight for targeting. And ammunition, too. Seven magazines, seven rounds each. Don't play around with this. Read the instructions carefully. Spend some time practicing with the dummy rounds until you get—"

"Wait—stop. What? Why are you giving me a gun?"

"A 9mm Sig Sauer with a padded grip and a laser sight for targeting. There's a custom holster, too. And extra ammunition, and a speed loader."

He pointed to a dark metal box tucked under my desk. I hadn't noticed it before. "You'll need it."

"No, I won't. Take it away. I'm not—"

Harlan leaned forward, a hard look on his face. "Yes, you will. You're going to save the world, asshole."

Coming from anyone else, I would have bristled. But when Harlan calls you an asshole, it's a term of affection.

"Please," said Dorothy. "It wasn't easy arranging any of this."

"It's complicated," said Older Me. "This timeline doesn't exist yet. We're trying to make it happen."

Dorothy said, "That book, the terrible history of the 20th and 21st centuries, the book—that's what's going to happen. That's what we want to stop."

"Wait. Stop. I'm confused." I wasn't confused as much as I had a terrible suspicion. "Is that what the gun is for?"

"Yes. I'm sorry, but yes."

"The people in the article—?"

"Yes."

"But those people are already dead—"

"Yes. And no," he said. "They won't be dead until you kill them."

"If they're already dead, then why do I have to kill them?"

"Because you already did. That is, you will."

"No, wait. That can't be true. I'm not a killer. I can't be. That would make me just as bad as them. Maybe worse. Because I'd have a real justification. Like a holy mission. No, there's gotta be another way—"

Older Me said. "There isn't any other way. We tried. It didn't work. You're the way, the only way."

Harlan interrupted. "Kiddo, this is on you. You might be an asshole, but you're the asshole we need."

"Thank you for sharing that," I said. Sarcastically.

"David," said Dorothy. "Please read the documents we've provided."

"You think that's going to make a difference?"

"We think so, yes."

"Um… I think you're wrong. I'm not exactly a big fan of guns."

"We know. Yes."

"So why me? Why not one of you?"

Older Me said, "We're not from this timeline. You are."

Harlan said, "Your timeline can't exist until you do what you have to do."

"And then what happens to you?"

"Dorothy and Harlan become two of your best friends," said Older Me.

"This was your idea, wasn't it?" His expression was answer enough. "Then you should know—"

"I know," he said. "Much better than you. I know your past, you don't know your future. I'm doing you an enormous favor here—"

"Fuck you," I said.

"Yes," he said. "I wrote that one, too. With a timebelt, it's possible."

"What's a timebelt?"

"It's a belt that lets you travel backward and forward through time."

"Sounds convenient. I'd like to see that."

"You will. We're going to give you the timebelt."

Harlan made a face, he looked to the others. "He'll believe in a timebelt, but not a laptop? Oh, yeah—he's the right kind of asshole."

I shrugged. "I can only believe six impossible things before breakfast. That was the seventh."

Dorothy said to Harlan, "Please stop calling him an asshole. It's not helping."

"Okay, I'll just call him a schmuck. Because that's what he is until he accepts the responsibility."

Older Me reached around to the hidden side of the chair. He brought out a flat box and passed it over. "This is the timebelt. It's the only one we have. We all had to share it. Now it's your turn. Take good care of it. When you're done with it, put it away in a safe place. Maybe get a gun safe."

"Don't you want it back?"

"I'll get it back, don't worry."

"And don't play around with it, kid," said Harlan. "The timelines are fragile enough."

Older Me looked like he wanted to put a hand on my shoulder, but he didn't. He said, "I wish I could sit and talk with you for as long as it takes, but… I can't. That doesn't work. Read the printout. Read the letter with the laptop. Read all the documents. There's everything you need to know. And a lot more. Then you'll understand. And then you can decide. Will you do that much at least?"

I nodded, a noncommittal assent.

"There's really only one good choice," said Dorothy.

"Good for who?"

"Good for you. Good for everyone," said Harlan.

"But especially good for you," said Older Me.

I didn't answer that.

I was tired of people telling me what would be good for me. Most of the time, they were telling me what would be good for them if I'd just please cooperate.

So yeah, I was pissed.

Pissed at the intrusion. Pissed at their presumed authority. Pissed for no reason I could identify.

There are a lot of emotions for which there are no words. I was experiencing several of them. Maybe several dozen. Confusion was at the top of the stack, but there was also annoyance, anger, upset, fear, curiosity, and even a sense of relief. Because whatever else this was all about, apparently I was important enough for Harlan and Dorothy and Older Me to travel through time to tell me to do something.

The problem?

Well, that's where the other emotions came pouring in. Resentment and outrage.

I'm not a killer.

I've never fired a gun. And I doubt I ever will.

I'm a strong believer in rational discussion as an alternative to violence. Except, of course, if you're dealing with Hitler. Maybe that was an exception. Maybe that was why they were here—?

There was still too much I did not understand.

"Look," Older Me said. "You don't have to decide anything tonight. You don't have to do anything tonight. Sleep on it. Read the documents tomorrow, or this weekend. Take your time. There's no rush. You literally have all the time you need. So do yourself a favor. Be the writer you want to be and allow yourself to imagine the possibilities. Will you do that?"

Dorothy added, "Please."

I thought about it. Finally, I said, "Okay."

They stood up then, ready to leave. Harlan said, "You gotta do the right thing, kiddo."

Dorothy said, "We believe in you."

Older Me said, "I wish there were an easier way. I really do. I know this is going to be hard for you. But... trust me, it's important. It's necessary. We need you to be a hero. The hardest kind of hero."

And then they were gone. Pop, pop, and pop. One after the other, they vanished.

I went into the kitchen, Dog followed, and I fixed his dinner without the usual conversation about how lucky he was to have the expensive wet dog food instead of the usual dry kibble. It didn't matter, he'd eat whatever I put in front of him. Even salads. Especially salads.

I called Steve. I hardly ever bother him at work. I hate the telephone. I've hated it since I was four. My mother had one surgically attached to her ear, and getting her attention while she was on a call was impossible. I learned at an early age that I was nowhere near as important as whoever she was talking to.

But talking to Steve always made me feel good—like everything was going to be okay, no matter what.

I told him I had some serious reading to do, so maybe he could pick up a pizza for dinner. That confused him—he said, "I thought we were going out tonight."

"Oh, right—um, I must have forgot."

I didn't ask for details. Maybe he had planned something. We'd sort it out later. He had to get back to work. He never objected to having me check in, but we tried to keep our calls short anyway.

I opened the bag and took out that thing they called a laptop. It didn't weigh very much. I put it aside. Whatever it was, I didn't trust it. Most future tech was a lie. Flat screen televisions had been predicted in 1955. They were still ten years in the future.

I picked up the spiral-bound manuscript instead. The pages were crisply formatted, and there were pictures on almost every page, many of them in color. However this thing had been printed, it was an impressive piece of work.

Dog and I curled up on the couch, and I began to read the horrifying history of the 20th century that hadn't happened. Not just what could have happened in the past, but also what could have happened in that future. I paged ahead to the end. This thing even predicted what the 21st century had become—oh, come on. That's just ridiculously stupid. We'd never—

Okay, I've read bad science fiction. I've even written bad science fiction. Maybe that's why I didn't have a career.

But I've read stuff by so-called professionals that was so bizarre, so deranged, so terminally stupid that even some of my worst efforts made more sense.

This book—this "printout"—this thing went from bizarre to insane to surreal to simply unhinged.

But it was so convincingly written. And supposedly there was even more evidence on the laptop: documentaries and videos and interviews.

If it was a hoax, then somebody had spent way too much money creating all of these pictures and photocopies of news articles. And if that laptop really had a couple thousand hours of video—hard to believe that—then the cost of that kind of fakery would have been in the millions. You couldn't have done it anywhere in the world, except here in Los Angeles—and if you had, the whole town would have been employed in the effort. And there would have been all kinds of chatter everywhere about the effort involved.

So no.

And there was one other reason it couldn't be a hoax.

Harlan and Dorothy and Older Me were the evidence that this thing—

A single sheet of paper fell out of the book. It said, "You want proof? Test the timebelt. Here's how."

I read the instructions. I put on the belt. I popped backward. Three hours. The bright sunlight of midday dazzled in the window.

Older Me was sitting in my living room again. Or still. Or before. Not certain of the phrasing. This time he was alone. Dog got down from his lap and trotted over to me. I appreciated that. He was going to get a special dinner tonight.

Older Me pointed to the desk clock. "Convinced?"

I swallowed hard and nodded.

He said, "Here's a thousand dollars. More than enough to pay off all your debts. But more important, before you do anything else, take Steve out to dinner tonight. You have a reservation at 7:00 PM at Musso and Frank's. Splurge. Order off the expensive menu. Have a great dessert. And tell him how much you love him. That he's the best thing that ever happened to you. There's the phone. Call him now."

I didn't need any encouragement for that. I called Steve and told him we were going out for dinner. Oh, now I understood our mutual confusion on the earlier—later?—other call.

After I hung up, Older Me said, "I want you to know something. Just you and me." He took a deep breath.

I waited.

"What?"

"You're stronger than you know. Remember that."

"Why? What do you know?"

He shook his head. He wouldn't explain. "You have to go now. You'll be home soon. You don't want to meet yourself, that would freak you out." Hmm, that was an interesting idea, maybe I could write a story about that.

Back in my own time, I picked up the printout and started reading in earnest. Each chapter had a summary, followed by a longer narrative, and then a thoroughly detailed timeline.

It was not comforting. Particularly the assassinations. And the mass shootings. And the—ohell, whoever had taken out these bastards was a hero. One of the greatest in history—

Oh, shit.

I put the manuscript down as if it were something evil. I stared at it for a long moment, then slid it into the desk drawer.

I stood up slowly, went into the bathroom, peeled off my clothes and stood in the shower, letting the hot water rain down on me—hammering on my head, splattering across my shoulders, draining down my back— letting it do its steaming best to soothe an ache that would not go away. Those terrible images, those disturbing words, they'd been stamped indelibly into my soul.

Damn them, damn them all! Older Me knew me too well. He knew I would want to do something—anything to end the pain in my head. Damn that bastard! Damn me!

I got dressed.

I met Steve at Musso and Frank's. He lit up when he saw me. And I let go of all my worries when I saw him. Steve had the brightest eyes and the most beautiful smile. He was my joyous red-haired completion. He was soul-filling. Conversation was unnecessary. Smiles were enough. Anything either of us said, the more important message was how much we relished being together.

Steve shared his day at work. I listened as if it was the most important news in the world. When he asked me how my work was going, I said, "Really hard to explain. I have this thing I have to figure out."

"Can I help?"

"I dunno. It's a story problem. Well, more of an ethical one. Would you kill Hitler?"

Steve's expression darkened. There were some things he didn't like to think about. "Killing is a mortal sin," he said.

"That's the problem. What if you could save many lives by taking one? Is the lesser evil acceptable?"

"The lesser evil is still evil. That's what Father Byrne says."

"I know. But what if those are your only choices. Big evil or little evil?"

He smiled, and I knew what he was going to say even before he said it. "You're the writer. You choose." He quoted my own words back to me. It made me laugh. I told him how much I loved him and he smiled and put his hand on mine, his way of saying it without words. He lit up my soul.

We went back to the apartment and spent the entire night wrapped in each other's arms. For just a little while longer, I didn't have to care about… the decision. When we were naked together in bed, just looking into each other's eyes, he sang to me. "You're just too good to be true." It made me cry. Now I know why there are love songs.

In the morning, I made him breakfast. The refrigerator was filled with a lot more food than I remembered buying. So we had bacon and eggs and hash browns and toast and jam and coffee and orange juice. He smiled in delight, hugged me tight, and kissed me deeply before heading off to work.

Leaving me alone with—that printout. That book. That decision.

The gun.

I hadn't opened the case.

I didn't want to kill anyone. I didn't know if I could.

Everything I'd read—sociopaths do it without caring. But real people, the kind of person I tried to be, wouldn't recover from the emotional trauma. It would become a permanent part of who you were.

On the other side of that equation—if there ever were crimes worthy of capital punishment, I now had a list. The crimes and the perpetrators and the days when they were supposed to have happened. And I had the power to stop them.

If I didn't stop them—the world I lived in today would not be the world any of us would be living in.

I kept reading, looking for a way out.

There wasn't one.

If there had been an alternative, then wouldn't Harlan and Dorothy and Older Me done that instead?

I'm very good at overthinking things.

There were detailed instructions in the box. How to handle the gun safely. How to load and unload it. How to take it apart and clean it. Everything.

Older Me had thoughtfully included dummy rounds. I practiced loading the magazines, I practiced putting the magazines into the gun. I practiced dropping them out again. I practiced everything but firing actual rounds.

It was an alien experience. And yet, curiously satisfying on a mechanical level.

The instructions included the address of a target range north of the San Fernando Valley, just off I-5. I wasn't certain it was a good idea, but not going was a worse idea.

The range safety officer questioned me about the gun: he'd never seen one like this. I couldn't tell him it hadn't been invented yet, so I said it was a prototype, designed for inexperienced users. I was testing it for the company. He accepted that explanation and told me that the gun was clearly built on the 1911 platform, whatever that meant, and would certainly serve well.

I told him I didn't have a lot of experience, that was true, so he taught me how to hold the gun—how to place my hands, keeping my finger out of the trigger guard, and using my left hand to provide a firmer grip. He showed me how to load a magazine, slam it home, how to drop it out one-handed, use your thumb on the button, and finally how to check that the chamber is empty—and then double-check that the chamber is empty. Then everything all over again.

Then, when he thought I was finally ready, he put up a paper target for me. I practiced shooting at the silhouette of the alleged criminal. The first time I shot, the recoil startled me, but after that I began to get used to aiming and shooting. By the end of the afternoon, I felt almost comfortable loading and shooting, reloading and shooting again. I surprised myself—I could hit the target in the chest at least five times out of seven. The misses were the head shots.

I drove home with my fingers stained with gunpowder residue and my whole hand aching. My index finger was sore as well.

But I could do this—the physical part, that is.

The emotional?

I tried to imagine what it would be like to shoot someone—to face a man and kill him.

I couldn't.

This wasn't a movie—death wasn't a convenient plot point.

Something someone said to me once—all great stories are about revenge. Maybe that was what was missing from this—I couldn't see these shootings as vengeance.

And maybe that was what was missing from my writing too. I couldn't do revenge. Is that what was missing from my psyche?

But according to Dorothy and Harlan and Older Me, if I didn't find a way to do this, we'd stumble into a much worse future.

It was the classic grandfather paradox, only turned inside out. If you don't kill your grandfather, you inherit a shitshow.

The book of horrors scared me. There was no shortage here of men (and a few women) the world would be much better off without. Serial killers. Mass murderers. Assassins. And a couple of billionaires who'd put their thumbs on the scales of liberty. Promoters of bigotry and corruption and greed, creators of ignorance and poverty and despair. It was a horror story.

But here—I was living in a world where they never had a chance to commit their atrocities. Didn't I want to save this world?

President Robert F. Kennedy had inherited a booming economy from his brother, President John F. Kennedy. The Cold War was over. We had a base on the moon. We had the first legs of high speed rail running up and down the eastern corridor. We had the minimum wage pegged to the cost of living. We had government-insured health care. We had expanded civil rights and voting protections for all citizens. And the Beatles were talking a reunion album.

The alternative—? This goddamned printout was a great argument for becoming a serial killer.

Just not me.

And I really couldn't talk to anyone about it. Couldn't share the problem. They'd think I was crazy. Or they'd think I was trying to plot another dreadful sci-fi novel. "You still haven't given up, have you? Still trying to write your little stories?"

The only one who believed in me was Steve—and I wasn't going to drop this on him. I couldn't have him doubting me.

There was only one thing to do. I'd known it from the beginning, I just hadn't wanted to admit it to myself. I had to find out for myself if I could face a monster and squeeze the trigger.

I picked one. Not at random. Someone local. Not the worst, but bad enough. It would be a test.

Then I practiced with the timebelt.

I could target a specific moment, even a specific place. I would arrive at an instant of stopped time. I could find a clear space to pop in—like right in front of my target. Then I could raise the gun. I could fire it two or three times, however many times I thought necessary. The bullets would hang unmoving in the air. Then, if I was satisfied with my aim, I could pop in and out of real time—inserting myself and the gunfire for only the briefest fraction of a second, but in that tiny flicker of time the bullets would be traveling at 900mph. They would penetrate the target instantly, tumbling through their flesh like jelly. In stoptime, I would see only a frozen explosion of bloody bits.

In theory, anyway.

What actually happened—I saw three rounds suspended in front of me, all poised to send this someday killer into oblivion, this sad little man who would never know what hit him or why—

But he looked so pathetic, like a poor dumb homeless hippie.

—so I walked around the motionless rounds and pulled him sideways. My bullets would shoot past him and thump into the distant hillside beyond.

I popped in and out of real time. The sound of the gunshots startled him, he jumped sideways, then I popped out and he became a statue again.

I didn't know what he might someday do to deserve this, and I didn't care—but I couldn't be the agent of his destruction. I was not going to kill Charles Manson or anyone else.

I hit the return button and sank down on my bed, shaking and gasping and sobbing. I couldn't do it.

I couldn't.

Dog came over and put his head in my lap. I picked him up and held him tight, rocking him like a baby. I kept telling myself, it's not a weakness. It's a strength. But it still felt like a failure.

Whatever his eventual crime, he had to be stopped. But not this way. There had to be a better way. But if Harlan and Dorothy and Older Me hadn't been able to come up with a better way, how the hell could I?

And if he was already dead, then why did I have to do it?

None of this made sense.

I dropped the clip out of the gun. I put it and the gun in the box. I shoved the box under my desk.

By the time Steve showed up, I was almost human again. He looked at me oddly, then just held me for the longest time without talking.

He finally asked, "Are you all right?"

I shook my head. I wanted to tell him everything. I didn't have the words. I couldn't speak. I just sobbed into his shoulder while he held me tight. I felt safe in his arms. And scared as well. I never told him how afraid I was—about everything, but most of all that I wasn't good enough for him, and that maybe one day he'd feel that way, too.

"I don't know what this is all about," he said. "I don't need to know, but I can see you're hurting. Whatever it is, I'm here for you." He held me tighter and whispered in my ear. "I'm not going away. You can stop worrying about that. I'm not leaving you. I'm here forever."

Eventually we crawled into bed, and Steve held me close all night. I relaxed in his arms, finally accepting his certainty, and drifted into a dreamless oblivion.

Slivers of light replaced the dark. Sparkles of dust floated in the light. Morning invaded the bedroom, demanding a trip to the bathroom and then coffee.

Stretching awake, I felt strangely at ease, as if everything had sorted itself out. As usual, Steve and I showered together without much talk, still drifting in the land of afterward, punctuated only by the usual fits of giggling in surprise as we soaped each other up. It was clear now, Steve was important, nothing else.

After he left for work, I gathered up everything. The gun, the laptop, the printout, the extra ammunition. I put it all in my battered old suitcase and zipped it up. The suitcase sat in the middle of the living room floor, almost an accusation.

"You're the writer," Steve had said. "You choose." They were my words, but now a shared joke.

Choice. That's the question.

We all have choices. Every day. Every moment.

Those people, the ones listed in the printout, they'll choose whatever they choose. They'll be whoever they choose to be.

I choose not to be one of them.

Dog and I got in the car, the suitcase in the trunk.

We headed south to Santa Monica. I bought a round-trip ticket on the ferry to Catalina Island. Halfway to the dock at Avalon, I dropped the suitcase into the water. It disappeared in the ferry's wake. A nearby steward looked oddly at me. I said, "I'm not diving in after it."

Dog and I walked around Avalon for an hour, then caught the ferry back to Long Beach.

We drove home, and I gave Dog a belly rub and a cookie.

I went to hang up my jacket—

The closet was half-empty. All of Steve's clothes were gone.

I stood there, staring at the emptiness. He'd promised me—

The bathroom, his toothbrush, his razor, his shampoo, everything, there was gone too—

No, this was wrong. All wrong.

I deserved an answer, an explanation. Into the living room, my desk, I picked up the phone, dialed his work number. An unfamiliar voice answered, a woman. She said there was no one there by that name. That didn't make sense. Wasn't this his company? No, you must have a wrong number—

Maybe. I dialed again—same woman. Sorry to bother you, and hung up confused.

The car—I fumbled with the keys, panicking now, driving recklessly, impatiently across Hollywood, straight to the office— except it wasn't there. The building was gone. Instead, a decaying strip mall filled the lot.

I felt odd. Headaches and double vision. Hallucinations like memories, but not—ugly fragments of thought—

Terrified, hurting, screaming, crying, the bottom dropping out of the world, a screeching pain in my gut, somehow got back to the apartment, grabbing Dog and holding him close. Fearing the worst—

I woke up, as if from a dream, my mind churning with bad memories. Terrible ones. Things that happened in 1963 and 1968 and 1969 and—

Oh, no, no, no, no, no!

T he day I decided to kill myself, they came back.

Older Me was playing with Dog. "I missed him," he said. "He was always the best."

Dorothy and Harlan were sitting in the only two chairs I had. Nobody was sitting at my desk. That was my sacred space. Older Me must have told them.

They had the timebelt—and the laptop, the book, the gun case, and the ammunition—all of it, on the couch.

I didn't offer him a Coke. I didn't offer them anything.

"I threw all that in the sea," I said.

"You threw a later iteration," said Harlan. "This is an earlier instance."

Dorothy added, "The timebelt you threw overboard had several hundred years of experience before it got to you, including this visit."

And Older Me finished the thought. "There's a story idea you might want to consider. Time machines always uninvent themselves."

"What do you want?" I said.

"Do you want a second chance?"

I didn't have to think about it. "Yeah, I do."

"You sure about that, kiddo?" That was Harlan.

"Fuck you," I said.

Harlan shut up. It might have been the first time in his life.

Dorothy said, "We know you're hurting—"

"Stop it! Just stop it! Nobody knows anything. And I can't tell anybody. Nobody understands—I can't even tell anyone who he was, what he meant to me. Not now, not here, not anywhere. Nobody knows how alone I am!"

"I know," said Older Me.

"Fine. Then just give me the gun and get out. Everyone else can just eat shit and linger."

They understood. They stood up.

"Write like that," Harlan said. "Write like that and you'll do okay."

Dorothy said, "We know. And we care. And someday, you'll know it too."

Older Me looked—I don't know how he looked. He was unreadable to me. Maybe he was sad. Maybe he was something else. I couldn't tell. "It's gonna be a long hard road, but—well, I'll see you on the other side."

"You knew from the beginning that this was going to happen, all of you? Didn't you?"

Older Me nodded. "I knew. They knew. I was you."

"So you know how this is going to work out?"

"Yes, we do."

I picked up the gun case, opened it. Looked inside. Closed it again. "Okay, give me the timebelt."

Dorothy didn't look happy. She said, "Go find out who you are."

Older Me stood up, leaving everything on the couch. "I'd say, let me know how it all works out, but I already know."

Harlan stopped at the door. He looked like he wanted to say something else, but he stopped at, "Seeya, kiddo."

After they were gone, I sat down at my desk and put my head in my hands. Yes, I was going to do it.

And I did.

The details don't matter. I went after that bastard and his so-called family. I popped up in front of them like a demon from hell. I didn't bother to freeze time. I wanted them to know terror. And they did. They screamed and died.

I set the timebelt for home. I was barely able to press the button. I was shaking. I felt a familiar dizziness. The timeline was rewriting itself.

Steve's clothes were in the closet.

I unpacked my gear and pushed it all under the bed.

I took a long shower. And a nap.

When I woke, it was dark, Steve was lying next to me. "Are you okay?" I could hear concern in his voice.

"I don't know." I rolled over and looked at him. I was still feeling it. All of it. "You have no idea," I said. "You do not know what I have done for you. You will never know."

"What are you talking about?" He looked at me strangely.

I didn't know what to say. I wasn't going to explain. I rubbed my eyes. "I had a bad dream." It was a lie. The first lie I'd ever told him.

"Oh, okay—" He pulled me into a hug. I relaxed into his arms. But I couldn't feel complete. Not now, not yet. Not while I knew that reality was so fragile.

I held him tight. I wanted everything to be all right again.

Only it wasn't. It couldn't be.

Because now that I knew I could do it, now that I knew it was necessary, I had to go after the rest—as many as I could. I didn't want to do it—and I did. I needed to prove something to myself. To Harlan and Dorothy and Older Me.

Every afternoon, while Steve was at work, I went to work. I set myself a quota. Three, six, ten. I wanted to get it over with as soon as possible.

I went after the assassins first—presidents and candidates and civil rights leaders survived. And then I took out the mass murderers—the massacres didn't happen and families thrived. The most violent murderers went next—she lived, they all lived. And then the kidnappers too—the children got to grow up with loving parents. The arsonists—the buildings stood, the people survived. The child molesters—the children deserved a chance to grow. The abusers of all kinds—their victims lived. The drunk drivers who killed families and children, they survived—I just shot out their tires, the first time anyway.

I went down the list methodically. Sometimes I screamed at them. Sometimes I didn't. Sometimes I was incoherent with rage. I didn't care who was on the list or why. If they were on the list, it was enough. Someone—my older self—had decided that these lives were dangerous to others, and that was enough.

After the first few, I fell into a terrible rhythm. I won't say it was easy, but after a while it wasn't hard either—I won't say I was good at it, but after a while I was efficient. I wanted to get in and get out, get it over with as fast as possible. My days became a blur of splatter and gore. Familiar and different every time. I wanted to believe that I'd made the world a little better, but all I'd seen of it was death and horror.

And every time, I felt the same strange dizziness as the world rewrote itself. I'd lie in bed waiting for my heart to slow, waiting for the memories to reassemble.

I couldn't stash anything under the bed anymore. I didn't want Steve to find it. I had no better place, so I put it all in the trunk of my car. Not just the gun and the ammunition and the book and the laptop, but the cash, too—thousands of dollars, from all their wallets. I had made the killings look like robberies. Where I could, I grabbed their wallets and took the cash. Maybe I'd donate it somewhere. Maybe I'd burn it. But I'd probably spend it stupidly. Consider it my fee.

I weakened. I bought a new television. I bought a new stereo. Steve didn't ask where the money came from. He asked other questions instead. He asked me why I smelled of ammonia. He asked me where I was going during the day. He asked me why we weren't making love anymore. "Is something wrong?"

I just shook my head. I said, "It isn't you, it's me. I'm working something out."

"Are you trying to solve a writing problem? Maybe I can help. Do you want to talk it out?"

I hadn't written anything in weeks. I hadn't even tried. I shook my head. "No, it's not that. I'm sorry, I can't explain."

Steve looked hurt. I should have apologized, but no. Sorry is not an eraser. I couldn't be with him right now. I didn't know what else to say. Finally, I blurted, "I just need to be alone."

He didn't say anything. He just got up and walked out. I heard the front door close behind him. I felt abandoned and empty. It was my own fault, but I didn't know how to fix this. I felt so bad I wanted to kill someone. I went and got the timebelt and the gun and the list. At least that was something I could do.

L ater, much later.

We hadn't given up. We still had moments. But the chasm between us was growing wider—and you can only build bridges if you're building from both sides. I'm not sure who gave up first. Probably me. I don't know why. I just didn't feel love any more. Not even lust. Nothing. Where once we were lovers, now we were strangers.

It was inevitable. Steve said, "You've been spending a lot. Where is all that money coming from."

"Odd jobs," I said.

"You're not writing. You haven't shared anything with me in weeks."

"I'm working it out," I said.

"No, you're not." He faced me. He was still the most beautiful man I'd ever known, red hair, green eyes, porcelain skin, all of him, but now his expression was the most painful I'd ever seen. He was sad and hurting. I wanted to grab him and hold him, but I couldn't. "You're not the same person anymore. I don't know what happened. We used to be special. Now, we're nothing. There's something happening here, I don't know what it is, and you won't tell me. I think I should move out."

"I know," I said. "I'm sorry."

He packed his things the next day.

I wanted to hate him. I couldn't.

I sat alone for a long dreadful time, I don't know how long. Then I put on the timebelt.

I went after the serial killers. I'd been avoiding them, I didn't know why. They were strange, broken men. I watched them from a safe distance. They looked like normal human beings. But they weren't. They were monsters. So I shot them in their beds. I splattered their brains across the walls. I walked away, shaking. And then I reloaded and consulted the list. It was something to do. Something no one else could do, so I had to do it. Over and over again. There were just too many of them—

Until one horrible night, lying alone in my own bed, staring at the ceiling, the recognition hit me, washed over me like a wave of acid fear.

I was no better.

I was one of them.

Dog whined at me. I pushed him away. I got up, took a shower. A long hot shower. It didn't work. I couldn't wash the pain away. I couldn't wash the guilt away. I had become a bigger monster than any of them.

I should kill myself now. It would be justice.

I put on the timebelt. I chose the setting carefully. I gathered everything. All of it. I pressed the button.

I found him sitting alone in my apartment, playing with Dog. Older Me.

"You're a monster," I said. "A bigger monster than me. You knew what I would become and you let me do it anyway."

"You had to know what the choice was," he said.

"I lost Steve again."

"Sit down," he said.

I sat. I waited. I held Dog on my lap and buried my face in his fur. He smelled doggy.

Older Me waited until I looked up again. "There is no timeline where you and Steve can stay together," he said. "Believe me, I tried."

"The timeline we were in. If you had left us alone—"

"That timeline was already broken. It was an illusion. Untenable. I've been trying to fix it."

"You've just made a bigger mess."

"It looks like it, yes."

Something about the way he said it. I stopped. "But—?"

"But nothing is ever what it looks like."

"I don't understand."

"Most people don't. We don't see things as they are. We see things as we are."

"Fine, thank you. It still hurts."

Older Me looked at me sharply. "What kind of a person do you want to be?"

"I don't want to be this person. I want to be a good person."

"Are you willing to pay the price?"

"Is there a price worse than the one I'm already paying?"

"That's up to you to decide. This part of the timeline—this loop. Now that you know where this choice goes, do you want to get out of it? This is where we choose. What do you want to do?"

"I don't want to be a killer. I want to go back—but that's not possible, is it?"

Older me nodded. "Actually, it is. But I needed to hear you say it."

The day I decided to kill myself, he came back.

I didn't offer him a Coke.

"What do you want?" I said.

"Do you want a second chance?"

I didn't have to think about it. "Yeah, I do."

"So do I," he said. "But there aren't any. We stumble through life and we get what we get. Then we either learn to live with it—or we don't. That's the harder choice."

"That's it?"

"That's it."

"It sucks."

"Yes, it does. But this is it. There isn't any other." He stood up. "But I can tell you this much. You're going to be okay. I know you don't believe it, I know you won't feel it for a long time. You still have a lot of stupid mistakes to make first. None as bad as the ones you've already made, but you are going to be okay. Maybe even better than okay."

"Yeah, right. Thanks. Now go to hell."

"There isn't anything I can tell you that will make any of this easier. But I know this much. There are possibilities in your future that you have yet to imagine. One day, you will ask the right question, and one day, you will make the right choice. And one day in 1992—well, just do it."

"What happens in 1992?"

"Your chance at redemption." He made as if to go. "Oh, and one more thing. Take good care of Dog. He might be your only friend for a while." He stopped at the door. "You won't be seeing me again."

"Promise?"

"Well, not until one day a long time from now, when you look in the mirror and say, 'Oh, there I am.' And you'll laugh. It'll be good."

I wanted to believe him. Maybe one day I would. But right then, I just crawled into bed and cried. Maybe it was a good cry. I don't know. But Dog snurfled next to me, and that had to be enough for now.

Punching Muses
S.W. Sondheimer

Sappho, Kusama Yayoi, and Frida Kahlo walked into a bar in Boston in 2003. The lights were low, the music was trance, and the clientele consisted mostly of children clad in various shades and textures of black, further adorned with silver hoops and gauges, rings, chains, and pendants whose size seemed to correlate to pecking order.

There was also quite a bit of leather on display as well as inexpertly applied, transfer-ink tattoos keeping lower backs and ankles warm until such time as desire and law came into alignment. "Tramp stamps, ahoy," Frida commented to Kusama, who snorted.

The knitting circle and their bright yarn was an unanticipated presence. "Can I have a moment to ask them some questions?" Kusama asked. "Look at their webs!"

"Maybe later," Sappho sighed.

They were not there, in a bar in Boston in 2003, to make artistic inquiries.

They were there because Oscar Wilde was dead in the middle of the floor.

Again.

It wasn't the first time Oscar Wilde had ended up dead in the middle of the floor in a bar. It wasn't even the first time Oscar Wilde had ended up dead in the middle of the floor of *that* bar; the goth children did so love the man and his drama, both lived and written, and they were undoubtedly as excellent a source of nourishment for their muse as he was of creativity for them.

Or at least what *they* viewed as creativity.

"Oi! Listen up!" Sappho called with her orator's voice and poet's tongue. "We are Muse Recovery Squad F. We're here for the body and to gather any evidence any of you may have seen, heard, smelled, felt, or tasted regarding the death of Mister Oscar Wilde, duly appointed muse to the arts of drama, literature and poetry. This is the seventy... third—"

"Eighth."

"Eighth?" Sappho asked.

Frida shrugged.

"Have you been seeing other recovery squads?"

"You've met me, sí?"

"*Hussy.*"

"Damn straight."

"As though straight as anything to do with this," Kusama said, examining the myriad tiny, perfect polka dots on her fingernails.

Frida smirked.

Sappho raised an eyebrow. "Seventy-*eighth* time we've been forced to process Mister Wilde's death, track his soul, capture it, and return it for reembodiment, so if one of you could possibly give us a hand to make this rotation of the hamsterwheel just a little bit less creaky, that would be fan-fucking-tastick."

After a single beat, everybody in the place returned to *exactly* what it was they had been doing before Sappho had asked for their attention.

"May they all have to search eternally for the word they need to finish their magnum opus."

"Absence makes the heart grow fonder," Kusama said. "Or is it fungus? I can never remember."

"That would make a great painting," Frida said, contemplating the empty air in front of them, then tracing light strokes through it.

"Can we get this over with?" Sappho asked, hands on her hips, "so I don't have to spend the rest of my eternal life wondering why this dipshit is a muse and I, after two and a half millennia and serving as the inspiration for an entire sexual orientation, am still cleaning up his messes?"

"I mean… " Kusama offered, tapping dots of brilliant light onto what Frida had already painted with reality and dreams. Frida opened their eyes wide and nodded enthusiastically, placing one hand over their heart and wrapping their arms around Kusama's waist from behind. "We all know *why.*"

Sappho frowned. "But…"

"It's his dick," Frida supplied.

"There are women…"

"Yes," Kusama agreed. "The nice ones. The compliant ones."

"The blonde ones, mostly," Frida added. "Also, have you noticed that they all have two eyebrows?"

"But Wilde was—"

"Gay. Sure. But he was from a good family. He was well connected. He was famous during his lifetime. Look, we walk up and down time. We, of everyone, know some things change and some things don't."

Sappho sighed. She snapped her fingers over Wilde's body and it vanished. "Let's just… go," she muttered and turned back to the broom closet where the portal had dumped them out.

"I am *not* going back through 1518," Kusama declared, disentangling from Frida and putting her hands on her narrow hips.

"Fuck's sake," Sappho muttered.

"Did *you* enjoy the dancing plague in Strasbourg? Because I have enough intrusive thoughts without a psycho-social mass delusion prying its way into my brain."

"Ugh. I forgot about that. Why can't mass delusions ever be nice? 'Does everyone see those flowers? Aren't they pretty, let's make crowns.'"

"Let me tell you a thing about flowers," Kusama told her. "My first hallucination was a flower, and he was an *asshole*."

"Counterpoint," Frida offered. "The old Ukrainian lady at the corner always gives us the evil eye, throws garbage at us, and then sics her Maine Coon on us when we try to make the portal in the alley."

"I thought that was in 2020."

"Chica, 2020 is Covid-19, not even muses go there. So. 'Dance 'til you barf, 1518' or Baba Yaga's older, meaner sister with a compost fetish and a mountain lion?" Frida looked at her cohorts.

"Wicked witch of Central Square," Kusma said without hesitation.

"Second," Sappho decided after a brief hesitation.

"Prepare your defenses then," Frida crowed. "We ride!"

"**W**hat *is* this?" Kusama asked, pulling lank, wet, rotten *strings* out of her wig.

"Don't ask questions you don't want answers to," Frida suggested, gagging as they scrubbed at a spot on their trousers. They frowned at a rusty splotch on their tie, stuck their tongue out, and yanked it over their head, tossing it into the garbage bin. "*That* is chicken blood. Madre de dios."

Sappho emerged from the marble-tiled bathroom, her chiton spotlessly white, rubbing her squeaky hair with a towel. Kusama gestured a "go ahead" to Frida, who flashed a smile and sprinted for hot water and soap. They sprinted everywhere they could. Kusama leaned against the worktable and smiled to see it, knowing it had been impossible for her friend in life.

And the comfort of knowing death had its perks.

She turned to the map of the galaxy on the wall, covered with what appeared to be fireflies, the spots of light actually markers that indicated where in time and when in space each of Calliope's muses was.

Wilde's swirl of crimson, persimmon, and sharper, more-acidic-than, vibrating-neon almost-turquoise, "is definitely missing," Sappho confirmed as Frida exited the facilities, clean, perfectly pressed black trousers and French-cuffed, blue shirt already on. Their sunflower tie was thrown over their shoulder, suit jacket draped over one arm. "Which means he's…" Sappho shrugged and then let her hands fall to her sides. She skirted the corner of the desk, opened a drawer, pulled out paper and a pen, and started scribbling. After a moment, she paused. "Can I pretend 'castle' rhymes with 'asshole' if it's just for a limerick?"

"Don't you think best in the meter *you* invented for your own personal use?" Kusama wondered.

"No, I *seduce* best in the meter I invented for myself. I *think* best in rhyming dactylic hexameter—hear that, *Homer*? *Rhyming* dactylic hexameter. But before I can *think*, I need to be not *annoyed*, and that means a limerick. So. Can I pretend 'castle' rhymes with 'asshole'?"

"Yes?"

"Good. 'There once, from Dubl*i*n, was an asshole…'"

"Mira, mi amor, I don't think that's how you're supposed to pronounce 'Dublin' en ingles."

"It's the only way the meter works."

"If it makes you happy," Frida said, holding their hands up, palms out and turning their attention back to the map. "A ver, donde esta?" Frida muttered. "He exists and therefore he must be. Surely, we'll be resolved by la cena debajo de las estrellas."

"It's always dinner under the stars somewhere!" Kusama called back.

"Not helpful!"

"Or extremely helpful, from a certain point of view!"

Sappho scribbled. Frida considered.

Kusama emerged again in nothing but her waist-length hair. "Alas, the wig was not to be saved."

"The wig was an abomination."

"Exactly."

"The only thing I can say in Wilde's favor," Frida declared, "is that he continues to get us into very fine throuples." They produced a deep rust sunflower from the air and added it to the neatly braided nest of their hair, then a peony, and finally, some marigolds.

"Queerplatonic *is* an excellent 21st century clarification," Kusama agreed.

"Alas, business before pleasure lest we find ourselves interfered with. Señor de poemas. ¿Donde se esconde?

"Yes. Where *did* he go while the three of you were standing right there?"

"He was gone when we arrived and you know it, Calliope," Sappho said, straightening and twisting her hair into a bun, shoving the cheap, ballpoint pen through the knot to secure it. "Perhaps if you kept better tabs on your employees we wouldn't be looking for this one for the seventy-eighth—"

"Ninety-second," Frida corrected. "I remembered a few more."

"So you'll really do this with just anyone now?"

"I'll do a lot of things with just anyone. You know what you signed up for." Frida winked at Sappho. Sappho ran her tongue over her teeth and bit her lower lip.

"Are you two done?" Calliope asked.

"No," they chorused.

Kusama laughed, an unexpectedly bright sound, deep summer oranges and star fruit muffled by her hand with a hint of filling on foil as it drifted away on the currents of warm air.

Calliope raised a golden eyebrow, the rest of her features composed into the Platonic ideal of neutral. Kusama raised a dark one back, a nascent smirk only just curling the left side of her mouth upwards. "Muses require a certain amount of freedom so they can be where and when they're needed. Most of them are wise enough to choose steady, if some-times bland nourishment, certain to satisfy. Those who choose adventure may achieve some greater satisfaction, but ultimately fail and come crawling back. We have to allow it, or the next big thing may never be."

"Some of us would be happy to follow the rules."

"If only you weren't so good at *your* job, Sappho."

"You promised me that if I—"

"Institutional change comes slowly, darling. Do you have any idea how many ulcers I've developed over the millennia? I can't even enjoy a dish of ambrosia without wishing I'd never been born anymore. Honestly, I'm doing you a favor. Once you get started, you'll never go on vacation again."

"Yes, I enjoyed my last vacation very much. Where did we go, friends? Oh, right. Nowhere. I haven't had a fucking vacation in two and a half millennia. Frida?"

"Going on sixty-seven years."

"Don't look at me, I'm not even dead yet. This is a dissociative episode," Kusama reminded them. "There will probably be a boat made of plush, purple dicks when I get back."

"Definitely not a vacation," Sappho clarified. "Even if it was seaworthy. It's never a vacation when there are *that* many dicks involved."

"*Anyway*," Calliope continued, "there's no rest for the well-behaved, the wicked, the dead, or the dissociated until you find Wilde."

"This is cruel and unusual punishment," Frida declared.

"Pardon?"

"He still owes me a scarf," Sappho grumbled. "A red one. For the one he stole in Paris and gave to his lover."

"Just find him and bring him back. *Again*." Calliope stalked out, followed by chimes and flowers and random lengthy words that glittered and smelled of roses.

"She's such a cunt," Kusama yawned. "And if she were going to make you a muse, Sappho, she'd have done it already. She knows you can do her job better than she can, and someone will notice."

"I don't want her fucking job," Sappho rolled her eyes. "Why would I want to waste my time throwing mediocre white men at mediocre white men? Fuck's sake."

Kusama tossed her hair behind her shoulders and found a marker in her pocket, started to draw interlocking teardrops on her forearm. "They made me help retrieve Jackson Pollack so they could musify him. And being not dead, I was forced to look not only at *his* garbage, but at trashfires *inspired* by his garbage with my own human eyes."

"The *horror*," Frida said, sticking their tongue out.

"To the point," Kusama said. "Unlike Pollack, Wilde *is* taking a risk. The reward would have to be commensurate. Because old muses *don't* die. They just... scream into the void for eternity."

"And can you imagine anything worse than someone with the balls to believe themselves an inspiration watching the last person who believed them to be one dying?" Sappho continued.

"Por eso," Friday asked, "what's the opposite of that? Being remembered?"

"No," Kusama said. "Something… alive. Praise?"

"Fame," Sappho said. Sibilant. Sharp. Echo. Bells. Harp strings, catch, flow. "Living, breathing *adulation*." She pulled the pen out of her hair and wrote something on her palm, then curled her fingers over it and nodded. "We should go. Now."

London, 1895

"**N**ope," Frida said. "No. Un desastre. Necesitamos salir. *Ahora*."

"Why? He's *right there*!" Sappho argued, thrusting a finger at the back of a head in the second row. An opalescent aura swirled around it, dancing, seething, roiling, and generally making a ruckus only the three of them could see.

"Because, he's also right *there*," Kusama countered. "And the man currently blocking his exit, face going puce and fist drawing back is the Marquess of Queensbury. They aren't supposed to meet here. Wilde had the Marquess barred from entry, but whatever deal the muse made with his living incarnation has clearly fucked the timeline—"

"But what's the difference? Whether he dies here or in three years after imprisonment—"

"He still has a *terrible* memoir to write," Frida sighed.

"Does he though?"

"Yes."

"But what if we just—"

"Come on, Sappho."

"Ugh. Fine."

Paris, 1896

"**C**orsets," Sappho said. "Fucking corsets. Again."

Frida, gorgeous, and mobile, in a tailcoat and a white, albeit overly starched, shirt, drew her arm through theirs.

"Frida?"

"Hmmm?"

"Paint me like one of your deconstructed girls."

"Bits and pieces everywhere."

"Sorry, sorry." A woman with an absolutely dreadful wig the color of twenty-first century traffic cones hurried up, body swathed in a green and purple striped circus tent cinched at the waist with a wide leather belt.

"Kusama?" Sappho said.

"Yes?"

"Saph, it's Paris," Frida pointed out.

"He can't come here," Kusama said. "He's in prison. Sodomy. We need a convergence, this is a paradox. Wrong singularity."

"Well, fuck," Sappho declared. "Do you know how long it took me to get into this thing."

"Sure, but now you can take it *off*."

"Well, fuck this for a lark, what are we still standing around for?"

Dublin, 2021

"We should have thought of this first."

"Definitely a convergence," Kusama agreed.

"The actors who have studied and loved the work," Frida counted off on their fingers. "Shockingly rabid fans who have adored Wilde's plays across years, and the man himself with his pride and his proof."

"It would be nice if Calliope saw fit to grace her muse hunters with muses," Kusama said.

"Would you really want Sherlock Holmes up our asses?" Sappho asked.

"I do like his hat. Besides, at least we have some decent choices in that category. Agatha Christie? Long Chau? Nie Huaisang?"

"Please, like she'd let us have any of the good ones."

"Well, that is some bullshit." Kusama pushed strands of another, obviously synthetic, but more hair-like, fuschia bob behind her ears and smoothed her polyester minidress emblazoned with her signature pumpkins. Her knee high boots were covered with gold-painted macaroni.

Frida rejoined them, wiping lipstick off their jawline.

"I thought you were reconnoitering," Kusama grinned.

"Oh, I reconnoitered," Frida grinned back. "He's dead center. Con todos los colores. All bright and swirly. It's a little terrifying, to be honest. Takes a lot of faith to have that much faith in yourself. What happens if you feel even a modicum of imposter syndrome? An atomic millisecond of doubt?"

"You'd blow a hole in reality," Sappho said.

"So how are we not all atoms?"

"Calliope must kill them before they doubt. Which means... they don't actually come."

"But we've retrieved... and seen them..."

"Have we? Or do we just think we have?"

"So why isn't *Wilde* dead? Every time he runs, there's a risk..."

"Calliope... fuck me with a quill," Sappho said. "She gets some of what each of her muses gets, right? That's how she survives without inspiring directly?"

"Sure," Frida said. "Cost of doing business."

"How much," Sappho asked, "do you think she gets from Wilde?"

"Oh," Kusama said. "Oh, shit."

"She lets him go when she needs a boost," Frida said. "And reels him back in before he gets too powerful and becomes a threat."

"That *cunt*," Frida spat.

"We're still going to make this super embarrassing for him, right?" Kusama asked.

"Hades, yes," Sappho agreed. "But swords can cut both ways."

"Mami, you are feral right now. Te amo."

They waited.

Wilde exited the auditorium surrounded by people, the man himself incandescent.

Sappho raised her arm and waved. "Oscar. Yoo-hoo. Oscar! Run. I dare you."

Wilde froze for a moment, surrounded by his entourage, their entourages, and their entourages' entourages, every hand clamoring for a touch, each eye for a glance, each voice for his attention.

"If you'll all excuse me for a moment," he said, buttery smooth, honey sweet, coffee dark, "I have a small matter to attend to."

He strode over to meet them.

"Well played," he said. "You almost had me in London. I heard about Paris as well, I would have liked to see that dress, Kusama-san."

"I'm sure I can recollect it for you."

"Do you really think you can take me right now?" Wilde asked.

"I think you have an ego the size of Jupiter," Sappho said, "or we'd all have been blown out of existence a long time ago."

"And there we have the rub, my dears, because if you take me, then there *is* a hint of doubt, my supermassive black hole of an ego *does* take a hit, and every person, place, and thing in space/time suffers. If, however, you let me go…"

"Your vastly inflated self-worth remains inflated. And we all survive. And Calliope continues to stuff her adoration sack."

"Until I challenge her."

"We sure as shit don't want you as a boss," Frida said.

"I don't want to *be* the boss," Wilde said. "It's a lot of work. I absolutely *despise* work. So allow me to offer you a deal."

"Satan said that to me once," Kusama yawned. "Turned out badly for him."

"I get rid of Calliope. Your little triumvirate takes control of the muse network. Advance your… agendas. Whatever. And you leave me alone."

"How do we know you won't keep the corner office?" Sappho asked.

"Have you met me?"

"And that you won't suffer a crisis of conscience or confidence?" Frida asked.

"*Have you met me*?"

Sappho, Frida, and Kusama shared a quick three-way glance.

"On one additional condition," Sappho said.

Wilde spread his arms. "I'm at your disposal."

Sappho grinned, showing all of her teeth, then swung for his nose.

"I suppose I had that coming," Wilde said muzzily from behind his hands.

"Oh, you definitely had that coming," Sappho assured him. "You'll be in touch?"

"Give me forty-eight hours."

"We've found you ninety-three times, Oscar. We can find you again."

"Of that I had no doubt. Ladies, gentlethem, a pleasure doing business."

He walked away, handkerchief pressed to his nose.

"I need a cigarette," Sappho decided.

The trio wandered the streets until they found the Liffey. Kusama pulled a pack of cigarettes and a lighter out of her boot.

"Have any cake in there?" Sappho asked.

"'We just fucked around to see what happens' cake? 'We're so fucked' cake? Or 'Congratulations on our promotions' cake?"

Kusama nodded and lit her cigarette, passing one to each of her compatriots. They took turns with the lighter, their feet dangling over the dark, roiling, filthy water.

"This," Frida said, "is not what I expected as the next step in my career path. La jefa? I mean… raro."

"I guess if you can't beat 'em, taking part in a coup to tear them from their seat of power is the next best thing," Sappho agreed.

"Might be fun," Kusama said. "Casual Fridays can have a whole new meaning. I have a lot of mass produced pasta to spray paint."

Wednesday Night at the End Times Tavern
James A. Moore

Francesco Tignini struggled and screamed, but it did him no good. The girls with the chainsaw meant to have his head, and there was nothing he could do about it.

Robert E. Howard watched the man struggle with horror and fascination in equal parts. This was the fourth time he'd seen the Vampire of Naples killed, and despite himself, he couldn't look away.

Tignini was strapped to a table, and he fought valiantly to be free. His thick arms bulged, the muscles straining with unnatural strength, his entire body bent into an arc of effort, but to no avail. The ropes and chains that bound him in place were too much.

The girls went about their grim task with faces made old by sorrow and determination. According to the stories offered in the program, the girls were Tignini's daughters, and they were fulfilling a duty that they had no desire to accomplish. They were honoring their father in his time of need and removing the stain of evil from the world.

"I don't know if I believe in vampires."

The man next to Howard nodded his head and spoke softly. "It does not matter if you believe in them. They will feast on your blood just the same if given the chance." Prince Radu of Walachia spoke from experience, at least according to the tales he told. He said his brother was a vampire, and he had initially come to the End Times Tavern to see the best way to kill the undead once and for all.

The older of the girls shook her head and pulled the starter cord on her chainsaw. Tignini hissed, and shook, and cursed in Italian. Bob wished, not for the first time, that he spoke the language, but he could guess the sorts of threats the dead man made. That he was dead was obvious. His skin was pale and peeled slowly from his face. His eyes were glowing red coals in sallow flesh, and his canines were too long and pointed.

The younger of the girls grabbed at Tignini's hair and forced his head back with a mighty effort. The vampire hissed again and tried to fight back, but with no real chance. His daughters were determined to have their father rest in peace instead of being damned to eternal torment as the pawn of an undead force of evil.

When threats failed the vampire tried begging, but his older daughter got her chainsaw working and revved up, drowning out his piteous sounds.

The dour man on the other side of Radu leaned forward and stared at Tignini as the two young women fought on, struggling to hold him in place and then to run the roaring chainsaw across his neck.

The end was a foregone conclusion, really. The vampire hissed, then screamed, and thrashed and bucked as the whirring blade carved the dead meat from his neck. Three seconds after his head fell away, the corpse began to decompose at a furious pace, withering, shriveling and then collapsing in on itself, aging the five or more years it should have aged since Tignini had become a member of the undead.

Bob watched on, mesmerized as he was every time he saw the vampire killed.

The End Times offered strange entertainment. Every night, seven little known deaths played out for all to see. They could not be stopped; they could only be witnessed. As always, the End Times Tavern was busy. He had come each Wednesday since he heard of the bar, and he was drawn again tonight. Not by Tignini's death, though he had to admit to himself if to no one else—that the beheading was hard to look away from, and the unsettling decomposition kept his attention.

No, it was another short while before what he thought of as the main feature took place. The notion unsettled him, made his stomach twist in a way that was mostly unpleasant.

Wednesday nights. The rest of the time he didn't much care about the place, really. It was an interesting notion, and he had no idea how it worked, but each night there were seven deaths, played out in real time, with sound and color and scent. Yes, even now he could smell the rot of Tignini's corpse, though the image and odor were both fading away as the proprietors prepared for the next show.

Waitresses moved around the room, taking orders from people from every imaginable era. There was a Pict over in the corner, sitting with four of his friends, who were dressed in clothing from different eras, though they all spoke the same tongue, near as he could tell.

A waitress slid smoothly over to speak to the dour man, who ordered a strong tea and scowled at the price. Still, he was civil enough. He was a preacher, apparently, and a witch hunter. His name was Cotton something or other, and under the circumstances Bob wanted to chat with him. He was fascinating in his own right, and claimed that he had hunted down and killed several witches, held trials and tests for them. He was vague on details, but fascinating to speak to. He was here to see Tignini's death, just in case he should ever run across a vampire.

Bob had a notion for a Puritan sort of character in his mind, and though the man did not fit the image that played in his thoughts, he felt inspired by his table companion just the same.

"Do you believe that vampires also have free will, Cotton?" Bob asked the question because the man had already volunteered that witches chose to serve the devil, and therefore knew exactly what they were doing, and deserved their fates.

"No." The man shook his head. "They are corrupted before and after their deaths by unnatural means. They are enchanted by other vampires, seduced, or forced into taking the blood of the beast into their bodies, and then possessed by the devil's spirit upon their death. They are forced to do so against their will, and become little more than instruments of continued damnation," He frowned and paused. "Is that correct, Prince Radu?"

Radu nodded, his face a calm, neutral and expressionless mask. "My own brother was corrupted in this fashion. He was a noble man and fearsome warrior before the devil came for him." Radu paused for a moment to sip at his goblet of wine even as the waitress came to replace the drink. Before anyone could protest, the man was paying for Cotton's tea and Bob's beer.

"Much obliged, Radu. The next round's on me." Bob smiled tightly, and the prince smiled back, bowing his head in thanks. Radu was speaking in a different language entirely, but he had no trouble understanding the foreigner's words. The same was true of Cotton, who spoke English, but his words may as well have been a different language. He talked more like Shakespeare than he did a modern man. That was one of many things that Bob did not understand about the bar he was in. Why was it on the corner of Euclid Avenue, not far from his home? How was it that no one else seemed to know about the place? He'd have bet a dollar that each person entering the tavern came in from a different location, just as surely as they came from different eras in history. He was sitting with a medieval prince and a Puritan from the 1600s, just to drive that point home. He half expected Cotton to scream about witchcraft at the very notion, but no. Like Bob, he simply accepted that the rules of the End Times Tavern were not normal.

The place was comfortably appointed, with a few fireplaces and a dozen tables as well. Everything was pleasantly modern, but Bob had a suspicion that if he could see the place through Radu's eye it would look entirely different.

Madness, but then so was the show the proprietors put on. Seven deaths a night, and he had already been through four. After the next one there would be the execution of a man named Edgar Lucerne, a wretch who had killed seventeen young boys before he was caught, and the night would wrap up with a horrible train wreck where only one person died, a drifter without a known name, who was unfortunate enough to be looking out a window when the train rolled and then a tree forced its way through the window where he'd been staring. It was a graphic nightmare of a scene.

But before those moments, there was one more death that mesmerized him every single time.

"Ten minutes before our next death," intoned the calm deep voice of the show's narrator, whom Bob had yet to see, but only heard speaking calmly as he made note of the history of the next dead man waiting to be watched. "Ten minutes before famed pulp writer Robert E. Howard cuts his life short at the height of his career. Howard is best known as the creator of the fictional character Conan of Cimmeria," the narrator's voice continued on, and both Cotton Mather and Prince Radu of Wallachia stared at him with mild surprise. So, they could be shocked after all.

Bob watched his own death once per week. Suicide. After seeing his death nine times, he still could not quite make himself believe that what he was about to witness was true. He could think of no reason in the world why he would end his own life. Seeing the event unfold continued to baffle him and unsettle his nerves.

He didn't like to think of himself as a coward. He didn't want to speculate on a reason why he would end himself before his time. Was it love gone wrong? Did his career fall apart? He felt he was stronger than that. It made no sense at all.

"Why would you?" Radu stared at him.

"I wouldn't. Never. Not ever." Bob waved aside the idea as he would an irritating fly.

Cotton looked at him and nodded slowly. "We see a show. Sorcery of some sort. There are no guarantees that what we see is truth," the man lied comfortably. Bob could see his real opinion in his eyes.

Not that it mattered, not really. At the end of the day, this was why he was here. He needed to understand the mystery of why he would commit suicide when everything seemed so good in his life and the sales of his stories were becoming very nearly a guaranteed thing.

Why would any man willingly seek his own end?

Surely that way lay madness.

In the area where the image would be presented a darkness lay, a void where soon there would be a motion picture, laid out in full color and as real as anything he had ever seen in his life. So real that he should have been able to touch it, to reach out one hand and prevent the madness from happening.

God knew he had tried before, only to find that his actions prevented nothing, that his death was a certainty, at least according to the moving images at the center of the End Times Tavern.

He would not try to stop it again. He had been assured that if he did, he would no longer be allowed into the comfortable bar. Much as he hated it, he felt compelled to come in on Wednesdays to see the show, at least until he could properly convince himself that what he watched was a lie.

The waitress came over, a polite smile on her pretty face. Bob ordered another round for himself and his two viewing companions. They nodded their thanks and settled back, eyes shifting from the glow that preceded the death scene over to him and then slowly back again as the first drawn-out image began to appear.

He reached for his beer.

He had no doubt that he looked at his own face in that image. It wasn't a close resemblance; it was spot on. Maybe a few years older, but he knew every detail of that image, knew the eyes he looked at in the mirror every day when he prepared to shave.

The expression was different. Determined, but oddly haunted.

Still, he couldn't imagine a time when he might consider killing himself.

Bob watched on as his older doppelganger lifted the revolver and stared at it for a moment. The older version of himself looked at the weapon as if it might be his salvation, and Bob shook his head. "No. Not again."

He didn't mean to. He had told himself he wouldn't do it again, but he lunged from his seat and ran for the man holding the pistol as if he might, somehow, stop the inevitable from happening.

"Don't you do it! There's nothing in the world that makes that right, and you know it!" He found himself filled with a sudden fury. That anyone would so easily toss aside a life was something he could barely understand on the best days, but that he would end his own life? Not possible.

The bouncers were there in seconds, two brawny fellows who caught his arms and pulled him back with unsettling ease. Bob was a big man and an accomplished pugilist, but the men were ready for him, and they were bigger than life.

"Mister Howard, you've been warned before." The man spoke calmly and respectfully, and Bob forced himself to calm down as much as he could. The bouncers were just doing their jobs.

Though he had reached out to touch the older version of himself with the pistol, his fingers had moved through the moving image as easily as they would through smoke. There was nothing to touch, nothing to stop, and the images continued to play out, undisturbed by his foolish actions.

The men turned him, prepared for any actions he might make, and Bob closed his eyes as they led him away from his table and the strangers he'd been having conversation with since entering the End Times.

He did not fight as he was escorted to the door of the establishment. "I'm sorry, boys. It got the better of me."

"The situation is delicate, Mister Howard, and we understand that, but you were warned. You will not be allowed back in the End Times, I'm afraid." The man was polite, and the fury in Bob's chest faded away, replaced by a cold dread.

They were firm, and he didn't want to make a scene. Bob took his coat and hat when they were offered, and nodded his apologies.

The night outside was warm enough, and though he could have taken his car, or even called for a cab, he decided to walk home. There was just enough beer in his body to make him careless, and he didn't like the notion that he might do something foolish behind the wheel. It wasn't that bad a walk in any event.

He thought long and hard about his actions, about his future self's actions, and whether he believed he could ever commit suicide as he walked and drank in the nighttime air.

In the morning, after spending a sleepless night trying to calm his overly active mind, he walked back to the building where his car still waited for him. The structure was the same as ever, but the decorations were different. The End Times Tavern was no longer there. Instead, Lowell's Bakery stood in the same spot, and the smell of freshly baked bread filled the air, and three cars were parked near his, along with a delivery truck that was being loaded with baked goods.

For one moment Bob felt panic sink fangs deep into his guts, and anxiety gripped his mind, but he pushed that aside. The world didn't always make sense, it was just that simple. The bar was gone? All the better. He didn't need to watch that particular show again. He needed to move past the obsession.

Besides, he didn't feel suicide was an option in his life. It never had been. It never would be.

Simple as that, really. Bob settled in his car and thought about it for a minute, then climbed back out and headed for the bakery. A good loaf of bread and maybe some muffins. It was time for a fresh start.

A Christmas Prelude

Peter David

I.

Bartholomew Wendell Scrooge had never had much appreciation, affection or tolerance for his son, Ebenezer. He had good reasons, to be sure, or at least they were sufficient to him and he never felt any need to share them. When the boy reached the minimum age wherein such things could be done, Bartholomew immediately whisked him off to boarding school so that he no longer had to tolerate those looks of infinite hurt in the boy's eyes as he would stare wanly up at his father and wonder —albeit to himself because he never dared voice his considerations— what in the world he could possibly have done to engender such hostility from his father, and what tasks he could possibly undertake in the future that might earn him some morsel, some crumb of affection from the great loaf that was his father but never shared.

Ebenezer thus adjusted his life to residing at the boarding school and adjusted his expectations to the existence in which he resided.

His dear younger sister, Fan, was the one light in his life. He dreaded the notion of the poor child likewise being shipped off to a boarding school, where the inner light that shined in her eyes would doubtlessly be stomped out by the older and surlier children. But that happenstance was not to be, at least not initially. Despite his surly attitude toward the world, there was something about the little girl that utterly enthralled the typically dyspeptic Bartholomew. Indeed, he even considered shipping her off, but he eventually pushed away the information about the potential school, and resolved that he was going to keep the child around. There was no need to inquire as to his wife's preferences, since the shrew had done him the courtesy of dying of consumption some months previously. The fact was that, as ill-fitting as their marriage had become, he had indeed loved her once, and there was something in the child that reminded him of his wife's former innocence and virginal view of the world. In short, he found that he liked having Fan about and so preferred to, at the moment, keep her around. All men should have some source of inspiration to get through the day.

Bartholomew was certainly familiar enough with children in general. He was not particularly enamored of them. Moreso, he actually disliked them. Even moreso, he definitely despised them. He had to deal with them every day in his position as the master of the local workhouse which served as a refuge for the poor, the downtrodden, the unskilled, and oftentimes the mentally deficient. It was his job to keep matters running smoothly and maintain the proper progression of work, and that he did with a formidable iron hand. The local council had appointed him to the job, probably out of recognition as a formidable money lender in the town, and therefore he seemed a fit appointee to the job.

He was utterly unaware that Christmas was rearing its ugly head. He had no patience for Christmas, its carols and carolers, its trees, its decorations, its sentiments, its worshippers, its prayers, and, oh yes, its savior and reason for existence. He was not particularly enamored of Jesus's obsession with helping the poor, providing handouts, transforming water into wine, and multiplying fish so that everyone would be able to eat, instead of teaching them how to fish and thus learn to fend for themselves. Nothing good ever came from providing handouts to those in need, because eventually they will deplete the supply of whatever they've been given and have a need for more. So what, indeed, was the point?

And so his inattention to Christmas is doubtless what prompted him to neglect bringing his son home for the holidays. As long as the boarding school was up and running, he saw no need to go to the expense of retrieving his not-especially-welcome son, despite the fact that Fan kept inquiring after him and requesting his presence at home for Christmas.

"He does not like to travel," Bartholomew finally told her in desperation. "The lengthy journey would ill fit him, and he would arrive here cranky and unhappy and burden the home with his darkness, so please, child, cease requesting his presence."

Fan knew this was nonsense. She was not a stupid girl, after all. But it was Christmas Eve and she had been hinting about the prospect of bringing her older brother back for a visit to home, and thus far her father had been avoiding the subject in as clumsy and ham handed a manner as he could devise. But finally he had addressed it directly, and even though she knew that as an explanation it was utterly pathetic and untrue, besides, she sensed that it was the best that she was going to acquire from her intransigent father.

And so Christmas Eve imposed itself upon the Scrooge household in the same manner that it was foisted on the rest of the world. Bartholomew and Fan ate their dinner in silence, which they typically did, but this was a different silence. Usually it stemmed from having nothing of any importance to discuss, but on this day its reason was that there was something Fan Very Much wanted to talk about and her father Very Much did not, and since he was the man of the house, that was where it ended.

Bartholomew then did some idle paperwork around the house, just to keep his mind busy. He knew that it was time to retire for the evening. He knew it intellectually, and yet did not quite understand why he was loathe to go upstairs. It was as if something was warning him, something that he did not quite understand. Some inner loathing was preventing him from ascending to his bedroom.

So instead he remained ensconced in his sitting room. The fire in the fireplace had been roaring rather fiercely, but now it was starting to diminish. He could not find within himself the strength to stoke the logs and bring the fire back to full life. Situated above the fireplace was the portrait of his late wife. He would have preferred to take it down, but Fan seemed rather enamored of it, and so he allowed it to remain there in order to accommodate the child, since generally she asked for so little.

He sat there in his chair, which was certainly the most opulent piece of furniture in the room. It was a quite elegant Bergere chair that he acquired during a sojourn to France some years ago, and no one else in the house (meaning servants and Fan) were allowed to sit in it. He relaxed into it, interweaving his fingers, gazing up at the old shrew's scowling expression and feeling the shadows in the room getting longer. Sleep, it seemed, was coming for him regardless of where he was.

And then he stiffened in his chair, his eyes going from slowly closing to snapping open wide as he saw the image in the painting begin to move.

This was, of course, an impossibility, and it was his instinct to attribute it to shadows being thrown by the dying fire. An illusion, to be sure.

But then the image drifted forward, off the painting, accompanied by a low and irritated moan that his wife typically made when she stood up and the joints in her body protested even the slightest hint of exercise.

Bartholomew's lips moved, but there was a distinct lack of words emanating from them. Finally he managed to whisper a name: "Louise?"

"*How nice that you remember me. And where, may I ask, is our son?*"

"He… he is in boarding school… how… how are you here—?"

"*How is he not?*" she rejoindered. "*How can you exile our child from his home at this time of year? Keep him away from his sister, his family? How can you ignore him so?*"

"You know why," he said. "And why am I bothering to speak with you? This is merely a dream. Obviously, I fell asleep and you have invaded my slumber. You cannot be here. Ghosts do not exist; they are merely fancies of an imaginative mind. Here, I will awaken myself and end this foolishness."

And he slapped himself as viciously as he could, positive that doing so would be enough to rouse him from his slumber. It was an effective and powerful whack, and the slapping noise reverberated through the room.

He didn't awaken.

He slapped himself again.

He didn't awaken.

"*Here, allow me,*" said the spirit of Louise, and she whipped her hand around and struck him so fiercely that it nearly knocked him out of his chair. "*That was most satisfactory. I have long wanted to do that.*"

Scrooge's resolution was severely shaken. The pain from her slap reverberated through his head, and yet he gave no indication that he was awakening. And since pain was most atypical, that realization was slowly pushing him in the direction of the inevitable realization that he was, in fact, awake.

"Wh-what do you want?" he managed to say.

"*I want you to change your mind about our son. Cease exiling him from the house, the family, and your life. Bring him home. Love him as a father should.*"

"I…" He hesitated. "I scarcely know him."

"*That is by choice. But it is no longer your choice to make. I am going to guarantee that.*"

"How?"

"*By providing you visitors who will remind you of who he is, and more, of who you are.*"

"And how are you going to do that?" he asked.

Slowly her image began to withdraw into the painting. And now, much to his surprise, he begged her to remain. The woman he had come to loathe, the symbol of everything that had gone wrong in his life, he urged her, begged her, pleaded with her to remain with him for even five more minutes, then one minute, then however long she desired to stay.

But she did not attend him, and seconds later, she was gone, having returned to the image that she customarily was, gazing at him with that same distant indifference that she had customarily displayed in life.

Bartholomew stood there for a long moment, and then his lips twisted in annoyance. "Typical," he muttered, and then decided that he had had enough. He tromped straight upstairs and retired to his bedroom, determined that if he was going to have fantasies, it might as well be in his bedchamber where he could do it out of sight of the eyes of anyone else.

II.

Bartholomew flopped into his bed, trying to forget the image of the damnable woman that had had the nerve to haunt him during what was indisputably his transition from waking to slumber and then obviously full waking once more. That had to be it. She had inhabited those transitory moments, coming to him when he was so on the verge of slumber that the reality of his world was blurry.

As he lay there, trying to get his head comfortable on the pillow, which seemed to have transformed from goose down into rock, he saw a soft light burning in the adjacent room. He had no idea what it might be; it appeared to be being generated by some manner of lantern. Slowly he lowered his feet, all hints of slumber having evacuated his poor, tortured body, and he made his way to the door and slowly opened it, fully expecting to scold Fan for lighting a lantern and delaying his finding rest.

It was not Fan.

It was a man, a slender man with dark skin who looked vaguely Arabian. He was wearing sizable Turkish trunks, and a loose fitting blue and white jacket. A sizable turban sat perched atop his head, and a scimitar dangled from his hip. He was standing with his hands akimbo, looking as if he was ready to launch himself into an adventure. Perched on the floor next to his leg was the oddest-looking creature Scrooge had ever laid his eyes upon. His skin was a deep purple, and his belly protruded over the belt of his own Turkish trunks. In that regard he was dressed similarly to the man next to him, but there the resemblance ended. He could not have been taller than four feet tall, and his face was impossibly and perfectly round, with several chins hanging down.

"Greetings!" said the taller man. "Perhaps you have heard of me. I am," and he bowed deeply, "Ali Baba, and my companion is a genie I picked up in my adventures. I have been dispatched to show you your son's past."

"I know my son's past," said Bartholomew. "I was there for it."

"Really," said Ali Baba. He glanced down at the genie, and an unspoken understanding passed between the two of them.

And suddenly, with no warning at all, the room dissolved around them, and reformed into his office at the workhouse. He stood there and watched himself studiously shuffling through paperwork, as if he hoped to be able to discern some answer to the mysteries of the universe.

He could also see that he was younger. There was no gray in his hair, and the crow's feet that he had developed and which sorely irritated him had not yet formed on the edges of his eyes.

"Can he… I… see me?" he asked tentatively.

"No, not at all. You are simply an observer to what has already occurred."

Bartholomew watched silently as there was a knock at the door. His assistant entered tentatively and said, "Sir? Mr. Scrooge?"

"I am quite busy, Jacob," Scrooge said to him with clear disapproval in his voice. "What do you need to say that requires my attention?"

"You… you have a son, sir."

Scrooge looked up in surprise. And Bartholomew recalled that he had scarcely interacted with Louise in the final days of her pregnancy with Ebenezer. That had been by design, of course.

"I do?" said Scrooge. Then he "harrumphed" somewhat. "Are you sure?"

The question seemed to surprise Jacob. "The midwife sent word, yes. She was quite specific. She wants to know if you will be coming home straightaway."

"I will be home when it is my time to be home, Jacob," and he tapped the work spread across his desk. "Other matters require my attention."

Jacob was visibly surprised at his indifferent reaction. "Sir, they can certainly wait. Others would understand if you—"

"If I what?" and he lay his pen down in quiet irritation. "Ceased doing my job? Left those who reside in this workhouse to their own devices so

I can rush home to stare at a sleeping infant? I am one of those individuals who prioritizes his work above all else, and this workhouse is filled with people who count on me to maintain that attitude. They know me and know that I will work until my last breath to keep them gainfully employed. Nothing will distract me from that. Certainly not some mewling infant. Is that quite clear, Jacob?"

Jacob managed to nod, and he kept his face impassive, but his disdain for Scrooge's dismissal of any priority for seeing his son clearly aggravated him. "I will leave you to your work, then."

Scrooge simply nodded, and Jacob exited the room, bobbing his head slightly as he did so.

Ali Baba stared silently at Bartholomew, saying nothing. And finally, Bartholomew spoke, saying the words he had never spoken aloud, although he had thought them repeatedly.

"The child wasn't mine."

Ali Baba raised an eyebrow as he studied Bartholomew silently.

"My wife had... relationships... with another man," said Bartholomew. "Ebenezer was not mine; he never was. If she could have left me to be with him, she would have done so. But he never asked her. In fact, shortly after the child was born, he departed England and went to live on his plantations in the colony of Virginia. I imagine he wanted to be as far from her as he could get."

"Is that what you imagine?" said Ali Baba, and before Bartholomew could respond, the genie who sat crouched next to him gestured, and the room dissolved around them once more.

He was now standing within the nursery which had been meticulously prepared for the infant Ebenezer. Louise was sitting in the rocking chair, cradling the child, and then there was a knock at the door. Louise glanced up and the nurse was standing there, saying, "Mr. Crockett wishes entrance."

"Send him in," said Louise.

"This is him," said Bartholomew. He was pointing and his hand was trembling in barely contained fury. "Russell Crockett. The landowner. Watch. You watch. He is going to inform Louise that he never wants to have any contact with her again."

The door swung open and Crockett entered.

Ali Baba let out a low whistle. "Quite the handsome fellow, isn't he."

Bartholomew stared at Crockett's pleasant face, his gentle eyes, his square jaw, his thick and copious brown hair. "To some, I imagine," he said with much indifference. "Certainly to Louise, one would presume."

Crockett strode across the room and stood there, beaming down at the infant who was dozing in its mother's arms. "He's beautiful," he whispered.

Louise nodded. "He is indeed."

He knelt down and rested his hand upon Louise's. It was hard for Bartholomew to watch, but at the same time he could not bring himself to look away. His mind was split right down the middle, uncertain of how to react.

"Louise," he said, then paused before he continued as if summoning the strength. "I am going to be departing England. I'm going to be relocating to my plantation in Virginia. Tobacco is the wave of the future, and I want to be at the crest of that wave. I cannot do it here." He squeezed her hand. "And I want you to come with me."

Bartholomew gasped in incredulity. He could not believe it. Here was the hated Crockett, propositioning his wife right here, in his home. The man knew no boundaries, had no heaven-sent sense of decency. How was it possible that one man could have so much nerve?

Then, to Scrooge's shock, Louise slowly shook her head. "I cannot, Russell. I am married to Bartholomew. I am holding his son—"

"My son," Crockett corrected her.

But she continued to shake her head. "No, Russell. *His* son. He is my husband. I swore an oath before man and God to remain with him until death does us part, and I cannot walk away from that vow. I cannot. I may have twisted it, bent it... but I cannot abandon it."

"It's another country," he said dismissively. "He will not even know where you are. You will be here one day, gone the next. You will vanish into the wilds of Virginia, be the mistress of my plantation. Raise Ebenezer to adulthood in an entirely new land. Wake up every morning with a man whom you know loves you. When did you last get that feeling from Bartholomew?"

She looked so wistful that it nearly broke Scrooge's heart. "Not for quite some time. His indifference is what drove me to you."

"And now let it drive you away. Come with me, Louise. No one in the colonies will ever know."

She stared levelly at him. "I will know," she said firmly and sadly, as if inwardly she was sobbing her soul out of her body. "And God will know. And when my time comes to step before the Pearly Gates, how will I stand there awash in my sins and hope to step through. There is more to life than what we derive in Earthly pleasure, Russell, and I believe you know that. So I beg you, depart for Virginia, and think well of me. Hold me lovingly in your thoughts, but that is the only place henceforth where you will ever be able to embrace me from this day forth."

Crockett knelt there, clearly utterly crushed, and Bartholomew, despite the circumstances that he was witnessing, could not help but feel a brief bubble of sympathy for the man. He had genuinely loved Louise, had begged her to accompany him, and she had refused to do so. She had had her dalliance on the side, had produced a child with him, but nevertheless in the end her loyalty had remained with Scrooge. She had remembered who she was, and set her commitment to him above all else, up to and including her own happiness.

"As you say," Crockett managed to utter, even though it was clearly a strain for him to do so.

"Louise," whispered Bartholomew, and he started toward her, but even as he approached her the burning lights within the room faded to blackness, and when he strode forward his shin bumped into something, which he was not expecting. In the dimness of his room he recognized his surroundings, and realized he was back in his bedroom.

III.

In the distance, he heard the faint clanging of a clock. He imagined it was the grandfather clock whose pendulum monotonously swung in its sizable casing down in the sitting room. It clanged once, which made sense because he had gone to bed shortly before midnight, so one hour had progressed. That certainly made a sort of internal sense. It made him wonder if the ghosts were arriving on an hourly basis. That would certainly be rather precise of them.

He had to stop his wondering for a moment to ponder the fact that he was beginning to accept that he was indeed being visited by ghosts. There had been no tottering on the border between wakefulness and slumber; he had indeed been awake when Louise had come to him, had indeed been awake when Ali Baba had presented himself. He was not dreaming; he was actually experiencing a bevy of alternate beings who were parading through reality as if it was the most natural thing in the world.

And who knew? Perhaps it was. Perhaps believing that the real world and unnatural world never had congress with each other was in fact the ludicrous belief to adhere to.

That was when he heard the oddest noise outside of the door to his room. It was a steady clip-clopping, as if a horse were approaching him. But that was absurd. What in the world would a horse of any sort be doing coming down his hallway? How could it climb the stairs? Could a horse even mount a flight of stairs? Was that an equine possibility?

Then the door burst open and a knight rode in. Except he was unlike any knight that Bartholomew had ever seen. For one thing, he was remarkably skinny. He also was older than one would expect a knight to be, seemingly somewhere around fifty years of age. He sported a breastplate that had been thoroughly scrubbed and polished to within an inch of its life, and he wore a helmet made of pasteboard. His arms were unencumbered save for sizable metal gauntlets and metal plates upon his thighs and shins, and he was wearing metal boots as well. He was holding a lance that was gently balanced upon the horse's back, and Bartholomew stared at him in disbelief and bewilderment. He had literally never seen anything like the man in the entirety of his existence.

"Greetings," declared the man, and there was a Spanish lilt to his voice. "I am Don Quixote de La Mancha, a knight errant, seeking the man known as Bartholomew Scrooge. Would you be he that I search for?"

It occurred to Scrooge that he could just lie to the man. Just dodge his attentions. Deny his name and send him on his way. But somehow that did not seem… gentlemanly.

"I am," he admitted.

The knight smiled. He had a thick mustache and a goatee beard extending from his chin. He extended a hand to Bartholomew and said, "Accompany me."

"To where?"

"Where I take you, of course."

That was not the most detailed of responses he could have hoped for, but somehow it seemed consistent with the man as he had presented himself. Realizing that there was no point in pushing the conversation beyond its limits, he took the extended hand and allowed Don Quixote to pull him up onto the horse's rump, perching himself on the back of the beast, wrapping his arms around the knight's mid-section so that he did not fall off the creature's back.

"On, Rocinante!" he commanded the horse. Scrooge then assumed that the beast would leap into a gallop. Instead, the poor creature let out what sounded like a heavy sigh, as if it would rather just rest, be fed and groomed, and otherwise be left to its own devices. It did not seem to have any galloping left in its body. Instead, it trudged forward at a steady clip, not particularly fast, but just speedy enough to not be slow. She moved toward the window, which was hanging open, and then clambered through it. Bartholomew braced himself, certain that the beast was going to plummet to the ground, breaking its own aged body and likely killing Bartholomew as well.

But that did not happen. Instead, impossibly, the horse remained airborne, as certainly as if it were a Pegasus being kept aloft by great wings. She moved across the sky, trotting down a road that only she could perceive and traverse.

"Are you taking me somewhere else in the past?" asked Scrooge.

"You have already been to the past. There is nothing more to show you there. No, this Christmas Eve, I am taking you to see your son."

"*Her* son," Bartholomew corrected him.

But the knight errant would not be deterred. "You are the only father the boy knows. He is unaware that his true sire is currently laboring in Virginia, getting rich from his plantation and wistfully recalling the woman he wanted to accompany him… while he indulges in affairs with female slaves who labor in his fields when he is so inclined. The truth is that the boy would likely be happier with his true father than with you, but such have the fates dictated that he is stuck with you as his father, in truth if not in actuality. And if you could look beyond your own hostilities toward him and what he represents, perhaps you could accommodate him."

"With what could I possibly accommodate him?"

"With the love of a father for his son."

Scrooge waved off the notion. "The boy is better off without me. Why should I bring him home for Christmas? He is certainly content at the boarding school, where his needs can be most easily accommodated."

"Is that a fact," said Quixote. He sounded very neutral in his question. "Let us see if you are correct in your assumption."

The horse, Rocinante, abruptly seemed to change course, and angled down toward a building that Bartholomew immediately recognized as the boarding school where his son resided. Despite the fact that the ghost had ostensibly arrived at one o'clock in the AM, nevertheless it appeared to be only early evening. Rocinante landed smoothly on the ground, never so much as missing a step, and then walked into the school, the door opening before them as if being manipulated by an unseen hand.

Bartholomew kept a firm grip on Quixote's midsection as they moved through the deserted hallways. Scrooge couldn't help but notice how empty the building was. It was amazing to him. He knew intellectually that most of the residents were likely heading home for the Christmas holidays, but he had just assumed that it would remain populated. Not *all* the children, one would think, were being retrieved home, and certainly not the entire staff would abandon the place. There definitely had to be *someone* around to keep Scrooge company.

But no. There was no one. The entirety of the building had been vacated, and when he finally encountered his listless son, the sight crushed his heart. They had reached a room in the back. It was a long, bare, melancholy room, made barer still by lines of plain deal forms and desks. At one of those desks, a lonely boy was reading near a feeble fire.

Something stirred in Bartholomew's chest, something unrecognized. It was his heart, feeling the boy's loneliness, his miserable emptiness. The solitude in the empty red brick mansion was absolutely crushing. Bartholomew had never considered it, never given it the slightest bit of thought. Knowing the other children were leaving was one thing. Witnessing the child's miserable loneliness was crushing, and knowing that he himself was responsible for it all…

"The boy does not know his father, nor his origins," Don Quixote pointed out. "His mother never shared the knowledge with him, nor did you. He has spent his life wondering what in the world he did to aggravate you so, to earn the obvious contempt that you feel for him, and you have provided him no love, no guidance, no fatherly obligations…"

"All right, all right," said Bartholomew angrily, gesturing that the knight should hold his tongue. "Perhaps… perhaps I did not do right by the boy…"

"*Perhaps?*" echoed Don Quixote, doing nothing to mask the incredulity from his voice. "You are not certain still, after seeing the boy with your own eyes?"

"What I see," said Bartholomew slowly, "is a boy who is capable of surviving on his own. He does not depend on anyone else for survival, especially not his father."

"Especially not," Quixote agreed.

"And... and this is something that will be of benefit to him," Scrooge continued. "To learn to be dependent on himself rather than upon loved ones. Loved ones, that I apparently need to remind you, can betray you at any time. Loved ones are an unnecessary extravagance, and no sane or rational individual chooses to depend on them and so leave themselves open to betrayal at some random point in the future. Loneliness builds character. By leaving him to his own devices, I am preparing him to face the reality of his future. I am giving him strength."

At that moment, young Ebenezer let out a low, agonized, pathetic sigh, and tears began to dribble down his face. Seconds later, he was full out sobbing, and he slumped his head forward and wet the pages of the book he was reading with the moisture that was seeping freely from his eyes.

"Oh yes," said Don Quixote pitilessly. "He seems very much the model of strength."

Bartholomew couldn't stand seeing the boy's misery. "Stop it!" he bellowed angrily, as if he was capable of making himself heard by shouting at the hapless child. "Stop crying! It is a vicious world out there, and a man needs to stand up to it. To show others what he is capable of!"

"He is showing you," said the knight. "And you are just incapable of, or unwilling to, see it. You are punishing the boy for your own actions that drove your wife into the bed of another man. What I am seeing is unbridled cruelty on your part."

Bartholomew slowly disembarked from Rocinante. He approached the child, gripped emotionally by the boy's unbridled misery. He knew that the knight was correct; that the boy had done nothing to deserve the disdain with which his father had treated him. That he was tormenting the boy over his own actions.

Slowly he tried to reach out, to gently touch the child, to minister to him in some manner, to provide fatherly comfort to him somehow.

His couldn't move. He felt paralyzed.

"Let me touch him," he whispered, his voice scarcely audible.

Don Quixote did nothing but stand there and watch in silence. There was nothing he could offer the frustrated father by way of consolation or advice.

"What is this infernal crying!" bellowed a new voice.

Bartholomew spun and saw that the school master was there. The boy was not abandoned. Someone apparently remained to keep him company.

"You know I detest blubbering!" he thundered, and advanced on Ebenezer waving a long, wooden rod that he was obviously going to use upon the child to stem his sobbing.

The elder Scrooge let out an angry shout and stood directly in the school master's path. "Put that down this instant!" he bellowed.

Even as Don Quixote shouted "No!" in desperation, the school master strode right through him. Instantly a massive pain slammed through Bartholomew, and it was easily the greatest agony that he had ever suffered in his life. It was as if a thousand needles were simultaneously piercing his skin, all over his body. He had never felt any discomfort like it, and he staggered, gasping, grabbing at the air in an effort to keep himself righted.

It did not work. He collapsed to the ground, and then he heard the sound of the rod behind him, slamming into Ebenezer's skin.

And Ebenezer made no noise. He suffered in silence.

The dim fire that was flickering in the fireplace at the end of the room was diminishing and the shadows of the room extended themselves, slowly reaching out with their icy tendrils and caressing father and son before enveloping them both.

IV.

Bartholomew blinked several times, and the world began to come back into existence around him. He was lying on the floor of his bedroom, gasping for air, and then he heard a clearing of a throat.

He looked up, and the most oddly dressed person he could imagine was standing there gazing down at him. He was dressed in clothing that would have looked at home in the Elizabethan age. He was attired entirely in red, sporting a red velvet jacket, a red doublet and scarlet hose. Around his neck was a large red ruff. Astoundingly, his skin was also red, and his slicked back hair was deepest crimson. His face was amazingly triangular, and his eyes were glittering yellow.

And he seemed disappointed when he studied Bartholomew.

"You're not Faust," he said, clearly annoyed that Scrooge was not this Faust individual.

The name was familiar to Bartholomew, but he couldn't place it. "No, I am not. I have no idea who this 'Faust' individual is, so if you would not mind being on your way…"

"You don't know Faust?" said the red-skinned man in astonishment. "Are you not remotely literate?"

"I have little patience for fantasies. My son seems enamored of them, considering that he typically seems to have his nose buried in a book, even during the times when he was residing here. But that remains the interest of children, not adults who have to work to earn a living." He hesitated and then his curiosity got the better of him. "Who is this Faust? And who are you?"

"Faust was a doctor. A German doctor who was far more interested in the pleasures that the world has to offer than anything having to do with the spark of the divine. And as for me," and he bowed deeply, "I am Mephistopheles. I would like to think that you have heard of me."

"The… the devil," said a stunned Bartholomew. "You are the devil."

"Who better to show you your future, my dear fellow," said Mephistopheles. "You are, after all, set to be damned. You will be coming to my realm soon enough, so naturally it would be my province to show you how you arrive there."

"I… I am to be damned?" said a stunned Bartholomew. "But… but I have led an exemplary life. For what could I possibly be condemned to the pit?"

"Are you that oblivious, truly?" said Mephistopheles, making no effort to disguise his incredulity. "In your career, you have been brutal and uncaring about the lives of those who reside in the work house, if you can use such a benign word as 'reside' to describe their situation. They sleep on the floor, they have scraps to eat, they work in brutal jobs such as cracking rocks and breathing in the dust of the rocks they are shattering. Children are dying and their little corpses are being tossed into ditches and unmarked graves. And you are profiteering off their work, leasing them out to people who are having them do horrific jobs for scarcely any money at all while pocketing bribes."

"It's not bribery!" said Bartholomew desperately. "It is… incentives. Gifts. That is all. It does not impact on how I do my job."

"Really. Someone thinks differently."

Mephistopheles pointed icily at the bed with one long, red finger. Bartholomew turned and stared in shock at what he now saw.

It was himself, which made sense since it was indeed his bed. He was clearly some years older than he was now. His hair had long since departed his head, and the crow's feet had moved from the corners of his eyes and commandeered the entirety of his face. He was lying still, staring up at the ceiling, and for a moment Bartholomew wondered if he was even alive. Before he could bring himself to inquire, however, there was a noise at the door. He turned and saw Jacob, of all people, walking into the room. Jacob likewise looked older, and there was an expression of grim determination on his face, as if he had come to deliver bad news.

"Jacob," Bartholomew said from his bed. His voice was scarcely above a hoarse whisper, but he sounded rather self-possessed. "You will be happy to know that I am feeling much better. My lungs are clearing; the illness is disappearing. I am quite certain I am going to recover."

"I am afraid you are wrong, Mr. Scrooge," said Jacob, and with no more of a pronouncement than that, he stepped forward and snared the pillow out from under Scrooge's skull. His head fell back on the bed, and an expression of pure astonishment appeared on his face. At which point Jacob didn't hesitate, but brought the pillow down over his dumbfounded visage and kept pressing. Bartholomew cried out in terror, both the one being smothered and the one who was looking on. However, the one with the pillow on his face was severely muffled, and although his panicked fists slammed into Jacob's arms, they did nothing to deter his strength and obvious determination.

"Your man seems not especially enamored of you," observed Mephistopheles, and it was certainly impossible to argue with his observation. Meanwhile the struggles of the man in the bed were slowly diminishing as, deprived of air, the strength began to depart his body. Long seconds passed, and then finally he ceased struggling, and Jacob fell back on the bed and exhaled deeply.

"It's done," he whispered. "It's done."

Then a soft voice came from the doorway, a single question: "Father?"

Bartholomew spun and stared at the image of his son, Ebenezer. He was no longer a child, but a fully grown man. He was quite the handsome young fellow, it appeared, and there was a look of only mild surprise in seeing Jacob perched on the end of his father's bed.

Jacob had yanked the pillow clear when he had first heard noise from the door, and when he spoke, his voice cracked. "I... I found him like this," he managed to say, and it was clearly one of the worst lies in the history of lying. Jacob had obviously not expected to be caught, and the presence of Ebenezer had thrown a sizable spanner into the works.

Now Ebenezer would see that justice was done. He would challenge Jacob, would press him on his murder. It would not take much, for Jacob was clearly scarcely holding himself together. At the very least, Ebenezer would summon the authorities, and they would certainly break Jacob in no time at all.

All of this was plainly evident to Bartholomew, and he waited for Ebenezer to hurl an accusation that would easily destroy any attempts at sang froid on Jacob's part.

For a long moment Ebenezer was silent, and then he spoke.

"Good."

That was all he said, that one simple, indifferent utterance that completely detached him from the scene and endorsed Jacob's obvious crime.

"*No!*" screamed Bartholomew, and for just an instant, Ebenezer seemed to react, as if he was able to hear his father's hysterical reaction from the other side of the veil. Then he shrugged in indifference and turned back to Jacob.

"Attend to whoever needs to be contacted, would you, please, Mr. Marley?" he said.

Jacob Marley bowed slightly. "Of course. I will take care of it. You will have nothing more to worry about."

"No, I don't think I will," said Ebenezer, and a brief smile played across his face.

Bartholomew sank to the floor, his world reeling around him. "Tell me this is not inevitable," he said, his voice scarcely above a gasp. "Tell me this can be avoided."

"Are you attempting to make a bargain with me?" asked Mephistopheles. "I feel obliged to warn you, such deals do not traditionally go well for those who initiate them."

"No, no deal," said Bartholomew frantically. He might have been unaware of the fate of Doctor Faust, but he was aware of the lack of wisdom displayed by those who attempted a bargain with the devil. "Just… just tell me if I can avoid his horrible fate? This being murdered in my bed, and having a son who so despised me that he is indifferent to it. Why would you show me this scenario if I am beyond all hope?"

"Why, Bartholomew, why else? Because it's Christmas." He began to laugh, and his laughter became louder and enveloped the room. Bartholomew sank to his knees, clapping his hands over his ears to try to block out the sound, but it did not help. Nothing helped, and the laughter became louder and louder, until it threatened to consume him body and soul.

V.

Young Ebenezer Scrooge was sitting alone in the empty classroom of the boarding school. Then the door opened, and a little girl, much younger than the boy, came darting in. Putting her arms about his neck, and often kissing him, she addressed him as her "Dear, dear brother."

"I have come to bring you home, dear brother!" said the child, clapping her tiny hands, and bending down to laugh. "To bring you home, home, home!"

"Home, little Fan?" returned the boy.

"Yes!" said the child, brimful of glee. "Home, for good and all. Home, for ever and ever. Father is so much kinder than he used to be, that home's like Heaven! He spoke so gently to me one dear night when I was going to bed, that I was not afraid to ask him once more if you might come home; and he said Yes, you should; and sent me in a coach to bring you. And you're to be a man!" said the child, opening her eyes, "and are never to come back here; but first, we're to be together all the Christmas long, and have the merriest time in all the world."

"You are quite a woman, little Fan!" exclaimed the boy.

She clapped her hands and laughed, and tried to touch his head; but being too little, laughed again, and stood on tiptoe to embrace him. Then she began to drag him, in her childish eagerness, towards the door; and he, not loathe to go, accompanied her.

Now…

Ebenezer was unaware of the existence of telepathy, or even of the word itself, which makes a sizable degree of sense, since the word would not actually be coined until the 1850s. Telepathy involves doing things with the mind that would seem impossible to any others. That was something that Ebenezer did routinely, so routinely that he did not even consider it special. For instance, the previous day, he had conjured up an array of characters, including Ali Baba, Valentine and his wild brother, Orson, and a parrot named Robin Crusoe, and Friday, Crusoe's companion. That was his ability, to create the most formidable of illusions so that the subjects of his attention could not distinguish between fantasy and illusion.

And, feeling isolated and desperately alone, he had unknowingly turned his attentions to his father and bombarded him with a series of telepathic illusions that set his father's nature straight.

He was unaware of this, of course. Just as, decades later, he would be unaware of it when he wound up subjecting himself to a series of illusions that would straighten out his own twisted, tortured, miserly personality.

But that, of course, is another story....

Cornwallis's Gift

Heather McKinney

"General Washington?"

Washington looked up from his papers to see a soldier peeking through the entrance to his tent. The lantern from his desk cast just enough light to show the outline of his face. He motioned him in.

"General Washington, this came for you." The soldier saluted him and moved closer to the light. Washington took in his threadbare blue coat, tattered breeches, and boots held together by scraps of rags, but his eyes locked on the small wooden chest the young man held. "From Cornwallis. He sent it from England. There was a note. A gift for you as a show of respect."

The papers dropped from Washington's hands. "Bring it here, Private." Taking it into his hands, he was surprised by its light weight. "What's in it?"

The private averted his eyes. "The note did not say. The instruction was that you open it alone, General."

Washington raised an eyebrow. "Well, that is disconcerting, I must say. Better stand near my tent just in case, Private, er—"

"Private Gates, sir." The young man stood at attention.

"Private Gates. Yes. Please stand ready near the entrance in case this is some trap."

Private Gates saluted and moved out of the tent.

Washington examined the chest, turning it over in his hands. It was plain but made of rich, sturdy mahogany. The only adornment was a bronze hasp secured vertically by a small pin on a chain.

He sat the chest on his desk and stared at it. The last time he had seen his adversary was nearly two years ago, when Cornwallis surrendered to him. Now that the war was over and the Americans victorious, it seemed an odd time for a gift.

"I should just throw it in the fire," Washington muttered. "Nothing good can come of this." He picked it up, tucked it under his arm, took a step toward the tent's opening. Then he froze. "What can it hurt? It would be a waste of a well-made chest. I can always use it to store my important documents."

He placed it on the desk, grasping the pin between his fingers. Lifting the pin out of the hasp, he flipped up the latch. There was not a hint of a squeak. He grasped the lid in both hands, took a breath, and raised it. Peering inside, he found emptiness.

Washington struck his desk with his fist. "Damn that Cornwallis. Does he think I have time for jokes?"

A loud bang rang through the tent, followed by a warm push of air that caused his powdered wig to slip to one side. He gripped his desk as his eyelids fluttered.

"General!" Gates threw open the tent flaps and rushed inside.

"It's all right, Gates. I am fine. Just a little trick from Cornwallis." He adjusted his wig. "You are dismissed."

As he heard the private's footsteps fade, a voice spoke over his shoulder. "What gives, Chuck?"

Washington spun around to a man several inches taller than him, adorned in shiny black pants with a matching jacket and a white low-collared shirt. The man slowly ran a comb through his dark hair, his eyes facing the ceiling.

Washington caught his breath. The man's feet hovered above the ground.

The man tucked the comb into his jacket and heaved a short sigh. "Jesus, Chuck, out with it, I ain't got all—" the man brought his gaze level with Washington and raised an eyebrow. "Who the fuck are you? Where's Chuck?"

"Chuck?" Washington's voice squeaked out.

"Yeah. Chuck. Cornwallis. Whatever. Where is he?"

"I… I don't… he sent me this box." Washington pointed at the desk.

The man looked over at the chest and rolled his eyes. "You gotta be fucking kidding me. He sent that to you? Well, how nice. After all my years. So, what's your name, buddy?"

Washington stood tall and crossed his arms. He had faced insurmountable odds before and had never been intimidated. "I am General George Washington, Commander-in-Chief of the American Army."

"Is this a joke? Never mind, I don't give a shit. Okay, what do you want?"

"Look, good sir. I am terribly sorry, but I am not sure what is going on here. Who, or should I say, *what* are you?"

The man brushed at his jacket. "For Christ's sake. Look, I'm a genie. I've been in the service of the Cornwallis family for centuries. So, chop-chop, what's your wish?"

"A genie?" Washington paused, confused. "A genie? A genie that grants three wishes?"

"Three wishes? You've read too much of that *Thousand and One Nights* shit. Name's Maurice. Yeah, I grant wishes. How do you think the Cornwallis clan got their money? Look, time's a-wasting. Mom wants me over for dinner. So, what do you want?"

Washington went quiet. This was clearly a trick. Fine, he'd play along for now. "Very well, *genie*," he said, sarcastically emphasizing the word, "we are just breaking up camp to head home. It will be several weeks before I see Mount Vernon. I'd love to be home now instead of waiting."

Maurice let out a sigh. "I don't want to hear all your deepest thoughts and dreams, Mack. I just need the wish. Look, let me help you. You say: 'I wish' and fill in the fucking blank. Think you can handle that, genius?"

Washington nodded and gave an exaggerated bow. "Very well, Mister Genie. I wish that I could be back in Mount Vernon."

"Fine. Your wish is my command." Maurice clapped his hands, and a puff of smoke filled the air.

W ashington roused from his sleep, recalling his dream of a strange man all in black with a foul mouth. He laughed to himself and muttered, "What a crazy dream."

As he stretched, he became aware of the foul odor that engulfed him—the unmistakable scent of cow manure. He could not imagine why there would be cows in the camp. He turned on his side. A chill moved through him, and he realized his back was damp. He sat up and blinked. Early morning sunlight accosted his eyes. As the world came into focus, he realized he was lying in a field a few hundred yards from his home.

Standing slowly, he glanced around to find all his personal property lay around him. Chests of clothes and papers were strewn about the field, as if someone had grabbed the contents of his tent, wadded them up, stuffed them in his traveling chests, and dumped them around him.

There, in the middle of it all, was a small mahogany chest.

H is homecoming was met with the appropriate amount of excitement and fanfare, combined with surprise at his early arrival without a carriage or soldiers. Martha ordered a special dinner, and the servants prepared a warm bath afterwards. He felt clean and content for the first time in years.

He and Martha retired to the bedroom, where she gave him another homecoming present. People thought she was prim and proper, but he knew another side of her. Once he was sure she was asleep, he slipped up to his study.

The chest lay on his desk, untouched.

He slowly moved his hand toward the chest's latch, and then paused. Was it true? Had he imagined it? What other explanation could there be?

He turned toward his door to leave, but felt the pull of the chest and the possibility of endless wishes inside. His found his hand moving back toward the chest, easing the pin out, and opening the latch. Bracing himself, he lifted the lid, hoping not to rouse the house.

Maurice hovered over his desk. "What is it, Georgie?" He wore only a pair of white boxer shorts with red polka dots. His ample hairy belly hung over the waistband. "I was in the middle of a massage." He made air quotes with his fingers.

"Maurice. Yes. Sorry to bother you. Martha wants to have a party to celebrate my homecoming. I really want to liven it up. It's the end of the war. It needs something big."

Maurice sighed. "I'm not hearing a wish in there, Mack. For future reference, have the wish ready when you call me. In case you haven't noticed, I'm not one for chitchat."

Washington went quiet as he considered the wording.

"Holy shit, man, this girl charges by the hour. Tick tock, tick tock."

"Well, that's just it. I am not exactly sure what I want. I just know I want a prominent political leader to attend, someone foreign, to add some color. And the best entertainment. I am just not sure who to ask for. I'm sure you must know people."

Maurice huffed. "Yeah, sure. I know people. Now make your wish before I get your wife to finish my massage."

"Right, then." Washington took a deep breath. "I wish for a great foreign leader to attend my party. And I wish to have the greatest entertainer. I wish for my party to be something no one ever forgets."

"Yeah, it will definitely be unforgettable." Maurice clapped his hands together and disappeared with a bang, leaving Washington sitting in a smoky office.

Invitations were sent to every prominent family in the country. New carpets gifted from a French diplomat were on display. The servants and slaves spent the next few weeks cleaning, painting, and repairing the main house. Guest rooms were provided with the finest linens. Dozens of lambs, chickens, and cattle were slaughtered for the feast. Fresh vegetables and fruits were harvested from the garden.

On the day of the party, George and Martha stood in the entrance to greet the guests. Ben Franklin arrived first, followed by Thomas Jefferson and his young daughter. Other dignitaries were greeted and ushered in.

Washington's eyebrows rose as a tall, slender woman in a long brown velvet dress approached. Her long train was held by two servant girls who looked to be no older than fourteen. The girls wore simple white dresses, cinched at the waist by white cords. They kept their eyes trained to the ground as they walked. The woman held her head high and her back straight as she glided through the door.

Her dark hair was piled high, woven into intricate twists and turns. A finely stitched lace headpiece pushed up from her hairline, secured with ornate gold pins inlaid with sapphires that sparkled in the late afternoon sun. She lifted her chin and offered the back of her pale hand to Washington.

He accepted it and pressed his lips against her clammy skin. "Good evening, madame. I am George Washington, and this is my wife, Martha. Forgive me, but I do not recognize you."

The woman's dark brown eyes flared. "Countess Erzsebet Bathory. In this country everybody calls me Elizabeth."

"And where are you from, good lady?"

Elizabeth groaned and rolled her eyes, "The Kingdom of Hungary, of course. I belong to the richest, most powerful family in the land." She made a wide sweeping motion with her hand. Her stiff neck ruff bristled. "Do you have a lot of guests whose uncles are the king of Poland?"

"Uh, no. I think you must be the only one."

She nodded, her eyes darting over the crowd. She took a step forward and leaned in closer to his ear. "So, tell me, what's your servant situation? Can you spare a servant girl or two?" The girls holding her train raised their heads in unison and locked eyes with Washington. They shook their heads sharply, causing the train to ripple in their hands. Elizabeth raised an eyebrow and spun her head toward them. They returned their eyes to the ground.

Before Washington could respond, John Adams and his daughter Abigail approached, "John, I would like you to meet someone. This is the Countess Erze… Erz… uh, how do you pronounce it?"

"I said to call me Elizabeth, you glorified peasant!" She threw her hands in the air.

"Well, then, meet Countess Elizabeth Bathory from the Kingdom of Hungary. She is one of the foreign dignitaries who will be joining us tonight."

Adams bowed and kissed her hand. "It is a pleasure to have you here, madame. And may I present my daughter, Abigail."

The countess took Abigail's hand in both of hers. "Such soft delicate skin." She lifted her hand to her lips. "I could really sink my teeth into skin like that. Tell me, are you still a virgin, dear?"

Abigail blushed as she tried to pry her hand from the countess' grip. Adams took hold of his daughter's shoulders. "I am going to have to insist you let go of my daughter's hand, madam."

Elizabeth bared her teeth at Abigail and growled before uncurling her fingers from the girl's wrist. Adams cut his eyes toward Washington before steering his daughter through the crowd.

"Are all the people in your country prudes?" Elizabeth patted her tall coif, motioned to her servant girls, and moved into the main hall.

Martha watched her go and turned toward him, an eyebrow raised. He shrugged. "It's probably some Hungarian custom, asking about one's virginity." Martha shook her head and turned toward the next guest.

"Will you excuse me a moment, dear?" Washington slipped up the stairs and went into his study. When he summoned Maurice, he was thankful to see he was again wearing his black jacket and pants.

"Maurice, I don't have a wish. Just more of a question, really. Do you remember me asking for a foreign world leader to be at my party?"

"Yeah, and I brought you one. Born in sixteenth century Hungary. No need to thank me."

"The sixteenth century?"

"Yeah, you know, the one right after the fifteenth century. I'm so glad you understand such complex concepts. I can see how you beat the Brits."

"It's just… when I asked for a prominent world leader, I meant a modern one."

Maurice rolled his eyes. "Look, I ain't a mind reader. When you make a wish, be specific. You said a prominent world leader. I brought you one from one of the most powerful noble families in Hungary. And here you are, bitching."

"I don't want to appear ungrateful. But could we maybe swap her out for another?"

"There's no undoing a wish. She is here for your party. End of story. If we're done with the twenty questions, I have a poker game to get to."

Dozens of tables had been brought into the main hall for the evening, and they were piled high with food, desserts, and drinks. The main course had just been served when the countess' shrill voice rose above the crowd. "This is wine, you imbecile!"

Washington craned his neck to see his servant Victor retreat from her table, narrowly dodging the glass Elizabeth flung at him. He apologized to Martha and the guests at their table, rose from his seat, and went to investigate the ruckus. As he approached, he heard Victor say, "I am so sorry, madame, red wine is served with the main course."

"What seems to be the problem, Countess Bathory?"

"I'll tell you what the trouble is. This fool brought me red wine."

"Do you prefer a white, or maybe a brandy? We are happy to accommodate your tastes."

Elizabeth struck the table with her fist. "What kind of a place is this? I specifically requested a cup of virgin's blood. To cleanse my palate. Or are you keeping it all for yourself, you savage?"

Washington cleared his throat. "We simply do not keep much blood on hand here at Mount Vernon, virgin or otherwise. We import our red wine from the finest vineyard in France. I think you'll find it satisfactory if you give it a chance." Washington turned toward Victor, who was pulling at the brass buttons on his blue coat. "Victor, kindly bring our guest another glass."

Victor bowed, and slipped off to the kitchen.

The countess rolled her eyes and sighed. "I guess I will make do. You Americans live like monks."

After dinner, a servant informed Washington that the entertainment had arrived. Washington went to the entrance to find a slightly built man with long wavy dark hair cascading down beneath a curious black hat. He wore a pair of black pants with buckles all over them and a jacket of a similar style.

"Good evening." Washington extended a hand.

The man took his hand, smiled shyly, and said in a high-pitched voice, "My name is Michael and I am here to sing and dance for your party."

Washington beamed. Music and dance! That would be entertaining. "Thank you so much for coming. We were just finishing dinner. If you would follow me into the main hall?" He led the young man to the musicians, and Michael handed them some sheets of music.

Washington bowed and turned to his guests. "Ladies and gentlemen! We have some entertainment arranged for the evening. The floor is yours, sir." The audience gave Michael polite applause as Washington went to his seat.

The orchestra began playing an unusual driving beat that Washington moved his body to without thinking. This was different.

Michael slid out into the middle of the floor, sliding his feet backwards and kicking up his leg. He spun for several rotations to the applause of the crowd.

"An acrobat!" Martha said.

Michael slid his hat down over his eyes and began to sing "Bad." He made high pitched sounds to the beat of the music. As he spun around the floor, he seemed to hover over the floor, defying gravity. He spun around and grabbed his doodle, jerking it up and down to the beat. Washington sat forward in his chair, Martha turned to face him, her eyes wide. Michael did it again.

Gasps ran through the crowd. Women covered their eyes and swooned. The young man leapt on one of the tables and let out a guttural yell, hurling decanters of dessert liqueur to the ground. He yelped with each explosion of tinkling glass. He made more indecent gestures from his new perch.

Washington pushed through the crowd, making his way over to Michael, apologizing to his guests as he went. He waved the musicians to stop, and then reached up and touched Michael's arm, bringing the act to a halt. "Thank you very much for coming out, but I'm afraid your act has shocked our ladies. I am going to have to insist you end it here, sir."

Michael grinned, waved to the room, and shouted, "I love you all! Good night!" Then he jumped down from the table and disappeared out the door, walking backwards.

The countess rose from her seat. "I have never seen anything more disgusting in my life! Bring him back here and I will burn his eyes out with a hot poker."

Washington put a hand on her arm. "That is a generous offer, madame, but it won't be necessary. Why don't we just start the dance?"

No one paid Washington any heed. The room buzzed with outraged voices. Chairs scraped the floor as the guests rose and began filing out. Within minutes, only the Washingtons remained.

L ate that night, after Martha had gone to bed, Washington tiptoed up to his study.

There, on his desk, was the chest.

The cursed chest.

His fist tightened around an iron hammer as he crashed it down on the chest with all his might. Again and again and again.

Not a splinter came loose.

Breathing heavily, he opened it, dropped the hammer to the ground, and collapsed in his chair.

Maurice looked down at him with crossed arms. "Geez, it's almost like it's magic, huh, genius?"

Washington looked up at him. "What *are* you?"

Maurice rolled his eyes. "I told you. I'm a genie. I grant wishes."

"You create nightmares. My party was a disaster. Between that crotch-grabbing spectacle and that creepy Hungarian savage, people could not leave fast enough."

"You asked for it. I did it. I never promised you a fairy tale, Mack."

"You're evil. The devil himself."

"Well, there's a lot of debate on that subject. I mean, you wanted a big elaborate party to show off what a great guy you are. That ain't exactly Christian."

"You're a curse!"

"You defeated and humiliated ol' Chuck. Did you think he was gonna jerk you off?"

Washington rose to his feet. "I have to destroy you."

Maurice threw his head back and laughed. "I was with the Cornwallis family for generations. Don't you think if they coulda found a way to destroy me, they woulda done it already? You can't destroy me." Maurice scratched his hairy belly and burped. "I'm like the clap."

George William Fairfax was sitting at his breakfast table with his wife Sally, when one of the servants came in with a package.

"This just arrived by the post, sir. From General Washington in America."

Sally raised an eyebrow as the servant placed the brown paper package on the table. She and Washington had dated before he ended up marrying that awful Martha Custis. Sally and her husband George had been close friends with the Washingtons until her husband chose to remain loyal to the king, and returned to England when the war broke out. So why was he sending a package?

Fairfax untied the string from the package and opened the thick paper. "Well, look at this. A lovely mahogany chest…"

What You Can Become Tomorrow
Keith R.A. DeCandido

"Our greatest hopes could become reality in the future."
—Stephen Hawking

Sussex, England, Earth, 1849

"That was such a lovely journey," Jane Shelley said as she threw open the doors to the house she shared with her husband, Percy Florence Shelley, and her mother-in-law, Mary Wollstonecraft Shelley. The house in Sussex had been in the family of Mary's late husband, the poet and anarchist Percy Bysshe Shelley. Mary had been relieved to inherit it after the death of her odious father-in-law. It had become a most wonderful home for her, her lovely son, and her delightful daughter-in-law.

"I do so love traveling with you, Mary," Jane said as they opened the windows to air out the house after their absence. They had just returned from a jaunt to Italy, spending time in Venice and Siena. Percy Florence had gone to collect the mail. "It's no wonder you're the premier travel writer of our time."

"Hardly that, Jane."

"Don't be so modest. Your travel writings are the finest I've ever perused. Next time," Jane added, "we must go to Geneva and see the Villa Diodati."

Mary chuckled as they entered the house. "Perhaps. I doubt the current owners would appreciate our presence, though."

"That must have been a glorious summer."

"It was actually a miserable summer. It rained *constantly*."

"But that's what led you to write *The Modern Prometheus*."

Mary sighed. "The ghost-story contest that Albé proposed led me to write my novel of *Frankenstein*, yes, but that was the least of the literary accomplishments of that gathering."

"Who's Albé?" Jane asked, sounding confused.

Another sigh. Mary spoke very little of those insane days of her youth. Now she found much of it coming back. "That was Percy Bysshe's nickname for Byron—and Byron called my husband 'Shiloh'." A tear welled up in one eye. "I do miss them so."

Percy Florence came into the house just then, carrying several parcels. "What's wrong, Mother?"

Wiping the tear away, Mary said, "Nothing, my sweet boy, simply remembering my callow youth writing flights of fancy."

"Mother, stop that, your novels are excellent."

"I appreciate that, but they are only novels. What is in the parcel?"

Percy Florence smiled and handed it to her. "See for yourself."

She unwrapped the brown paper that concealed the package's contents, revealing a leather-bound volume.

Mary felt her heart skip a beat. It was a new printing of Percy Bysshe Shelley's works. "Oh, this is wonderful. You see, Jane, poetry, like that of my dear Percy Bysshe and of Byron and of Coleridge—those are the words that will ring down throughout history, long after my tales of monsters and immortals and Armageddon have been forgotten."

Shaking his head, Percy Florence started, "Mother—"

Holding up a hand, Mary said, "Please, sweet boy, I have a headache. I must go and have a lie down."

"Of course, Mother."

Slowly, Mary went upstairs to her bedroom. In truth, her head had been pounding since she awakened in the inn this morning, and throughout the carriage ride that brought them to Sussex. But she had grown accustomed to the headaches, so common had they become.

And they were most useful distractions from thinking about their financial state.

She still wrote, for it was a way to earn money. When her father-in-law, Sir Timothy, had finally been so kind as to shuffle off this mortal coil, Mary and Percy Florence inherited a portion of his estate, but it was a much smaller portion than she had been led to believe by Sir Timothy's lawyers.

Those lawyers were her only means of speaking to her husband's father. The funeral was the first time Mary had been in the same room with him since long before Percy Bysshe's death twenty-seven years ago.

But while she wrote to keep food on the table, it was her tireless work in preserving Percy Bysshe's legacy that fed her soul. And it had been working! More people knew the poems of Shelley now than ever had in his lifetime, and it warmed Mary's heart to know that his work was discussed among the intelligentsia—and not to criticize his radical notions, but to truly examine his work, as he deserved.

The bedroom was musty from the weeks of disuse, and she found her headache increasing in its intensity. Nonetheless, she lay down on the bed, shifting her weight on the straw, hoping sleep would ameliorate the pounding in her head.

And then everything changed…

Washington, D.C., United States, Earth, 1945

Josh Gibson and Grace Fournier stumbled out of the bar, the last of the patrons to leave before it closed for the night.

"Coulda given us one more goddamn drink," Grace muttered.

"Wouldn't help," Josh said. "'Cause I had me six drinks t'forget, and I ain't forgotten shit."

Grace grinned. "You tryin' to forget me, baby?"

Pulling her into a tight grip with his massive arms, Josh said, "Never for a minute, girl. B'lieve that. Nah, what I wanna forget is what Satch told me about Robinson."

Yanking herself out of Josh's embrace, Grace said, "I thought we was done talkin' 'bout Jackie Robinson."

"Toldja I couldn't forget, girl! That motherfucker's gonna play in the Major goddamn Leagues, and, and, and, listen to this!" He shook his head, trying and failing to clear the bourbon haze. "What Satch tol' me? Mr. Rickey of the Dodgers, he had himself a condition for ol' Jack. He got to turn the other cheek."

"What you mean, baby?"

Josh actually grinned at this, because the whole notion was *that* stupid. "It mean that when them white folks throw shit at him and call his ass names, he got to *take* it. And you know what I said to Satch when he done told me that?"

"What you tell him, baby?"

"I told Satch, I couldn't never be doin' that no-how. Jesus turned the other cheek, but I ain't no fuckin' Jesus. And then you know what Satch said to me?" Josh shook his head, the grin collapsing into an angry snarl. "He said, 'That's why you ain't goin' to no Major goddamn Leagues, Josh.' You b'lieve that?"

"Let's get a cab, baby," Grace said, stumbling toward a collection of cars on the corner.

The first cab in line closed his window and locked his car when they approached.

The second waved them off. "No coloreds."

The third, though, started, "I'm sorry, but—" Then his eyes widened. "Holy shit, you're that ballplayer! For the Grays! I saw you at the Negro World Series back in '42! Satchel Paige mowed you fuckers *down*! You're the black Babe Ruth!"

"Josh Gibson," he said quickly. He hated being compared to that fat white fuck.

"Yeah, I saw the ball you hit in the fourth inning, thought for *sure* it'd go out!"

That got Josh to smile. He'd taken Satch deep with two on and one out, but it didn't clear the deep fence in Griffith Stadium.

"Hey, you need a ride?"

"Yeah, me and my lady—"

The cabbie held up both hands. "Oh, hey, I'm sorry, Mr. Ruth, but I can only take you, not the girl. I mean, on account'a you bein' a celebrity and all. But that's it."

Grace had been standing unsteadily on her feet while the cab driver went on about how great Josh was, but now she got in the cabbie's face. "Oh *hell* no!"

Josh grabbed her and forcibly pulled her away from the cabbie. "Take it easy, girl! It's all right, it's a nice night, we just walk home."

The third cabbie had shrunk from Grace's advance, and now was practically leaping back into his cab. The fourth cabbie, meanwhile, had driven off.

As they continued down the street toward Grace's apartment, she spoke angrily. "I thought you weren't Jesus!"

"What you talkin' 'bout, girl?"

"I'm talkin' about you tellin' Satch you wouldn't turn no other cheek! So what the *fuck* was that?"

"Girl, I'm talkin' on the field. On the field, I'm Josh motherfuckin' Gibson. On the field, I'm the black Babe Ruth! But out here? I'm just another colored boy who's gotta walk his ass home."

They went the rest of the way to the apartment. Josh wondered what was going to happen when Grace's husband finally got back from the

South Pacific. The war was basically over now, so he'd be coming back, and Josh knew that Grace's insistence that she'd leave him was a load of bull.

No more war, which meant all the ballplayers that got drafted would be back on the ballfield. The shit baseball in the majors meant that Black Baseball was doing better than ever—not to mention that girls' league that Mr. Wrigley in Chicago put together.

But that was all gonna change. And if more people did like Mr. Rickey with that Robinson buck, and brought colored players to the majors, well, that was it for Black Baseball. The Negro Leagues were finished.

Which means I'm finished, too. I ain't turnin' no other cheek, and ain't nobody gonna bring my ass to the majors. Besides, all the home runs I hit, I'll break that fat fuck's record in nothin' flat, and ain't no way they'll stand for no colored boy hittin' more homers than the Babe.

They went up to the apartment, Grace struggling with the keys.

The moment they got into the small apartment, Grace collapsed onto the couch. Within seconds she was snoring.

Josh shook his head, an action he immediately regretted, as his skull was pounding. He went into the bedroom, and fell facefirst down onto the double bed alone, the springs straining against his massive frame.

And then everything changed...

Hampton, Virginia, United States, Earth, 1986

"So," Jim Johnson said as he walked with his wife Katherine to their car in the parking lot of the Carver Memorial Presbyterian Church, "you want to go out tonight?"

Katherine looked at him askance. "It's Sunday, Jim."

"So? Ain't like you gotta go to work tomorrow."

At that, Katherine laughed. She was still adjusting to being retired, and had indeed forgotten that she would *not* have to get up the following morning to report to the Goddard Space Center for work.

"We could go see a movie," she said as she climbed into the passenger seat of their Ford. "Miss Nichols has a new picture out."

"What, another *Star Wars* movie?"

"*Star Trek*, there's a difference."

Jim snorted. "It's all fake space travel. Seems to me, you helped the men that did the real thing."

"So?"

He turned the engine over. "So why you want to see a movie about it when you did it for real?"

"Because Miss Nichols is in it. She's a great lady. Spent most of the Seventies tryin' to get more black folks and more women into NASA— and not doin' what I was doin', but bein' actual astronauts." She smiled and shook her head as Jim pulled out of the parking lot. "Lord have mercy, I remember the night Mae Jemison was takin' off for the first time. Miss Nichols, she called to wish her well, and they kept passin' the phone around to everyone *but* Mae 'cause every one of them wanted to say hi to Lieutenant Uhura."

"That's fine, I guess, but that mean we gotta sit through a *Star Wars* movie?"

"*Star Trek*."

"What difference does it make?"

"Well, for one thing," Katherine said, "there's actual black people in *Star Trek*. Only brother in *Star Wars* is Billy Dee Williams."

Jim laughed. "So they got Colt 45 in space?"

"They must, yeah." Katherine yawned. "Whatever we do, it'll be after I have my nap."

"You sounded beautiful today, darlin'. Choir sounds more like angels every Sunday."

Katherine smiled, and then yawned again. "Well, soundin' like angels has got me all tired."

"I'll get you home and tuck you in, darlin', don't you worry."

Jim got them home, and he escorted her upstairs to the bedroom, tucking her in as promised.

After kissing her on the forehead, he said, "I'm gonna go read the paper."

Katherine nodded. Jim always liked to spend the time after church reading the Sunday paper. Even as he left the room, she faded into her nap.

She dreamt of being asked—by name—to verify the calculations of the orbit of *Friendship 7* back in '62. But in the dream, it was Nichelle Nichols, not John Glenn, who demanded that Katherine double-check the calculations of the first manned vessel to orbit the Earth.

And then everything changed...

Katherine Johnson University, Valles Marineris, Mars, 2312

Dr. Hannah Ward let out the breath she'd been holding when the three targets materialized on the platform.

"It worked…"

Mary Shelley looked around. "What has happened?"

Josh Gibson rubbed his eyes. "The fuck is goin' on?"

Katherine Johnson pursed her lips. "This dream has taken an odd turn."

"Please, don't be alarmed," Hannah said. "I'll return you to your homes very soon. I just wanted to test the equipment."

Johnson looked around at the alcove in which she sat. "Equipment?"

Hannah said, "You're sitting in the TD-73 prototype." Realizing that would be meaningless to the three of them—indeed, would be meaningless to anyone beyond her, the chair of her department, and her two graduate assistants—she added, "TD stands for Temporal Displacement."

Shelley's eyes widened. "Displacement in time?"

"Yes. My name is Dr. Hannah Ward, and I've brought all of you forward from your own times to the year 2312 C.E." Then she winced. "Sorry, you would call it 'A.D.'"

"Anno Domini is no longer used to delineate the era?" Shelley asked.

"It was changed to 'Common Era'."

Shelley nodded. "Thus divorcing the calendar from religion. Fascinating."

Gibson spoke. "Will someone tell me what the *fuck* is goin' on?"

"Mind your language, young man," Johnson said.

Hannah took a deep breath. "I wanted to test the TD-73, and I particularly wanted to bring forward the three of you: Mary Shelley, Josh Gibson, and Katherine Johnson."

Gibson frowned. "I'm supposed to know who they are?"

"Not necessarily. But I wanted all three of you to know something that I'm fairly certain you didn't in your lifetimes—and that's that *everyone* knows who you are now."

Shelley asked, "Why would anyone know who I am?"

"You wrote *Frankenstein*."

Gibson asked, "She wrote the movie?"

Hannah sighed. "She wrote the novel that the movie was based on. More to the point, it became massively influential—it's widely regarded as the first science fiction novel."

Johnson chuckled at that. "Never thought about it that way, but it makes sense."

Shelley seemed confused. "I'm afraid I do not understand. *My* work has endured? But what of Percy Bysshe?"

"Oh, he's regarded as one of the greatest poets of the nineteenth century—and that's also due entirely to your efforts after he died to make his work more widely known. But by the twenty-first century, you were far better known than him."

"Because of *Frankenstein*?" Shelley asked.

Hannah nodded.

"Remarkable."

Turning to the ballplayer, Hannah said, "Mr. Gibson, even though you don't get to play in the major leagues, eventually Negro League records were counted as equal to that of Major League ones. And while you didn't get the chance to break Babe Ruth's record, it was broken by a... a colored player."

"Hank Aaron," Johnson said. "I don't follow sports much, but I remember when Aaron hit the 715th back in '74."

Gibson stared at Hannah. "You mean to tell me a black man broke the Babe's record? And they let that shit stand?"

Hannah nodded. "And that record was broken by another player of color in 2007, and then *that* record was broken by a mixed-race player in 2099."

"Mixed-race?"

"Yes, the player's mother was white and his father was black."

"And they let his ass play?" Gibson sounded incredulous.

"Mm-hm. And they also inducted you into the Hall of Fame in 1972."

Gibson's eyes went wide. "For real? They put colored folks in Cooperstown?"

Hannah grinned. "Lots of them."

"Fuck."

Johnson shuddered. "Please, young man, if you don't cease with the foul language—"

The ballplayer snapped, "Lady, I'm Josh motherfuckin' Gibson. Who the hell are you?"

It was Hannah who answered, "She's Katherine Johnson. Right now, you're all sitting on Mars, in a terraformed habitat in Valles Marineris, in a lab in Katherine Johnson University. It's named after you."

At that, Johnson's eyes widened, and she almost fell out of the alcove. "Lord have mercy. Mars?"

"Yes. And your work in getting the space program started has been lauded for centuries now. Your name is spoken of in the same breath as Neil Armstrong and John Glenn and Steve Squyres and Maya Chen and Alberto Fontanarossa. And they named the first university they built on Mars after you."

Johnson put her hands to her mouth. "Well, I never…" She shook her head. "That's… that's remarkable."

Hannah looked at all three of them. "None of you were recognized properly when you were alive, but you were three of the greatest in your fields. I always thought it was horribly unfair that you didn't get the recognition you deserved when you were around to appreciate it, even though your legacies have carried on for centuries after you died. So I wanted you to know that, even though it feels like you were neglected or forgotten or not important—even though you lived in the shadows of other people who *did* receive the accolades in their lifetimes—you *are* remembered. You will continue to be remembered."

An alarm sounded. Hannah checked the console and was dismayed to see that the generator was starting to overload. If she didn't send them back soon, they'd be stuck here, and what that might do to the timestream didn't bear thinking about.

"I have to send you all back."

Johnson looked disappointed. "But I have so many more questions. We're on Mars?"

"We are," Hannah said, "but I can't tell you more than that. I shouldn't even have told you that much. I'm sorry."

"No, don't be, Dr. Ward. I appreciate the gift you've given us. Thank you."

"Yes," Shelley added, "thank you. Even more than what you say about my own accomplishments, to see a woman constructing such a device, knowing that such women as Mrs. Johnson here are in the future, fills me with tremendous hope."

Gibson let out a bark of a laugh. "Black man breaks the Babe's record. Don't that beat all."

"Goodbye, Mary. Goodbye, Josh. Goodbye, Katherine. Please wake up knowing that you will endure."

She sent them all back. Hannah had deliberately taken them when they were going to sleep, so that they would likely return from their odyssey thinking it a particularly bizarre dream.

And then the generator sparked and burned and shut down. She had exceeded the power requirements by six hundred percent. They'd probably make her pay the excess on next month's power bill.

All for what the department chair would probably think of as self-indulgent.

But to Hannah's mind, she got to right three wrongs. That was worth even paying the power bill.

Now she just had to figure out how to explain that she'd need to rebuild the generator. Again.

Nostradamus's Angels
Hildy Silverman

Michel de Nostredame laid out their mission. His voice echoed from a modified version of Edison's prototype telephone that sat atop a round Louis XIV tea table in the parlor-*cum*-control center of Le Petit Trianon du Temps. "A new disruption to the proper course of time has been revealed. I beheld a dire outbreak... of disease or violence, it was unclear, but it begins in Paris of 2018. If the city falls, the entirety of France shall follow. Your mission is to prevent this disaster. Madame, you have the coordinates?"

"Oui." Marie Curie adjusted brass knobs and levers embedded in the marble fireplace mantle. "Course is set."

"Then bonne chance, mes anges."

Marie Antoinette's eyes flared red in her pale face. "We must prevent this!"

"And so we shall." Mary Todd Lincoln reassured her. Despite having been violently deposed, Antoinette's noblesse oblige remained unwavering, which Lincoln found admirable.

She could understand why the great seer Nostradamus had revived and recruited Curie to protect the True Timeline. He too respected the scientist's vast intellect (although Lincoln found her unwavering agnosticism disconcerting). However, she remained puzzled as to why she and Antoinette had been chosen to join Curie. The only clue she had was the poem de Nostredame recited when he introduced them to one another:

> *Three who bear the name,*
> *of Holy Mother*
> *Misfortunes in life brought premature ends, now subverted.*
> *Against he who robbed the Tree of Life*
> *time's traveling angels shall prevail.*

Curie set a dial to *Pilote Automatique*. "Ladies, it is time to prepare. Choose garments from the 2015–2020, Popular Casual section of your cabinets."

Antoinette hurried off to her room. It took her a while to conceal her deathly pallor and the seam marking where her head had been reaffixed. de Nostredame had been able to revivify the executed queen with his alchemical wizardry only to the point of suspension between life and death. In contrast, the fully resurrected Lincoln and Curie bore no indications of having ever left the world of the living. At least, not visibly.

"I do look forward to seeing Paris again," Lincoln sighed. "My life there was pleasant despite the sorrows that brought me to it." She plucked at the black gown she always wore between missions, and started toward her rooms.

"Wait." Curie intercepted her. "You should know… the location of this anomaly is the Catacombs."

Lincoln shuddered. It seemed she could never escape death, not completely.

Curie gently squeezed her hands. "*Please* remember to take your medications."

Lincoln pulled away and folded her arms. "I do not care for those medicaments. They dull my wits."

"They also mute the voices." Curie tapped her temple. "We cannot afford for you to become, ah, overwhelmed."

So many spirits vying for her attention *could* make it difficult to remain rational, let alone on mission. "Very well," Lincoln agreed reluctantly.

Once within her apartment, Lincoln tapped pills from three different bottles into her palm. Curie meant well… but would she *not* need her senses sharp and her mind open to insights from beyond? Decided, she replaced two of the pills and swallowed only one.

The intrepid team exited Le Petit Trianon, now camouflaged as another low-rise townhouse within the Villa Adrienne enclave. "Might we assume this event is the work of our foe, Count Cagliostro?" Antoinette sneered his name.

Lincoln sighed. "No doubt *another* attempt to bring about the Biblical apocalypse."

"That is what de Nostredame suspects." Curie consulted the mission parameters jotted down in her notebook. "Either he causes or takes advantage of it to usher in his vision of a shining new age—under his *benevolent* guidance."

They strolled down the avenue drinking in the astonishments of twenty-first century Paris. Curie raised an eyebrow at the *Tesla* emblazoned along the rear of a motorcar, while Antoinette squealed at the delicacies displayed in a boulangerie's window. Lincoln thought it sweet that they retained such childlike wonder despite all they had seen and experienced. She only wished she, too, could find pleasure in such novelties.

A scream interrupted their orientation, one quickly echoed by another. Soon they beheld a crowd stampeding toward them like sheep fleeing a wolf.

"It appears we've arrived without time to spare," Curie sighed. "Shall we?"

They dashed (or in Antoinette's case, due to the ridiculous high heels she wore, toddled rapidly) down the avenue toward the Catacomb's entrance. Much like salmon swimming upstream, their passage was slowed by the current of humanity flowing in the opposite direction.

Finally they arrived on Av. du Colonel Henri-Rol Tanguy, where chaos reigned. Vehicles with wailing sirens and flashing lights blocked the street, law enforcers attempted with precious little success to direct the masses to safety—

—and there was something else. A susurrus that filled Lincoln's head like a swarm of bees.

The dead were screaming. And they were many.

They surged forth from the tourist entrance to the Catacombs. Barely more than skeletons encased within veneers of fascia, they nevertheless ambulated quite swiftly.

Antoinette sensed immediately they were like her—resurrected, but only partially. "The dead rise! Surely it is Judgment Day," she proclaimed.

"Nonsense," sniffed Curie. She could rationalize their personal resurrections as the results of de Nostredame's foreign, forgotten science, but refused to believe in Biblical fairy tales. "They are merely ill. Plague carriers of some sort."

A cluster of the swiftly shuffling wretches fell upon a screaming young man and drove him to the ground. They clamped teeth upon exposed flesh and began worrying it from his bones like starving hounds.

"You were saying?" Antoinette cast a sideways look at her skeptical companion.

Curie recoiled. "It would appear their pathology involves more than a touch of lunacy."

Lincoln clutched the sides of her head. "They are so loud... so many... such *hunger*." Her wide-eyed gaze darted between Antoinette and Curie. "They are incoherent with terror and overwhelming emptiness. They would devour the *world*!"

She screwed her eyes shut, sensing something beneath the noisome chatter. A directive had driven the dead from their subterranean sepulcher. She concentrated, seeking to sort command from cacophony.

Curie observed Lincoln's struggle empathetically. Each of them had experienced side effects from their revivals. Mary Lincoln's manifested as the ability to hear and visualize residual energies of the deceased— what the more fanciful called ghosts. Marie Antoinette developed enhanced strength and seeming invulnerability, as though her revivified body refused to be dragged back to the grave. As for her, an element of what had caused her brief demise remained within, now fully hers to control.

Curie observed as the afflicted fell on more terrified victims. Curiously, those who'd already gorged on the living were regaining more of themselves. Muscles thickened, veins inflated, and nervous systems branched across bones. Skin, albeit cankered and yellow-green, stretched to cover skulls, trunks, and limbs.

Curie began rubbing her palms together vigorously until her hands shone silvery-gray, then shouted, "Stop this madness! Please allow the authorities to assist you. Don't expose others to your disease!"

"Truly, Madame?" Antoinette rolled her eyes. "Mary, can you quell them?"

Lincoln attempted to reach one, then another, but these returnees from beyond the veil were insentient; naught but creatures of torment and craving and pain and... "I cannot," she managed through gritted teeth. "Their souls have not returned. Consciousness... gone. Only perception of the incomprehensible void remains."

"Mon Dieu." Antoinette wrapped her in a steadying embrace. "Madame, our Mary cannot reach them! You must *make* them stop."

Based on her observations and this input, Curie discarded her original hypothesis and accepted Antoinette's. At least the undead queen retained her fundamental humanity. These were monsters.

"Someone is behind this." Lincoln could sense the impetus driving the dead intermittently. "I feel... they are close."

Regardless of cause, Curie knew she must eradicate the symptom. These husks were insatiable, but that wouldn't stop them from trying to consume every last person in Paris. Resolved, she flexed her silver-gray fingers until they emitted a blue glow.

Glancing to her right, Curie spotted a terrified mother huddled over her small son, who had tripped on the curb. The starving dead closed in around them.

She thrust both hands, fingers splayed, at the monstrosities.

Her fingers emitted rays of blinding blue light. Ten of the reanimated exploded into flames and burned with such speed and intensity that, within seconds, only piles of ash remained.

Curie advanced, releasing her polonium beams. Unable to execute broad sweeps, the process was less efficient than desired. She clenched her jaw as beads of silvery perspiration bubbled out of her pores and evaporated, surrounding her in a bluish aura.

Antoinette knew from previous experience that Curie could only expend so much of the force within her at a time. Already her rays weakened, and there were still so many dead everywhere.

Her extensive travels through time had exposed Antoinette to multitudes of people and their struggles, of which she had been blissfully ignorant in life due to her privileged, isolated upbringing. Her empathy for others had blossomed over time, so the threat of innocents being slaughtered stirred desperation within her bosom. Grasping Lincoln's arms, she cried, "What shall we do?"

"You forget your strength, Your Majesty." Lincoln winced, but found herself grateful for the external pain. It distracted her from the maelstrom within, allowing her to recover a modicum of control. She tamped down the noise to a bearable, if steady, buzz.

"Apologies, dear friend." Antoinette released her.

Lincoln observed Curie's waning defense and pondered. Although Cagliostro had never before utilized necromancy, he was surely capable of such perversion. As if in confirmation, she heard the subliminal command to *rise* in his familiar accent.

"This *is* Cagliostro's heretical work." Lincoln clenched her fists. "Resurrecting so many in such a state—it is an affront to God!" She battled the throbbing in her skull to formulate a plan. "While these miserable corpses crave human flesh, they do not attack one another. Therefore, it is possible that because your flesh is not…" She fumbled for a polite way to state the obvious. "Since you, ah…"

Antoinette waved away her discomfiture. "Because my flesh is as dead as theirs, I might move among them unopposed."

"And escort me safely to the Catacombs' entrance. Then, while you and Madame Marie defend the living above, I will hunt Cagliostro below."

Antoinette's eyes widened. "Alone? No, this is far too dangerous!"

Lincoln forced a brief smile. "I must, for the sake of all these innocents. I am scant use in battle, but fully capable of locating our foe. And I sense he lurks beneath these streets."

Antoinette looked around and made a moue of uncertainty. "In Paris, the dead far outnumber the living."

Lincoln nodded. "They have the advantage of numbers. But they are also mindless, while we three have our wits and talents. I am confident we shall prevail."

"Bien sûr." Antoinette grinned and nodded. "Very well. Follow me."

She strode directly into a cluster of the reanimated. They paid the former monarch no more mind than they did one another.

One lunged at a teenaged girl. Antoinette grabbed its bony neck, hefted, and slammed it into the ground. Bones snapped like twigs. The teenager glanced at Antoinette, then fled shrieking into the crowd.

"Not even a merci." Antoinette mourned this era's lack of etiquette.

Plucking another corpse from its milieu, she hurled it against the wall of a nearby Metro station. Its skull exploded into powder in a most satisfying fashion. Antoinette clapped and exclaimed, "La reine des morts et arrivée!"

Her excitement grew as she dismantled every corpse that had the misfortune of crossing her path. Although she never dared confess it to her friends, a part of her reveled in these opportunities to let loose. She cackled gleefully while tearing the ambulatory corpses limb from limb and crushing their bones beneath her red-soled pumps.

Lincoln followed cautiously in her wake. She spied Curie across the way and waved, but her friend's attention remained on a phalanx of the dead ignoring bullets fired by the recently arrived gendarmerie. As officers backpedaled desperately, Curie sprang forward, fingers unfurling to release her beams.

They finally reached the entrance to the Catacombs. "Be cautious," Antoinette advised. "Cagliostro, he is a snake."

"I am all too aware, but we have successfully routed him before."

"Yet he always manages to slither free of permanent consequences." Antoinette's grudge against him was quite personal due to his involvement in L'affaire du Collier, the theft of a near-priceless diamond necklace that she was falsely accused of arranging. It resulted in her losing favor with the people of France, paving her way to the guillotine.

Lincoln reached for her friend's hands, observed they were dripping with gore, and patted her shoulders awkwardly instead. "Have faith in me, as I do in you and Madame Marie." Steeling herself, she plunged through the stone archway into the darkness below.

L incoln clung to the shadows and ducked into crevices to avoid the undead, but soon realized they were disinterested. It appeared their hunger for living flesh did not activate until they exited the Catacombs—a delay she realized Cagliostro must have woven into his working as a safeguard against falling victim to his own creations.

The command source strengthened as she approached its location. Squeezing through narrow openings and claustrophobia-inducing tunnels, she lit the way using a small electrical torch from her mission kit.

At last she emerged into a spacious cavern. Dozens of partially melted black candles had been set around its perimeter, providing enough light that she stowed her torch.

Then she spotted the body.

It lay in the middle of the cavern, next to a deliberately stacked pile of rocks. A frisson shook her, less attributable to the sight of the corpse than to what rested atop the makeshift podium.

She recognized the open book immediately. de Nostredame had sent them to retrieve it during their first deployment against Cagliostro: the infernal *La Très Sainte Trinosophie*, The Most Holy Threefold Wisdom, a tome of occult, alchemical, and divine mysticism. For ages, this fount of power had fueled its author, the wanderer Count St. Germain—and later his pupil, Cagliostro.

"But however did you retrieve it?" Lincoln murmured. Her team had seized the book after arranging for the Inquisition to imprison Cagliostro in the eighteenth century. They had safely deposited it in the Library de Troyes, where the librarians served as guardians of esoteric and dangerous literature.

She approached Cagliostro's body. No doubt it was him; she would recognize his bulging eyes, weak chin, and sparse white curls anywhere. "And how are you, who stole fruit from the Tree of Life itself, finally deceased?"

"These are very good questions, mio signora," said Cagliostro, or rather his shade, which rose from his corpse to face her in all its translucent glory. "I shall be happy to answer them, but only if you help me undo," he gesticulated at his body, "*this*."

"**H**ow could you let her go alone? She's vulnerable physically and mentally!" Curie's aura flared, then waned from exhaustion. The dead kept coming with no end in sight.

One advanced from Curie's left, jaws snapping. Antoinette ripped out its spinal column and the rest flopped to the ground. "You underestimate our sister-in-arms," she rebuked gently. "She might have been fragile in life, but in rebirth, our Mary is a force of nature."

Curie blasted the base of a light post, sending it crashing down on a column of undead. They thrashed helplessly beneath the steel pole. The uniformed schoolchildren they'd been menacing escaped into a nearby shop. "She follows voices in her head!"

"Which have helped us before."

"I remain unconvinced they are more than her own delusion mixed with intuition, and perhaps a dollop of extrasensory perception." The practical scientist sighed and rubbed already-raw palms together, preparing a fresh onslaught. "I wager she did not take her medication as advised."

Antoinette shrugged. "We may yet thank her for that disobedience, if it allows her to stop Cagliostro before his legions overwhelm us." She pulled off her shoes and regarded their broken heels, downcast. "Zut. I *loved* these Louboutins." She slipped them back on, growled, and surged through a cluster of corpses. Skulls and femurs and ribcages flew in her wake.

Curie narrowly dodged a grasping cadaver. "I hope you are right, for if we fail, the dead will conquer the living. And the rest of the world will have no choice but to destroy all."

"S o you stole the book, replaced it with a forgery so the librarians would not know, and used it to raise the dead... only to have it *backfire?*" Lincoln glared at Cagliostro's shade hovering beside her.

"The first bit was clever, no? As for the last... in my defense, the instructions were unclear." He twisted his thin lips wryly. "Master St. Germain, always too focused on flowery prose over clarity. And so I missed that the working required an immortal lifeforce."

He gestured to the book lying open between them. "Now repeat the words *exactly* as you envision through me, capisci? Any variation—"

"The wards will trigger, the dispelling will fail, and we will die," Lincoln snapped. "I understood the first time!"

"Forgive me if I am unused to placing my faith in the ignorante!" He hunched his spectral shoulders. "Eh, but given the dead cannot work magic, I have no other choice but to do so."

"So long as you understand my only goal is to save *their* lives." She pointed up.

"Cara, I do not give a single whit *why*, just so long as you *do*." He released a ghostly sigh. "Your ability is exactly what I require. You must see through the filter of my mind beyond the words and illuminations to the spell beneath. Shall we begin?"

Lincoln's heart pounded. Everything inside her rebelled at the thought of communion with the notoriously faithless Cagliostro. But without another option, she simply had to trust that so long as their goals aligned, he would not lead her astray.

C urie's beams abruptly blinked out. She fell to one knee, vision blurring, gasping for breath.

The dead marched toward her. She lacked the strength to rise, much less run.

The indefatigable Antoinette reappeared to smash and rend the advance. Though appreciative, Curie realized she could not be relegated to the defense of one person while others fell. "Go," Curie panted. "I will... manage on my own."

"Do not ask me to abandon you." Antoinette patted Curie's head. "I will clear these away, then pursue the rest."

Curie shook her head. "There are… too many. Even for a mighty queen." She struggled to regain her footing, but her body would not obey. "I just need… a moment."

Antoinette's nature was to deny the hopelessness of unwinnable odds. "I will give you that moment. Do not fret. Have faith in our Mary."

More corpses approached, at least ten deep. Curie swallowed against the growing knot in her throat. "Whatever Mary's plan, let's hope she executes it swiftly."

L incoln recognized few of the words she recited, as the chant shifted between multiple languages. Nevertheless, she felt its power. The cavern filled with golden firefly sparks.

Reading such blasphemy through the filter of Cagliostro's consciousness was sickening. She kept reminding herself that tainting her soul was a small price to pay for saving innumerable others.

Cagliostro's shade blazed brighter. "Tutto qui, one final passage!" He pointed a translucent finger at the image of a dark angel near the bottom of the page. "You see it, si?"

Words swam into focus beneath the illumination, and relief stirred within Lincoln's bosom. Soon she could sever the connection to this wicked spirit, and the dead would return to their rest. She sensed Cagliostro's anticipation, along with—

Something else. Something *wrong.*

The spectral count radiated eagerness for her to read the next passage. Probing his thoughts, she caught onto his game. "An impressive feint. You nearly fooled me."

His spirit dimmed. "Whatever do you mean?" He pressed his right hand to his chest and widened his eyes.

"I may not understand all these languages, but *you* do. Did you forget our thoughts were intermingled, deceiver?"

"Just say the words, you milquetoast mucca!" His shade elongated to loom above her, eyes shining black with fury.

Lincoln was unimpressed. Her gift had taught her that the rage of ghosts was mostly impotent—especially when facing someone capable of pitting her living will against the dissolute desires of the dead.

She stared defiantly into those blazing black eyes. "You might be an expert warlock in life," she snarled. "But as a ghost you are completely unpracticed... and outmatched."

Lincoln plunged deeply into Cagliostro's consciousness. She forced their gaze back to the book, and scanned for other phrases hidden within the page until she located one in particular—

"Not that!" The shade shrank down and flickered. "All right, bene! There is another conclusion to the spell."

"And which were you trying to trick me into reading?"

"The one that would... dannazione!" His head bowed. "Transfer my spirit into your body. Temporarily, mind you! Just long enough to figure out how to restore myself without withdrawing my lifeforce and terminating the reanimation spell."

Lincoln jabbed her fingertip at the phrase that had alarmed him. "So I should actually read this one, hm?" She intoned the first word.

The disembodied sorcerer waved his arms frantically. "Per favore, no! If you finish that, I cease to exist!"

"Yet the dead shall rest once more?" She curled her lips into a feral grin. "That seems an ideal outcome."

Cagliostro clasped his hands. "This is quite unnecessary. I apologize for my deception. Just... please, read this third passage instead, and all will turn out as originally agreed."

She glared at his pleading visage for several heartbeats before relenting. While he had attempted to betray her, and was already dead due to his own misadventure, eliminating his shade still felt like murder. And as the widow of a murdered man, she considered no act more despicable.

A ntoinette roared as she tore through a veritable platoon of the undead. Yet far too many eluded her wrath and continued pursuing the living.

Fortunately, most of the latter had found shelter indoors—even the police and gendarmerie had withdrawn. Unfortunately, the dead were fast. As they invaded surrounding neighborhoods, distant screams made it clear not everyone had found shelter in time.

Curie's palms bled. She needed more time to recharge. Ironically, that was the one commodity they lacked.

The dead closed ranks, cutting her off from Antoinette. They reached with rotted fingers curved into claws, slavering jaws snapping—

Then, as one, the animated corpses collapsed.

Curie blinked, unable to credit the evidence of her eyes. But it was true; the dead had fallen, bodies reverting to dusty, skeletal remains.

Antoinette returned to Curie's side clutching a pair of tibias. She tossed them aside merrily. "Triomphe!"

"It would appear you were right about our Mary." Curie chuckled, weary but relieved.

"Oh, I do like when you admit I am right." Antoinette grinned. "Shall we join our sister below then? She might yet require assistance with," she spat, "le serpent!"

B ack in Le Petit Trianon du Temps, the ladies were being debriefed. "Cagliostro lives," Lincoln concluded. "I know it was the moral and ethical choice to restore him, yet—"

"It's unfortunate the coward scampered off once revived," sighed Curie. "If only we'd reached you sooner."

"Oui." Antoinette cracked her knuckles loudly. "If only."

"But not all was lost." Curie glanced at *La Très Sainte Trinosophie* on the tea table. Lincoln had managed to wrest it from Cagliostro, who'd been weakened by his recent discorporation. "We'll return the real book to the Library of Troyes. Countless lives have been saved, and France stands."

"You performed admirably," de Nostredame assured them. "While this unholy disruption cannot be entirely erased, the authorities will proclaim it a terrorist attack. As those occurred periodically during this time, their obfuscation will ultimately minimize the damage to the True Timeline."

"Cagliostro raised an army of the dead with full intention of leading them into Armageddon." Lincoln shivered. "Thankfully he overreached, but I fear what he might accomplish with his ever-increasing audacity."

"Rightly so," said de Nostredame solemnly. "However, until I envision his next threat, please rest. Celebrate your victory. À bientôt, mes anges."

Curie gestured at the mantle controls. "Where shall we go to enjoy our downtime, my dears?" She winked. "Or should I ask, when?"

The Last Act at the Time Cabaret
Adam-Troy Castro

The great man tumbled through a gray void, not knowing where he was or how he had gotten here, a predicament that rankled him because he saw himself as an accomplished explorer and cartographer whose sense of place, and of the routes between places, was not subject to error.

He had been a soldier. He had been a would-be conqueror, intent on starting an empire in California. He had been an author and he had been a businessman and he had been a leader of men. He did not know the specifics, not even his name. All these names had been withheld from him, perhaps (he thought) because one could not be allowed full understanding of one's own deeds, before arriving at the destination that awaits us all. But he was confident. He had the sense of himself that he had always carried, that of a great man, a visionary and leader.

Still, he sifted through his fragmentary memory. The only thing he could recall was being wracked by illness, in the Virgin Islands, where he was doing what he had done many times, offer travelers the benefit of his expertise. Yellow Fever, somebody said.

Then he found himself sitting on the edge of a bed in a well-appointed hotel room. It was a soft bed, one of the most luxurious he, who had braved hardship in the pursuit of his goals, had ever known. The curtains were drawn to reveal a vast plain, beneath a merciless midday sun. The air was hot, but a powerful breeze blew through, and he detected colder weather, coming soon. It took the mountains in the distance, little nubs on an otherwise razor-sharp horizon, to identify the location for him. He remembered this place, but he did not remember why.

A man in an oddly-cut suit, without a collar or tie, stood before him. His complexion was neither white nor black, but sepia in the matter of an art that had been in its infancy, last he saw it: portrait photography. "Before you ask, Lansford Hastings. You are not dead, not in the way that the men of your time understood; and this place is neither Heaven nor Hell. You are on the terrestrial plane."

Lansford Hastings said, "Where am I?"

"The question is not where, but when. You are far in your future. We have technology that can reach back through the years and reproduce the essence of those that lived before us, for reproduction in our era. We use this to plumb history, to garner the wisdom of the ancients, and to recruit the talents of those who came before. We assure you that will not deprive you of one actual moment you enjoyed during your natural life. You are a reproduction, but in every other way, the man you were."

Hastings struggled with the concept. "I am... a time photograph."

"That is a simplification, but a helpful one."

"And you have chosen me for a purpose?"

"Yes, sir."

It was not this simple, of course. Hastings was a man of a simpler time, confronted by what his contemporary self would have considered madness. He came, in fact, from an era before "time travel" was a well-known fictional trope, and he required an explanation involving the fourth dimension and the premise of the photocopier before he accepted what he was being told. The conversation repeated itself many times. But in the end, the premise exerted himself, and he was not displeased. It was good to be useful, to receive confirmation that everything that was special about him would be valued by some future era. But then he said, "I don't know what use I can be when I do not remember my life in any detail."

"The memories will take some time to catch up with the flesh. They will come. You will be fully yourself by tomorrow morning."

"And tonight?"

"Tonight you will be our honored guest. I preside over a cabaret of sorts, where the great entertainers of the past are brought forth to amuse us and our honored guests. It is especially important in your case, as two of those entertainers will be critical to your task. You will watch both perform tonight. I promise not just that you will find them fascinating, but that they will be a fine prelude to the restoration of your full mental and physical powers."

Hastings felt good already. He had died a robust man—except for the dying part, of course—but he had by that age learned what all men must, that as soon as adulthood begins, the process of physical decay does too. He had catalogued the tasks that had become more difficult, the eagerness of pains to take root, the measurable differences in the effort it cost him to climb steep slopes. He did not feel fifty anymore; he felt like a robust youngster of thirty. He rose, discovering as he did that he was wearing a suit that he remembered being one of his favorites, once upon a time, and that it was as fine as it had been on the day he had first worn it.

It may have been the fog that persisted in concealing his memories, but he discovered that he was honored and looking forward to whatever challenges awaited him.

He was, after all, about nothing if not pride. "I am at your disposal, sir."

"Capital!" said Everett Fawn.

A maid came to draw the bath. It was steaming, just as Lansford Hastings would have preferred it, and as he soaked he was treated to cigars of exceptional quality, well beyond those available in his time. After a lazy afternoon he clad himself in the superb suit that had been provided him, one that befit the fashions of his time more than the apparent style of Fawn's, and he descended the stairs to the main hall, a place occupied by many dozens of men and women in many styles of clothing, most of which were bizarre to him.

Fawn came around and introduced him to some of the figures, including an Akira Kurosawa and an Amelia Earhart and a Nellie Bly and a Barack Obama and a Norman Borlaug and a Harlan Ellison and a Sally Ride and a Judi Castro, and he found them all charming puzzles whose own greatness in life could not be discerned before he was whisked away and introduced to others.

At length he was brought to the veranda, where he breathed deep of the cold desert air and looked out upon the mountains, majestic and familiar: the gateway to empire, he thought, though the relevance of that phrase remained a naggingly familiar mystery to him.

"This place was important to me," he told Everett Fawn.

"Yes," Fawn said, "indeed it was. This establishment can generate any environment, at any scale; and on this occasion we have chosen a vista critical to you, that will be vital to our purposes tomorrow. But come; the sun is setting, and the cabaret awaits."

He allowed Fawn to escort him through the vast and elegant interior of his establishment to a wing that featured a luxurious amphitheater where hundreds of fellow guests sat in semicircular booths overlooking a distant stage, and where he was directed to one particular table as Fawn's guest. The other two seats at the table were unoccupied at the moment, reserved for other guests who Fawn said would be joining Hastings in tomorrow's great adventure. Drinks were served, the lights came down, and the curtains rose, revealing a number of acts that while impressive never would have been headliners in Hastings's own time: a young woman with crossed eyes and an unfortunate nose who belted out songs of strange tempo in an operatic voice; four strangely made-up brothers running amuck to the consternation of an elegant society matron; a fellow who did rope tricks while regaling the audience with various bits of homespun wisdom. Each time the curtains closed, there was a long silence before the next act. Hastings sat through it all, not knowing how this theatrical exercise was relevant to him, or to anyone. But the food was sumptuous, and the drink even better, and it all rendered the confused Hastings as logy as he was game.

Then the four young British men with the oddly discordant music left the stage, and Fawn said, "The next two acts were recruited specifically to aid in your great adventure."

The curtain rose.

A man in a poorly tailored suit, tight jacket and baggy pants, emerged from off-stage, running backward to stay upright atop a careening barrel. He managed to make it look like he was terrified and like this ride was difficult, but it must have required great athleticism to perform this feat at all, and it was absolutely terrifying when the barrel crashed into an obstruction and the man went flying into a pigpen and landed atop a gigantic hog. The beast reacted to the sudden weight on its back by screeching and bursting free of its enclosure, with the man—apparently a clown of some sort—holding on for dear life. The audience howled as he was tossed free and deposited in a pile of debris, beneath a false brick wall that then collapsed on him. Thunderous applause ensued, and the curtain fell.

"Billie Ritchie," Fawn supplied.

"I do not know the name."

"Of course you would not. He convulsed his stage audiences, and later audiences of a medium called film that captured his antics for later display in distant locations, long after you breathed your last. You never would have heard of him. But he possessed an extraordinary, even foolish, daring. You can tell that he cared little for the risks he took, as long as he made people laugh. It made him a perfect partner for the enterprise that begins tomorrow."

The intermission lasted long minutes, and after a bit, Ritchie came by looking only a little worse than wear, among his injuries a great purple bruise on his forehead. His demeanor bespoke an intelligence greater than the buffoon he had played on stage. But he still wore his performance gear, that tight jacket and those baggy pants, along with a comically fllexible bamboo cane, all apparent measures to produce the persona of a vagabond who had clothed himself out of salvaged clothing. He tipped his funny little dome of a hat to Hastings, and took his place at the table.

"You are very funny," Hastings said politely—and it was only politeness, because he thought the act crass buffoonery—"but I found myself worried for you."

"That's what made it funny," Ritchie replied, in a heavy Scottish accent that reminded Hastings, somehow, of vaguely recalled pioneers from his travels.

"Do you always take such risks?"

"Guv, I would follow a laugh to my grave. That's the nature of the business. Anything to beat that talentless thief, Chaplin."

The name "Chaplin" had been spoken with such special vehemence that Hastings repeated it. "Chaplin?"

"I came to America years and years before that young pup did, and developed this character for the stage, long before he put on his own pair of baggy pants for the pictures. I tell you that he stole every gag he ever played from me, and it's been a case of him on top and me playing catch-up ever since. I tell you, it's time someone knocked him off his pedestal, and as soon as we make the next film, that's exactly what I'm going to do."

Fawn broke in. "Billie works with a very audacious director named Henry Lehrmann. His technique is always adding unexpected elements, that the performers have to confront and deal with. He once released actual African lions onto the stage, and got great laughs when the terrified performers leaped out the windows. And then, of course, there was the time with the high-pressure water hose that blasted Billie here thirty feet into the air."

"I didn't see that one coming at all," Ritchie admitted. "I almost broke my fool neck. But it got a colossal laugh."

"The next one will involve ostriches, am I correct?"

"Yes. I'm not looking forward to it, really. In the first place I've done it before, for this picture I did a few years ago; hopped on the big bird's back, and wrestled with it, and I have to tell you that my ribs hurt for days. Mean, nasty thing. But it's the nature of the business, as I say, and if I do it right, I'll make the rubes forget all about Chaplin. Why, if he—" Then he noticed the house lights dimming, and he grinned widely beneath his paintbrush mustache. "Oh, here comes the next one. I know of this fellow. I heard of him when I was a lad. He's a legend."

The amplified voice of an announcer cried, "And now, the toast of Paris: that brilliant entertainer Joseph Pujol, The Great Le Petomaine!"

The curtain rose, and a newcomer entered to thunderous applause. Something was wrong with his tuxedo, and Hastings puzzled over just what before recoiling in shock. The pants had been altered by cutting out the seat, revealing the man's pale white buttocks in what Hastings presumed to have been regarded as all their glory. They seemed no more special than other buttocks, and for one mad interval Hastings supposed that this man must have come from an era in which this was, God help all mankind, the fashion.

"Good Lord," Hastings exclaimed. "Are you saying that—"

Ritchie shushed him. "I don't want to miss this."

As the act went on, it became clear that the unusual tailoring was a necessary feature of the act performed by Pujol, which was—he carefully explained at the onset—that of a "Fartiste."

Because, yes, Pujol was a trick farter.

His intestinal control was superhuman.

He inserted a rubber tube into a jar of water, with the other end up his rectum, and inhaled it all, at which point he could lean over and expel the liquid twenty feet to extinguish a candle burning in a holder on the stage. He demonstrated that he could aim his expulsions of air with precision, announcing which of three burning candles he would blow out before keeping the promise.

He did impressions. One light fart was a virginal bride on her wedding night; the next was as deep as a tuba and represented the same maiden the next morning. He performed the fart of a proper gentleman avoiding scandal in church, and the great basso profundo the man was able to release once he was safely at home.

He farted in national accents: a German, an Englishman, an American.

He farted Mozart and Beethoven. He farted a composition from an era far beyond his own, which he called the theme from *The Good, The Bad, and The Ugly*. He farted bird calls. He lay face down on the ground and kept a pink feather dancing aloft, with multiple blasts.

His patter was in French, but Hastings had some knowledge of the tongue and got the set-up to each joke, not that it seemed Pujol needed it; as a comedian, his timing was impeccable, and as a performer, he had that combination of inspiration and stage presence that set the audience to hysterical laughter, even when the gaseous eruptions were in some way beholden to local French politics.

Ritchie applauded wildly. "The toast of Paris," he exclaimed. "I met someone who saw him perform once, and he never stopped talking about it. What a sensation!"

Hastings, whose shock had given way to embarrassed laughter, said, "And people actually paid money to see him?"

"More than once, sometimes. He sold out the theatre, for years, and I'm surprised that you're surprised. He's amazing, he is."

Pujol ended his performance by using his intestinal vapors to play the cannon fusillade to accompany the house orchestra's performance of the finale to the *1812 Overture*, and received a standing ovation. The curtain came down, and another intermission descended before whatever no doubt even more repellent madness arrived to up the stakes.

Hastings said, "What strange entertainments the future has!"

"The past as well," Fawn told him. "The Romans had the coliseum, the future has Thanos snapping his fingers. It is too bad Lady Gaga is not here with us tonight; she could likely outstage even Le Petomaine. But, ah, here is the man himself."

Pujol arrived at their table, all smiles and handshakes. He still wore the special cutaway pants, with the wildly accomplished buttocks still clearly visible, and as he slid into his place at the table, Hastings had maniacal thoughts about how the material of the booth must have felt, to his unprotected skin.

The two entertainers at the table started to praise each other at length. Pujol was effusive in his lightly accented version of English. "I am honored, my Scottish friend! You are such a master of the pantomime, I am humbled in your presence!"

"I'm good at falling over," Ritchie said, modestly enough. "But I only play the fool. You play your entire digestive system."

"Not the system in its entire, my friend. That would be an orchestra and I only have a flute. But I am very practiced in my one chosen instrument. Do you know that before I came to Paris I was in the army, and used my little gift to delight my fellow soldiers in the barracks? It was my uniformed friends who suggested that I take the act to the Paris stage, and so I did; and so I have prospered." He looked at Hastings. "And you are the mapmaker, Hastings? The one who will join us in our task, tomorrow?"

"I am," Hastings replied, "but I trust that you will not be offended when I report that I do not know what deed I can possibly be needed for, in the company of a man who wrestles ostriches and another who breaks wind for a living."

Pujol said, "I am told that it involves redress for a great injustice."

"That is new to me," Hastings replied, "I have been told nothing."

Ritchie plucked a roll from its basket, buttering it with a dainty flick of his knife. "It will be a great thing, whatever it is. I just hope it gets a larf."

About the time it became clear that the cabaret never ended, that there was always another act waiting in the wings no matter when in the course of the day a given audience member sat down to enjoy whatever spectacle the curtains separated to reveal, Mr. Fawn suggested that it was time Hastings rested up for his still-unspecified adventure the next morning. He escorted Hastings to his room in the highest reaches of the sprawling, labyrinthine passages of the way station.

"Bizarre people," Hastings said, as soon as he was sure that no one but Fawn would hear him.

Fawn chuckled. "If I have learned nothing about people in my career traveling through time, it is that history is random and influenced, mostly, by bizarre people. You were a strange man yourself, Hastings, with your ambitions of a new American Empire in California; in your belief that you could lead others to vast quantities of gold in the Amazon basin. Many of your time must have considered you mad."

"I prefer visionary," Hastings replied.

"As you wish."

"In any event," Hastings said, "I am not as mad as a man who performs gaseous eruptions for a living!"

"Pujol? I believe you do him an injustice, sir. He was as sane as a man could be, putting his one bizarre talent to use, earning enough to earn his keep for the rest of his life. He made people happy, and then he retired from stage performance for a life with his family. In his personal life, he was beloved. Those who knew him considered him a saint. That is not madness, sir."

"Then that Ritchie fellow. Wrestling with wild animals to make people laugh!"

"There you might have a stronger case, sir. We have spared him the memory of his fate, but not far in the future of the man you met, that wildly irresponsible director of his, Lehrmann, will set more ostriches loose on the soundstage, without any care to what they might do, and they will attack poor Ritchie into permanent disability. For the two years he will linger in significant agony, until a completely unconnected case of stomach cancer takes him, he will never leave his bed again."

Hastings winced. He had actually liked the Scotsman, and enjoyed his company. His personal contempt for the man's career choices—for the career choices of any entertainer, really, when there were more serious contributions to be made—had not translated to wishing the man ill. "The wages of madness, surely."

"Still not madness," Fawn said. "He is perhaps reckless and foolish. But mad? He lived in an era when performers fell down stairs, crashed through windows, and even fired real guns at one another, to create the spectacles that the audience expected; a time when his profession will spawn entire generations of what will come to be known as 'stunt performers,' people whose entire professional lives will be spent taking such risks to further the illusion of the stories being told. Billie Ritchie had the extra, added motivation of living in the shadow of that Chaplin fellow, an undisputed genius of comedy whose skill with character and pathos made him an international icon that Ritchie could never be. He and two colleagues named Buster Keaton and Stan Laurel were here the other night, sir, acting as a trio, and they were brilliant, absolutely brilliant, and if mad, mad only in the way that furthered their art. No, they do not fit my definition of madness."

"Ego," said Hastings.

"Absolutely. But not just ego, sir. Not in Ritchie's case. It was also desperation. Desperation for all the things we are all desperate for: appreciation, prosperity, advancement beyond what our humble beginnings dictate for us. Billie Ritchie had more character flaws than I perhaps have time to tell you, sir, notably a certain cruelty to his humor that may have been better hidden in the work of his great rival Chaplin, but in the end, Billie Ritchie only wanted to make his life better, and it was in the service of that dream that he allowed that irresponsible director of his to urge him toward ever-riskier risks, up to the very point of his own destruction. How is he different from so many of the desperate, the hungry, and the yearning from your own time? Those who also ached for their lives to be better, and whose only sin was finding counsel in the wrong places?"

Hastings had nothing to say to that. He could only offer, "But without risk, one cannot accomplish great things."

"Perhaps not, sir. But we should discuss this further tomorrow. It is late, and we are at your room."

Hastings stopped at the door, his hand on the knob, and for some time he stood there, head bowed with a silent discomfort that all but paralyzed him. He said, "Those others. Billie. Joseph. They may have been fools, but they knew who they were."

"Correct, sir."

"Why don't I know who I am?"

"You are Lansford Hastings. An important man. A man who wanted to create a new empire in California."

"And?"

"We should discuss this tomorrow morning."

What followed for Lansford Hastings was a night of uneasy dreams, followed by an early-morning visit to a valet who saw to it that he dressed in comfortable attire and followed him down a long corridor to an exit that deposited him in a part of the grounds he had not seen before.

There he found Fawn and Ritchie and Pujol waiting for him. And not just those three men, but behind them a flock of thousands of ostriches, larger in individual than he had ever known that exotic bird could be, all milling about with what amounted to politeness as Ritchie sat in the saddle that had been fitted to the largest and what seemed to be the fiercest of all the birds. Pujol stood not far away, clad in fresh pants with the seat cut out, and he looked odd, even by the standards of the prior night: colder, more furious. The familiar mountains were a grey line to the distant west.

"I... don't understand."

"The ostriches?" Fawn asked. "They are not the specimens you would find in Africa. They are a special engineered species, designed especially for today's activities. They are hardier and more durable and more intelligent, and they will be gentle with Mr. Ritchie... if not with you."

"I still don't understand."

"You are a madman, Mr. Hastings. You do not rant and rave, but you are capable of a sin that will cause more suffering than can be measured, in the centuries after yours. You treat expertise as a thing that you can achieve just by declaring it, and you lead unfortunate people to catastrophe just because they possessed the naiveté to believe in you."

Hastings was beginning to remember... something. It still remained foggy, though, and so he exclaimed, "In the name of all that is holy, tell me!"

"At a time in your country's history when ordinary people, families, packed their worldly goods in wagons and headed west to California in search of a brighter future—a risk as mad in its own way as what you attribute to Mr. Ritchie here—you drew a map outlining a faster and safer way over the mountains. You did this without ever visiting the region yourself. You called your route the Hastings Cutoff, and you told the people naïve enough to believe you that it would get them to California faster. But it was far more dangerous, Mr. Hastings; far more slow. It was a greater distance in miles, and it was across soft ground that slowed down the wagons, and through hostile territory where angry natives peppered their pack animals with arrows and gunfire.

"You, yourself, taking the same route only a few days ahead of them, managed to cross the divide before the snows laid an unpassable blanket over the mountains. But the party that came after you, the Donner Party, was fatally delayed by the additional hardships your fraudulent expertise laid upon them, and so they found themselves trapped in the pass by many feet of snow, which prevented them from going forward or going back. They starved, Mr. Hastings. Trapped for four months of 1846 and 1847 with minimal supplies and no means of finding food, they began to waste away, and those who lived were the ones who resorted to murder and cannibalism to survive. About forty men, women and children died, Mr. Hastings; and many of those who made it through were never the same."

Hastings remembered now; remembered every damn minute of it. He recalled the horror when the news came, and his own reaction to it. He protested, "But I led the rescue party! I went back into the mountains to save them!"

Fawn's gaze was pitiless. "Yes, you did."

"I made it! The people who came before me made it!"

Fawn smiled. "They did, sir. The Donners were slow. They were last in line. That cannot be denied.

"And that might have been enough to spare you the ordeal to follow, were it not for one thing.

"You did not learn a damn thing. Your next popular thesis, directed to the general public just as if you had any knowledge on which to base it, was a means of seeking gold in the Amazon rain forest. Another place you had never been. People died because of that one, as well.

"You were incapable of learning, Mr. Hastings—just as all the flat-Earthers and anti-Vaxxers and inane conspiracy theorists who followed you were incapable of learning. You eschewed the actual experts and took whatever came off the top of your head as knowledge, presented what would have been convenient to believe as gospel. You killed people, sir, and the sin you represent has persisted throughout the centuries, to the current day, still killing people.

"And so this is what we decided to do, to commemorate that, in the name of all the lives you destroyed. All the lives the people like you continue to destroy.

"The mountains to your west are the Sierra Nevada. It is late autumn, and if you start walking right now, and never rest except for sleep, taking the path you know, you might be able to forge your way past them, to a safe arrival in California, before the first snow comes. And it will come, Mr. Hastings, sooner than you would ever dare to believe. All you really require is speed.

"Mr. Ritchie, here, will make sure you keep up the pace. The ostriches he will lead will not take kindly to any delays, any pauses to rest. You will get rations to fuel you. You will get water to refresh you. You will get fifteen minutes of rest every two hours, a few more, all you can spare and not one minute more, at night. But if you ever pause longer than that, the ostriches led to Mr. Ritchie will start to peck and kick—and I promise you he can testify that it is very unpleasant. You will not be allowed to fall to your knees and give up. You will be pressed on, ever on. I believe that it will be close, but you might make it. If you press yourself to absolute exhaustion."

Now wild-eyed, Hastings regarded the flock of angry ostriches to his immediate east. They looked restless, hungry for the damage they were capable of inflicting on a fleeing man. They seemed pitiless, and they seemed to know that he was beseeching them. Billy Ritchie, seated aboard the flock leader, had the same expression, only sillier; whatever cruelty had fueled his humor in life was now distilled, fueling a dedication to his task that was only natural for a man who would do anything, go anywhere, for a laugh. Hastings could tell that the man would not show him mercy. Maybe this copy of him was crueler by far than the real man had been, maybe not. But it would not matter. Whatever he did, whatever he led his ostriches to do, would be cruel enough.

"Wait," said Lansford Hastings.

"Sorry," Mr. Fawn said. "Your time is short enough as it is. Daylight's wasting."

And then he turned to the man who performed under the name Le Petomaine and spoke the words that began the ordeal of Lansford Hastings.

"Mr. Pujol? If you'd please? Starting pistol in five seconds."

Joseph Pujol offered a courtly smile, and an expressive squat.

Never Meet Your Heroes
Eric Avedissian

The plan goes sideways when John Dillinger points a gun to my head.

Nose wrinkled, signature pencil-thin mustache twitching, Dillinger has other ideas about the heist.

My heist.

"Sorry, kiddo. We do things my way," Dillinger says, and clocks me in the mouth.

I taste copper and yank my rubber gorilla mask off. Blood droplets fall onto the tile floor. My legs buckle and I go down. A siren trills loudly.

Dillinger removes the ChronoJumper from my wrist.

Things never go as you plan. Every permutation of this job fails catastrophically, and my faith is about as shattered as my jaw.

"This is the most valuable item I've ever scored," I brag to my partner at dinner. We're in a posh Manhattan restaurant, the kind where you wipe your fingers with a hot napkin between courses.

Carly twirls linguine on her fork and stares at me with those baby blues.

"I don't see why we're celebrating. It's OmniGlom, Nick. The biggest corporate leviathan in the world. I can't hack into surveillance cameras and wipe you from their data logs forever. It's only a matter of time before they nail us," she says.

"Relax, Bisetti." I pull up my right shirtsleeve, revealing the metallic band strapped to my wrist. "We've got nothing but time now."

The band is sleek, silver, and all mine. A touchscreen flickers on, its liquid crystal display bursting with colorful icons from the most complicated software ever created.

Carly blinks. "Is that…"

"A ChronoJumper? Yes. Yes, it is."

"Holy crap, Nick! Why are you wearing it?"

"Because I lifted it from OnmiGlom. It could come in handy."

"Handy? What are you planning?"

"We're going to do a heist."

"A heist?"

"A heist."

Her eyes narrow. "What's the score?"

"Enough money for a private island far from OmniGlom's reach. Mixed drinks in our hands, swimming in caviar, newly minted members of the nouveau riche," I tell her.

"Nothing is far from OmniGlom's reach." Carly looks at her plate of half-eaten pasta, then back at me.

"Come on, Carly. I can't do this without you" I tap the time machine on my wrist. "And this little baby."

"Another heist, Nick? Really?"

"Hey, filthy lucre is the best kind of lucre."

"Who do we get for the crew?"

"That's the brilliant part. We go back in time and recruit three of the most notorious robbers from history. Three people who aren't barcoded and who OmniGlom can't track, but with enough skill to do the job."

Carly smirks. "Wait. This is *Time Bandits* meets *Bill and Ted*, right?"

"I see your love for vintage cinema is paying off."

Her smile vanishes. "Who do you have in mind, genius?"

"My heroes," I tell her. "Every one of them my heroes."

Extracting them from their times with the ChronoJumper was easy. Getting them acclimated to 2028 wasn't.

Edward Teach, known to history as Blackbeard, cowers and quakes under the safehouse's halogen lights. He reeks of rum and fish, and his coat is frayed and threadbare.

"Me ship! Where's the *Queen Anne's Revenge*?" Blackbeard asks. "Where's me crew, ye stinkin' bilge rat?"

"This isn't the Caribbean in 1717, Captain," I remind him.

Jesse James is young, rakish, and has crystalline clear blue eyes. He pulls a bandana from his face, revealing a stubble-coated chin. His hands reach down to his holster, but his signature Schofield is missing.

He grinds his teeth. "What'd you do with my hogleg, tenderfoot? Where's my brother Frank? And who the blazes are you, anyways?"

"The name's Nick Hugo, and I admire your exploits, Mr. James," I reply. "Your gun will be returned to you once you're back in 1876."

"What do you mean once I'm back…" James says, and trails off. "This ain't Northfield, Minnesota?"

"Far from it." I lift my tablet from the table and turn it on.

"Then where the Sam Hill am I?" James asks.

"The future." John Dillinger bolts upright, his sinewy body dominating the room. He runs his hands down his pinstripe jacket and flicks his fedora's brim. "Ain't that right, Nick?"

"That's right, Mr. Dillinger. Welcome to the year 2028."

Dillinger cracks his knuckles. "I knew something was up. You nabbing me at that bank in Ohio in '33. Saw you fiddling with that bracelet on your arm like Buck Rogers. You got some big idea for bringing us here?"

"A heist. We're hitting The Spire. Part private club, part bank, and all-exclusive. The Syndicate wets its beak regularly from its clientele, making this job particularly dangerous," I say.

Dillinger removes a cigarette case and flips it open. "You ain't some kind of G-man? One of Hoover's boys?"

"I assure you, J. Edgar is very dead," I reply. "As I said, I recruited you all for a heist."

Dillinger flicks a Zippo lighter and carefully unites the cigarette and flame. He takes a long drag and asks, "Let's hear it, hotshot. What's the score?"

"For me? Information I can sell to my black market contact. For you three? More money than you've ever seen," I tell them.

"A horde o' doubloons and pieces of eight? That'd fill me coffers nicely." Blackbeard rubs his hands.

"Don't get too excited, Captain. You've never defeated a 21st century security system." I point to the map on the flat screen, and control the presentation from my tablet. "If you finesse your way past the front desk into the elevators and bypass the security cameras to the tenth floor, if you don't set off the motion detectors and attract too much attention, you'll get to the executive offices before you reach the vault. Breaching those two-foot thick steel walls requires the manager's keycard and passcode. Alpha Team—a security force of cyborg soldiers—responds when the alarm is tripped, and in every simulation I've run, the alarm is always tripped. All we can do is buy ourselves enough time. That means precision, gentlemen."

James removes his Homburg. "Why us, mister? You coulda taken anyone from history, right? Why us?"

"In your own eras, society regarded you as renegades and criminals. Outlaws. Each one of you has the exact skills I'm looking for," I tell them.

"Skills?" Dillinger squints. "What skills?"

"You execute robberies with surgical precision, Mr. Dillinger. Jesse has firearms proficiency, while Blackbeard's strength and commanding presence make this a formidable crew. Carly can hack into the surveillance system, while my familiarity with the building's layout ensures this job's success." I tap the tablet and run the boys through a virtual simulation of the building's schematics.

After we discuss the plans, the boys explore the safehouse. They stare dumbstruck at the food in the refrigerator: the oat milk, kale salad, and veggie burgers on gluten-free bread. Dillinger blows smoke rings while gazing out the window at passing cars. The indoor plumbing and toilet mesmerize Blackbeard. James flips through channels on the plasma screen TV and lands on a classic Hollywood western.

While the boys are occupied, Carly pulls me aside.

"We worked together for seven years, and in all that time I trusted your judgment, but I have to be honest here." She sucks on the vape pen and puffs smoke from the corner of her mouth. "This isn't going to work, Nick. You could train circus monkeys to pull off a heist better than these three."

"Think of what we have here, Bisetti. History's most infamous thieves. They aren't afraid to dirty their hands." I'm practically beaming with every word.

Carly flips her pink hair from her eyes. "Really? What I see is a grown man playing with a pirate, a cowboy, and a gangster. Three things little boys play with each other. Tell me you're not regressing, Nick."

"Just because my heroes happen to be a pirate, a cowboy, and a gangster is irrelevant. Also, Jesse James wasn't even a cowboy. He was a guerilla fighter and militiaman before he turned to a life of crime." I flick the tablet, and the schematics for The Spire vanish.

"He was a pro-Confederate and his family owned slaves. Blackbeard sold captured slaves. All of them straight-up murdered people. You actually admire them?"

"Hey, nobody's perfect."

Carly nearly chokes on her vape pen. "Excuse me? I list why you should avoid these three assholes and your comeback is 'nobody's perfect'? What's next? Inviting Hitler, Lucrezia Borgia, and Caligula over for lunch?"

Recruiting a benevolent historical figure might be a logical choice for your average time traveler, but such lofty platitudes didn't interest me. Keep Abraham Lincoln, Gandhi, and Harriet Tubman in the past. To rob The Spire and stick it to the Syndicate, I need the best of the worst history has to offer.

That'd be my boys John Dillinger, Jesse James, and Blackbeard.

T he Spire is a cavernous tower of black marble, quartz, and polished steel cutting through Manhattan's cosmopolitan heart.

Carly, waiting in the escape van, hacks into the security system and disables the cameras on the ground floor.

We ascend via elevator (which Blackbeard and James think is a vibrating closet) to the trading room, and don our boiler suits and rubber gorilla masks.

I arm the boys with .357s.

"If anyone gives us trouble, wave your handguns at them like we planned," I say.

The elevator door opens.

It's show time.

Several people in business attire sit at computer terminals, busily typing on keyboards or talking into headsets. Before I can process anything, Dillinger shoots a junior executive in the throat. Blackbeard takes down another. James blasts one by the watercooler. Chaos erupts.

A klaxon sounds. We have a minute after tripping the alarm before Alpha Team rips through the outer office doors.

We corner the manager in his office. This isn't his first hostage rodeo, but unlike the drills he's practiced, the guns we have aren't firing blanks. Blackbeard and Dillinger frog-march him to the vault door. The manager refuses to cooperate. He's stalling, knowing we're struggling against a deadline before his armored protectors burst in guns a' blazing.

Jesse James levels his .357 to the manager's head and fires.

My ears ring from the shot. I wipe bits of the manager's brain from my boiler suit.

"What the hell did you do that for?" I demand.

"Ain't got no time for useless jawin' from him or from you." Jesse holds the gun to my temple. "Looks like I'm the one in charge of this here robbery now. Open the damn safe."

He grinds the barrel to my forehead. It hurts like hell. I can't breathe and my pulse quickens.

"I can't open the safe. The manager has the code, and you shot him." I point to the fresh corpse.

James whips off his mask. Perspiration glazes his face.

"Open it or I'll shoot you next," he says. "I shot Yankee blue-bellies and Pinkertons. Don't make no difference to me if you die, too."

"You have no idea what you're doing." I raise my hands above my head slowly. "Jesse, put the gun down. We don't have time for this."

James rubs his eyelids and lowers the .357 with a disgusted grunt. "This is my job now, you hear? With or without you."

He squeezes the trigger and sends a bullet into my shoulder and out the other side. A crimson stain seeps through the boiler suit. I tumble backwards and hit the ground.

Alpha Team breaches the hallway, their electric eyes glowing an ominous red. The Syndicate's logo is emblazoned on their black body armor, and their metallic hands clutch assault rifles.

My fingers graze the ChronoJumper's touchscreen. James stands over me. He's getting ready to fire again.

Lesson learned. Don't arm these assholes, I think before vanishing.

I reappear a half hour earlier and don't pack the guns except one I keep on me. My wound disappears, along with the bloodstains on my boiler suit.

This time, we make our way to the manager's office, grab his passcode, keycard, and knock him out cold. I fidget with the card in the vault's electronic lock. That's when I peer directly into the security camera over the vault.

The alarm sounds.

"What's happening, Nick?" Carly asks through the earpiece.

"Cameras," I tell her. "Can you disable them?"

"Working on it." The sound of her fingernails clacking on a keyboard fills my ears.

"I'll sends 'em to Hell, me buckos!" Blackbeard pulls off his mask, jams tiny candles into his thick beard, and strikes a match. Nonchalantly and with a strange finesse, he lights each candle. Flames and smoke shoot from his beard. Screaming wildly, he charges Alpha Team like a crazed berserker.

The security team freezes when they see a hulking buccaneer, facial hair ablaze, rushing towards them. Without hesitating, the cyborgs level their automatic rifles at Blackbeard. The pirate takes several rounds in his chest before hitting the ground like a bag of wet cement.

I slide my fingers across the ChronoJumper's screen and depart before another lethal salvo strikes Dillinger and James.

O n my next attempt, before we get to the manager's office, I ask Carly to take the security cameras offline.

In this timeline, I input the manager's passcode, swipe the keycard and the metal vault door glides open with a hiss. Rows of safe deposit boxes line the walls from floor to ceiling.

I locate one—my score—and insert the master key. The box swings open, revealing a slender cylinder. I pop the lid and a single flash drive spills out. I pocket it and turn around, only to stare down the barrel of my own gun.

One inattentive moment and Dillinger lifts my .357 from the holster. That mistake is costing us time and probably my life.

"Sorry, kiddo. We do things my way." Dillinger strikes my head with a glancing blow.

Dazed and bloodied, I'm kissing the floor. Dillinger removes the ChronoJumper from my wrist and slides it on his.

He scoops up the master key and unlocks a few boxes.

"Okay, you mugs. Empty it out," Dillinger orders.

My boys loot the vault, throwing out boxes and dumping their contents into the duffle bags.

"Nick!" Carly's voice crackles in my ear. "Talk to me. What happened?"

"John Dillinger hit me." I'm immediately awestruck at what I said. *"Whoa. John Dillinger hit me."*

"Focus, Nick. Where's that Depression Era gangster now?"

Dillinger scrutinizes the ChronoJumper's screen.

"Once I figure out this gizmo, I'll return home," he says. "Then those egg-sucking Feds will pay."

"Trust me, John. You don't want to do that." I spit blood. "Give it back."

"In a pig's eye I will." Dillinger taps the touchscreen and flinches in agonizing pain as electricity fries his hand. He sinks to his knees, and the ChronoJumper skids across the floor towards me. I grab it.

"I warned you. It's not calibrated to your specifications. Shocking, isn't it?" I slip the ChronoJumper on and pull myself up.

Dillinger wraps a hand around his swollen wrist. "I'll put you six feet under, you hear?"

The alarm sounds. While we struggled, the cameras must've come back online. Alpha Team is heading our way.

"It's yer fault, ye scurvy dog," Blackbeard hisses at Dillinger.

"My fault? What're you talking about, mac?" Dillinger asks.

"Maybe if you two greenhorns weren't flapping your jaws, we'd empty this here vault and vamoose." James throws down his duffle bag. "Y'all cost me my money."

"*Your* money?" Dillinger says. "If anyone's getting a larger cut from this job, it's me. This lettuce is mine, see? You and Captain Ahab over here get whatever I decide."

"Like hell you will," James protests.

"Who be this Captain Ahab and why's he looking to plunder me booty?" Blackbeard empties another box into his duffle bag.

"Shut up!" I cry. "You're supposed to work together, boys. We're on the same crew."

Dillinger chuckles darkly. "Same crew? You think we'd work together? Boy, are you a sap."

Alpha Team breaches the vault and fills the air with lead. Staccato bursts from their automatic rifles echo around us. I dive to the floor. Blood mist and bone fragments erupt nearby. Someone's ear flops on the floor in front of me.

I flick the ChronoJumper again for what seems like the millionth time.

A round we go again. Every time the boys screw up, the ChronoJumper circles back a few minutes and I get a do-over. It takes us several tries to hit the vault without incident. I get my flash drive and the boys bag their riches.

We finally escape The Spire and scramble into the getaway van.

Carly looks over her shoulder from the driver's seat. She mashes her foot on the accelerator, and the van's electric motor hums like a million angry hornets. The van careens towards the interstate with flashing lights and sirens in pursuit.

On the expressway, the police have a clean shot at us. The van is struck repeatedly. The driver's side window shatters. Carly's head jerks forward. We flip over.

Blackbeard slams against the roof. Dillinger smashes into James. My shoulder hits the window and I reach for the grab handle. Crunching metal. Broken glass. The airbag explodes into my face. Sirens grow louder. Carly isn't moving. Someone in the back groans. The world turns on its side. Blood drips from my scalp. My fingers tremble and activate the ChronoJumper. A sickly pale light from the screen bathes my face. I shut my eyes and tap the touchscreen.

On my next do-over, I tell Carly to take a side street instead of heading onto the interstate. One hairpin turn and we lose the pursuing patrol cars. I lean back in my seat and exhale, but it's not over. A blinding light strikes us from above. The police helicopter's rotor blades sound like a million angry hornets.

Carly veers off from the main road and steers the van towards a large opening in a culvert. The van travels for one hundred feet through thick wastewater before Carly parks in a cistern.

We exit the van. Dirty water soaks my shoes, but I don't care. Even the foul stench doesn't dampen my spirits. At this point I'm coasting on pure adrenaline.

Carly boots up her laptop and plugs the jump drive into an open slot. With a few keystrokes, she's unlocked the virtual blockchain vault and pilfered priceless digital artwork. I contact my buyer, who forwards ten million to my account when we upload his files. Every one of those pixilated tokens are worth a sizable fortune, according to the numbers on Carly's computer.

Dillinger, James, and Blackbeard unload their haul; duffel bags loaded with cash and jewelry.

Carly breaks out a bottle of champagne and passes it around to the boys.

"Congratulations, gentlemen. Biggest score ever," I tell them as we toast our success.

"Let's swig rum and get three sheets to the wind, me hearties!" Blackbeard crows.

"About that. Unfortunately, this partnership's run aground like your ship, Captain." I point the ChronoJumper at him. One tap and a red beam engulfs the pirate. Blackbeard is frozen in a silent scream and returned to 1717.

James cringes, mouth agape.

"Hey! What'd you do?" Jesse asks like a child told there's no such thing as Santa Claus.

"Sorry, Jesse. All good things must end. Give my regards to Robert Ford, you sociopathic hick," I tell him.

"What?" James asks before I push the button. The outlaw's dumbstruck face is the last thing I see before he vanishes.

Dillinger stares me down, his eyes black and watery. "I met some double-dealing, two-bit back stabbers in my day, but nobody like you."

"I learned from the best, namely you, John," I say.

Dillinger spits at my shoes. "Go on. Do it. Send me back. That's what this whole damn thing was anyway. A con."

"Like I said. I learned from the best."

Dillinger shakes his head. "It don't matter with this score. In the end, it's never big enough. You do more and more, but it ain't about the money. It's all about the thrill of breaking the law, of getting away with it. I see that in you, mac. Don't make no difference if it's a hundred years before me or a hundred years after me, it's all the same."

"You did this to yourself." My finger hovers over the touchscreen.

"How do you figure?" Dillinger asks.

"When you lifted my gun and the ChronoJumper. That's when I knew you couldn't be trusted, that you were playing by your own rules," I say.

Dillinger exhales. "Boy, you sure are a dip. You knew who we all were; me, the kid, the grouchy pirate. You knew and still you trusted us."

"*The Scorpion and the Frog*," I mumble to myself.

"What?"

"A fable," I tell him. "The scorpion wants the frog to carry it across a river. The frog hesitates because it's a scorpion. The scorpion promises not to sting the frog. Reluctantly, the frog agrees. Midway across the river, the scorpion stings the frog, dooming them both to a watery death. As the frog sinks, he asks the scorpion why it stung him even though it promised not to. The scorpion replies, 'I couldn't help myself; it's my nature.' That's you, John. You're the scorpion."

"And you're the gullible frog." Dillinger cracks his knuckles. "Only a fool would idolize me, Nick."

Touché, Mr. Dillinger, I think.

"Come on, hotshot," the robber says, growing impatient. "Push those buttons and make the gadget do its thing. Don't matter if you send me back. I'll always be with you, Nick, as will Jesse James and Blackbeard. Deep down, you know you're just like us. A cold, rotten bastard who pulls one more job because he can."

The sight of a smug John Dillinger makes my stomach lurch. I flick the touchscreen counterclockwise and tap the "return" icon.

"Have fun at the Biograph, Johnny," I say before every one of John Dillinger's atoms disintegrates from my timeline.

Carly turns to me and says with her usual snarky tone, "Damn. That could've gone better."

I grin. "Yeah. Well. That actually happened."

"I told you that combination wouldn't work. Too violent. Not enough strategy."

"Who should we get for the next job? Bonnie and Clyde? Pancho Villa? D.B. Cooper? There are many despicable people in history who want to make a quick buck. The talent pool's endless," I say.

Carly wraps her arms around me and draws herself closer.

"How 'bout I pick the next team? Let me run a job for once?" she purrs.

"An excellent idea," I reply. "I'm tired of meeting my heroes. They were disappointing. Every one of them."

We load the money, laptop, and gun into the duffel bag. I strip off the boiler suit and don my blazer and jeans.

Carly kisses my cheek.

"Let's go recruit some real baddies, then," she whispers into my ear. "Bet you five grand I can pull off the heist without time jumping more than five times."

I grasp her hand and shake. "You're on."

That's my partner. Carly Bisetti always knows how to make things interesting.

Without blinking, I fiddle with the ChronoJumper's settings, turn the switch backwards, and tap the touchscreen.

The Adventure of the Confounded Writer
Jonathan Maberry

-1-

The Grenadier Pub, Wilton Row, London
1912

"**I**f you could go anywhere," said the stranger, "where would you go?"

The man being addressed set down his pen and leaned back to look up. The question was audacious and without preamble. The stranger who spoke was young, perhaps not yet thirty. He was well-dressed in country tweed, though they were out of date and unfashionable. He also wore a droopy mustache that was more in the American railroad style than British. His accent, however, was a somewhat generic local one—London, with perhaps a soupcon of Kent.

"Do I know you, sir?" he asked.

"I must apologize, Sir Arthur," said the young man, fidgeting a little. "I just finished reading—devouring, quite frankly—your extraordinary novel, *The Lost World.* Bravo, sir, on a remarkable work."

The seated man smiled with more politeness than warmth. "Yes, I perceive a copy of it peering over the hem of your coat pocket. Are you seeking an autograph…?"

"No, sir," said the young man.

"Don't tell me you are a journalist inquiring as to when or, indeed, *if* I will write another Sherlock Holmes story. Because I will tell you flatly, sir, that it is no one's business but my own and, to a much lesser degree, my editor."

"Oh, no, sir. Although I greatly admire the Holmes stories, I have quite another matter I would like to discuss. And, in case it occurs to you, I am not trying to sell you anything, nor interest you in a great investment scheme. Nothing like that. Perhaps I can buy you a drink or—"

"May I ask who you are, sir?" interrupted the older man. He was Sir Arthur Conan Doyle, and after all these years as a published author, it was not at all uncommon to be accosted in such a fashion. It was seldom agreeable to Doyle, who valued his privacy unless he was giving a lecture or a public reading. In quiet pubs like this, however, he preferred the anonymity afford by good manners. He rested his hand on the journal in which he had just begun making notes for another Professor Edward Challenger novel.

"My name is Wells, sir," said the young man. "But my friends call me Bertie."

"You are a writer?"

Wells smiled. "Did you deduce that from the ink upon my shirt cuff, the spatulate structure of my fingertips, or—?"

"Yes," said Doyle flatly. "Now, please, sir, if you have a point, I would appreciate you getting to it so that I can return to my work."

"Ah, yes… to be sure, Sir Arthur. But please… may I sit for just a moment? What are you drinking? I see that your glass is nearly empty. Please permit me?" Without waiting for a proper answer, the man slid into the chair opposite and signaled to the publican. Randklev, the pub's owner came over, eying the young man suspiciously.

"Is everything all right, Sir Arthur?" he asked.

Doyle sighed. "Yes, Tom. All's well. Please bring me another."

"I'll have the same," said Wells, "and please put it on my tab."

Randklev raised a single eyebrow at Doyle, who gave a reluctant nod. The publican went away and returned with two glasses of excellent Buchanan's Whiskey. They did not toast but instead each took a small sip before setting their glasses down.

"And now, Mr. Wells," said Doyle bluntly, "what is it that you feel is so important that you felt compelled to intrude upon my privacy. You asked a peculiar question."

"I did, sir, and will repeat it now," said Wells, his eyes glittering. "If you could go anywhere, where would you go?"

"Why do you ask? And why ask it of me?"

"If you would indulge me, Sir Arthur, I think it would make more sense if you answered first."

"Are you American, sir?"

"Me, sir? No. What makes you ask?"

"Lack of manners," said Doyle, and he took another sip.

Wells gave a self-deprecating laugh. "Fair point, sir, fair point. Nor do I mean to be so random and strange."

"And yet you manage it, sir."

"I do. And for that I apologize," said the young man. "I had thought that such a singular question might spark your curiosity."

"So far it has not," said Doyle, drumming his fingers very slowly and deliberately on the cover of his journal.

"Let me try it another way, sir," said Wells. He looked more amused than nervous. "If you could visit any place or any *time*, where might you choose to go?"

"Is that a serious question?"

"Very serious."

"Any 'time'?"

"Yes. If that power were available to you for a single trip, where and when…?"

Doyle took another sip, then he sighed. "Very well. If this will hurry this along to a conclusion, I'll play along. Where would I go? You mean the future or the past?"

"Either, sir. I have found that most people say they would travel to ancient times. To the land of the Pharaohs or the Greek senate. To the Roman circus or Camelot."

"Camelot is a myth."

Wells sipped his scotch and did not comment.

"Not the past," said Doyle, after giving the question some actual thought.

"The future, then?"

"Yes, I suppose."

"May I ask why?"

"Because I already know what happened in the past. I mean, as well as any other reasonably educated person. But of the future I know nothing. It is unwritten and even the most insightful and predictive scholar can only watch certain cultural and scientific trends and make guesses."

"I agree, Sir Arthur. I fully agree," said Wells with excitement. He leaned closer and dropped his voice. "The future is full of surprises."

"By its nature, yes. What is the point of the question?"

"If someone were to tell you that it was *possible* to visit the future, observe it, and return to the exact moment when you departed, would that not excite and inspire a writer of your nature, sir?"

Doyle began to dismiss the comment as frivolous, but then he smiled faintly. "It would. But, alas, that is one door closed to even the most enthusiastic and determined adventurer."

"Except," said Wells, "it is not."

"What do you mean?"

"What if such a traveler could provide proof that time travel is, in fact, quite possible? That it is a scientific reality."

"Ah, now I get it," said Doyle. "You are an aspiring writer and have come here to run an idea by me for a book or, perhaps, a short story."

"You are partly correct, Sir Arthur," said Wells. "I *am* a writer. I have published, however, and I know without a shred of doubt that I will continue to write and publish for many years."

"Congratulations," said Doyle dryly. "Now if you will allow me to return to my work?"

Wells grinned, dug into an inner pocket of his coat, and removed a digest magazine of average size and thickness. The young man placed it face-down on the table and kept the spine turned away, effectively hiding the magazine's title. He placed his open hand flat on the back cover.

"Sir Arthur," he said, "would you be more inclined to believe that I am speaking truth rather than sorting through the plot for a potential work?"

Amused, Doyle said, "That, sir, would depend on the proof."

Wells reached across the table with his other hand and tapped the corner of the notebook in front of Doyle.

"What if I could tell you something about the novel you are just now beginning to outline?"

"That would be some trick," said Doyle. "And I warn you that I am not fond of tricks. While I may have a sober view of the larger world— that which is unseen but not unfelt—I do not believe that you can look through the closed cover of this journal and tell me about an idea I had only this morning. I have barely made three pages of notes and have shared it with no one else."

"Exactly, sir," said Wells triumphantly. "You build a compelling case for how I can prove to you that time travel is a very real possibility."

Doyle sipped his whiskey, and then set his glass atop the closed journal.

"As I am sitting with my back to a wall on which there is no mirror," he said slowly, "there is no chance you stood behind me and peeked nor saw its reflection. So, yes, let's play this game. And once you have revealed your hand as having no winning cards, I'll thank you to pay for the drinks and go."

"That is a fair bargain, sir," said Wells.

"What is it you can tell me about my as-yet unwritten novel? My guess is that, because of the success of *The Lost World*, you'll deduce that I am writing another book in the same vein."

"Same character," said Wells.

"That is so easy a guess it's a bit of a cheat."

"No, sir, it is not," insisted Wells. "Let me start by telling you the title of that work."

"Nonsense. I have not picked a title yet," laughed Doyle. "I have three or four possible titles jotted down but have not chosen one."

"*The Poison Belt*," said Wells bluntly.

Doyle stared at him. "The devil you say. How on *earth* could you know that?"

The smile on Wells' face was filled with mischief. He turned the magazine over and slid it across the table. It was a copy of *The Strand*. On the cover was a painting of an extravagantly bearded man on hands and knees as he stared down at a young man and woman who lay unconscious or dead. But Doyle barely noticed the artwork, staring instead in dumb amazement at the title of the feature story.

The Poison Belt
The Great New Serial
By A. Conan Doyle.
The date of the issue was May 1913.

-2-

The Grenadier Pub, Wilton Row, London
1912

"This is some kind of trick," snarled Doyle as he snatched up the magazine and opened it. There was a calling card in place as a bookmark, but Doyle ignored it and began reading the story. His eyes snapped back and forth over the prose, then he leafed through the issue to read snatches of prose here and there.

"You will admit," said Wells, "that this is your writing style. The story is the one you began outlining today. It is impossible to explain this by any reasonable means *other* than time travel."

"Clairvoyance," mumbled Doyle, but without emphasis. In truth, he was completely at sea over the magazine. He slapped it down on the table hard enough to make other patrons turn sharply to look. The publican began hustling over, but Doyle waved him back. He glared at Wells. "I do not know how you managed this nonsense, man, but I swear by God that I will…"

Once more his voice trailed off and he simply stared.

"Sir Arthur," said Wells gently, "how old do you think I am?"

"What…? Oh… I… twenty-five, perhaps. Thirty at best." His voice was vague, as if he was in a dream or very drunk. "Why?"

"There are two answers to my question, Sir Arthur," said Wells. "In terms of strict biological chronology, I am twenty-nine years old. However, I was born in 1866, which means that I am forty-six."

Doyle merely stared.

"I am not of this time," said Wells. "My older self is very much alive and at this moment he is playing golf with a friend right here in London. He does not, of course, know that I am *also* here. That two of us are in London, seventeen years apart in physical age but sharing the same day and hour."

Doyle's hand shook as he reached out to pick up the calling card that had marked the place in the magazine. He turned it over and read the name.

Herbert George Wells

Doyle looked up slowly.

"There is an author by that name."

"Yes," said Wells.

"He wrote a novel about… about…"

"About time travel?" Wells smiled like a hungry tiger. "Yes. It was my first novel. And from my current perspective, that book is still new. It's only now gaining attention, and I have my own notebook full of ideas for future works. Perhaps I've skewed my own path, or created some kind of paradox, but I've wandered through bookstalls and libraries, running my fingers over the covers and spines of works I have not yet written but know with absolutely certainty that I will write. *The Island of Doctor Moreau*, which I am only now close to finishing. *The Invisible Man*, *When the Sleeper Wakes*, *The War of the Worlds*. A book came out this year—*your* year of 1912—called *Marriage*, but I don't know what it's about. I don't know what any of those other books are about."

"How… can you not?"

"Because I haven't written them yet. Except for *Moreau, The Wonderful Visit*, and another I have outlined called *The Wheels of Chance*, I don't have any of those ideas in my head."

"Surely you must have read those works in the… in *your* future."

"Oh, lord no!" cried Wells. "It's bad enough that I risked madness by even seeing the titles, but I dare not read them. I have no idea what a paradox of that magnitude would do. It could wreck time itself. Or perhaps cast me adrift in it. I don't know. You are more likely to know my future works than I am."

Doyle shook his head. "I haven't read you."

Wells made a rueful smile. "Ah well, an honest answer at least. On the other hand, I have read you. I have read *all* of the Sherlock Holmes stories, all of the Professor Challenger stories and… well… everything else, I think. I've been rather obsessed with your work, and particularly with your essays and lectures on the unseen world."

"On…?"

"Future essays and lectures," said Wells quickly.

"You are actually saying that you travel in time?"

"Yes, Sir Arthur."

"Have you been to your own end? Your own funeral?"

"No," said Wells flatly. "And that's another reason I haven't opened any of the books I will someday write. I don't want to find that some are published posthumously, with cause of death and dates provided. Personally, I think I would run melancholy mad if I knew what and when my end would be."

"Do you know mine?"

Wells hesitated. "I do. But…please don't ask, because I will not tell you. I think you would agree—or will when the shock of all this wears off—that such knowledge can do a man no good at all."

"No… no, of course not…"

Doyle picked up his glass and tried to take a sip, unaware that it was empty. He paused, staring down into the tumbler as if confounded by that reality; then he set it back down.

"I do not know what to say," he admitted, his voice now trembling as badly as his hands. "I don't think I even know how to have this conversation."

"It is unique, is it not? Two gentlemen sitting in a pub over drinks, talking about time travel."

"That novel you wrote…? Is it an autobiography?"

"No," said Wells. "It's a work of fiction. The protagonist, whom I simply call the Time Traveler, is only loosely based on me. He is both more heroic and more tragic than I. He journeys far into the future and finds mankind fallen into nearly mindless hedonism, and discovers that the former unwashed working class—the machinists and laborers who are virtually unseen by those higher on the social ladder—have evolved into cannibal monsters who feed on the helpless descendants of the elite. I wrote it as social commentary and a bit of a cautionary tale. That Time Traveler then journeys onward from there until the very end of planet Earth, where the dying sun is a red swollen thing, and the only remaining form of life is a black tentacular blob. He then returns home, resupplies, and vanishes once more into the unknown, never to return." He paused. "Oddly, while writing that book I always assumed that I would write a sequel, but no such work was ever published."

"This is madness," said Doyle. He removed a pocket handkerchief and mopped his brow. "Madness."

"And yet you know it's not, Sir Arthur," said Wells. "You believe me."

Doyle licked his lips and shook his head. Then, a moment later, he nodded. Very slowly and with great reluctance.

"But why tell me? Me, of all people? I am no scientist, no social theorist. I am not of the clergy or with the government. What value is there in telling me these things?"

"Because," said Wells with a smile, "I've read your diaries. No, don't look surprised. You're a great man of incredible influence. Many publishers and universities have published excerpts of your private writings. I know that sounds terribly intrusive, but believe me when I tell you that your private meditations are as valuable to future generations as are your stories."

"Utter nonsense. I write mysteries and ghost stories and adventures. Of what possible value do they have to the future?"

"More than you know," said Wells. "And the reason I picked today to come and see you is because in one diary entry, the one you wrote last night, in fact, you wrote that you have become tired of Sherlock Holmes again. Your last two tales, "The Disappearance of Lady Frances Carfax" and "The Adventure of the Red Circle" were published more than a year ago. You wrote in your diary that you will not write any more about Messieurs Holmes and Watson. You even intimated that a new story that you had thought to write later this year or early next, "The Adventure of the Dying Detective" would, indeed, end with a victory for Holmes but at the cost of his life. And with Watson right there to witness without chance of mistake, the final death of his friend."

"And what of it?" snapped Doyle.

"I hope to talk you out of that decision."

"Oh, pish. If you have visited the future as you say, then you already know that I will or will not. The future seems, by what you've said, to be a fixed point. What good will this conversation do?"

"Ah," said Wells, "that's a curious thing. Singular. I have visited *two* futures and seen *two* distinctly different outcomes. I do not yet know how or why, but the future is not immutable. It is, apparently, quite fluid. That's why I am so hesitant to delve further into my own future. What if a thing I do disrupts what I call the 'true' flow of time, and instead warps it into something else? What if, for example, I visit my current self and he does *not* remember ever traveling in time, and my appearance drives him mad or bursts his heart? What if... well... I could play that game of wondering forever. Literally forever. Instead, in my travels I've perceived some—shall we call them—rules? The most correct tracks for the train of events to travel into the future. I have seen alternate versions where that train has been badly derailed."

"Even if that is true," said Doyle, "what of it? Had you not come to me now, my life would have proceeded according to the true set of tracks."

"No, Sir Arthur, I don't think so," said Wells. "One thing I've discovered is that there are certain moments that, like points on a set of train tracks, the future can go one way or another. I don't know why or how, but I have witnessed enough outcomes to understand that these turning points do exist. The future I saw where you and what you have written are of great social value are one direction; and the one without your influence is another. One direction is light, the other very dark."

"But, damn it man, that makes no sense. I write *stories*. Fiction. That's all."

Wells shook his head. "No, sir, you are much more important than that."

"You're mad."

"No," said Wells. "I'm not. And I would like very much to prove it to you."

"How?"

"There is someone I would like you to meet."

"Who is this person?" demanded Doyle.

"Oh… he's not here. He's in America," said Wells. "And he won't be born for another fourteen years."

"But…"

"Let's go find the man that as-yet unborn child will become."

Doyle was really sweating badly now. "This is madness… madness…"

Wells gave him a compassionate smile. "This is science."

"It's madness," insisted Doyle.

"Amounts to the same thing," admitted Wells.

-3-

Denbigh's Carriage Yard, London
1912

"There are many places and times I can take you," said Wells, and he helped Doyle strap himself into the back of the carriage.

The thing was built like a sled with a metal framework around it, nearly enclosing a pair of seats—more like saddles—that were suspended by leather straps. The machine was made from a number of metals—Doyle saw nickel and aluminium, with bits of copper and brass and steel. There were devices socketed into a panel in the front, and bars of crystal that glittered in the lamplight of the horse barn. Outside, carriages and wagons rattled past as the afternoon was darkening toward twilight.

Doyle had gone with Wells, accompanying the young man in a kind of daze. He was half convinced this was a joke, and equally convinced he—or perhaps the world—had gone quite mad.

And yet…

"I don't believe any of this," he said, and he repeated it quite often despite accompanying Wells to the barn and allowing himself to be secured in the second saddle.

"I know," said Wells, smiling.

"Who is this person you want me to see?"

"His name is Salvatore Lombino."

"Never heard of him. Oh... wait... he isn't born yet." Doyle rubbed his face with his palms. "God in heaven, how does one even *talk* about time travel?"

"A new lexicon will be required, I suspect," said Wells, as he climbed into the pilot's saddle. "New tenses, too, I suspect."

He laid a hand on one of the controls.

"Are you ready, Sir Arthur?"

"No... not in the least."

Wells grinned and shoved the lever forward.

-4-

Walton Lake, New York
2002

The old man sat on a canvas folding chair.

He wore a strange cap with a wide bill and the letters NY laid one atop the other on the front of the crown. His clothing was likewise unusual—trousers of a faded blue denim, a lightweight coat with a strange kind of interlocking metal closure running up the front, and beneath that a checked shirt. Instead of proper footwear, the man wore some kind of plimsoll shoes that had white rubber soles and black canvas uppers on which was a blue star in a white circle.

The old man reached over and gave his fishing rod an indifferent wiggle, but the line was slack.

"How are you doing?" asked Wells affably.

"Well," said the old man, "to be fair, it's called 'fishing,' not 'catching'." A moment later he said, without turning. "Wells?"

"Yes, sir," said the young writer.

"And... did you bring him?"

"I did."

The old man nodded and stood, eliciting popping sounds from his old joints. He turned and studied the newcomers. The man was in his early seventies, and though lean, he looked a bit stooped and tired. He had a gray beard that still showed some of the black hair he once had. Wisps of thin gray hair escaped the band of the strange hat. He stood looking at Doyle for a very long time. So long it became uncomfortable.

"Wells," said Doyle awkwardly, "perhaps an introduction...?"

"Ah, sorry, yes," said Wells. "Even I have some difficulty with moments like this. Sir Arthur Doyle, it is my very great pleasure to introduce you to Evan Hunter."

"Hunter? I thought we were meeting an Italian? Salvatore Lombino."

"Guilty as charged," laughed Hunter. "I had my name legally changed a long time ago." He stepped forward and offered his hand. "Arthur Conan Doyle... my god! What an incredible honor."

Doyle looked at the extended hand for a moment, then accepted it and they shook.

"To further confuse matters," said Wells, "Mr. Hunter is best known as Ed McBain."

"A pen name," explained Hunter. "For my crime novels."

"Crime...?"

"Yes," said Wells. "'Ed McBain' is one of the most successful and respected writers of crime fiction."

"What... I mean... *when* are we?" sputtered Doyle.

Hunter's smile was warm and filled with compassion. "It's May 19th, 2002," he said. "And, yes, if you fainted right now, I'd understand. Hell, I did when Wells took me on one of his little jaunts."

"You... *also* travel in time?"

"Just the once. That was enough for me."

"Where, if I may ask, did you go?"

Hunter glanced at Wells. "Okay to tell him. Yes? Well, Mr. Doyle, I had a nice afternoon in a bar in the Bronx. Well, technically it was Fordham back then. Not sure which of us was more shocked. But I have to say, Poe adjusted to it quicker than I did. Though, I'm more than half sure he thought he was having a hallucination. The man drinks. A lot. And maybe plays around with other stuff."

"Why did you go to see him?" asked Doyle. "Why not Shakespeare or Julius Caesar? Why not Homer or Cervantes?"

"Because Poe invented the mystery."

"He certainly did not."

"He invented the mystery short story. Or, at least, the detective story as we know it."

Doyle gave a grudging grunt of agreement.

Hunter looked Doyle up and down, then glanced at Wells. "Have you told him why you brought him here? Brought him to me, I mean?"

"Not yet," said Wells.

Hunter nodded. "Okay, guys, let's go back to my cottage. Doyle…I hope you have a strong constitution."

With that he set off, moving at a brisk pace for a man of his age. Doyle, who was fifty-three years old and not as thin as he had once been, did his best to keep up. Wells walked briskly beside him.

A path led to a lovely little cottage on a hill that gave it a splendid view of the lake. There was an automobile of a kind Doyle had never seen before parked outside. A Ford, but completely exotic.

Once they were inside, the word "exotic" hardly applied, and for the next three-quarters of an hour, Wells encouraged Hunter to explain the various arcane devices. Some were merely futuristic versions of things Doyle understood—a telephone, a stove, and others. But some were so bizarre as to have no context for Doyle's understanding. Words like "personal computer" and "television" begged for explanations. And Doyle spent several moments watching "cable news" and then a play of some kind in which women wore shockingly revealing clothing and everyone seemed to only manage foul language.

"Why bring me here and show me all this?" demanded Doyle, once he was able to fight past his shock and articulate a question. "I don't write scientific romances."

"We call that science fiction these days," said Hunter, "but I get it. No, Wells didn't bring you here so I could dazzle you with the electronic marvels of the second millennium."

"I can't help it," admitted Wells, looking sheepish.

"The real reason he brought you here," said Hunter, "is that he wants me to prove to you why what you write matters. And to encourage you to continue writing about Holmes and Watson."

"You brought me across time and oceans to tell me *that*?" cried Doyle. "You have a time machine and you waste it on something so trivial?"

"First," said Hunter, "Wells is doing a number of these little trips, and each one has a purpose. A genuine purpose, and he's doing some good with it. Maybe cut the guy a little slack."

"Slack…?"

Hunter ignored that and continued, "He brought you to me for a few very good reasons."

"And dare I ask what they are?" asked Doyle with asperity.

"Sure. Let's go into my office and I'll show you."

He led the way down a short hall to a room that was lined with bookshelves floor to ceiling. There were filing cabinets and a table on which were boxes and stacks of books, papers, and magazines. Facing a window that commanded a view of the lake was an oak desk whose lacquered skin was nicked and stained and had countless cigarette burns. On it was one of the "personal computers," which Doyle took to understand as a kind of typewriter.

Hunter went to one bookcase and swept his hand along the spines of dozens upon dozens of novels.

"I've written about ninety novels, give or take," said Hunter. "Most of them are crime novels. Your writing, your Holmes stories, were one of the most important inspirations for me. In fact, I can say flat out that if it wasn't for you, I'd have never become who I am. As egotistical as it sounds to say it, I'm looked at as one of the most important writers of police procedural fiction. No, I make no claims to have invented that, and I can actually name a half dozen writers, including some friends, who are better at it than I am. My books—the *87th Precinct* series—have sold millions of copies. More to the point, none of what I've written in that genre would exist were it not for Sherlock Holmes. For *you*, Doyle."

"Do not take offense at this," said Doyle, "but so what?"

"This isn't about me," said Hunter. "Not really. Wells wanted to make a point. There are a *lot* of writers like me who do this kind of fiction. Thousands. Around the world and going all the way back to your days writing for *The Strand*. There are more pastiches of Sherlock Holmes than I can count. At least half a million short stories, novels, plays, and other forms of entertainment. Don't even get me started on movies and television shows because that would take us down a whole different avenue. My point is that Sherlock Holmes is arguably the most important literary character of all time."

"As grand as that is to know," said Doyle, "again I say… so what? All writers hope to inspire the generations that follow."

"Ah, but there's where we get to the real reason Wells brought you here. The real reason he and I want to beg you not to stop writing Holmes stories."

Doyle walked over to the shelf of Hunter's novels and let his gaze range over them.

"Tell me, then," he said.

"It's not even Holmes who matters as much as you, Sir Arthur," said Wells.

"It's Holmes *and* you," clarified Hunter. "In your stories, you—a medical man—had Holmes focus on the science of collecting and analyzing evidence. We call that forensic science these days. In your stories, Holmes was constantly badgering Scotland Yard to stop relying on hearsay and pay attention to the details. Cigarette ash, footprints, blood spatter, chemical residue, ballistics, toxicology, fingerprints... and all the rest. You made that make sense, even if Lestrade and Gregson and the rest did not."

"What of it?"

"Even while you were alive, police departments around the world were borrowing the logic and processes of Sherlock Holmes. Now, every police department in every nation around the globe relies on forensic evidence collection. I don't even know if it's possible to *estimate* how many crimes have been solved because you inspired the law enforcement agencies of the world to rely on science—hard, provable, science. The collection of evidence and the scientific analysis of same is the single most important development in the entire history of crime detection and enforcement. Every criminal court case hinges on it."

Hunter came over and stood next to Doyle.

"Are you hearing me?"

"I... I am..." said Doyle. "However, I am finding it very hard to believe."

"Believe it," said Hunter. "And before Wells takes you back to wherever he found you—"

"A London pub," supplied Wells.

"—I need to tell you one more thing. The most important thing," said Hunter. "Something that you included as a key element in many of your stories. Something that is of inestimable importance since then, and will be critically important for all time to come."

Doyle kept looking at the books and not Hunter.

"Tell me," he said very softly.

"There are two parts of this," said Hunter. "Both are massively important."

Doyle nodded.

"Because of this science—the science whose use you are largely responsible for—so many criminals have been brought to justice. And I'm not talking just about grifters and pickpockets, or even common criminals who shoot someone in a moment of passion. No, law enforcement agencies have been able to stop mass murderers and repeat killers, what we call serial killers. You remember Jack the Ripper? He was bad, but he was nothing compared to Ted Bundy, Ed Gein, Albert Fish, and others like them. Some of whom killed scores of people. Serial rapists, child murderers, slaughterers of entire families. Police were able to find them and stop them because of you and Sherlock Holmes."

Doyle turned to him, eyes wide. But he still said nothing.

"Now, look at that from the other side," said Hunter. "Think of all of the people—hundreds of thousands at least around the world—who were not murdered or tortured or otherwise destroyed by maniacs. Every time a criminal of that kind is taken off the streets because of some piece of evidence, there is an echo effect that touches the lives of people who will never even know that they were saved because of you."

Doyle closed his eyes.

Hunter laid a gentle hand on the man's shoulder.

"Because of you, Doyle," he said. "You're not just a writer… you're an actual hero. You *are* Sherlock Holmes. God, how I admire you. And damn, what an honor it is to meet you."

Doyle's eyes opened and they were wet. "I… I don't know what to say. I…"

"Do us all a favor, man," said Hunter. "Let Wells take you back home. Sure, go ahead and write more Professor Challenger stories. They're fun. But, if you care about future generation, about saving lives… go write some more Sherlock Holmes stories. Believe me when I say that the world is waiting. And the world will be grateful."

Then Hunter surprised Doyle by embracing him and giving a fierce hug. Then he stepped back, and there were tears in Hunter's eyes as well.

-5-

The Grenadier Pub, Wilton Row, London
1912

Sir Arthur Conan Doyle sat at his usual table in his usual corner of the Grenadier. There was a glass of whiskey within easy reach and a cigar fuming silently in a tray.

Doyle had his notebook open, with all of his notes for *The Poison Belt*, the second Professor Challenger novel, there...waiting for addition.

He re-read the notes and made a few additions, but then he would drift away from that idea and stare at nothing. Wells had brought him back to the exact moment from when they'd left, and after a hearty handshake and kind words, had gone off. Traveling through time. Perhaps working on his next bizarre introduction.

If Wells had existed at all.

The real Wells, the writer. Doyle was tempted to find out where the *current* version of that man lived and ask him about this. Had this all, in fact, happened? No time had passed. There were no artifacts to prove that there had ever been a time machine, or a man named Evan Hunter fishing by a lake in New York. There was no proof at all.

No evidence.

Except...

Hunter's words echoed through Doyle's mind.

Echoed and echoed and echoed.

Doyle tapped the page with the point of his fountain pen, and then he turned the page. The new, blank page seemed to invite him. To call to him.

Then he began to write.

The Adventure of the Dying Detective

Mrs. Hudson, the landlady of Sherlock Holmes, was a long suffering woman.

And if the writer's hand shook... then who could blame him?

About the Authors

ERIC AVEDISSIAN is an adjunct professor and speculative fiction author with a penchant for the macabre and fantastic. His published work includes the YA steampunk fantasy *Gargoyles & Absinthe* (Aurelia Leo) and the pulp role-playing game *Ravaged Earth* (Reality Blurs). His short fiction appears in *Outposts of Beyond*, *Aphotic Realm*, and the anthologies *Across the Universe*, *Dear Leader Tales*, and *Bananthology*. His debut novel *Accursed Son* will be released from Shadow Spark Publishing in 2022. When not chained to his writing desk, he hikes the New Jersey Pinelands and wastes too much time on social media. Visit him online at www.ericavedissian.com or on Twitter (@angryreporter).

ADAM-TROY CASTRO made his first non-fiction sale to *Spy* magazine in 1987. His 26 books to date include among others four Spider-Man novels, three novels about his profoundly damaged far-future murder investigator Andrea Cort, and six middle-grade novels about the dimension-spanning adventures of that very strange but very heroic young boy Gustav Gloom. Adam-Troy's darker short fiction for grownups is highlighted by his most recent collection, *Her Husband's Hands And Other Stories* (Prime Books). Adam-Troy's works have won the Philip K. Dick Award and the Seiun (Japan), and have been nominated for eight Nebulas, three Stokers, two Hugos, and, internationally, the Ignotus (Spain), the Grand Prix de l'Imaginaire (France), and the Kurd-Laßwitz Preis (Germany). His web page is www.adamtroycastro.com

New York Times-bestseller **PETER DAVID** has had over fifty novels published, including *Sir Apropos of Nothing*, *Knight Life*, *Howling Mad*, and the *Psi-Man* adventure series. He is the co-creator and author of the bestselling *Star Trek: New Frontier* series for Pocket Books, and has also written other Trek novels, including *Vendetta*, *I, Q* (with John deLancie), *A Rock and a Hard Place*, and *Imzadi*. He produced the three *Babylon 5 Centauri Prime* novels, and has also had his short fiction published in *Asimov's Science Fiction* and *The Magazine of Fantasy and Science*

Fiction. Peter's comic book resume includes an award-winning twelve-year run on *The Incredible Hulk*, and he has also worked on such varied and popular titles as *Supergirl, Aquaman, Spider-Man, Spider-Man 2099, X-Factor, Star Trek, Wolverine*, and many others. Peter is the co-creator, with popular science fiction icon Bill Mumy, of the Cable Ace Award-nominated science fiction series *Space Cases*, which ran for two seasons on Nickelodeon. He has written several scripts for the Hugo Award-winning TV series *Babylon 5*, and the sequel series, *Crusade*. His web page is www.peterdavid.net

KEITH R.A. DeCANDIDO is a huge devotee of 19th-century literature (which was his focus as an undergrad in college), a massive baseball fan since the age of seven, and a total space program nerd, so picking his three time travelers for this anthology was the easiest thing in the world. His upcoming work includes the novels *Feat of Clay* and *Phoenix Precinct*, the *Resident Evil: Infinite Darkness* graphic novel *The Beginning*, the short story collection *Ragnarok and a Hard Place: More Tales of Cassie Zukav, Weirdness Magnet*, the *Star Trek Adventures* RPG module "Incident at Kraav III" (with Fred Love), short fiction in the anthologies *Devilish and Divine, Phenomenons: Every Human Creature, The Fans are Buried Tales, Tales of Capes and Cowls*, and *The Four ???? of the Apocalypse* (which he also co-edited), and nonfiction for the award-winning web site Tor.com, as well as for the "Subterranean Blue Grotto," "Gold Archive," and "Outside In" series. He's also a fourth-degree black belt in karate, a musician, an editor, and possibly some other stuff he can't recall due to the lack of sleep. Find out less at his hilariously primitive web site DeCandido.net

GREGORY FROST's most recent novel-length work is the *Shadowbridge* duology from Del Rey. It was an ALA *Best Fantasy Novel* pick. His latest short fiction, "Ellende," appears in issue #364 of the revamped *Weird Tales*.

His collaborative novelette with Michael Swanwick, "Lock Up Your Chickens and Daughters—H'ard and Andy Are Come to Town," won an *Asimov's* Readers Award in 2015. His novels and short stories have been finalists for the World Fantasy, Stoker, Nebula, Hugo, International Horror Guild, and Theodore Sturgeon awards. Since 2004, he's taught the

Fiction Writing Workshop at Swarthmore College. His web page is www.gregoryfrost.com

Ten-time Hugo- and Nebula-award nominee **DAVID GERROLD** is also a recipient of the Skylark Award for Excellence in Imaginative Fiction, the Bram Stoker Award for Superior Achievement in Horror, and the Forrest J. Ackerman lifetime achievement award. He was the Guest of Honor at the 2015 World Science Fiction Convention. Gerrold's prolific output includes teleplays, film scripts, stage plays, comic books, more than 50 novels and anthologies, and hundreds of articles, columns, and short stories. He has worked on a dozen different TV series, including *Star Trek*, *Land of the Lost*, *Twilight Zone*, *Star Trek: The Next Generation*, *Babylon 5*, and *Sliders*. He is the author of *Star Trek*'s most popular episode "The Trouble With Tribbles." His most famous novel is *The Man Who Folded Himself*. His semi-autobiographical tale of his son's adoption, *The Martian Child*, won both the Hugo and the Nebula awards, and was the basis for the 2007 movie starring John Cusack and Amanda Peet. His web page is www.gerrold.com

HENRY HERZ's speculative fiction short stories include "Out, Damned Virus" (*Daily Science Fiction*), "Bar Mitzvah on Planet Latke" (*Coming of Age*, Albert Whitman & Co.), "The Crowe Family" (*Castle of Horror V*, Castle Bridge Media), "Gluttony" (*Metastellar*), "Alien with a Bad Attitude" (*Strangely Funny VIII*, Mystery and Horror LLP), "The Case of the Murderous Alien" (*Spirit Machine*, Air and Nothingness Press), "Maria & Maslow" (*Highlights for Children*), and "A Proper Party" (*Ladybug Magazine*). He's written ten picture books, including the critically acclaimed *I am Smoke*. Henry has edited three anthologies. His web page is www.henryherz.com

JONATHAN MABERRY is a *New York Times* bestselling author, five-time Bram Stoker Award-winner, three-time Scribe Award-winner, Inkpot Award-winner, and comic book writer. His vampire apocalypse book series, *V-Wars*, was a Netflix original series. He writes in multiple genres including suspense, thriller, horror, science fiction, fantasy, and action; for adults, teens, and middle grade. His novels include the *Joe Ledger* thriller series, *Bewilderness*, *Ink*, *Glimpse*, the *Pine Deep Trilogy*, the *Rot & Ruin* series, the *Dead of Night* series, *Mars One*, *Ghostwalkers: A Deadlands Novel*, and many others, including his first epic fantasy, *Kagen the Damned*. He is the editor many anthologies including *The X-Files, Aliens: Bug Hunt*, *Don't Turn Out the Lights*, *Aliens vs Predator: Ultimate Prey*, *Hardboiled Horror*, *Nights of the Living Dead* (co-edited with George A. Romero), and others. His comics include *Black Panther: DoomWar*, *Captain America*, *Pandemica*, *Highway to Hell*, *The Punisher*, and *Bad Blood*. He is the president of the International Association of Media Tie-in Writers, and the editor of *Weird Tales* Magazine. Visit him online at www.jonathanmaberry.com

GAIL Z. MARTIN writes urban fantasy, epic fantasy, and steampunk for Solaris Books, Orbit Books, Falstaff Books, SOL Publishing, and Darkwind Press. Urban fantasy series include *Deadly Curiosities* and the *Night Vigil* (*Sons of Darkness*). Epic fantasy series include *Darkhurst*, the *Chronicles of the Necromancer*, the *Fallen Kings Cycle*, the *Ascendant Kingdoms Saga*, and the *Assassins of Landria*. Newest titles include *Tangled Web*, *Vengeance*, *The Dark Road*, and *Assassin's Honor*. As Morgan Brice, she writes urban fantasy and paranormal romance. Books include *Witchbane*, *Badlands*, and *Treasure Tail*. Her web page is www.ascendantkingdoms.com

HEATHER McKINNEY received her Bachelor of Arts in History from the University of Texas at San Antonio. She is currently working toward her Master of Fine Arts in Creative Writing from Regis University in Denver with dual genres of fiction and creative non-fiction. Apart from writing, Heather loves old movies, learning obscure historical facts, and just being an all-around nerd. She resides in Colorado Springs with her wife, their son, and two dogs.

JAMES A. MOORE is the award-winning, best-selling author of over forty novels in the horror, fantasy, and science fiction arenas, including the *Seven Forges* series and the *Serenity Falls* trilogy. He currently lives in the wilds of deepest, darkest Maine, with his wife, Tessa, and a small menagerie of critters. When he isn't writing he also spends a little spare time as a barista at Starbucks. His web page is www.jamesamoorebooks.com

JODY LYNN NYE lists her main career activity as "spoiling cats." She lives northwest of Chicago with one of the above and her husband, author and packager Bill Fawcett. She has written over forty-five books, including *The Ship Who Won* with Anne McCaffrey, eight books with Robert Asprin, a humorous anthology about mothers, *Don't Forget Your Spacesuit, Dear!*, and over 160 short stories. Her latest books are *Rhythm of the Imperium* (Baen Books), *Moon Beam* (with Travis S. Taylor, Baen) and *Myth-Fits* (Ace). Jody also reviews fiction for *Galaxy's Edge* magazine and teaches the intensive writers' workshop at DragonCon. Her web page is www.jodynye.net

A former teacher of English, **LOUISE PIPER** is an editor of academic texts and a writer of fiction, non-fiction, and poetry. Her spiritual memoir, *The Year I Lived With a Psychic* is available on Amazon; her essay, "A Long, Long-Term Lockdown," is published by WindyWood in *Gathering In: Covid-19 Silver Linings*. She has been published on the Tiny Buddha website and co-authored a comedy sketch, "Eyeshadow," which was streamed by the Theatre Arts Guild in Halifax. Her current projects include co-authoring a non-fiction book about the ways everyone may develop their spirituality. Louise lives in Halifax, Nova Scotia, where she is a member of Les Belles Lettres poetry group and Tufts Cove Writers' Collective. Find her on instagram: instagram.com/louise._piper

L. PENELOPE has been writing since she could hold a pen, and loves getting lost in the worlds in her head. She is an award-winning fantasy and paranormal romance author. Her novel *Song of Blood & Stone* was chosen as one of *TIME* Magazine's 100 Best Fantasy Books of All Time. Equally left- and right-brained, she studied filmmaking and computer science in college and sometimes dreams in HTML. She hosts the *My Imaginary Friends* podcast and lives in Maryland with her husband and furry dependents. Visit her at www.lpenelope.com

HILDY SILVERMAN primarily writes short stories for speculative fiction anthologies. Her most recent stories include "ROI" (2022, co-authored with Russ Colchamiro, *Phenomenons*: *Every Human Creature*, ed. Friedman), "The Bionic Mermaid vs. The Sea Demons" (2021, *Devilish & Divine*, eds. Ackley-McPhail and French), and "Raising the

Dead" (2020, *Bad Ass Moms*, ed. Fan). Her story, "The Six Million Dollar Mermaid," was a finalist for the 2013 WSFA Small Press award. She is a frequent panelist on the East Coast convention circuit, former publisher of *Space and Time Magazine*, and a past president of the Garden State Speculative Fiction Writers. For more information, please visit her website, www.hildysilverman.com

SHIRI SONDHEIMER is a pansexual crone and gore spirit who spent four years ranting about books and comics on Book Riot and The Roarbots. She continues to do so for her own edification. Her short stories can be found in *Unlocking the Magic: A Fantasy Anthology* with a focus on mental health for which she called on her own experiences with depression and anxiety, and *Women In Horror 2016*. Her article on the neurological connection between music and creativity was published in Issue 10 of *Fantasy Art and Studies*, and she has two chapters in Blackwell's *The Expanse and Philosophy*. Her creative process is Haikyu!'s Tanaka and Tsukishima in a hamster ball and a random generator once declared her genre "cactus garbage." In her spare time she is an amateur frog. She can be found in colorful language form on Twitter @SWSondheimer, in pictorial form on Instagram as @frankencroneink, in motion on TikTok as @frankencroneink, and at www.swsondheimer.com

ALLEN STEELE has published eighteen novels and nearly a hundred short stories. His work has received numerous awards, including three Hugos, and has been translated worldwide, mainly in languages he can't read. He serves on the Board of Advisors for the Space Frontier Foundation and the Science Fiction and Fantasy Writers of America. He also belongs to Sigma, a group of SF writers who frequently serve as unpaid consultants on matters regarding technology and security. Steele lives in western Massachusetts with his wife Linda and a continual procession of adopted dogs. He collects vintage science fiction books and magazines, spacecraft model kits, and dreams. His web page is www.allensteele.com

LAWRENCE WATT-EVANS is the author of fifty or so books, including fantasy, science fiction, horror, and nonfiction about popular culture. He is best known for two fantasy series, the *Legends of Ethshar* and the *Obsidian Chronicles*, and won the Hugo award for his short story "Why I Left Harry's All-Night Hamburgers." His web page is www.watt-evans.com

About the Editor

MICHAEL A. VENTRELLA writes humorous novels like *Bloodsuckers: A Vampire Runs for President*, *Big Stick*, and the *Terin Ostler* fantasy series. He has edited the anthologies *Release the Virgins*, *Tales of Fortannis*, *Across the Universe* (with co-editor Randee Dawn), and the *Baker Street Irregulars* series (with co-editor Jonathan Maberry). His own stories have appeared in other anthologies, including the *Heroes in Hell* series, *Rum and Runestones*, and *The Ministry of Peculiar Occurrences Archives*. His web page is www.MichaelAVentrella.com

Kickstarter Supporters

Jim Adcock
Linda D. Addison
Antha Ann Adkins
Heather Allen
Christopher Ambler
Lorraine J. Anderson
Anonymous Reader
Matt Aronoff
Atthis Arts
Axisor and Firestar
Carolyn B.
Tom B.
Stephen Ballentine
Emily Barnaby
Charles Barouch
John D. Barton
Melinda Berkman
Jennifer Flora Black
Mischa Boender
Jeremy Bottroff
Keith Bowden
Edmund Boys
Mihail Braila
Christopher Brown
Bugz
Margaret Bumby
Gary Bunker
Jan Burke
Bret Burks
Michael A. Burstein
D Cameron Calkins
Dana Carson
Mike Cassella
Mark Catalfano
Chickadee

Robert Claney
The Clemente family
Jamieson Cobleigh
Kelly J Cooper
Sarah Cornell
Joseph Cox
Mike Crate
Rodney J Cressey
Dylan Culver
Scott J Dahlgren
Geoff Dash
Todd Dashoff
Dawno
GraceAnne Andreassi DeCandido
Jim Dirig
V Hartman DiSanto
Kenneth Dodd
Elizabeth Donald
Regis M. Donovan
Ed Ellis
Ross Emery
Jessica Enfante
Patricia Erdely
Colleen Feeney
Bruce Fenton
Nathan Filizzi
Robert C Flipse
Stacy Fluegge
Doug Forand
Chicago Frank
Mary Gaitan
J-P L. Garnier/Space Cowboy Books
Pete Gast
Mark Geary
David Gian-Cursio

Rico Gilbert
Scott Gillespie
Erica V.D. Ginter
Niall Gordon
ND Gray
Cathy Green
Robert Greenberger
Jaq Greenspon
Damon Griffin
Ina Alexandria Gur
Carol Gyzander
Josh H
R.J.H.
HBW
Thuy-Duong Ha
Alexander Hale
Mervi Hamalainen
Wendy Happek
Thomas Harning Jr.
Brian T. Hart
Andrew Hatchell
Pat Hayes
Sheryl R. Hayes
James L. Haynes
Stephanie Heath
David H Hendrickson
Eric Hendrickson
Henry Herz
Mary Jane Hetzlein
Brita Hill
Mark Hirschman
Jeff Hotchkiss
Avery Hughes
Andy Hunter
R. Hunter
Sonia "Pyrobyrd" James
Norman Jaffe
Jerrie the filkferengi
Carol Jones
Mike Jones

Joye
Jeanette Juryea
Rachel Kai
Chris Kaiser
Cheri Kannarr
AL Kaplan
Kerry aka Trouble
Josh King
Ian Klinck
AJ Knight
Adam Knuth
Simin Koernig
Bill Kohn
Daniel Korn
Karen Krah
Mischa D. Krilov
Lisa Kruse
Peggy Kurilla
Lace
Leigh
Paul Leone
Kate Lindstrom
Lisa
Giuseppe Lo Turco
Beth Lobdell
Brendan Lonehawk
James Lucas
Lisa & David Lyons
Rachel Machinton
Laochailan Maghouin
Katy Manck - BooksYALove
ToniAnn Marini
John Markley
Glori Medina
Steven Mentzel
Jeff Metzner
E.M. Middel
Frankie Mundens
J.R. Murdock
E.J. Murray

N/A
Randee Napp
Mark Newman
Tina M Noe Good
None
Odd
Omar
Ruth Ann Orlansky
Joshua Palmatier
Michelle Palmer
Dennis Parslow
Mary Perez
Pers
Amanda Peters
Gary Phillips
Pekka P. Pirinen
Aaron Pound
Marc Quillen
Michelle R
Tom Randklev
Scott Raun
Ben & Babette Raymond
Aysha Rehm
Mr Revaco
Brad Roberts
Roland Roberts
L.J. Robinson
GC Rovario-Cole
Lawrence M. Schoen
Danielle Schulman
Milwaukee Scott
Adam Selby-Martin
Patti Short
Stan Sieler
Nina Silver Ch.
Alin Silverwood/PopSkull Press
Claire Sims
Roger Sinasohn
Chanpreet Singh
Steven M. Smith

Tali Smith
Dirk-Pieter Smits
Leila Soffen
Sola
Liz Spicer
Deanna Stanley
RP Steeves
Curtis and Maryrita Steinhour
Liz Stonehill
Luke Sullivan
Rosemary Swift
Ed Teja
Francesco Tignini
Sam Tomaino
Tim Tucker
Ian Tullock
Bess Turner
Stephanie Trinity Turner
Stephen VanWambeck
Dr Douglas Vaughan
Leane Verhulst
Ioana Vlad
Sharan Volin
Tauriel Naismith Vorkosigan
Vulpecula
Deborah Wafer
Laura Ware
Hiram G Wells
Rachel Wells
Piet Wenings
Margaret Wheeler
Jenn Whitworth
Dr. Rich Williams
E.L. Winberry
Polyphemus Winks
Mary Alice Wuerz
Deborah Yerkes
Yes
David Young, Jr.
David Zurek